THE DEMON'S CURSE

PART TWO:

THE END OF ALL THINGS

ALLAN C. HOWARTH

 **New Generation Publishing**

**TO ALL MY
FAMILY AND THE FRIENDS
WHO HAVE MADE THIS JOURNEY WITH ME.**

MAY THE ROAD RISE WITH YOU

One

The middle aged man stood by the graveside, shovel in his hand, slyly watching the young girl walk down the path towards him. She ran a hand through her long brunette hair, which shone luminously, even in the dull grey light of an overcast afternoon. She was probably about fifteen years old and walked with an innocent, yet coquettish confidence, which emphasised her youth and beauty. The gravedigger cast a leering glance and grinned wolfishly as she passed.

"Creep!" the girl hissed, as she cast him a contemptuous glare and then swiftly and deliberately turned her gaze away. The rapid motion made the girl's hair flow like silk in a gentle breeze. Dino Giardino laughed. Even a pretty young girl's contempt was a considerable bonus in the depressing monotony of days spent digging graves.

The girl walked towards the middle-aged couple standing in the middle of a paved, sunken patio, which bordered the back fence of the cemetery. The couple were engaged in a deep conversation. The elegant, beautiful, brunette woman was nodding in agreement as the man gesticulated furiously at the ground. As the girl approached the couple she noticed that each paving stone bore an inscription of some sort, each relating to a departed loved one. It was one of the stones that the couple seemed to be discussing, judging by the man's animated gesticulation. The man ran a hand exasperatedly through his thick brown hair in which a silver streak was beginning to appear at the front.

"I mean why can't they do anything right?" The girl heard him complain loudly.

"I clearly wrote: born 1927 on the instructions and they've put 1928."

The girl snorted:

"God, Dad, take a chill pill. It's only a year. Surely it's the message that's important, not the date."

The man appraised his daughter thoughtfully, while the woman smirked.

The girl pulled her luscious hair back into a ponytail, exposing her large pointed ears.

The man blew out another sigh.

"Yes, I suppose you're right, darling." He crouched and traced the engraved words on the damp paving stone with his finger, whispering the words as he wiped away the growing traces of moss:

"Frank Higginbotham, born 1920, died 1979. Doris Higginbotham born 1928, died 1998. Words cannot thank you both enough."

Wayne Higginbotham wiped away a tear as he stood, while his wife, Natalia gently patted his shoulder. Katie Higginbotham, Wayne and Natalia's fifteen-year old daughter, frowned.

"He was your hero, wasn't he?" She whispered gently.

Wayne nodded, sadly.

"You would have liked him, Katie. Your granddad was a very gentle, kind man. Yet when it mattered, he was capable of doing amazing things. He once vaulted over a huge wall in a single bound that I would have taken half an hour to climb. He saved my life, you know."

Katie rolled her eyes.

"Er, like we know Dad. You've like, told us that story at least a thousand times. The wall, the punch, the bad dude getting knocked out. Anyway, I thought your Dad was buried at the Catholic church?"

Wayne smiled sadly. He had told the children a sanitised "magic-free" version of the story. If only they knew the truth.

Wayne cleared his throat.

"He was, this stone just sort of re-unites them in my head. He spent almost his entire life putting widgets on to thingummys and then sticking them into boxes, while Doris cleaned other people's houses and pubs. This stone, a few photos and my memories are all that I have left of them."

"And his medals, dad."

A young male voice piped up from just behind Natalia, as Frankie, the Higginbotham's eleven-year-old son emerged from behind a bush where he had been exploring.

"You've still got his medals." Frankie repeated earnestly.

"Shut up, you moron!" Katie Higginbotham hissed as her brother started to itemise the Second World War medals that Wayne had inherited from his adoptive father.

"Can't you see that Dad's upset?" Katie continued as she glowered at her younger sibling.

Frankie looked up at his father's face, just as Wayne wiped away another tear.

"Are you alright, Dad?" The boy asked; his voice laced with concern.

"Like, durrrr." Katie hissed.

"I thought you were supposed to be clever?"

"Come on guys, we'll go back to the car and leave Dad alone for a few minutes."

Natalia urged as she gestured for her children to follow her. She smiled sympathetically at Wayne then turned to walk back to the black Audi estate car, parked in the cemetery's small car park. Wayne smiled back, appreciatively.

Katie punched Frankie's arm causing the boy to squeal:

"Mum she just hit me."

"Didn't!"

"Did!"

"Didn't"

"Did!"

"Liar!"

Wayne smiled as the sound of bickering slowly faded as his wife and children disappeared behind an ancient oak tree.

The harsh cackling, cawing of innumerable crows in the bare, leafless trees surrounding the cemetery, soon became the only sound Wayne could hear. He looked around and shivered as he pulled his coat tighter around him.

He had definitely become less attuned to the cold, harsh, winter winds of Yorkshire in the twenty-odd years he had lived in the South of England. Yet he had so many memories of his years in Shepton. He stepped away from the paving stone and stared at his surroundings.

Over the back fence of the cemetery and across a neat patchwork of fields, he could see the grey bulk of Carelton mill with its tall chimney. A little bit to the left was the medieval church tower. Carelton was the small village where his adoptive mother, Doris and his Aunt Margaret had grown up. Beyond that loomed the imposing grey-green moors that stretched over into Lancashire.

In the opposite direction he could see the green hills and grey stone fells of the Dales, between the bare, skeletal trees. Much nearer were the dark stone rows of rooftops and few remaining smokestacks of Shepton.

When he had been very small this cemetery was where he had come to see Ellie-May, his adoptive grandmother buried. He remembered how Doris and Margaret had wept at the graveside, while he and his cousin Cedric had played hide and seek around the gravestones.

Wayne shook his head. It had all been so long ago. Even Doris' funeral now seemed to be almost a piece of ancient history. That had been the last time he had visited Shepton.

Katie had been little more than a toddler then, while Frankie hadn't even been born.

"You'd have liked him, Mum." Wayne whispered.

"He's not got the ears and he's as good as gold. Practically perfect, just like your Trevor, probably."

Wayne couldn't help the bitter barb and bit his lip in regret as soon as he'd said it.

He thought back to the weekend so many years earlier when he'd come up to Shepton with Natalia and little Katie to visit Doris.

Wayne visited his adoptive mother at least once every eight weeks and hated every single minute of every single visit. Doris had moved into sheltered accommodation on the Longhill Road after a serious angina attack not long after Wayne's graduation. She had become increasingly cantankerous with old age. Nothing that Wayne did was ever right, or remotely good enough, as far as Doris had been concerned. In her view, Wayne had abandoned her after University and had left his poor mother "to rot" in Shepton. How could he have done such a thing and her with her bad heart? His decision to go off to work in London after graduation had been greeted with scorn:

"Going to look for your real mother down there are you?" She had spat, when he had announced that he had taken a job in marketing, based in Chiswick.

"Nowt good ever comes out of London. I'll give you six weeks before you're coming back up North with your tail between your legs." She had added with a sneer, which had made Wayne feel great, as that was where he had been born.

It had been fortunate for Wayne that Doris had never found out about his reunion with Terri and his wider O'Brien family. She had suspected that some major event had occurred in the weeks following his adventure in Ireland, yet Frank had denied any knowledge of such an event and Wayne had eventually used his magical powers of persuasion to expel any such thoughts from her mind.

That last weekend with her had been so different. None of them knew it was going to be the last weekend, of course. For Wayne and Natalia it was just going to be another hard slog up the motorway to Yorkshire with Katie in tow. For Doris it was probably just going to be another chance to share her misery with her errant son and his stuck-up wife. Yet, for some reason, that usual chain of events, just didn't happen. Doris had been unusually pleasant, kind, lovely to Katie (although she always was) and as tender to Wayne as she had ever been. Wayne had even expressed his suspicions to Natalia that he thought she might be "up to something."

One week later Doris had suffered a massive heart attack and had died on her doorstep as she had tried to get to a neighbour's for help.

Wayne grimaced as he stared at the paving stone, which he had commissioned some ten months earlier and which had now been in place for eight weeks. It had replaced an engraved urn that had stood in the cemetery's chapel since just after Doris had died.

"Did you know?" He whispered.

"Did you know that was the last time I'd ever see you? Was that why you finally forgave me for leaving you here? I know I never replaced Trevor in your heart, but thanks for everything, Mum. And Dad, we named Frankie after you, you know. I hope he'll be as nice and kind as you."

Wayne wiped away one last tear, then walked away from the memorial stone and headed back towards the Audi.

He had two more things to do in Shepton before he could leave and then he would probably never visit the town again. The first thing was to visit his Aunt Margaret.

Margaret Houghton-Hughes still lived in the large house on the Ripon Road that had driven Doris mad with envy, but now she lived alone. Stanley Houghton-Hughes had died one year before Doris, also suffering from a massive, fatal heart attack.

Wayne's cousin Cedric was now living in a croft in the Highlands of Scotland.

Cedric and Wayne still got on well, on the rare occasions that they saw one another, which mainly now amounted to funerals.

Margaret was delighted to see the Higginbothams. She had always been fond of Wayne and had never liked the way that Doris had continually denigrated him. She was also particularly fond of Natalia and the children.

The second thing that Wayne had been determined to do during his sojourn in Shepton was to enjoy a brimming plate of proper Yorkshire fish and chips. So, after leaving Margaret's house, the family walked through the town in the direction of Eastwood's Fish Restaurant.

It had been in Eastwood's that Wayne had once attempted to woo Stephanie Fleming in the guise of a cool American called Mickey Finn. The exercise in shape shifting had almost turned into a disaster as Wayne had got progressively drunk and forgotten exactly what his American persona was supposed to look like.

As the family struggled through the throng on the bustling High Street, Wayne smiled at the memory of that evening. Had it really been over twenty years since he had used any sort of magic?

Over twenty years since he had last seen his real father, Aillen Mac Fionnbharr?

It was strange, but being back in Shepton brought all those memories back to the forefront of his mind.

The day he had nearly been caught in the chemistry lab by Dai Davies and had been forced to use invisibility to escape.

The day he had escaped the fire on Cavendish Street by telepathically communicating with the twin sister he had never met.

Wayne grimaced as he remembered how James Malone had rescued him, only to be murdered in his own home in L.A. just a few years later.

Suddenly, Wayne was snapped out of his reverie by the awareness of a vaguely familiar face walking slowly towards him, amidst the crowd on the busy High Street.

"Mrs Ball?" Wayne asked tentatively.

He really couldn't believe that the old lady in front of him could be the teacher he had admired so much, so long ago.

The old lady stopped and peered at him myopically:

"Is it, is it, it can't be, Wayne Higginbotham?" She asked hesitantly.

"Yes. Yes it is. How are you?" Wayne exclaimed with a huge grin and a bear hug for the old lady.

She held his arms for a second to appraise her old student, as a curious Natalia, Katie and Frankie gathered around and the hordes of Saturday shoppers and tourists grumbled and griped their way around the sudden obstruction in the middle of the pavement.

"My goodness, you're going grey, Wayne." Mrs Elizabeth Ball announced.

Wayne laughed.

"And fatter, let's be honest, I'm well on the wrong side of forty now, I'm afraid."

Mrs Ball clapped her hand to her mouth.

"Is it really so long since you were at Gas Street? I'll never forget that time you ran away to Ireland?"

Wayne nodded.

"Via London, if you remember? Anyway this is............"

Wayne introduced his family, while a shocked Mrs Ball tried to recover her equilibrium.

"John died." She stated simply after relating her tale of the race to London to find Wayne and then the subsequent trip to Ireland with Frank.

"I heard about your dad, I'm sorry." She murmured.

Wayne bit his lip and acknowledged the sympathy with a curt nod:

"Doris died back in the late Nineties." Wayne informed her.

Mrs Ball shook her head.

"Oh dear, when you get to my age, everyone around you seems to be dying, or to be affected by death. What happened to that nice young Irishman who I found looking for you here on the High Street, all those years ago?"

Wayne shook his head sadly.

"He died too, I'm afraid. He was murdered by a burglar in his own home in Los Angeles, over twenty years ago now."

Mrs Ball sighed sadly.

"Oh. I'm so sorry to hear that. See what I mean? "In the midst of life, so we are in death.""

She looked totally anguished before smiling at Wayne's wife and children.

"Anyway, you have a beautiful family, Wayne Higginbotham. You are a very lucky man. I am so proud of you."

Wayne smiled and nodded:

"I know. I don't deserve them." He laughed.

Elizabeth Ball peered at him again. A wry smile creased her lips.

"Oh you do, Wayne, you do. I'm so glad you're happy and successful, young man. I always knew you would be, but…………"

Again she peered at the man before her who she had not seen since he was a gawky adolescent.

"You don't look fulfilled. There is something missing in your life. You are not totally happy, Wayne Higginbotham, are you?"

"What did she mean by that?" Natalia asked as the car rumbled to a stop in the drive-in queue at the "Happy Boy" Burger Bar. Eastwood's had closed and was now a canal side art gallery so, much to the kid's delight, Wayne had agreed to stop for a burger on the return journey South.

"By what?" Wayne asked as he fumbled for change in his wallet and tried to study the seemingly infinite permutations of a quarter-pound cheeseburger on the menu.

"By "there is something missing in your life?""

Natalia stated by way of clarification.

Wayne shrugged.

"I don't know. Maybe she's gone a bit batty. She wasn't psychic or anything when she was younger."

The thought stayed with him all the way home, however. Visiting Shepton had revived so many memories that had been hidden by the veneer of his routine, middle-class life in rural Berkshire.

Wayne Higginbotham had abandoned his destiny, the very meaning of his existence.

How had Mrs Ball known that?

Later that night as he grabbed a glass of Merlot and switched on the Ten p.m. news, Wayne Higginbotham wondered if he had done the right thing by denying his magical heritage all those years ago. After all there hadn't been Armageddon on the 31st December 1999. The Four Horseman of the Apocalypse obviously still hadn't left the stable despite 9/11 and Iraq, Afghanistan and so on.

The world seemed to have survived just fine and dandy without him and his magic.

In fact, if people believed the mass hysteria surrounding climate change, then the world was going to end long before the evil one even had a chance to destroy it. That amused Wayne. He thought of the devil sitting on the burned out, shrivelled up rock that had been the planet earth, sulking:

"But I was going to destroy this, not mankind. They ruined all my fun!"

Wayne smiled, then took a sip of the satisfyingly smooth, warm red wine, put the glass down on the coffee table nest to his armchair and felt his eyelids begin to droop. He heard the newsreader announce:

"And finally tonight......"

The announcement at this point was always frivolous: Dancing Donkeys, or a cat that watches TV.

Wayne felt the fuzzy sensation of sleep creeping up on him. He was sinking into a dark, warm, abyss. Yet he could still hear the news anchors amused voice droning on in the background:

"During the Eighties he was the biggest star on T.V. playing the lovable rogue in smash hit shows like "The Amishers" and "Beach Patrol." In the Nineties he was the biggest thing in pop music with ten number one singles on both sides of the Atlantic. Now, Movie Star, Luke Lively has announced that he's retiring from Show business to take up a career in politics. His father, veteran Republican Senator Aurelio Vitalia said............."

Wayne Higginbotham was staring wide eyed at the plasma screen in front of him.

The eyes that had once scared the hell out of him in his nightmares, were staring right back at him once again from the screen.

The child, whose murder had supposedly been Wayne's destiny, was going to run for the Presidency of the most powerful nation on Earth, while still in his thirties.

Two

Terri Thorne could not believe her ears. She emitted a faint gasp of surprise and asked her son to repeat what he had just told her.

Marco Vitalia grinned:

"I said, Mom, that I asked Aoibheall Vasquez to marry me, last night and believe it or not, she agreed."

Terri shook her head in disbelief. Marco and Aoibheall had been friends since junior High, while Terri had known her since she had been a baby. Her son, Michael, or Wayne as she had now got used to calling him, had asked her to look after Carrie Malone in the immediate aftermath of James Malone's murder. Terri had been short of genuine friendship at the time and had struck up an immediate close bond with the young Californian widow and her infant daughter. That relationship had now endured for over twenty years and four marriages, three of them Carrie's.

Carrie's fourth husband, Miguel Vasquez was a fine man, so much so that Aoibheall had agreed to be adopted by him at the awkward age of sixteen, bringing to an end a three-year period of shocking adolescent behaviour and teenage rebellion that had brought Carrie close to a nervous breakdown. It had been the first time Terri had seen Carrie truly happy since the untimely death of James Malone.

As for Terri's own second marriage, that had lasted precisely three weeks. All of her children had been opposed to the union with Hans Schneider, a German sea Captain who had been in charge of a Cruise Liner that Terri had worked on in the mid Nineteen Nineties, but she had married him in Vegas anyway. Terri had been the ships entertainment officer and love had blossomed in the claustrophobic, frenetic atmosphere of the ship. On reflection, on dry land and once the euphoria of the wedding and the Honeymoon had faded, both Terri and Hans had realised that it had been a rash and impetuous act and on the third week of their marriage, she had found him amorously engaged with one her young dancers. Terri had vowed never to marry again and she had been true to her word.

Terri Thorne was now the owner of a very successful beauty salon in Malibu and could number many famous faces amongst her clientele. She had a fine house in Chatsworth, which, while not as grand as the house she had shared with Dean in Coldwater Canyon, was spacious and extremely comfortable. She had two kids she could be proud of, three if she counted Wayne and her two fine grandchildren. She had raised Marco and Marina almost single-handed. Her sister Annie had helped as much as she could and Carrie had been an absolute Godsend. Life had been a struggle but they had pulled through.

Dean, of course, had lost interest in his own offspring as soon as his second wife gave birth. Marina had been unceremoniously dumped from the "Amishers" as soon as she grew out of the toddler stage and was required to deliver complex lines of dialogue, while the part that had been promised to Marco never materialised at all. If he saw his children more than twice a year, then Dean Vitalia was being extra attentive. He was now partially retired, having made a fortune on "The Amishers." Most of his time was spent playing golf in Palm Springs with his old Hollywood cronies. The rest of his time was spent looking after Luke Lively, the TV star, movie star and successful pop singer.

Terri threw her arms around her son.

"That's wonderful news Marco." She gushed: "I love Aoibheall. I really always hoped that this would happen but never really believed it would."

Marco laughed.

"Seems Carrie and Aoibheall want a spectacular wedding. Carrie's found a place in Mexico that would be way cool."

Terri looked amazed:

"Wow, you're discussing venues already? What about a date?"

Marco shrugged:

"We thought August 31st would be pretty cool. Wayne's kids will be on vacation and the weather will be perfect."

Terri laughed:

"My God, Marco, you guys are really planning this aren't you? Have you told Marina?"

Marco shrugged again.

"Not yet. I'll ring her later."

Terri stepped back and her face suddenly became serious.

"What about your Father?" She asked in what was little more than a whisper.

Marco blew out a huge sigh.

"Like, what about him? He'll get an invitation, I guess. If he wants to come that's up to him."

Terri nodded and tried to force a smile, unfortunately it looked more like a grimace.

Marco looked hurt.

"I've gotta invite him, Mom, after all, he is my Dad."

Terri threw up her hands.

"Sorry Marco, that wasn't what I was thinking. What I was thinking is; is Aoibheall's Mom going to be OK about the Dean and James thing?"

Marco looked stunned:

"Mom, I thought that was put to bed years ago. Dad swore that he didn't have anything to do with James Malone's murder. He's sworn it to me, personally. I know you hate him, but whatever Dad is, he isn't a murderer."

Terri nodded and apologised. The news was just too good to ruin with a family row about things that had happened so long ago.

Terri hugged her son.

"Are you going to ring Wayne and the Irish crew? I wish Daideo was still alive to see this."

Marco grinned:

"No, you can do all that. Don't forget August 31st is provisional."

He turned and left the house.

Terri watched her tall, dark, handsome son through the kitchen window as he climbed into his Ford pick up truck. His looks were a definite Italian-Irish fusion with his dark hair and his green eyes. Aoibheall was quite a beauty too, long blonde hair from her Mom's side and deep brown eyes just like her Dad's.

Terri took a deep breath and pursed her lips as the truck roared out of her drive.

Carrie would not be looking forward to the man she suspected of having ordered her husband's murder being present at her daughter's wedding.

"I can't believe you are going to invite Marcy's Dad." Carrie screamed, using her daughter's pet name for her fiancée.

Aoibheall's face set in a determined look that informed her mother that she would not broach any nonsense and that the subject was not open to negotiation.

"Mom, we have been through this, like a thousand times. Marcy has looked his father in the eye and asked him outright if he had anything to do with Dad's murder. Dean has said categorically not. I know Dad wrote you a letter incriminating Dean, but you said yourself that the murder was carried out by Hispanics. You saw them Mom. I mean I don't want to be racist but there's a big difference between a young Mexican and a middle-aged Italian American, even when they're wearing masks."

Carrie closed her eyes and sat down at the old familiar table. She was still living in the house in Box Canyon that she had owned since long before she had met James Malone.

She thought back to the day that she had picked up a long haired, scruffy, Irish hitch-hiker on the outskirts of Santa Barbara, all those years ago. Poor James.

"OK." She conceded: "I guess it's your day."

Aoibheall grinned:

"Thanks Mom. It will be your day too."

The beautiful, tall young woman spun around and walked out of the house in which she had been raised.

"See you Saturday." She called as she waved cheerily.

Carrie watched her go and felt a warm surge of pride in her stomach.

"You would have been very proud of her, James." She whispered.

Although Carrie loved Miguel Vasquez and he was a charming and entertaining companion. She had never found anyone quite like James Malone. His daughter was so like him in many ways: stubborn, opinionated and occasionally moody, but most of the time she was like a ray of sunshine.

Carrie poured herself a coffee and went out into the yard. The bougainvillea that James had so loved had grown almost wild and surrounded the entire garden. The activity centre that he'd put together for Aoibheall to play on when she got older was long gone. Carrie missed it. It reminded her of many happy days watching her brave young explorer climb and swing. She couldn't think of anyone she would rather have as a son-in-law than Marco. He was a lovely kid and was so much in love with Aoibheall. It was just that he was Dean Vitalia's son and Carrie was still convinced that Dean had arranged the murder, just like James had said in his letter. She was not looking forward to having to meet him at the wedding.

Three

Lucy Sherman was absolutely delighted. Pangfield College was just perfect for the twins and Jonathan, for once, was in total agreement. It had turned out to be an excellent visit to the old country for the chic New York lawyer couple, after something of an inauspicious start. The couple had spent almost the entire flight to London arguing about the decision to school their twins privately in England. Jonathan had not understood Lucy's desire to use the English Public School System, when Private Schools in the United States were equally as good, if not better. He had even considered sending them to a local state High School to let them experience some of what he called: "real life." Jonathan T. Sherman had attended a Boston Military Academy before Harvard and had been determined that his unruly offspring needed some discipline if they were going to go down the fee paying route. As far as he had been concerned, an English boarding school, with its aura of class privilege and exclusivity, would only serve to reinforce the twins' precociousness, elitism and arrogance.

Lucy on the other hand had been absolutely determined that the twins would be taught quintessential English manners and would receive a far more rounded education in a traditional British school, like the prestigious boarding school she had attended.

It had been a protracted struggle but eventually Lucy had managed to persuade Jonathan to at least look at some English private schools, so the affluent family of four had travelled to Europe with that aim in mind.

Lucy had managed to fit in a short visit home to Jersey, while Jonathan had researched the schools that they had short-listed, from a base in a five star London hotel suite. The twins had accompanied their mother, as visits to their Grandparents always resulted in tons of "booty."

Both of Lucy's adoptive parents were still alive, although Rupert Hetherington had been suffering from a prolonged period of ill health. For most of his daughter's visit he had sat in an armchair facing the French windows and a glorious view out to sea, with a blanket over his knees and a "medicinal" Cognac by his side. It had soon become apparent to Lucy that the twins had irritated him. Rupert had never been fond of the fact that his grandchildren were being raised in America and had developed all the brash, loud and confident behaviour that was seen as being so typical of American kids.

Melinda, however, had been on top form and had been delighted to see the twins, Jonathan Junior and Jemima. It had been two years since the Hetheringtons had seen their grandchildren, so a huge fuss had been made and when the children had arrived back in London, Jonathan had been horrified by the piles of presents that they had obtained.

"They really need a good dose of reality." He had moaned to Lucy.

"They're twelve years old and if we carry on spoiling them like this they'll be insufferable by the time they're eighteen. Plus, how on Earth are we going to get this stuff on the airplane?"

Lucy had laughed.

"Jonathan, dear, you will never stop grandparents spoiling their descendants and we will simply have to buy more luggage. Plus, if we choose a good school they will not turn into insufferable brats. So, have you narrowed that list down?"

Jonathan sipped his coffee and grimaced painfully.

"Jeez, I'd forgotten how lousy English coffee is."

He walked over to the desk in the sumptuously comfortable suite and picked up a couple of prospecti.

Jonjo and Jem, as they were known to family and friends rushed up to Jonathan to try and snatch the documents out of his hand.

"Let's see Pop, aww c'mon."

Jonathan held the documents above his own head, teasingly way out of reach of the two twelve year olds.

"I've spoken to these guys and they can accept the terrible twosome in September."

He handed Lucy a glossy brochure heralding a college in the west of Berkshire that compared itself to Eton, Harrow and Westminster.

He then handed her a second prospectus that appeared somewhat nautical in appearance:

"This place, however, is awesome. It's got a real Naval tradition, they even do parade drill."

Lucy eagerly grabbed the Pangfield college brochure and quickly rifled through the pages, her eyebrows raised approvingly.

Both twins groaned in unison.

"Drill? Like you've gotta be kidding."

Jonathan grinned.

"We're seeing the Principal there, tomorrow at 2:00pm and the Dean of the other place on Tuesday at 10:00am."

"Headmaster, Warden, or simply Master, darling. Only American schools and colleges have Principals and Deans." Lucy informed her husband, haughtily."

She finished flicking through the brochure.

"It looks just fine." She admitted, passing the Pangfield College brochure to Jonjo who was immediately jumped on by Jem:

"Let me see, let me see." She shouted.

Jonathan and Lucy Sherman had been incredibly successful since graduating from Oxford and had a wonderful multi-million dollar home in Connecticut as well as the large apartment on West 72nd Street on Manhattan Island. Jonathan's law firm: Sherman General Law Inc. had a huge presence on the East Coast and was still growing. It had been founded by Jonathan's father, John H. Sherman in the early fifties and had a superb reputation for integrity, economy and most importantly success.

Lucy had taken the American Bar after completing her studies at Harvard and had been a successful lawyer in her own right. Indeed it had been Lucy that had initially expanded her husband's company over to the West Coast and had set up the entertainment division in Los Angeles. Lucy had given up work when the twins had been born, however, and had spent the last twelve years living the life of an American socialite, amongst the white picket-fenced estates of New England. Winters had been spent in New York, summers in Connecticut and the Hamptons, with frequent vacations at Martha's Vineyard.

For Jonjo Sherman and Jem, Pangfield College would come as something of a shock. Not only was it in a foreign country with strange accents, habits and behaviour predominating, but it was run on the lines of a military Academy, with Parades, drill and cadet manoeuvres being a mandatory part of the curriculum.

Jonathan and Lucy loved their visit to Pangfield and signed the twins up before even looking at the second school.

It was on the journey home that Lucy expressed her first doubt:

"Are you sure you're OK about this darling? It is a long way away, after all."

Jonathan T. Sherman placed his glass of bourbon down on the First Class table by his seat and shook his head.

"Lucy, honey, only you could spend five years nagging incessantly for the twins to go to boarding school in England, as soon as they hit thirteen and then, when you've won me round and we've gotten them into a school we both love, you say "are you sure?" Goddammit woman, of course I'm sure."

He looked at the twins, Jonjo engrossed on his PSP games machine and Jemima lost in her iPod world.

"I mean look at them. That Head guy dude said they'd even learn how to make their shoes shine like mirrors. Now that, I can't wait to see."

Lucy smiled contentedly.

"Are you going straight out to L.A. when we get home?"

Jonathan glanced out of the 747- 400 series window at the expanse of grey cloud below them.

"Next Monday, honey. It looks like we really could be hitting the big time with this one. Larry has set up a meeting with some kid who used to be in that "Amishers" show and his agent. They want Sherman General to be their lawyers when he runs for President, sounds good to me."

Lucy laughed:

"He's much too young to be President and anyway, the rumour is, he wasn't even born in America. According to the tabloids, anyway. Supposedly, he was adopted as a small child, by that awful Senator Vitalia. They say he was actually born in Italy. They also say his mother shot herself rather than live in Senator Vitalia's odious company. Anyway, isn't the Senator tarnished by all those Mafia rumours?"

Jonathan nodded and gazed admiringly into his wife's eyes.

"Those are some of the issues they want us to work on. They consider that a reputable firm like us should be able to dispel all the negative gossip and it is all just rumour and gossip. From what I've seen I think Luke Lively, or whatever his stage name is, will make a fine President of the United States of America. He's young, yes, inexperienced, yes. But isn't that what we need right now? A fresh start? Someone not tainted by the stink of political intrigue and corrupted by power? I think he'll be a breath of fresh air."

Four

Wayne Higginbotham was almost as excited about the flight to Los Angeles as he had been as a teenage boy, so many years earlier. It had been ten years since his last trip to Southern California and that had been a brief stopover on the way to Hawaii.

It hadn't been his decision to not visit his family in their home environment. Wayne absolutely loved California. Terri, however, had been fiercely determined to keep her first-born son a long way away from Dean Vitalia. Terri had always strongly suspected Dean of being involved in James Malone's murder, despite his constant and consistent denials and even though no connection had ever been made by the police. She had never forgotten Dean's suggestion that Wayne might have instigated James' investigations as a form of revenge for Dean's divorcing her. She had seen her ex-husband's vicious streak on more than one occasion in the years that had passed since their divorce and had become totally convinced that even if he was not personally capable of murder, he was capable of arranging it.

When Marco's engagement and proposed nuptials in Mexico had been announced, however, Wayne had insisted that he would be visiting Los Angeles and attending his brothers wedding, irrespective of any risks. He had over-ruled Terri's objections over the phone with a determination that had taken her by surprise.

"Mom, I am not a little boy any more. I am a father of two. I am heading for fifty. I am as large as life and twice as ugly. Dean is an old man. I think I can deal with him, don't you?"

"It isn't Dean, honey, it never was." Terri had pleaded desperately: "It's the young thugs that he could pay to do his dirty work."

Wayne had laughed.

"Mom, you worry too much. I'm coming to my little brother's wedding and that's final!"

That call had taken place months before and now as the August 31st date neared, Wayne's concerns were more about the amount of luggage that Natalia had packed for the trip and what to buy his brother and Aoibheall as a wedding present.

Wayne had been more than delighted when he had heard that his little brother was dating James Malone's daughter. He had kept in touch with Carrie by Christmas card and the occasional letter. Even at his most wildly optimistic, however, he had never expected to see her again. Poor Carrie had been totally devastated by James' death and

Wayne had felt that she had become a little bit weird in the years immediately following the tragedy. She had always been very Californian in her adoption of the latest trendy beliefs and habits, but her behaviour had seemed extreme even by Californian standards. She had been a caffeine-free, militant vegan, a Buddhist pacifist, anti-war protestor, an eco-warrior and an animal rights activist in the years leading up to her marriage to Miguel Vasquez.

That marriage seemed to have calmed her down a bit and Wayne had found her last two letters much more palatable than some of her previous lecturing rants. Now he was actually looking forward to seeing her again. After all, she was now the only person on earth who knew that Wayne Higginbotham was not just a boring, English businessman with a wife and two children.

"Poor old James, if only he'd lived to have seen this." Wayne had laughed one night over supper with Natalia.

"He'd have died at the prospect of being related to me."

Natalia had squeezed his hand:

"I think he'd have been delighted." She had smiled reassuringly.

Wayne had returned the smile but the thought crossed his mind that James might not have been so pleased to see his daughter marrying the son of the man who might just have signed his death warrant.

The evening before the flight Wayne had been like a little boy on Christmas Eve. He had hardly been able to sit still and had excitedly regaled Frankie and Katie with his tales about Los Angeles and the Pacific coast. The prospect of facing Dean Vitalia at the wedding had not even crossed his mind, his only concerns had been would they get to the airport on time and how difficult would it be to get through security with all the family baggage intact.

It was in the middle of the night that he awoke in a cold sweat and sat bolt upright in bed. Natalia was fast asleep and breathing heavily next to him and at first he had no idea why he had woken up. The room was pitch dark, only the red neon readout of his alarm clock cast any light in the gloom. Had he been dreaming? Wayne couldn't remember. He listened carefully, but couldn't hear anything out of the ordinary, nothing that would have woken him from his sleep anyway. He sipped from a glass of water, then settled back down on to his pillow and closed his eyes.

As he began to drift off to sleep he was conscious of a figure standing silently before him. A tall, faceless figure, swathed entirely in black. The figure did not move or speak but seemed to be staring at the ground before it. Wayne slowly approached the figure.

It was as though he was trying to walk through thick cloying mud.

He could hardly lift his feet.

The figure did not move.

It reminded him of something he had seen in a dream, a long time ago and far, far away. It was a dream that he had not had for many, many years.

The figure looked up towards him and Wayne recognised the eyes.

They were the clear blue, cold, merciless eyes of his tormentor.

The same figure that had called him a whelp, all those years ago.

Now, however, the eyes were sad, lost even and they weren't looking at him.

They were staring down, straight down at the ground.

"Who are you?" Wayne demanded, as he struggled through the mud.

The figure remained totally impassive.

"Who are you?" Wayne repeated.

The figure raised its head and glanced at him, there was no face, just those eyes.

Wayne was bemused. Where were the taunts? Where was the arrogance? Had his victory been so complete all those years ago?

The figure bowed its faceless head low again and Wayne heard a low voice rumble.

"My fault, it's all my fault."

Wayne pulled a foot free from the mud with a huge slurping, gloopy sound.

"What's your fault?" He shouted.

The figure groaned:

"This, all of this."

The figures arms rose as it seemed to indicate everything around it.

Wayne looked down.

He wasn't walking in mud, he was struggling through blood. An ocean of blood, splinters of white, broken bones and raw meat.

Yet it wasn't meat, Wayne realised, but body parts, red and brown organs, acres of torn flesh, faces, men's faces, women's faces, children, hair.

He was sinking.

He wanted to scream, but his voice wasn't working any more.

He looked up at the figure in front of him as he struggled to breathe.

He could smell the blood, taste it. He felt himself begin to gag.

The figure pulled back its hood.

Wayne Higginbotham's own face stared back at him.

"It was all my fault." He moaned.

Wayne sat bolt upright in bed again. He was shivering and felt incredibly sick.

"What's the matter?" He heard Natalia's voice in the darkness.
"Nothing." He gasped.
"A bad dream, that's all. Go back to sleep darling."
Sleep eluded Wayne for the rest of that night.

Five

The press speculation in the United States had been intense. Why had Luke Lively, the good looking young actor and pop star, decided to run for President at a ridiculously young age? Not only was he way too young, he was going to run as an independent candidate, which everyone agreed was absolute, total and utter madness. The major Democratic and Republican candidates had already been canvassing for over a year and had secured most of their hard-core support. Luke had no political experience beyond being the adopted son of a Senator with a somewhat dubious background and reputation. He was of Italian descent and no Italian had ever been President. He was a Catholic and only JFK had reached the presidency as a Catholic. Supposedly, he hadn't even been born in the U.S.A. constitutionally he was therefore ineligible, unless he could provide a birth certificate to prove otherwise.

The whole thing was absolutely insane.

It was undeniable that he was incredibly popular amongst certain demographics, particularly females of all ages and the gay lobby. The young lusted after the pop star, whilst their mothers wanted to mother the cute kid from "The Amishers."

It was also a fact that he possessed enormous charisma and had already spoken out on green issues and had controversially adopted an anti-war stance.

But to run for President?

Every single Political columnist and leader writer in the United States had been flabbergasted by his announcement and had been quick to ridicule him and his chances of ever reaching the oval office. All had agreed that it must be some sort of elaborate publicity stunt to enhance Luke's career, to give him a more mature image and maybe to promote some movie about politics.

Every single chat show host and stand up comedian quickly developed a repertoire of Luke Lively jokes. From sea to shining sea, Luke Lively became the laughing stock of every political pundit and so called expert in the land. If enhancing his image had been the aim of his announcement then everyone was in agreement that it had backfired spectacularly, unless one subscribed to the view that any publicity constituted good publicity.

Was his father, Senator Aurelio Vitalia, advising him? If so this was probably the end of his political career.

Was his manager, Dean Vitalia, advising him? If so this would probably be the end of his now limited career in Hollywood.

One thing was for sure, people were certainly talking about that kid with the cute blond hair and the cheeky grin, who had had the audacity to state that he could run their lives for them.

Luke's first appearance since the announcement, on the Saturday Night David Bannerman show was, therefore, eagerly anticipated by almost the entire nation.

What could he possibly say that would justify such a ludicrous decision?

As the second guest on the show, after the hilarious Scottish comedian, Billy Connolly, Luke was greeted rapturously by the already much amused studio audience. As Bannerman announced his entrance, both he and Billy Connolly stood and shook Luke's hand in turn as he grinned and waved confidently at the audience and the cameras, before taking his place on the sofa next to the Scot.

Bannerman waited for the audience to quieten down as he shuffled some cue cards in his hands. Finally there was near silence in the studio.

"So Luke Lively, maybe better known as the cute Hans Kirsche of "The Amishers." We, er, hear that you, errr, want to be our next President?" Bannerman asked, somewhat sardonically.

Luke smiled and looked slightly abashed.

"Yes, sir. I sure do."

Bannerman grinned at the cameras.

"Most guys, your age are still packing away their short pants and discovering girls, aren't they?"

Luke smiled at his interviewer and rubbed his chin thoughtfully.

"Oh, I packed the short pants away a long time ago, David, but I've decided to leave the girls until I am President, power seems to work as a bit of a turn on, an aphrodisiac, you know?"

He looked directly at the camera and gave a Hans Kirsche toothy grin:

"I mean it seemed to work OK for Bill C., didn't it?"

The audience hooted with laughter, especially when Billy Connolly shouted:

"Aye, I'll say so and he's no' talkin' about me folks."

Bannerman grinned again and waited for the clamour to die down. Assistants hushed the audience with hand gestures out of the view of the cameras.

"But why now?" Bannerman leaned forward aggressively, fixed grin on his face.

"Ronald Reagan retired from acting before running; surely you've got a hell of a career in Hollywood before you, why now?"

Luke coughed and cleared his throat:

"Because, to put it simply, David, I don't have long on this earth. The last time I was here, I was only allowed to get to my early thirties, so this time I thought I better act quickly."

There was a stunned silence in the studio, just a couple of nervous coughs and a faint murmuring.

Billy Connolly turned, looked at the studio audience conspiratorially, grimaced and raised his eyebrows.

Before a clearly surprised Bannerman could react, Luke suddenly stood and approached the live camera:

"You see folks. It's time I cut to the quick. I am the Messiah. I have returned to Earth, to save all of your mortal souls. I will no longer be known as Luke Lively, but by the name I was raised by: Luca Vitalia. I am the light and I am life and to prove my point, here is my first miracle: A thousand blind shall see." He waved his hand towards the camera, smiled his gleaming white toothy smile and then turned and returned to his seat.

Billy Connolly and David Bannerman were both staring at him with their mouths open, while the studio audience muttered, murmured and coughed. It took several seconds for Bannerman to recover:

"Well, Ok, errr, Luca, so you believe you are actually the, errr, Son of God?" His tone was now extremely sardonic.

Luca smiled beatifically.

"Why, yes, Sir, I am. Check your glass of water, David."

Bannerman reached for his glass and turned to the audience and cameras with the sort of expression that showed his scepticism and amusement at unfolding events:

"This is better than Cruise on Oprah." He quipped as he took a sip from his glass.

His expression changed immediately and there was a collective gasp from the audience as the translucent liquid turned red before their eyes.

"Who put wine in my glass? " Bannerman asked, glancing around the studio nervously.

"I did." Luca stated simply.

Billy Connolly lifted his glass of water and to laughter, whoops and cheers asked his neighbour:

"Hey, Jesus Jimmy, could you turn this into 12 year old Scotch?"

Luca grinned and waved his hand over the glass. The liquid inside turned from clear to amber. Connolly took a sniff and then a sip:

"Bloody Hell." He exclaimed: "This guy's better than Copperfield. This is really bloody good!"

Bannerman swung nervously towards the camera:

"We'll be back straight after these messages."

All over the country people were gasping in amazement. Some had dropped to their knees, others argued about conjuring tricks. Some were crying with happiness, others in fear that judgment day might be just around the corner. Most snorted with derision at the lunatics in Hollywood and the TV studio's cheap tricks.

Meanwhile, a thousand blind people cried and shrieked with delight as the world around them came into view for the first time in their lives.

Six

The Mexican bar was raucous and loud laughter permeated the air. Terri Thorne, wearing a fetchingly crazy, enormous sombrero staggered back from the Ladies room and plonked herself precariously back on her bar stool. Carrie Vasquez turned and blearily examined her friend:

"I am shoo glad we're going to be related." She slurred.

"We've been friends for shoo long."

Terri nodded as she squinted her eyes and peered at her Margherita.

"Yesh, 1 know. It's like it was always meant to happen. You know, you and James and James knowing Michael, I mean Wayne and Aoibheall meeting Marco and, you know, all, all that stuff."

Aoibheall wandered over from her table of rowdy young women. Her stagger was less pronounced than Terri's but she was obviously very merry.

"Is this the most awesome bridal shower ever, or what?" She yelled at the top of her voice.

Her long blonde hair was tied up in multi coloured ribbons and her short white mini-shift dress had writing all over it as her friends wished her well in her forthcoming wedding.

Carrie laughed:

"Sure it is baby. Are you having fun?"

Aoibheall grabbed the table to support herself:

"Whooah!" She exclaimed. "What does it look like?"

She turned and bumbled away, back towards the cheering throng.

"Your daughter is so beautiful." Terri informed her friend, as though she was confiding something really secret.

Carrie nodded her agreement:

"And your son is great too, in spite of his schmuck of a father."

The women clinked their glasses in agreement.

Carrie thought for a moment.

"Ish your other son, you know, Michael, no, Wayne, coming to the wedding?"

She asked as she wobbled unsteadily on her stool.

Terri pondered the question as though she had been asked a particularly difficult riddle.

"Yesh!" She replied, eventually.

"He's a naughty boy though. I told him not to come, because Dean will be there and he still thinks Wayne got James to....well, you know."

Carrie nodded.

"At least Wayne has got the powers to blast him into obli, oblivi, pieces, if he attacks him."

Terri readily agreed:

"He's put weight on and Dean is in his sixties now. Wayne would murder him."

Carrie shook her head:

"No, I don't mean physical powers, I mean his magic powers. You know, as the last of the Tuatha."

Terri frowned and looked confused.

"What do you mean?" She asked, perplexed.

Carrie pulled her head back and tried to focus her eyes on Terri's face.

"You know, that leprechaun, or whatever he was, whatever, who got you pregnant. He passed his magical powers on to Wayne. James told me he saw him blasting lightening out of his hands, like some sort of comic book superhero dude."

Terri screwed up her face and laughed:

"Michael's father was from Tupelo, Mishishippi. He looked like Elvish, not a leprechaun."

It was now Carrie's turn to look confused:

"What's the difference between an elf and a leprechaun?"

Terri shook her head:

"I meant Elvish Presley, not the little, pointy eared people." She giggled:

"Though he does have very, very, big pointy ears."

Somewhere in the subconscious, sober recesses of her brain, the memory of Danny Finn from Mississippi morphing into Aillen Mac Fionnbharr emerged. That had been what had given her that first nervous breakdown. Then she remembered the disembodied voice by her pool when she had still been married to Dean.

Was it even remotely possible that it had all been real? That she had not imagined it? That her son's father really did have magical powers and that her breakdowns had been caused by real events, rather than being the products of her own febrile mind?

Terri Thorne suddenly felt cold and so much more sober.

Carrie had always been interested in the occult and mysticism, but she had never mentioned Wayne's powers before.

Terri leaned back towards her friend, who was still going on about the "little people." Terri's sombrero bashed into Carrie's face, which caused much guffawing.

"I'll ask you more about this, when we're sober." Terri announced.

30

"The little sucker's never done any magic for me. Mind you, neither did Dean although he always promised it."

The women giggled again.

It was at that moment that someone burst into the bar and shouted urgently:

"Turn on the TV, turn on the TV."

There was a great deal of protesting by the merry bridal shower party, but the barman dutifully turned on a TV suspended high above the bar counter and slowly a hush descended on the bar as the clientele watched a repeat on the news bulletin of the evening's earlier events on the Bannerman show.

"Oh my God!" Carrie gasped: "Is he for real?"

Terri sat in stunned amazement as she watched her ex-husband's cousin's boy perform miracles on the TV.

The news anchor woman continued by stating that reports were slowly emerging from all over the country of blind people miraculously regaining their sight.

As soon as the bulletin ended the TV was switched off and where there had been a party atmosphere, the mood was now serious and the whoops and yells were replaced by heated discussion.

"My God, do you think he could be, like, the Son of God?" Carrie asked Terri.

Terri considered the question, thought about Lucien Vitalia, Luca, or Luke Lively as he was known to millions.

"No!" was her eventual succinct response, then, after a few more minutes thought:

"He's an arrogant, sneaky, selfish and incredibly egotistical little brat."

"Oh!" Carrie sounded disappointed.

"He seemed like such a nice boy when he was in "The Amishers.""

The next morning Terri awoke with a screaming hangover. The bridal shower had ended pretty soon after the TV interlude. The gaggle of girls had been unable to raise their spirits with the prospect of judgment day being just around the corner, even though most commentators were dismissing the claims of Luke Lively, as they still insisted on calling him. The breakfast TV news was still full of the previous evening's Bannerman show.

It appeared that Luke had abruptly left the studio after changing Billy Connolly's water into Scotch, although he had announced to the audience that he would explain much more soon.

David Bannerman and Billy Connolly had been unavailable for comment since the show had ended.

Terri popped a couple of aspirins into her mouth and swilled them down with soda.

It wasn't only the Bannerman show that was playing on her mind, but something that Carrie had said about her son, Michael, or Wayne. Although she couldn't remember Carrie's exact words, she had definitely stated that James had seen him blasting lightening out of the palms of his hands. Therapy had twice convinced Theresa O'Brien, as she had been known when she had first met Danny Finn; that he had been no more than a simple boy from Tupelo, Mississippi, who had run like the wind when he had thought he might have to bear the responsibilities of parenthood. That half remembered dream she had had, when he had revealed himself to be a "faerie" had been just that, a dream, hadn't it? The reflection she had seen in the pool at Coldwater Canyon and the weird voice she had heard when she had been pregnant all those years ago. That had been her mind, hadn't it?

Terri Thorne slowly convinced herself that Carrie was just a crazy hippie chick who believed in things like "faeries," even so, she decided that she might have a question or two for Wayne when he arrived in Southern California.

Seven

The fallout from the Bannerman show soon spread across the oceans. The internet was buzzing with clips of Luke Lively miraculously changing water into wine or whisky and declaring him self the "Son of God."

Monsignor Doyle had been informed within a few hours of the shows transmission and was not surprised when His Holiness the Pope summoned him to his private chambers early the next morning. Pope Gregory XVII had been known as Cardinal Pietr Warzowski until his elevation the previous year and had been fully involved in the search for Cardinal D'Abruzzo's missing "child Messiah." He had personally committed Father Reichmann and his assistant Father Doyle to the search, until the former had died suddenly during a trip to America. Father Abraham Reichmann had suffered a massive coronary failure just as he was about to tell the then Father Doyle about a significant breakthrough he had made. The memory of the kindly German Priest's demise still haunted the Irishman.

When Monsignor Doyle entered the Pope's chambers, he found the old man, unsurprisingly, in a state of nervous agitation.

"Have you seen it?" The Pope demanded before any greetings had been exchanged or formalities entered. Doyle knew immediately what the Holy Father was referring to.

"No, Your Holiness." He answered with a resigned shake of his head.

The Pope was stood looking out of his window over the Piazza.

"Sadly, neither have I. However, my sources tell me that the tricks performed on this "chat" show, so stunned the presenter that he has been taken quite ill. He, for one, is totally convinced that this boy is indeed the second coming of "Our Lord." What do you think, Monsignor Doyle?"

Doyle took a deep breath, but before he could speak the Pope turned from the window and approached him:

"There are three possibilities: The first is that this boy is a charlatan, a conjuror of cheap and childish tricks, albeit a very good one.

The second possibility is that this truly is "Our Lord" returned among us, just as he promised. This could be the very boy that Cardinal D'Abruzzo sheltered within these walls. The boy's age is right and the description of a blond cherubic child fits perfectly. If this is the case then we must prepare for a joyous judgment day.

The third possibility and the one that frightens me, is that this is D'Abruzzo's boy, but as our friend, the late Father Reichmann suspected, he is a demon of unimaginable evil."

The Pope paused as he considered the unlikely possibility that the boyish actor, Luke Lively, could indeed be the Son of God.

Monsignor Doyle was about to speak when the Pope interrupted him again:

"My view, for what it is worth, is that the boy is a cheap conjuror drumming up publicity."

Monsignor Doyle opened his mouth, but the Pope suddenly wagged his finger.

"However, if he is a demon we must find out very quickly. I can not imagine "Our Lord" wishing to take high political office, but I can imagine a demon trying to take charge of the biggest nuclear arsenal in the world."

The Pope rubbed his forehead, his face anguished.

Doyle waited for a moment and then spoke:

"Your Holiness, my humble opinion is precisely your first considered possibility. Indeed the American news media seem to be of one mind about the issue."

"What about the "miracle" of the blind?" The Pope shot back as he retired behind an ornate desk.

"It is being reported that hundreds of blind people, or their relatives are ringing TV stations and newspapers saying how they got their sight back, as soon as the boy stated that: "a thousand blind shall see.""

Monsignor Doyle shrugged:

"Mass hysteria, the Americans are known for it. Your Holiness."

The Pope clasped his hands together as though he was about to pray.

"Monsignor Doyle, we must know the boys intention. If he is our saviour then I am surprised at the route he is taking. If he is just a blundering fool, then he needs to be exposed and very quickly. If he is "Our Lord" we must ensure that we are the first to welcome him and that the "Church of Rome" gives him all our support and protection.

If he is a demon, he must be destroyed. Abraham Reichmann once mentioned to me that there was someone as powerful as this demon and that he would provide balance. This person must be found."

Monsignor Doyle nodded.

"Yes, Your Holiness."

The Pope sighed:

"You will take charge of this exposition, Monsignor Doyle. You will use any means at your disposal to identify the true nature of this boy's intentions. For this purpose, I am immediately reactivating "The

Sacred Order of Saint Gregory." You will be at its head Monsignor Doyle."

Monsignor Doyle bowed and reached out to take the Pope's hand to kiss his ring.

"Thank you, Your Holiness."

The Pope acquiesced to the Priest kissing the symbol of his authority.

"My namesake and predecessor had the best intentions when he originally created "The Order." However, I fear that in its hunger for success, "the Order" created the monster that became the agent of its own destruction. Your new "Order" will be more careful. Father Reichmann said that you were a brilliant young Priest. This will be the most important task of your life, Monsignor and a chance to repay the old man's faith in you."

Doyle nodded:

"Yes, Your Holiness." He stated flatly.

"I will not fail you."

The Pope watched the Irish Priest turn and leave his chambers:

"It is not just me you would fail if you make a mistake my friend. The plight of every mortal soul on this Earth is in your hands."

Eight

Wayne leaned over his son and stared out of the 747-400's small oval window at the familiar mountain range, burning red in the late afternoon sun.

"You know, I can still remember the thrill I got the first time I saw those mountains." Wayne commented wistfully.

"I used to love coming to L.A." He continued, as the mountains became the outer suburbs of the city's inland empire.

Frankie nodded.

"Yeah Dad, it looks really cool. I can see loads of swimming pools down there."

"Your Grandma used to have a pool." Wayne whispered as he remembered Terri's house on Coldwater Canyon with its magnificent pool on the patio that overlooked Beverley Hills. He remembered the beautiful young Californian girl who had crashed the party, hoping to get spotted and had ended up making love with him. It had been Wayne's first time. He strained his mind in a desperate effort to remember the girl's name; all he could recall was that it began with a J. and that she had been tall, blonde and incredibly gorgeous.

He remembered Aurelio, Dean's older, fat cousin from the East Coast and felt a slight cringe as he remembered his cheek being tweaked patronisingly and the limp, cold handshake that the sweaty, then prospective Senator had given him.

Most of all, however, Wayne remembered Aurelio's son, the boy with the strange eyes.

The boy with the same eyes as the faceless figure in black that had taunted Wayne in his adolescent dreams and had cursed his magic.

The boy who now just happened to be running for the office of the most powerful man on earth.

The plane's cabin director interrupted Wayne's reminiscences by announcing that the cabin crew should take their seats for landing as the giant plane dipped towards the runway at LAX.

Would Luke Lively be at the wedding? Wayne wondered, as he grinned reassuringly at Katie and Natalia across the narrow aisle. It was doubtful. According to the press, Luca Vitalia, as he now wanted to be known, was avoiding public appearances until his upcoming guest spot on the Oprah show, due in just over two weeks time.

Luca had guaranteed another miracle, but had stated that would be his last, as he did not want to become known as a mere magician. He would fight the forthcoming election on an independent platform and would deal with the issues facing America and the world as both a politician and a spiritual leader with links to all three of the great Abrahamic faiths.

Wayne snorted derisively. Whatever Luca Vitalia was, he was certainly not the second coming of Jesus Christ. Yet, somewhere, deep in his subconscious mind, Wayne could not help but wonder if Luca was who he claimed to be. After all, wasn't it Wayne Higginbotham who had killed a man, not Luca Vitalia?

Wasn't it Wayne Higginbotham who had destroyed the mind of a child, even if he was a psychopathic bully, not Luca Vitalia?

And wasn't it Wayne Higginbotham who had effectively raped and given a girl a nervous breakdown, probably ruined her career and made her pregnant?

Luca Vitalia might not be Jesus Christ, but Wayne Higginbotham wasn't exactly a pearly white and innocent Saint either.

Wayne wondered what might have happened to Sabine. He hadn't heard from her since he had graduated, then again, he hadn't made any effort to contact her. An overwhelming sense of guilt flooded his senses. What a stupid, shallow youth he had been.

Wayne Higginbotham had been blessed with the sort of magical powers that every child dreams of. Every child wants to be a comic book super hero and Wayne had had it all, except for the ability to fly, super strength, spider sense and all that stuff that filled Frankie's Marvel comics and DVDs.

Yet, he had been cursed to waste his gifts on greed, lust and violence, hence why he had not performed any magic at all, in well over twenty years.

The thing that really worried Wayne was the possibility that had he carried on using magic to further his own ends, he might have tipped over to the dark side and become the evil one that the "Sacred Order of Saint Gregory" had attempted to eliminate. Was that possible?

The plane touched down and the Higginbotham family entered Southern California for their first proper visit. Terri was in the terminal to greet them, almost lost amongst the throng of taxi drivers, family members meeting loved ones and bewildered looking tourists. Terri hugged her grandchildren first, then Natalia and finally Wayne. She looked concerned:

"You've lost weight." She gasped urgently, brushing a strand of grey hair back off his forehead. Wayne grinned:

"You always say that, Mom, I'm fine, just older and fatter if anything. You on the other hand look great."

Terri grimaced bashfully:

"I'm old, fat and very, very stressed." She stated, rolling her eyes sardonically.

Wayne laughed. Terri Thorne was still incredibly beautiful and looked at least twenty years younger than her actual age. Yet he did think that beneath the confident veneer, there existed an edge that evidenced her worries about her son being in California, in the vicinity of Dean Vitalia.

The first two days of the vacation were spent fitting tuxedos and dresses. Frankie had been given the honour of being the ring-bearer at the wedding ceremony, while Katie was to be a maid of honour. Wayne himself was to be a groomsman for his younger brother and felt very honoured to be asked. The strange fact was that although Marco and Wayne had been raised on different continents and had an effective seventeen-year age gap, they were very similar as individuals. The little time they had spent together had been extremely rewarding and the brothers had developed a very close sibling relationship. Despite Wayne being a typically British be-suited academic, while Marco fulfilled the role of the cool Californian artistic dude, excelling in art and music, the brothers shared exactly the same sense of humour and were at one in just about every single interest.

Without any help from his famous father, Marco's band had just released their first album and the feedback had been extremely positive. Wayne was as proud of his little brother as it was possible to be.

The icing on the cake for Wayne was that it was James Malone's daughter that Marco was going to marry. Wayne had never quite understood why James had named his daughter, Aoibheall, after the evil Banshee that had tried to kill him, all those years ago. But even he couldn't deny that James and Carrie had produced a beauty the equal of any mythological being.

It was on the journey down to Mexico that Wayne began to consider the bizarre series of co-incidences that had led to the wedding of Marco Vitalia and Aoibheall Vasquez in Rosarito, Baja, Mexico and how the boy from the Yorkshire Dales had ended up in the middle of it.

As the mini van they'd hired lined up to cross the busy, chaotic border at Tijuana, Wayne wondered about everything that had happened to him since Baz Thompson had put him into hospital in 1974. No matter how much he tried to deny it, there did seem to be something going on that was bringing a few people towards an inevitable and potentially cataclysmic convergence.

What was even more bizarre was the fact that the daughter of his best friend was marrying the little brother he had never expected to have.

For the first time in his life, Wayne Higginbotham contemplated the possibility of a grand design. It was just all too convenient, too perfect to be pure happenstance. Maybe something, or someone out there was pulling the strings. Wayne didn't know whether that made him feel more, or less comfortable. It all depended on who exactly was pulling the strings and whether he was going to be on Wayne's side, or not.

For over twenty years, Wayne Higginbotham had lived the life of a normal family man, primarily engaged in first building a solid career and a happy marriage, then in building a secure and happy family. Magic had had absolutely no place in his life. Aillen Mac Fionnbharr had become a distant memory, almost like something embarrassing that had happened in his childhood.

It was in the bar in the "Las Palmas Resort Hotel" on the night of their arrival in Mexico, however, that Wayne realised that his prolonged efforts to deny his birth-right might be coming to an end.

The first thing that happened was when his mother, Terri, asked him quite out of the blue:

"Wayne, what do you know about your father?"

Wayne had almost dropped his lime-plugged bottle of Mexican beer. Natalia had taken the kids to bed and Terri and her son had found some time to be alone for the first time in many years.

Wayne blew out a huge sigh:

"Well, mainly what you've told me, of course. He was an American, from Tupelo Mississippi, I think. His name was Danny and that's about it." He shrugged and shuffled uncomfortably.

Terri smiled wistfully and looked around the cantina styled bar area. It was nearly empty; most of the other guests were due to arrive the following day. She looked back at her son.

"I will never forget that day, when I first saw you on Daideo's farm, running down the hillside as I got out of the taxi. That was a long time ago. Yet in all that time I've never really talked about your father, have I?"

Wayne coughed:

"No, not really, you don't have to, you...."

Terri held her hand up to interrupt him.

"I've never told you the full story because I always believed that you would think that I was mad." She laughed as Wayne shook his head.

"Well now you know that I am mad, I don't see what difference it makes."

Wayne tried to speak but Terri hushed him:

"I really did think that Danny was from Tupelo, Mississippi. That's what he told me. He was a handsome devil and had all the charm and blarney in the world."

Her eyes misted over as she drifted back over four decades to an Ireland that now only existed in the memory and the imagination.

"Danny used to take me to dances in Tourmakeady, Finney, Cornamona and all over. All the other girls were so jealous. I will never forget the first time he kissed me. It was like a sip of champagne and a bite of a strawberry at the same time as a million Fourth of July fireworks exploded over my head. Of course one thing led to another as it tends to when you are young, impetuous and ruled by the body rather than the brain and…"

Terri noticed her son's slightly glazed, uncomfortable expression and she laughed again and gripped his hand:

"Don't worry I'm not going to go into the sordid details. It was what happened afterwards that I want to tell you about."

Terri Thorne took a deep breath and leaned in towards Wayne. She swallowed as though her throat had dried up, but she managed a low whisper.

"Just after we had, well, you know, your father revealed his true self."

Now it was Wayne's turn to gulp. Terri closed her eyes and visibly steeled herself.

"Your father changed into one of the faery folk, one of the little people."

Terri's breath came in short sharp bursts as she opened her eyes, to see if her son was laughing at her, or whether he was just looking at his evidently mad mother in abject horror.

To her surprise Wayne looked quite calm.

"Your father, well I guess he was not human, Michael." Terri stated as serenely as she could manage, using the name she had not called her son in many years. She averted her eyes in embarrassment.

"I decided to tell you all this now, because Carrie seems to believe that you are some sort of faery yourself."

Wayne laughed:

"The cheek of the woman. I always thought I came across as quite macho."

Terri and her son laughed easily, but Wayne could see the plaintive look in her eye. She needed reassurance that she was not insane.

40

Wayne grinned at her:

"Did my Father tell you that he was Aillen Mac Fionnbharr. Last High King of the mighty Tuatha de Danaan. That he was immortal and could shape shift at will, as well as being able to become invisible and all that stuff."

Terri's face froze. It was as though Wayne had hit a raw nerve.

"Are you mocking me? You think I'm mad, don't you?"

Wayne smiled sympathetically:

"No Mom. Think back, those would have been his actual words, as near as makes no difference. You see, I actually met my father before I met you. I was there. I was there the night he died. I saw my father pass away."

By the time he had finished his sentence, Wayne's eyes had misted over, somehow, unconsciously, mother and son were holding each other's hands tightly.

"So you see I don't think you're mad. Not one little bit."

Terri searched Wayne's eyes for any hint of mockery as Wayne continued.

"That was how I met James Malone. When I was eleven, I found out that I'd been adopted when I heard some doctors whispering in the hospital where I was recovering after a fight. Once I'd found out it was really true, I ran away to find you and eventually I ended up at Daideo's house. My father found me there. I was there when Father James Malone, as he was then, tried to help my father fight off the assassin who had been sent by the "Order" to eliminate Aillen, or Mickey Finn as everyone knew him locally. I was the assassin's target once he'd stabbed my father. It was my adopted dad, Frank, who saved me that night."

Terri nodded frantically:

"We all knew Mickey Finn. He was just regarded as an old eccentric farmer."

Her face creased in horror:

"So you mean, my Danny, was actually dirty, smelly, old Mickey Finn?"

Wayne nodded and grimaced playfully:

"Dan Joyce was another of his favourite guises."

Terri made a retching sound:

"Dan Joyce and Mickey Finn? But they were dirty old men. I was only sixteen."

Wayne couldn't help but smirk:

"They were one man and he was so much older than you could ever imagine."

Terri leaned back in her chair and burst into tears.

"All these years, I've thought I was soooo mad." She wailed before wiping her eyes and turning crossly towards Wayne:

"Jesus, Michael, why didn't you tell me you knew all this stuff thirty years ago?"

Wayne shrugged:

"Same reason you didn't tell me. Like, it's not exactly the sort of thing that comes out over a cup of tea, is it? Oh, by the way, did I tell you your Father was a leprechaun? Or hey Mom, what's it like to make love to one of the faery folk?"

A waiter approached the couple, who were suddenly laughing like lunatics.

"Er, nothing for me thanks, er, gracias."

Wayne asked his mother if she wanted anything.

"No thank you. I think it's past my bedtime." She responded as her face took on a serious expression again. The waiter nodded curtly and wandered off.

"You do know you have a sister?" She asked, tentatively.

Wayne nodded:

"Of course. Molly told me that when I was eleven, before I'd even got as far as Daideo's."

"Ah." Terri nodded.

"I don't suppose…"

Wayne shook his head as he predicted what she was going to ask:

"There's no trace of her Mom. Maybe one day she'll find us."

There was a long silence.

Terri took another deep breath:

"Do you have any, like you know, special abilities?"

Wayne rubbed his forehead and sighed.

"I once, you know, did a few things that could be described as magic, I guess, but that was a long, long time ago. It scared me. I wasn't mature enough to wield magic."

He snorted:

"I'm probably still not."

Terri nodded:

"Does Natalia know?"

Wayne shook his head.

"Nobody, just you and Carrie. James told her that I had some, errr special abilities, as you just called them."

Terri smiled as she gave her son's hand a squeeze:

"You have no idea what a weight that is off my mind."

Terri Thorne reached out her hand and gently traced her index finger around Wayne's left ear.

"I should have known it was all true when I first saw your pointed little ears when you were first born. Your sister had them too."

"Little?" Wayne queried sardonically.

Terri kissed Wayne on the forehead, bade him goodnight and wandered contentedly back off to her room. Thirty years of doubt and pain had been partially ameliorated.

Wayne sighed heavily as he watched her walk away. If only his sister would make contact with one of the organisations that reunited families affected by adoption, then his mother's primal wound could be healed. The time she had lost with her first-born twins could never be replaced, but at least she would know what had happened to them. His life hadn't been perfect, but it could have been so much worse. He smiled sadly, held up his glass of tequila and toasted Frank and Doris Higginbotham from that little market town in the Yorkshire Dales for everything they had ever done for him.

It was at that moment that Dean Vitalia walked into the bar accompanied by a pneumatic blonde girl less than half his age.

Wayne felt the hackles rise up on the back of his neck. He saw Dean cast him a cursory glance and realised that although he recognised Dean, after a period of over twenty years, Dean did not recognise him.

It was at that moment that Wayne decided that he would find out the truth about the murder of James Malone at some point during the wedding. He would find out the truth for once and for all and following his discussions with his mother, he knew exactly how he was going to do it.

Nine

Lucy Sherman did not like Aurelio Vitalia. She did not like him one little bit. Not that she had ever met him, they moved in very different circles, even within the tight knit legal and political social arenas, but Lucy had read a great deal about him and knew people that were well acquainted with him. The word most commonly used to describe Vitalia, whether in the press, or on people's lips was "sleazy". His reputation as a former Mafioso had dogged his political career and had ensured that a seat in the Senate House would be the apogee of his political career. There had also been a gamut of rumours about his many affairs with much younger women and about the apparently suspicious suicide of his wife of only a couple of years, over two decades earlier.

The most remarkable thing about Aurelio Vitalia and the thing that puzzled Lucy most, was how he had managed to get elected in the first place and how had he kept his seat in election after election? Although rumours abounded about bribery, corruption and sharp practices in his electoral campaigns, no one had ever managed to substantiate any of the evidence presented against him. Senator Teflonia had become the nickname most commonly apportioned to him by the tabloid press. The few that had tried to prove that he had engaged in dubious practices had been successfully sued in Court, with Vitalia always representing himself and playing "the son of the poor immigrant, so unfairly discriminated against," card.

His favourite line was: "So, I'm of poor Italian, Catholic stock and my granddaddy didn't roll in on the Mayflower, but that don't make me a crook and it don't mean I'm involved in organized crime. Is every Irishman a drunk? Every German a Nazi? Every Frenchman a coward? Every Englishman a faggot? No! So don't go assuming that every Italian is mafia. In any case, I am a true blue American first, foremost and goddam forever!"

One thing that was certain was that Vitalia had been a damn good lawyer. Even Lucy had to admire his pugilistic courtroom style and he had taken the same aggressive approach into the Senate house where he had been fierce in his sponsorship of several populist policies designed to benefit blue-collar workers. Certainly the Union vote had been crucial in his electoral success.

Lucy had run into Dean Vitalia a few times when she had been Chief Executive of Sherman General Law Inc. (Los Angeles) during the early Nineties. However, she had found him comparatively charming, albeit somewhat predatory, certainly nothing at all like his rotund, slimy, sweaty cousin.

It was not, therefore, with the greatest of enthusiasm that she had greeted Jonathan's news that the Vitalia clan wanted Sherman General Law Inc. to represent them during Luca Vitalia's Presidential campaign. Although Lucy had been a fan of the "Amishers" and Jemima, her daughter, had had a crush on Luke Lively during his pop star period, she found the whole thing totally and utterly ridiculous. Luca Vitalia was no more than a boy for goodness sake. As far as she was concerned, association with such a doomed cause could irrevocably damage Sherman General Law Inc. Not that she was going to say as much to her husband. Jonathan T. Sherman had stated many times that when it came to the home she was boss, but when it came to Sherman General, that was his baby, just like it had been his daddy's. They had had many rows about his professional intransigence in the early years, but since she had given up work, she had decided to let him get on with it, for better or for worse.

Aurelio Vitalia's adopted son's declaration of his intention to run for President had initially been greeted with hilarity by the mass media, considering Vitalia senior's reputation, but the "Bannerman miracles" had quickly changed that initial perspective to incredulity, scepticism and no small degree of doubt.

Lucy had been one of the many people who had not seen the Bannerman show and had immediately decided upon hearing about it, that it had been a well-managed publicity stunt. The "miracle of the blind" was obviously just down to mass hysteria and people saying they had been cured in the hope that they would be interviewed on TV and gain their fifteen minutes of fame.

Lucy expected the whole thing to die down quickly, but events quickly spiralled out of control. There were riots in several Southern Cities and in the Middle East, millions took the street and burned American flags and beat their chests in protest at what was perceived as a mockery of one of Islam's revered prophets. The press across the Western World speculated furiously about what Luca Vitalia's intentions were, above and beyond a brief burst of publicity. After a week, small voices began to emerge giving the erstwhile actor and pop star some credence, especially in the Southern States. One thing was for certain. Whatever conjuring trick Luca had lined up for the Oprah show, it had better be bigger than anything any magician or illusionist had ever achieved before.

It was much to Lucy's surprise when the usually composed Jonathan came home to the Manhattan apartment one evening, about a week after the Bannerman show, looking very agitated and worried.

"What on earth is the matter, darling?" Lucy asked, her precise English accent having lost none of its clipped tones, in nearly two decades in America.

Jonathan sat at the shiny stainless steel breakfast bar and looked out of the kitchen window at the brightly lit, steel and glass skyscraper opposite.

"I need a drink." He gasped.

Lucy had never seen her usually calm and collected husband so traumatised. She poured him a large twelve-year-old Scotch.

Jonathan T. Sherman knocked the amber liquid back in one gulp and held the glass out for his wife to refill. Lucy shrugged and poured him a similar sized shot, which he downed in one, again.

"Are you going to tell me what the hell is going on?" Lucy demanded.

Jonathan rubbed his eyes despondently.

"I met the Vitalia kid today." He whispered.

"I think we ought to bring the kids back from England."

Lucy snorted derisively:

"Good grief, they've hardly had time to unpack their trunks. What could possibly have got you so upset?" Her face suddenly tightened into a mask of concern:

"Has the company folded?"

Jonathan shook his head.

"It wouldn't matter. None of it matters. Nothing matters any more."

Lucy grabbed Jonathan's shoulders:

"What is going on, Jon?" She was now clearly worried and was sounding sympathetic, although she didn't know why.

Jonathan stood and poured himself another large Scotch.

"I met the Vitalia kid. He's, well he's........."

Lucy laughed:

"He's what? A loony? A smart cookie whose got the attention of the entire World? An odious little creep, like his father?"

Jonathan T, Sherman shook his head slowly:

"No, it's worse than that. Much, much worse."

Lucy laughed but this time her laugh was short and sounded panicked.

"What do you mean?" She gasped.

Jonathan T. Sherman looked up into his wife's beautiful eyes.

"He's the real thing, honey. I think Luca Vitalia is truly the Son of God."

Lucy Sherman raised her eyebrows derisively:

"Jon, darling. You are absolutely the last person I expected to be taken in by this charlatan. He's no more than a conjuror for God's sake."

Jonathan started to cry. Great big heaving sobs shook his shoulders. He dropped off the stool and fell to his knees on the kitchen floor, his hands clasped in prayer.

Lucy stepped back away from him, amazed and disgusted in equal measure.

The man she had been married to for fifteen years. The man she had known for more than twenty years, ever since she had bumped into him outside a bookshop in Oxford was at that moment totally and utterly unrecognisable.

The incredibly intelligent agnostic had become a blubbering convert within minutes of meeting Luca Vitalia.

"Please forgive her for she knows not what she says." He repeated, mantra like, over and over again, through racking sobs.

Lucy Sherman suddenly felt very lonely and an awful long way from home.

Ten

The intense Mexican sunlight played on the water behind the happy couple, providing the perfect backdrop as they tenderly kissed beneath an arch of blood red roses. The cliff top location was beyond perfection and as a ten-piece Mariachi band marched towards the bride and groom, wearing huge black sombreros and singing a Mexican love song, the seated audience of wedding guests broke into spontaneous applause.

Marco and Aoibheall Vitalia, nee Vasquez, were now man and wife and the ceremony could not have been any more spectacular, nor could it have gone any better.

Terri Thorne and Carrie Vasquez were both wiping away tears of joy as the happy couple were joined by their maids of honour, Marina Vitalia and Katie Higginbotham and by their ring bearing nephew, Frankie Higginbotham, for the official photographs.

Marina had chosen the little girl of a neighbour as her flower girl and she too ran eagerly towards the fairy tale couple looking for all the world like a picture book nymph.

Wayne snapped multiple photos as Natalia looked on proudly. Young Frankie maintained a cool and sombre demeanour, befitting his outfit, a junior James Bond in his smart black Tuxedo, which he had kept tightly buttoned up despite the heat of the late Mexican afternoon.

As the hundred or so guests stood and began to wander over towards a huge marquee for the reception, Wayne noticed Dean glowering at him from just underneath a palm tree near the main hotel reception. Wayne forced a smile.

"So you know who I am now, Deano?" He whispered under his breath.

The photographer called for all the groomsmen and the fathers to attend the bride and groom. Dean, along with Miguel Vasquez, a High School friend of Marco's and Wayne, gathered by the happy couple under the arch of roses.

"OK Smile!" The photographer ordered.

"Hello Michael." Dean hissed through a fixed grin.

"I've only just realised that it was you."

"Really?" Wayne hissed back,

"Have I changed that much?"

Dean cast him a furtive glance.

"Yes. You've gotten old. Plus everyone is calling you, what is it? Wayne now?"

Wayne grinned for the camera again.

"That's 'cos it's been my name since I was six weeks old."

Dean nodded and then fixed another grin for the photographer.

"So this is your boy, huh?" His voice whistled through his teeth as he nodded towards Frankie who had been told to join the male group.

Wayne nodded:

"Yep, that's my boy, Frank."

Dean whistled:

"Fine boy you got, good name too. Did you name him after Sinatra?"

Wayne shook his head:

"No, Higginbotham, Frank Higginbotham."

Dean raised his eyebrows as the photographer shouted:

"OK that's a wrap. Thanks guys."

The men strolled away from the cliff top as the flower girl and maids of honour approached the arch.

"I haven't seen you in what, twenty years or more?" Dean stated as he appraised Wayne.

"Yeah, I guess." Wayne responded coolly, "I think the last time I saw you, was at a party in your back yard, when you introduced me to your cousin and his son."

Wayne had to admit that Dean, despite the fact that he must have been over sixty, was still looking incredibly good. His hair was still jet black without a single strand of grey, which Wayne certainly couldn't claim. His figure was unnaturally trim, his tan still a perfect shade of brown and the cut of his tuxedo impeccable. His only real signs of ageing were the lines by his eyes and just above his top lip.

"Yeah, I remember." Dean muttered as he pulled a silver cigar case from his inside pocket.

"You're looking very well." Wayne stated, almost mechanically.

Dean nodded:

"Yeah, I work out and I stay young by dating young women."

He laughed and slapped Wayne's shoulder.

"Talking of young women, I guess that's your daughter."

He nodded in Katie's direction.

"She's beautiful." Dean added, "as is your wife."

"Thanks." Wayne muttered.

It was true. Katie looked a million dollars in the shiny pink dress, with her long luscious shiny brunette hair done up with ringlets, while

Natalia had pushed the boat out and was wearing a silky white designer evening dress that displayed her svelte figure perfectly.

"Yeah, you gotta nice family." Dean muttered, almost threateningly.

"Dean, Dean." A woman's shrill high voice permeated the air.

"We'll talk later Michael. It's good to see you." Dean stated insincerely as he patted Wayne's back, smiled at the younger man and wandered off towards the young blonde woman Wayne had seen him with the previous evening.

Wayne was immediately reminded of a crocodile. Funny, he'd never noticed that about Dean before.

"So that's your brother's father?" He heard Natalia's voice as she strolled up behind him.

Wayne nodded:

"Yeah, that's him. Let's go get a drink!"

The reception went off without a hitch, although Wayne did feel that Dean's eyes were burning into him a couple of times, yet when he looked up, his mother's ex-husband's eyes were only on his girlfriend. Wayne had to admit that Dean made a moving and witty speech about the happy couple; he even managed a humorous aside about his protégé's claim to be the Son of God:

"He'll either be the President, the Pope, or have the best luxury, designer padded cell in Beverley Hills."

It was during Dean's performance that Wayne noticed Carrie's eyes, however. She clearly had not forgotten James' posthumous accusation that Dean Vitalia would be responsible for his murder. Wayne had never seen a beautiful woman look so venomous.

The hot afternoon swiftly turned into a warm, sultry evening and the sky became an immense panoply of stars. As the revellers became more and more intoxicated, the laughter got louder and more raucous and the disco music pounded, like ancient war drums.

Wayne tried to limit his alcohol intake. He needed to be sober to carry out his planned activities, but drinks just kept appearing and the champagne flowed like water.

Carrie caught him by the arm just before eleven o' clock, while Natalia was taking Frankie off to bed. Wayne had just been wandering between the Marquee and the main garden when Carrie had caught up with him. She must have been on her way back from the loo, despite the fact that she had a drink in her hand.

"How are you, Wayne?" She slurred slightly. Wayne had already had a long chat with her earlier in the day, when her focus had purely been on her daughter and any potential problems in the dresses and the ceremony.

"Fine, Carrie." Wayne gasped as his friend's widow stumbled slightly and dug her nails into his arm.

"How are you? You look absolutely stunning. Poor Aoibheall must almost feel outshone."

Carrie grimaced and ignored the compliment. Whilst sober she had had too much on her mind to allow any bitterness to surface and she had been determined not to ruin her daughter's big day.

Now, however, after a few drinks, the bad memories had floated to the surface of Carrie's mind, like a bloated corpse in a river.

"Can you believe the audacity of that man?" She spat as she clutched her tall crystal glass of champagne and wobbled slightly on the spot.

"Mr Nice guy, Mr Show biz. He must have balls of solid steel to even turn up here after what he did."

Despite the volume of the pounding disco music, Wayne was aware that Carrie's voice was rising above the general level of laughter and conversation that emanated from the marquee and the strident volume of the crickets and tree frogs that echoed around the Hotel grounds.

"I mean." She grasped Wayne's arm again for support.

"He killed my daughter's father, my husband, my lovely James and now he pretends to be the perfect Father in Law. If he ever harms one hair of my daughter's head, I'll kill him, I swear."

Wayne smiled beatifically.

"There was never any proof, Carrie. It's hard but........."

Carrie pushed Wayne back and turned the same venomous glare on him that had been directed on Dean earlier.

"Shame on you, Wayne Higginbotham. You were his best friend. He loved you like a little brother." Carrie's normally beautiful face was twisted grotesquely:

"He was always there for you. He saved your life, Goddammit. Yet, you with all your supposed special powers, you didn't do anything for him."

Wayne glanced around. Two or three of the younger guests were stopping to observe what looked to be developing into a major row. Carrie wobbled on the spot but managed to stay upright.

"Carrie, shhh, I..."

The music stopped in the Marquee, momentarily.

"Don't you shush me, Wayne Higginbotham. James Malone was murdered by that slimy, Italian, mafia schmuck in there. You know it, I know it, James knew it. I will never forgive him and I will never forgive you for not doing anything about it."

Carrie shouted then burst into tears and fled towards the hotel, leaving a Cinderella-like slipper on the grass.

Wayne leant and picked it up. He was suddenly aware of a small red light growing in intensity just off to his left. A cigar end was being dragged on. Dean Vitalia emerged from the shadows and blew a plume of smoke into the starry sky.

"Women, huh?" He murmured.

"Sometimes they say the Godamned craziest things."

Aoibheall appeared, looking worried, still in her wedding dress.

"Wayne, was that Mom I heard shouting?"

Wayne nodded as he handed Aoibheall her mother's slipper:

"Yeah, I think she's a little bit the worse for wear. It's been a hell of a long day for her."

Aoibheall smiled:

"I'll go and tuck her up. I guess she won't be feeling too good tomorrow." She wandered off towards the brightly lit hotel with three or four of her young friends.

Dean drew on his cigar again.

"People really shouldn't make accusations they can't substantiate, even when they're drunk. Even so, I guess I'm related to the late Mr Malone's poor widow now, so I won't sue her."

He grinned, his perfect straight teeth gleaming unnaturally white in the darkness.

Wayne sighed.

"She's just a bit drunk."

Dean smirked:

"So what about you? I know it's all like ancient history now, but did you think I had anything to do with your buddy's murder."

Dean was almost whispering. In the half-light cast by the nearby hotel and through the canvas walls of the Marquee, his face was shadowed, taking on an almost vampiric appearance with his black hair, slicked tightly back over his head.

The shrill sound of a million cicadas was overtaken by the monotonous thud of the disco beat again.

"James was investigating your past, I believe." Wayne whispered as he shrugged.

"He wrote a number of letters saying that if anything happened to him, then we should look no further than you."

He looked Dean straight in the eye.

Dean grinned again and drew on his cigar. He rolled the smoke around in his mouth and then exhaled straight towards Wayne.

"But what do you think?" Dean persisted. "The cops said it was two illegal aliens from down here. A robbery that got out of hand."

Wayne shrugged again.

"It's not for me to say. It was a long, long time ago."

Dean nodded.

"You know, for a long time I thought you might have put him up to it, you know, his sniffing around me, digging up the dirt on my past. You know, because I was divorcing your Mom?"

Wayne shook his head:

"No, it was nothing to do with me. He was a journalist. He'd just started working for a new paper. I guess he thought you'd be the source of a good story."

Dean grimaced and nodded:

"The lady seems to want you to take some sort of revenge."

Wayne smiled:

"Like I said, she's a bit drunk."

Dean walked straight towards Wayne, stopping inches from the younger man.

"I always liked you, Michael. I even considered you to be like my own son. I've never had a girl like Terri and I sometimes wish I could turn the clock back. You know, I felt betrayed that a friend of yours would do something as vindictive as to try to ruin my good reputation."

Dean put his hand on Wayne's shoulder:

"When your buddy started poking his nose into places that he shouldn't have, I guess I automatically assumed you were behind it."

Wayne stared straight back into Dean's dark brown eyes as the older man continued:

"Family is real important to me. Michael. I'm Italian, I love family. In a way you are still part of my family. You're the half brother of my son and daughter. The best buddy of my daughter-in-law's late father. You gotta beautiful family of your own now too, Michael."

Dean patted Wayne's shoulder.

Wayne cocked his head to one side.

"What do you mean by that, Dean?"

Dean dragged on his cigar and blew out yet another plume of smoke.

"Nothing! I'm just saying that a family should stick together, especially with Judgement day being possibly just around the corner."

Wayne smiled:

"I can't help but feel that there was an implied threat there, Dean."

53

Dean grinned then brushed past Wayne and took a couple of steps towards the Marquee, pausing to suck on his cigar. The tip glowed angry and red in the darkness. He turned back towards Wayne:

"Big things are happening, Michael. Big things, things that are way above our heads. Luca don't need the past being dragged up if it's going to do any damage to his campaign. As his agent, I'm a part of that campaign. We gotta brilliant new lawyer who'll sue anybody defaming anyone in Luca's camp. I am not threatening anyone, Michael, but people should think before they open their big mouths, especially family. So the Lady's drunk, I can forgive that. It's a party for Christ's sake. It just seems slightly too much of a coincidence though, that I haven't seen you in twenty years, yet as soon as you show up people start talking about the mafia and me somehow being involved in the murder of some schmuck of a journalist. Just remember, nobody never proved nothing linking me to organised crime."

His voice was becoming angrier by the second.

"Nothing can harm this campaign, Michael. I'm not threatening you. I'm just giving you some good advice. Big things are happening, buddy and nothing can get in the way and I mean nothing. What's past is past."

"James Malone said you'd kill him. He died soon after. You can't blame people for adding two and two, Dean." Wayne responded quickly."

Dean laughed:

"Yeah, and some people can't do the math. They add two and two and come up with five. Even Carrie knows it was a pair of Latinos who killed her husband. Not me. Like you said, buddy, it was all a long, long time ago. You look after your good-looking little family, son and mind your own business. I'll mind mine. I'd feel real bad for Terri if anything was to happen to any of her grandchildren, you know what I mean?"

He turned before Wayne could respond and walked back into the Marquee.

Wayne took a deep breath of clear Pacific air and smiled. Flickering candles that marked the path to the bathrooms in the hotel shone in his eyes.

Dean Vitalia didn't know it, but he had just disturbed something that had lain dormant for many years. Dead men were about to be awakened and the secrets of the past exposed.

Eleven

Any hopes that Lucy had that Jonathan would have recovered in the morning were quickly dashed. He had certainly sobered up and lost the pathetic, hopeless demeanour of the previous evening. Indeed, he seemed almost back to his normal, professional, business-like self, but when Lucy asked him as she poured his morning coffee at the breakfast bar, if he had rationalised any of the conversation that they had shared, he simply said:

"No, I believe that Luca Vitalia is truly the light of the world and is our saviour reborn."

Lucy slowly and calmly replaced the carafe of coffee back onto the machine's hotplate.

"Jonathan, darling. You have always been, what I would describe as a practical man."

She suggested, hesitantly as she placed a slice of hot toast on to his plate.

Jonathan T. Sherman grunted.

"You have always had a fierce, independent intellect that has, on occasion, bordered on arrogance, when confronted by those less gifted than yourself."

Jonathan shrugged as he munched his slice of toast.

"You have always, at least to my knowledge, questioned what you perceive as the irrational norms of our society and gone out of your way to dismiss and I think I quote you: the superstitious, primitive mumbo jumbo that is the basis of all religious faith."

Jonathan sighed and wiped his mouth with a piece of kitchen roll.

Lucy continued as she picked up the dirty plate and placed it in the dishwasher:

"It came, therefore, as something of a surprise when you came in yesterday evening in such an agitated state. I mean can you understand how taken aback I was when my Harvard and Oxford educated husband came in ranting that his latest client was the son of God?"

Jonathan stood and smiled:

"IS the Son of God," he corrected his wife.

Lucy stared at him incredulously as the noise of the morning rush hour in New York City rose the twenty floors to their apartment.

Jonathan took a deep breath.

"Lucy, you know I love you more than life itself and I know that this is an awful damn lot to take in, especially from me, but I know what I've seen. There is no doubt in my mind that Luca Vitalia is what he claims to be, no doubt whatsoever. I've got to go to Los Angeles on Friday. He's doing Oprah and has promised one more miracle. I would sure like you to be there with me. Anyway, you are as much a part of Sherman General as me now, so we are both going to be working for the man."

Lucy continued to stare as she tried to process what he had just said in his calm, measured tones. Jonathan T. Sherman was quite incapable of playing a prank or of acting, so, she deducted, he must really be convinced.

"I'll come." She whispered, "After all the kids are now safely at school in England. What's to stop me?"

Jonathan didn't notice the half-hearted laugh at the end of her sentence.

"I can't wait for you to meet Luca." He grinned:

"I'm sure you'll love him, he may even make you a disciple, like me."

Lucy sort of smiled and winced at the same time:

"Oh, he's letting girls join the club this time is he? Gosh and I'm not even a hooker like Mary Magdalene."

Jonathan caught the inherent sarcasm in her voice. His smile did not reach to his eyes.

"I hope you'll be respectful when you meet him. I would hate to have to consider a future without you."

With that mind numbing statement, he pulled his jacket off a hook on the back of the kitchen door, picked up his briefcase and left.

"No kiss for the kaffir this morning then." Lucy whispered, using the Islamic word for an unbeliever to describe herself. She poured herself a mug of hot steaming coffee and walked over to the window. She had decided to work from home on this day. She had a pile of paperwork to catch up on and it just never got done if she ventured into the office.

Yet now she wished she had gone in. At least it would have been a distraction.

Way below, the sidewalks were crammed with bustling commuters struggling to get to their offices, shops, banks, or whatever job earned them their daily bread. All over the City, millions of people were doing the same thing. They were like ants. Lucy felt a tear run down her cheek. She had known Jonathan for over twenty years and had admired and loved him equally as long, yet overnight he had dropped a bombshell that had turned her world upside down. This was worse than him declaring that he found another woman; at least that would have been down to uncontrollable, irrational hormonal urges. This was intellectual infidelity. She mulled over his last words:

"I would hate to have to consider a future without you."

That was tantamount to an ultimatum. It was almost:

"Lucy, either you are with us, or you're against us. Make your choice."

Lucy watched the ant-like people way below. There was, of course, the faint possibility that he was right and that this actor or singer or whatever he was, was just who he claimed to be. Then everyone's lives would change irrevocably. All those people down there, how would they react? What if judgment day was at hand?

Lucy immediately thought about the twins, Jonju and Jem, why had she sent them so far away? Her first response was to grab the phone and ring her mother, but she stopped before a connexion had been made.

"Poor mummy has enough on her hands with daddy, without all this." She muttered as she replaced the digital receiver. It would be the end of the Michaelmas term in a few short months anyway and she had planned to go to England to collect the children to school.

The question was, would she come back?

Twelve

James Malone stared out of the bathroom mirror. His hair was long, thick, dark and curly, his sideburns long, almost Victorian. His eyes were also brown, or at least Wayne Higginbotham was sure he remembered them as brown. Slowly the face in the mirror changed back into Wayne's own features.

For the first time in over two decades, Wayne Higginbotham, born Michael Sean O'Brien, son of Aillen, son of Fionnbharr, the last of the royal line of the immortal Tuatha de Danaan, the last of the little people, had performed magic and it felt good.

Even though the reformed "Stone of Fail" was over five thousand miles away and hidden under a pile of rocks, the magic still worked. Mind you, Wayne had been able to use magic without even knowing it, long before he had ever heard of, or come into contact with the fabled magical "Stone." The magic was in the heart of the Tuatha de Danaan the "Stone" merely acted as an amplifier. Wayne morphed his face back into that of James Malone and grinned at the reflection in the mirror.

It almost felt like James was alive again:

"Ah, how're you doing you soft eejit?" James asked. Wayne even had his friend's distinct voice and lilting Irish accent still lodged in the back of his mind, even after all these years.

"I'm fine. You should have been here today, mate. Aoibheall looked like a Princess. Believe it or not, she's gone and married my little brother, Marco. He's a nice guy, you'd have liked him."

James' face looked surprised:

"Me little girl, married already, well there's a fine how do you do and me barely cold in me grave."

"Barely cold? It's been more than twenty years you fool. By the way, Carrie looked beautiful too, you would have been so proud."

The face of James Malone twisted regretfully:

"Ah, t'would have been nice, but hey. Tell me young Higginbotham, have you finished off those maniacs that did me in, yet?"

There was a knock on the bathroom door:

"Wayne? Who are you talking to in there?" Natalia's voice emanated from the other side of the door.

Wayne gazed at the face of James Malone for a couple of seconds then whispered:

"No, my friend. That starts tonight, with a little help from you."

The face of James Malone was slowly replaced by Wayne's own familiar features:

"No one, darling." He replied a touch indignantly, "Why?"

"I definitely heard you talking to someone." Natalia persisted, her voice betraying her concern. Wayne opened the bathroom door and grinned sheepishly:

"OK, I admit it, I was talking to the mirror." He admitted sheepishly. Natalia glanced around the white marble hotel bathroom, just to reassure herself. It was empty except for her blushing husband, standing in his underpants.

Natalia frowned, pursed her lips, put her hands on her hips and with a twinkle in her eye, looked straight into Wayne's eyes:

"They say it's the first sign of going mad, you know."

Wayne shrugged and grinned again.

"I was just arguing with myself and at least I always win those arguments."

About three hours later Wayne woke with a start. He glanced at the time on the red neon alarm clock, three thirty a.m.

"Perfect!" Wayne whispered and climbed softly and quietly out of bed. Natalia murmured in her sleep and Wayne stiffened in the darkness, hardly daring to breathe. If Natalia woke up, it would ruin everything. Wayne's wife pulled a sheet over her shoulder and turned onto her side. Wayne crept silently towards the chair, where he had left his clothes and pulled on a tee shirt and shorts. Then he tiptoed to the bedroom door, opened it, pausing slightly as it gave a slight creek, then he crept out, through the sitting room area of the suite they had hired, where Katie and Frankie were snoring gently, to the main door that led out to the Hotel corridor. He heaved a sigh of relief as he closed the Suite door behind him. He put his ear up against it for a moment, just to check that neither of the children had woken up, then he walked off down the corridor.

The knock on Dean Vitalia's bedroom door was sharp and loud. He woke up and groaned, blearily checked the time on his watch and groaned again. His girlfriend, Cindy, had also been awakened by the sharp report on their bedroom door.

"What was that?" She muttered sleepily.

Dean shrugged:

"Someone fooling around, I guess." He grumbled as he settled back down in the bed.

"Dean, Dean Vitalia."

The voice was little more than a loud whisper, but Dean heard it. It sounded like someone outside, on the corridor.

Dean jumped out of bed and turned on the bedside light:

"Damn kids." He groaned as he pulled on the hotel-supplied robe, he was about to open the door when he thought better of it and pulled a gun out of his bedside drawer:

"Be careful, honey." Cindy simpered as Dean slowly opened the door onto the brightly lit corridor. He looked left, then right, nothing. Then he heard the voice again:

"Dean, Dean Vitalia."

It sounded more like a hiss than a loud whisper and seemed to be coming from round a corner of the corridor, just past the ice making machine.

Dean furtively put the gun in the pocket of his robe but kept his hand on the stock and his finger ready on the trigger. He walked slowly down to the bend in the corridor.

"Deano."

The voice was now behind him. He turned quickly:

"Who are you? What the hell do you think you're doing?" Dean demanded angrily.

"Deano."

The voice this time drifted from around the bend in the corridor, Dean ran round the corner. At the end of the corridor, about ten yards from where he now stood he saw a figure with long brown curly hair and a pale white face grin at him, then disappear.

Dean ran the ten yards, barely able to contain his fury.

The corridor opened into a deserted lobby area. Dean noticed the figure disappear out into the night-time shadows of the ornate hotel gardens:

"Hey, you." He bellowed as he pursued the creep who'd disturbed his sleep.

The night was sultry and the hum of the cicadas and tree frogs much less intense than it had been earlier. The sky was clear and millions of stars lay over the resort like an immense sparkling curtain. The rhythmic pulse of gentle rolling waves, ebbing and flowing on the Pacific shore punctuated the darkness.

Dean stared up at the sky for a moment, as an Angeleno he wasn't used to so many stars due to the City's light pollution and the sight took his breath away. Then he remembered what he was doing and gave chase to the figure, who had just disappeared behind a manicured hedge.

Dean ran after him, his hand still on the trigger of the gun.

"Hello Dean." The soft Irish sounding voice greeted him as he rounded the corner of the hedge.

Dean gulped and pulled the gun from his pocket:

"Who's there?" He shouted, "why are you doing this?"

His eyes swivelled manically in the darkness. The rhythmic chirp of the cicadas sounded like mocking laughter.

The disembodied voice spoke again, this time chilling Dean Vitalia to the bone.

"I want to know why, Deano? Why did you murder me?"

Suddenly, a figure began to materialise in front of the terrified Hollywood agent.

The handsome young man, probably in his mid-thirties with brown corkscrew curls and dark brown eyes was vaguely familiar, but Dean couldn't remember where he had seen him before:

"Boo!"

The figure joked as Dean tried to lift the gun in his shaking hand.

"I don't think that thing'll be doing you any good, old man. You can't be shooting the dead, you know."

The accent was unmistakeably Irish.

"Who are you?" Dean stammered, his eyes wide, terrified.

"Tsk, tsk. Have you forgotten me already? Now that's just plain disrespectful, Mr Vitalia, so it is."

The figure mocked Dean as he stood frozen to the spot.

"Y, y, you're, J, J James M, M, Malone?" Dean could hardly spit out the words as he remembered the photographs he had seen of the murder victim James Malone in the newspapers.

The figure snapped its fingers triumphantly:

"Got it in one. Obviously the old memory still functions then, Deano, despite the cruel ravages of the advancing years."

"Wh, wh, what d, do you w, want?"

Dean asked as he blinked rapidly and surreptitiously pinched his arm, hoping that he'd wake up and find that all this had just been a bad dream.

"Just three things." The ghost of James Malone grinned wolfishly:

"First, you will confess to me now that it was indeed you, who ordered my murder and that the random burglary story was so much codswallop."

The phantom figure crossed his arms and waited as Dean Vitalia tried to moisten his throat enough to speak:

"It wasn't me, I swear. It was Aurelio. I told him you was trying to dig up some dirt on me. He knew that would impact on him and his run for the Senate, so he loaned me some of his old Vegas boys, real professionals. They carried out the arrangements. They hired the Mexicans, not me."

Malone's shade smiled:

"But it was what you wanted, wasn't it?"

Dean cast his eyes to the ground.

"No, I wanted them to frighten you off. I thought they'd just, you know, rough you up."

Malone shook his head:

"I think you're lying to me Deano. I think you ordered your cousin's boys to kill me."

Dean's eyes were wide in terror.

"I didn't, I swear."

The ghost of James Malone leaned towards the petrified agent.

"Swear to me on the soul of your mother."

Dean closed his eyes, his head dropped, his chin fell onto his chest. He sighed heavily and sadly.

"I swear!" He whispered in a barely audible voice.

Malone grinned:

"So old Aurelio was involved, was he? Now, now, there's a surprise. The father of the supposed Messiah is no more than a two bit gangster."

Vitalia fell to his knees:

"Luca will forgive us our sins. He has told Aurelio that when he judges the eternal souls of all men, he will forgive us."

Dean Vitalia put his hands together as if in prayer.

"Will you forgive me, James Malone? I didn't want you dead. You was my stepson's buddy. I liked the kid. I wouldn't have killed his buddy."

Malone shrugged:

"You didn't have to. People like you have people who do their dirty work for them. Ah, 'tis too late now, Deano. The dies have been cast. However, they do say confession is good for the soul, and as yours is about to be judged, just think how clever it would be to unburden yourself, just before Judgment day. If you don't want to see me again, you will carry out my second request and tell the police what you did to me and about Aurelio's part in my murder. You will do it as soon as you get back to L.A. OK?"

The phantom's face took on a fierce look that promised untold horrors to come if Dean failed to do its bidding.

Dean's face now looked even more horrified. He tried to speak but the words caught in his dry throat. He felt a warm, wet sensation running over his legs.

Malone's face softened again as he glanced at the growing dark puddle at Vitalia's feet:

"Oh dear, good job you're in that robe and not in one of your expensive designer suits, Deano. Anyway, my third request is a much more simple thing. You will be nice to me old mucker, Wayne Higginbotham and extra nice to my daughter. Who would have thought that me own killer would become me daughter's father in law? Life's weird isn't it?"

The ghost shook its head in feigned amazement.

"But I have to admit, you know, being dead is weirder! Anyhow, just to confirm, I would hate for you to be hurting anybody else that I love, because I can be pretty scary. Now remember, you will confess, or I'll be back and next time I won't be so nice."

The face of James Malone grinned as the flesh fell off his face leaving a white skull, flames appeared in his eye sockets and then he slowly faded into the darkness.

Dean Vitalia stayed on his knees and silently wept, dropping the useless firearm onto the gravel path.

"I'm sorry, I'm so sorry." He moaned as he crouched and then rolled into the foetal position.

Dean Vitalia was now faced with the prospect of either betraying his ruthless brother and potentially the Messiah himself, or of being haunted by a vengeful Irish phantom. Lying in the darkness, Dean began to slowly pull himself together:

"Man did I have too much to drink. I'm actually seeing spooks. Maybe someone slipped me something hallucinogenic."

Ghost or not, figment of a guilty imagination or not, or the product of a surfeit of Vodka, or even drugs that Dean couldn't remember taking, Malone was dead. What could he do to the Hollywood agent who actually represented the Messiah reborn? Dean Vitalia's sharp mind began to function clearly again. All he had to do was ensure that he had a bargaining chip the next time the "ghost" paid him a visit and Dean knew instinctively what that bargaining chip was. The "ghost" himself had betrayed his weakness in his third request. A quick visit to his shrink and his therapist as soon as he got back to the Valley would sort out his fear and the next time the "ghost" appeared, he'd be ready.

Dean Vitalia climbed to his feet:

"So Mr. Malone, my little Irish friend." He whispered into the clear night air.

"You weren't so clever when you were alive and you still ain't too clever now that you're dead, are you?"

Wayne Higginbotham crept silently back into the hotel suite and made straight for the bathroom, taking care to close the door before turning on the light.

The face of James Malone appeared in the bathroom mirror:

"Well, I think that went well, old friend." The face of James Malone said with a wink:

"And now at least we know the truth. Aurelio is as guilty as his slimy brother. For a plastic paddy, you did quite well there, Higginbotham."

Malone's face melted into Wayne's own features and he blew out a sigh of relief:

"Well James, they say revenge is a dish best served cold. I think we can safely say that after over twenty years, the dish is very cold indeed."

Thirteen

A scruffy, bearded man in a long robe suddenly awoke from a long, deep sleep. He blinked in the smoky atmosphere and peered around in the gloom. Bodies were stretched out everywhere. Moans and grunts periodically emerged from the darkness and a loud snore erupted from somewhere nearby. The searing rasp of a forced fart split the air and echoed in the rafters.

An enormous grey hunting dog opened one eye and raised an ear laconically before murmuring and settling back down to sleep. The man cleared his throat and wondered why he had woken up in the middle of a seemingly endless night. He reached out and took a sip from a brass goblet, immediately spitting out the liquid with a groan and a muted curse. Stale ale never tasted good. The man wiped his mouth and levered himself up and stretched like someone who had slept far too long. As his mind cleared Aillen Mac Fionnbharr, the last King of the Tuatha de Danaan grinned. He knew why he had woken up:

"So, it starts!" He muttered.

"It finally starts!"

The man began to laugh. The hunting dog snapped into a sudden alertness and slowly, all around him, eyes began to open and heads began to rise.

The whisper of magic had travelled all the way to Tir Na Nog.

Monsignor Declan Doyle waited outside the Pope's chambers in a state of extreme excitement. He couldn't wait to tell the Pontiff about his latest discoveries and was hopping from leg to leg like a small boy desperate to use the bathroom. He glanced at his watch. The visiting dignitaries would be leaving in less than five minutes. Father Reichmann, had he still been alive, would have been delighted by Doyle's discoveries and even more satisfied in the knowledge that it had been his own diary that had led the Priests of the reinvigorated "Sacred Order of Saint Gregory" from a small town in upstate New York to a convent in Sicily.

It was a full ten minutes before the delegation left the Pope's chambers and his chief secretary was by that time, in a complete fluster about the Pontiff's schedule, even so, Monsignor Doyle was not about to be bumped off the Papal timetable just because some technocrats from some Central American dictatorship had overdone their toadying.

Monsignor Doyle's news was the most significant information any Pope had received since Saint Peter himself had arrived in Rome.

"Declan, I hear you have news." His Holiness Pope Gregory XVII exclaimed as soon as Monsignor Doyle had entered his palatial chambers and bent to kiss his ring.

"Yes, indeed Your Holiness." The Irishman grinned:

"And I'm delighted to say, I think it's extremely bad news."

His Holiness frowned:

"I do not understand, Declan. Please sit and explain to me what the new "Order" has discovered."

The Pope waved his hand towards a chair by his working desk. A Papal official who just happened to barge in was summarily dismissed, along with the stressed looking secretary who closed the door behind him with a haughty and dismissive glance at the dishevelled looking Irish Priest.

The Pope walked around his desk, scratching his head:

"Extremely bad news, you say, Declan. Yet you are pleased. Please explain."

Monsignor Doyle nodded eagerly:

"It's difficult to know where to begin Your Holiness, but the best place is probably here in Rome, just after poor old Father Reichmann passed away. I was given his diary. It appears that the good Father had discovered that a young novice from the Convent of the Blessed Virgin, in the Sicilian town of Bagheria, had been brought to Rome by His Eminence Cardinal D'Abruzzo."

The Pope nodded patiently as the Irish Priest took a proffered small glass of water and took a sip.

"It appears that she was given a grace and favour apartment here in the Holy See."

The Pope scowled:

"She was his mistress?" He almost growled.

The Irishman shook his head:

"It was said not, but she was pregnant and a baby was delivered. When the baby was five years old, His Eminence died suddenly and the Nun and her child simply disappeared."

The Pope stroked his chin and leaned forward. His forehead was creased as he concentrated on every detail of Monsignor Doyle's story:

"How was she able to simply disappear?" He asked, bewildered by what he was hearing.

Monsignor Doyle held up his hands:

"I don't know, but what is important is the date she disappeared. Father Reichmann used some of his contacts in the police to discover that a single woman and a small blonde child matching the description of this novice, Maria Francesca Giardina, had booked into the Hotel D'Inghilterra on that very date."

The Pope nodded again as Father Doyle continued, his speech getting faster as he approached the significant details of his tale:

"According to Father Reichmann's sources, this same woman, met an American, one Aurelio Vitalia, in that same hotel."

He punched his right fist into the palm of his left hand triumphantly:

"But this is the best bit, Your Holiness."

When he died, Father Reichmann was working on this case in New England. He had discovered that Aurelio Vitalia's young Italian wife had shot herself, over twenty years ago. Only three years after moving to America."

The Pope raised his eyebrows:

"Do we have proof that this is the same woman who D'Abruzzo brought to Rome?"

Monsignor Doyle grinned:

"Young Father O'Rourke, the local Catholic Priest in the town where Mrs Vitalia died, he's my latest recruit to the "New Order of Saint Gregory" by the way, faxed me this, just yesterday."

He handed the Pope a piece of paper, which the Pope read, having perched his reading spectacles precariously on the edge of his nose:

"Details confirmed. Name of dead woman: Maria Francesca Vitalia, nee Giardina.

Place of Birth, Sicily, Italy. Luke Lively was born as Lucien Giardina in Rome in 1975. There was no father on the birth certificate. He was legally adopted by Aurelio Vitalia in 1981."

The Pope placed the fax face down on to the desk in front of him and muttered something inaudible. Monsignor Doyle coughed politely:

"That's not all, Your Holiness."

The Pope held up a single hand to silence the Irishman:

"Two things first, Monsignor."

Doyle raised his eyebrows at the Pope's suddenly much less friendly tone:

"Is this child, D'Abruzzo's? Or is he the miraculous product of a virgin birth?

And secondly: How can any of this be described as "pleasing bad news?""

Monsignor Doyle shrugged:

"It is unlikely that the child was D'Abruzzo's. Even now, Luca has blonde hair and blue eyes, while both the Cardinal and Maria, his mother, had very dark Italian complexions and jet black hair."

"But is he the product of a miracle?" The Pope exploded, interrupting the Irish Priests musings.

Monsignor Doyle shrugged:

"It's a possibility." He stated nonchalantly.

The Pope stood impatiently:

"Yes, or no, Declan, for the sake of Christ himself." He almost shouted.

Monsignor Declan Doyle smiled:

"Ah Your Holiness. You see I don't really think it matters."

The Pope's mouth dropped open and he slumped back into his chair:

"What? You don't think it matters? Luca Vitalia, as he now wants to be known, says he is going to perform a miracle on the Oprah show this Saturday. He is then going to be running for President of The United States Of America. In just over a year he could be the most powerful man on Earth. The first Primary is in January next year. The Oprah show will have the largest TV audience ever in the history of the medium. I will be expected to pass comment, to give my approval or to voice my disdain as soon as the show finishes and you don't think the circumstances of his birth are important."

By the time he had finished Pope Gregory XVII was actually shouting. His face had become flushed and his eyes betrayed his panic.

Monsignor Doyle sighed:

"Forgive me Your Holiness, but it does not matter, because whether his mother was a virgin or not, Luca Vitalia is not Our Lord. Judgment day is not imminent. That is why I said it was pleasing bad news."

"How do you know this, Monsignor Doyle?" The Pope asked suddenly sounding extremely weary.

"How do I explain to a billion of the faithful that the boy they have just watched perform a miracle on the TV in their living room is not Our Lord, re born to save our souls?"

Monsignor Doyle pursed his lips:

"Ah, I see, Your Holiness. I can't help you with that. I suggest you play a politicians game and suspend judgment for a while. I can tell you this, however. The last person to see Father Reichmann alive was Luke Lively. I found this scribbled note in his diary. This is why I am convinced that our young friend is not the Messiah."

The Irish Priest passed a piece of lined paper to the Pope. It had obviously been crumpled at one point, but it was still legible:

"Monday 4th August.

Today I was in the Church in Wellsboro, researching the circumstances of Maria Vitalia's death. She did come from Sicily. Met Aurelio in Rome. I am sure she was Cardinal D'Abruzzo's Virgin. Bumped into Luke Lively as leaving Church. He said he visits his mother every day when he is home. The boy has dead eyes, evil eyes. I felt him burning into me, searching my soul. He knows what I am doing. Don't think I gave away the English boy. He is our last hope. D'Abruzzo delivered us a demon."

The Pope's eyes widened with every staccato sentence. He looked up at Doyle.

"This was to have been his last entry?"

Monsignor Doyle nodded.

"Father Reichmann wrote in German, his handwriting was almost illegible. One of my people in Munich provided this translation. As you can see, he screwed up the paper because he was sure he must have made mistakes. He had not. Father Reichmann died at 4pm on Monday 4th August. I was due to meet him the next day in New York City."

The Pope stared at the piece of paper again.

"Who is the English boy?"

Monsignor Doyle smiled again:

"Do I have your permission to speak freely Your Holiness?"

The Pope looked surprised.

"Why, yes of course, Declan."

Monsignor Doyle noted the Pope's apparent return to a less formal tone with a degree of relief.

"Do you remember when you stopped Father Reichmann's investigations into the demise of the "Sacred Order of St Gregory?" some twenty years ago."

The Pope nodded:

"Poor old Abraham was heartbroken. He was on to something even then. Even I had my orders, however. It was only when my predecessor became so infirm that he hardly knew what day it was, that I could let Father Reichmann off the leash as it were."

Doyle nodded knowingly.

"Well it seems in the period prior to your instruction. Father Reichmann made the acquaintance of a young Englishman who, it seems, had been the primary target of the "Order" in its last days."

The Pope gasped:

"God's Assassin?"

Monsignor Doyle nodded eagerly:

"Father Reichmann only told me about him in the weeks before he died. He had become convinced that this English boy was a power for good, not evil. That he was a weapon of God, not a weapon to be used against God."

The Pope closed his eyes:

"That was what he would not tell me all those years ago. He was protecting this boy."

Doyle nodded eagerly again:

"Indeed, Your Holiness."

The Pope looked at his watch and stood abruptly:

"Declan, I have kept some very important Bishops waiting. I must end this meeting. However, know this. I will hold my approval on whatever miracle this Luca Vitalia performs on the TV. Find this Englishman that Abraham protected.

The "New Order" must be dedicated to protect him, if Vitalia does indeed prove to be a demon. If Abraham Reichmann believed him to be our only hope, then so do I."

Doyle kissed the Pope's proffered ring and turned to leave.

"Oh, Monsignor Doyle." The Pope shouted as the Irish Priest reached the ornate door of the Papal chambers:

"I see what you mean now. I will confess. I wasn't quite ready for judgment day either.

This is somewhat pleasing "bad" news."

Fourteen

Lucy Sherman was nervous, very nervous. She was about to meet the man who had effectively taken the husband she loved from her and that was a scary prospect. Lucy had never deferred to anyone intellectually, except for Jonathan T. Sherman. He was the one individual who she would always have readily admitted to having been smarter than her. The only lawyer she considered better than her. Yet now he had shaken her entire world by his slavish devotion to some two bit Pop star with political ambition and the delusional belief that he was the Messiah.

Lucy had decided by now that she would have been much happier if she had caught her husband having an affair. At least that would have been normal. At least it would simply have been a matter of lust overcoming good sense. Even the cleverest men, Presidents and Kings, were often slaves to their libidos.

She watched the blanket of cloud covering the Midwest, way below the plane carrying them from New York to Los Angeles and wondered what had happened to effect such changes in her man.

Maybe he had suffered a breakdown. She knew incredibly successful people who had found the stress of family and career just all too much and who had snapped and hit the hippy trail to India in search of an elusive inner light. Yet Jonathan?

Maybe he'd turned gay and was wildly in love with Luke Lively, or whatever it was that he wanted to be known as now. Things hadn't been great in the bedroom for a while and Lucy had simply put it down to tiredness on both parts, but what if he was gay?

Lucy shook her head. No, this was more than just some sexual infatuation. It was a far more profound change that had obviously undermined the very foundations of Jonathan's agnostic belief system.

Lucy turned and stared at the greying man sat next to her, dressed in a sharp grey Armani suit, his hair expensively and perfectly coiffured, his designer specs perched on the end of his nose. Was he still the same sartorially disastrous geek who she had literally bumped into in Oxford? Was he still capable of being intellectually brilliant? Could he still display a sceptical wit that was a sharp as a scalpel and could dissect pomposity and pretension like a hot knife cuts through butter?

A member of the cabin staff offered Jonathan a snack and a soda, his head snapped up in surprise at the unexpected interruption, he had been totally engrossed in reading emails on his blackberry device. His spectacles dropped off his nose and he bumbled around trying to catch them as the stewardess smiled at him patiently, obviously thinking: "what a dork." Lucy grinned. Jonathan T. Sherman had always been a dork and that was one of the reasons she had fallen in love with him. She was the power behind the throne. She chose his clothes, his stylists, even his shoes. Left to his own devices Jonathan would still be wearing a sweat shirt, checked golf pants and loafers.

"Water please!" Lucy said to the stewardess as the woman's eyes flicked dismissively from Jonathan to his companion. Her accent was still as pure as crystal water in cut glass. Jonathan turned to her and smiled:

"You're going to love Luca, honey! I swear." He whispered as he gently squeezed her hand.

"Betcha, I won't!" Lucy thought as she smiled encouragingly at her spouse and squeezed his hand back.

A couple of hours later, a shiny black Lincoln limousine pulled up by the Beverley Hills Four Seasons Hotel entrance lobby. Lucy placed her sunglasses on as she began to clamber out of the air-conditioned car into the blistering heat and glare of the L.A. afternoon. She was suddenly aware of a few flashes as an enormous pack of press photographers, clutching cameras bearing unfeasibly huge lenses, surged towards the car. Lucy's film star grin faded, however, as soon as the paparazzi realised that Luke Lively, as everyone still called him, was not a passenger in the Limo and the uninterested photographers turned away almost as one body.

"Gosh, that was almost like being a film star." She gushed as she encountered her husband on the other side of the Limo.

"They're like locusts." Jonathan glared at the press in disgust:

"They're desperate for Luke to make one mistake, make one faux pas and they'll be on him like a pack of rabid Hyenas. These guys make the Pharisees look like boy Scouts. Parasites!"

Lucy was taken aback by the sheer amount of vitriol in Jonathan's voice. That wasn't really like him, either. As the couple strolled into the hotel lobby Lucy couldn't help thinking that it wasn't just Jonathan's beliefs that had changed. His entire personality seemed to be undergoing a transformation. As soon as he stopped his Clark Kent like bumbling, then she would be really worried.

The Sherman's were shown to their room and so missed the furore that erupted in the parking lot almost as soon as they had disappeared into the elevator. As soon as Luca Vitalia's limo had arrived, photographers had literally climbed over one another to get the best shot. Flashbulbs had exploded everywhere as reporters bellowed for the ex child actor and pop star to grant them a few words:

"Luke over here!"

"Luke this way." Voices bellowed as Luca's security team who had arrived just before the Limo in two huge SUVs, struggled to force the baying press pack back. The grinning, waving, prospective young President rushed into the sanctuary of the hotel foyer without even removing his shades. It was left to Senator Aurelio Vitalia to address the horde as they surrounded the hotel entrance, much to the consternation of the door staff and a number of guests who had been caught up in the melee.

Aurelio held up one hand imperiously and slowly the pack fell silent like hunting hounds disciplined by a sound handler.

"As you all know...." Aurelio began, " Luca will be appearing live on the Oprah show tomorrow night. He has promised the World the most important event in the history of television, or any other medium, will happen during that transmission. I'm sorry folks, but until then neither I, nor my son, have any further comments to make. Watch the show and BELIEVE!"

Aurelio bellowed the last word like some Southern evangelical Baptist minister, then he turned just repeating the words "Watch the show" mantra like, to answer the questions hurled at him as he disappeared into the hotel.

Neither Lucy nor Jonathan spoke much while they were getting ready, Lucy, because her mind was in turmoil, Jonathan because he was so excited. Not only was Lucy worried about Jonathan's mental state, but she was also worried about meeting Luke Lively. What if he was the Messiah? What if he could see right into her soul? What if there was a heaven and hell and he condemned her to the latter for being at best a faint hearted believer, or at worst a sceptical agnostic. She had certainly wavered between the two positions most of her adult life. This certainly put being sent to the Headmaster's office at school into perspective. Finally Jonathan straightened his black bow tie for the hundredth time, glanced at his watch and asked if she was ready. Lucy stared at her reflection in the mirror. The blue dress had served her well on one previous occasion and it still looked good. She had deliberately decided not to buy anything new, despite Jonathan's appeals, just to display how churlish she felt about the whole thing. The dress looked fine, but that face. When had she gotten so old? She mentally slapped her own wrist for thinking in American English and then, casting herself one last critical, disappointed glance, declared that she was ready.

There were probably thirty people in the function room when Jonathan and Lucy walked in. Aurelio Vitalia rushed over to greet them. Lucy noted with distaste that he had managed to get even fatter and was perspiring more than usual despite the over efficient air-conditioning:

"Good to see ya Jon and wow, Mrs Sherman, Lucy if I may. I've often seen you perform in the Courtroom. I'd even go as far as saying you're almost as good as me." He laughed at his own little joke while Lucy smiled politely.

Oblivious to his faux pas, Aurelio blustered on:

"You look a million dollars, baby. Are you guys excited? Luca is going to meet all his new campaign team tonight and after tomorrow's Oprah show, we are going to walk all the way to the White House. Lucy, I hope you don't mind but your Jon is gonna be working his butt off over the next few months, but I tell ya, he's the luckiest lawyer in the land. Luca has decided that Jon is going to be his key contact at Sherman General. No disrespect to yourself, of course."

"None taken." Lucy almost hissed.

Vitalia pumped Jonathan's hand furiously and then kissed Lucy's right hand.

"You guys were meant to meet Dean, my cousin and Luca's agent tonight, but he's still at his son's wedding in Mexico. I'll introduce you after the Oprah show."

Lucy smiled as pleasantly as she could.

"I know your cousin quite well, Mr Vitalia. I do have a lot of legal experience in Hollywood."

"Sure you do, honey." Aurelio grunted, his attention already flitting to the next couple.

The rotund Senator walked off and Lucy shivered. She could feel the icy moisture from his grip on her hand.

A beautiful young girl offered her a glass of Champagne from a tray. The fact that the girl must have been an out of work actress crossed Lucy's mind. She turned to make a comment to Jonathan, but he had disappeared. Lucy looked around, almost in a panic. The room was well lit and the furnishings were standard for a hotel of that quality, but it was so cold. Lucy wished she'd worn a wrap over her bare shoulders, which she always did in New York, but in Los Angeles she just hadn't expected to feel so cold. She peered out of the nearest window and was startled as a flash-gun went off outside.

"Man they're like crazy, those guys. If anyone goes near a window the flashes are like a July 4th firework display."

Lucy heard the friendly female voice and turned to face the owner of the voice:

"Hi, I'm Carol Anne Riley." The tall, thin, elegant blonde woman stated confidently, holding out her right hand.

"Lucy Sherman." Lucy replied taking the hand and shaking it.

"Oh, awesome, Jonathan's better half!" The woman declared:

"My God, what have you guys taken on? You are going to be soooooo busy over the next few months. I mean I'm sure every girl Luca has ever kissed will be selling her story, let alone the more salacious of his conquests. I'm his press secretary by the way."

Lucy smiled. Wasn't it funny how the one woman on Luca's staff just happened to be drop dead gorgeous?

"Yes, I don't suppose we'll be seeing much of him, back in Sherman General, New York." She chirped, as cheerily as she could manage.

"But I'm sure we'll manage."

"You have kids, I believe?" Carol Anne asked; her interest just a bit too intense to be genuine.

"Yes. A boy and a girl. They're at school in England." Lucy replied. By now she was so cold she was even considering making an excuse to go outside just to warm up. Why was hotel air conditioning on L.A. always too cold to be comfortable?

"In England?" Carol Anne repeated incredulously.

"Well, I guess at least they're well out of the way then. I mean after tomorrow this place is just going to be insane."

Much to Lucy's relief someone tapped the toothsome, smiley press secretary on the shoulder and distracted her attention. Lucy slipped towards the door, but just before she could make a swift exit, the double doors opened and Luke Lively swept in surrounded by several huge men in sunglasses and black suits. One of them ushered Lucy back into the room:

"LADIES AND GENTLEMEN MAY I PRESENT, MY SON, LUCA VITALIA, THE NEXT PRESIDENT OF THE UNITED STATES." Aurelio Vitalia bellowed as Luke grabbed the hand of the nearest guest and pumped it furiously. Lucy couldn't help but notice that he did look incredibly young and angelic. His short, neat, blonde hair was still curly, his eyes were a distinct bright blue and his teeth straight and dazzlingly, pearly white. He looked every inch the actor and pop star, but he was far too young to cut it as a politician, Lucy caught herself thinking. She was amazed therefore, when he seemed to cast her a sudden glance and broke off from pumping someone else's hand to move towards her:

"You must be Jonathan's beautiful wife." He grinned and lifted her hand to his lips.

"Welcome on board, Lucy, it's gonna be one hell of a ride. Sherman General are going to be the biggest law firm in the world." He winked at Lucy and turned to the person stood next to her.

Lucy Sherman would never be able to explain what happened next. Firstly she felt like she was going to faint, then she thought she was going to be sick. She had never felt so cold, nor had she ever felt so, violated. In the very few seconds that his eyes had been on hers she had felt him reach right into her. She might as well have been stood there stark naked with all her diaries open in front of him. Now she knew what people meant when they described a cold sweat. The image of his eyes was burned into her memory. Lucy Sherman had not known what to expect when she met the Messiah, if Messiah he was, but revulsion had not been on the list of prospective reactions. No matter what everyone else was saying, Lucy Sherman had for the first time in her life felt total repulsion, a sense of palpable evil. She staggered back to a table and used it to support herself.

"Isn't he just soooo incredibly awesome?" She heard Carol Anne Riley gush.

"Amen to that." A male voice answered the saccharin Press secretary. Lucy glanced over and saw Jonathan. His eyes glazed, staring at the grinning prospective Politician. Lucy felt sick all over again.

Someone handed Luca a microphone, which he took and jumped onto a chair:

"Ladies and Gentleman." He boomed:

"Thank you for coming tonight for this little gathering. Tomorrow night the world as you know it will have changed IRREVOCABLY!"

Everybody in the room whooped their approval, save Lucy Sherman who was still using the table to stop herself from falling over. Luca waited for the cheering to subside before he continued. His grin was as wide as the Grand Canyon.

"Tomorrow night, I will perform a miracle on the TV that people will still be talking about in two thousand years." He punched the air to the sound of more whoops and cheers.

"In five months time, I will be taking part in the Iowa caucus. In six months it will be Super Tuesday, there will be twenty Primaries right across this great nation and you know what?"

The audience mumbled their ignorance. Luca Vitalia grinned an even wider grin:

"I don't expect any challengers at that Iowa Caucus, or at those twenty, or any other Primaries. I don't expect any Democrat, or any Republican, to challenge me. I mean after tomorrow night, who in their right mind is going to stand against the SON OF GOD!"

Luca Vitalia punched the air again:

"In what amounts to no more than a few months I will be the President of this Great Nation, the Greatest Nation on earth and I tell you this. No one will be asking for my birth certificate. No one will care where I was born."

The small audience, laughed whooped and cheered as Luca continued:

"The Kingdom of God will soon cover the entire earth."

He almost whispered the last few words then he jumped off the chair, passed the microphone to his Father and resumed "pressing flesh."

Lucy Sherman couldn't stop shivering. Why was she having such a strange reaction to this man? She couldn't help thinking about the early days of the Nazi party. She could imagine the peculiarly Aryan Luke Lively in a black SS uniform, punching the air like Hitler at a Nuremberg rally. She felt quite guilty. What if he was the Messiah and she was mentally comparing him to Hitler? If he was the Messiah, then surely he would be benevolent, like the Priests always said. He would forgive her scepticism. After all, she had never done anything wrong. Even so she couldn't help feeling that her gut instinct was right. Luke Lively was no more the Messiah than Jonathan was Brad Pitt.

"Are you Ok, Honey?"

Jonathan was looking down at her, his face concerned. Lucy hadn't even noticed that she had slipped onto a chair by the wall.

"You don't look well. Too much champagne huh?"

Lucy smiled weakly and nodded.

"Yes, it must be something like that."

Jonathan smiled:

"You must be overcome as well. I saw him kiss your hand. How many women can claim the Son of God has actually kissed their hand?"

Lucy smiled weakly again:

"Not many. Look, I'm going back to the room, is that OK?"

Jonathan looked disappointed, but he nodded:

"No, that's fine honey. I understand. I guess I felt overcome the first time I met him."

He helped Lucy to her feet and escorted her to the door. Lucy staggered off towards the elevator, grateful for the chance to escape. It was strange how much warmer she felt by the time she was stood in the elevator. Yet although she tried to think of other things, those eyes just seemed to stick in her mind, she felt as though his fingers had run over her entire body, inside and out, prodding, probing, sucking her deepest secrets from her most secure hiding places. At least there was a mini bar in the room and Lucy definitely needed a drink.

Back in the function room Luca approached the star struck Jonathan:

"Hey Jon, it's great to have you guys on board." He gushed through those pearly white teeth.

"I guess you're gonna be busy. Those suckers out there are gonna be going for my jugular after tomorrow." He laughed.

"You sure have a beautiful wife. Is she OK? I just caught her leaving out of the corner of my eye."

"Yes thank you, she's er f, fine." Jonathan stammered:

"Just a little too much Champagne and I guess she's, you know, overcome at meeting you."

Luca grinned all the more:

"Yeah, I guess. Look after her."

He moved swiftly along the line, until he'd had a chat with everyone in the room.

Aurelio handed him the microphone. This time Luca didn't climb on to a chair. He just put one hand into his pocket and seemed to think for a minute:

"You know, you guys are gonna get some dirt thrown at you over the next few months. The forces of Satan are always at work. They will do anything to prevent the coming Kingdom of God. The agents of Satan are everywhere, working with their unwitting allies, the non-believers. There are even some in this room tonight."

There was a collective gasp from the small audience as people turned and glanced nervously at each other and wondered who the traitors were. Luca held up his hand:

"Hey, they're gonna be everywhere. I'm prepared, are you?"

There was a tentative "Yeah" from the audience.

"I SAID, I'M PREPARED, ARE YOU?"

This time the response was an almighty bellowed "YES!"

Luca grinned:

"That's better. Ladies and Gentlemen, We've got one hell of a long road to travel, it ain't gonna be easy, but tomorrow I'm going to give us a helluva start. Thank you and good night."

With that he slipped out of the room, closely surrounded by his Vitalia security detail, Aurelio trotting along side his son like an overweight puppy.

The tumultuous applause, whooping, whistling and cheering was almost deafening. Lucy Sherman could hear it up in her room. The press corps could hear it outside.

Jonathan T. Sherman defied his bookish quiet intellectual nature to whoop and holler with the best of them. Yet everyone in the room had to admit to a slight feeling of disquiet. Who had Luca been referring too when he had said that there had been agents of Satan in the room that night?

Jonathan finished his champagne and made small talk with Carol Anne Riley. It was unusual, he decided, to find a woman as smart as she was beautiful. He then remembered that Lucy was alone in their room.

"Well, that was one hell of an evening and the best is yet to come." He said to no one in particular, but several people gave his back congratulatory slaps as he moved towards the exit. Jonathan was crossing the foyer when he heard his name being called. He turned and saw a heavily perspiring Aurelio bustling through a crowd of Hotel guests:

"Hey Jon, you going up already?" He panted as he reached the tall lawyer.

"Yeah, Lucy wasn't feeling too good. I guess the occasion just got to her." Aurelio nodded sympathetically.

"Yeah, Jon, look, walk with me a while. We've gotta talk."

Jonathan frowned:

"What's the matter? Have we got trouble already?"

Aurelio sighed. He looked around and guided Jonathan towards a quiet corner of the hotel lobby.

"Look buddy. This is real hard, but it's about your wife."

Jonathan raised his eyebrows:

"About Lucy?"

Aurelio nodded:

"Yeah, that's right. It's about Lucy."

Fifteen

Wayne Higginbotham was more than a little surprised to see Dean Vitalia at breakfast. He was even more surprised to see how relaxed he looked. After all Wayne's efforts the previous night to give him nightmares that would haunt him until the end of his days, Dean looked as though he had slept like a log. He cast Wayne a cheeky wave as he caught the younger man staring at him, then he said something to his young blonde girlfriend who cast Wayne a blatant glance and giggled. Wayne slumped into his chair.

How could he have failed? When he, or the ghost of James Malone, had left Dean, the man was a pathetic broken wretch. Now, just a few hours later, he looked like he had just won the State Lottery.

Natalia, Katie and Frankie joined Wayne at the table:

"Why so grumpy, Grumpy?" Katie asked, as she noticed her father's scowl. She often called him Grumpy whenever he looked cross, or irritated. Something that seemed to be a much more common occurrence as Wayne got older.

"Nothing." He muttered unconvincingly.

"Hang-over, dear?" Natalia asked with slightly too much relish for Wayne's liking.

"No!" he snapped. "Nothing's wrong. I'm going to grab something from the buffet."

Wayne stood as his wife and daughter exchanged knowing smirks. He just couldn't understand how his perfect rendition of James Malone's shade had failed to reduce Dean Vitalia to a bumbling nervous wreck. He was so engrossed in his bewilderment that he failed to notice who was stood in line in front of him and ended up bumping straight into Dean at the buffet counter:

"Sorry! Oh, Hi!" Wayne murmured.

Dean nodded and grinned.

"Hey Michael, funny thing. After we had our little chat last night, I had a dream about your old buddy." Dean stated as he held out his plate for a fried egg.

"My old buddy?" Wayne repeated dully.

"The Irishman, Malone." Dean explained as he picked up some bacon and hash browns.

Wayne collected a fried egg and followed Dean's example with the bacon and potato, but also added a small pancake.

"Yeah, can you believe that?" Dean grinned. "Me being haunted. It was like that Willis movie, you know: "I see dead people.""

Wayne grimaced:

"So did James have any message for you?" Wayne asked drily.

Dean pondered for a second:

"Yeah, as a matter of fact he did. He told me that we're going to have a new President. He told me to watch the Oprah Show and he also told me that he was sorry for upsetting me all those years ago. Can you believe that?"

Wayne shrugged.

The pair wandered back towards the main restaurant.

Dean shook his head.

"He also told me that his old buddy Michael was a good guy and would always be nice about the Vitalia family when the press start digging for dirt on Luca, which they inevitably will."

He said: "Michael loves his family and won't let nothing happen to his wife and kids, especially not for just a few lousy bucks from the gutter press. Remember what I said to you yesterday Michael. Nothing can get in the way of this campaign. Big things are happening."

Dean started to move away from Wayne, but Wayne was now totally incensed. His own failure to break Dean's spirit had annoyed him every bit as much as his step-father's implicit threats.

"Hey Dean." He called.

"I saw James last night too. He told me that you'd got down on your knees, cried like a baby and confessed all to him." Wayne grinned smugly.

"Or maybe, like you, I was just dreaming."

The look that Dean cast in Wayne's direction would have curdled milk at a hundred paces. Wayne grinned at the older man, then pointedly turned away and retook his place at the table.

"Bullseye!" He muttered under his breath. Natalia frowned as she sipped her orange juice.

"Good grief, did you just upset your Mom's ex. He's glaring at you as though you just told him he had a bad body odour problem."

Wayne finished chewing a piece of maple syrup laced pancake, swallowed and sighed contentedly:

"Oh it was far worse than that." He stated happily.

"Much, much worse."

At eleven o'clock all the wedding guests gathered on the hotel's main car park to wish the newlyweds goodbye and a happy honeymoon, before checking out themselves and setting off back up towards the border at Tijuana. Marco and Aoibheall looked blissfully happy as they hugged, kissed and thanked everyone for coming. Terri and Marina were in floods of tears, while poor Carrie looked desperately sad but was trying her best to be cheery and to cover up her sadness at the loss of her daughter. Wayne gave her a huge hug:

"I'm sooo sorry about yesterday evening." Carrie started to say, but Wayne put his finger to his lips.

"You know that if there had been anything I could have done. I would have done it." He whispered as he gripped his friend's widow's shoulders.

Carrie stared into Wayne's eyes and Wayne performed his second piece of magic in over twenty years.

"Be happy." He urged from the innermost core of his being.

Carrie broke into a wide smile and gave him a huge hug.

"Thank you." She whispered. "Take care, Leprechaun man."

Wayne nodded and grinned at her.

"Don't worry about me. I have been biding my time and let's just say that, well, as someone said to me, big things are happening."

Terri was the next to hug her son:

"I'm the mother of two married sons and a Grandma. That must make me feel sooooo old."

She quipped.

"You'll never be old, Mom." Wayne laughed. "In fact I don't think you've aged a day since I met you, back at Daideo's, all those years ago."

Terri frowned sarcastically:

"You were only meant to kiss the Blarney stone when you first went to Ireland, not swallow the bloody thing."

She teased her son playfully.

Wayne laughed.

Terri noticed Dean glaring at them from across the car park.

"Wow, he looks pissed. He must have fallen out of the wrong side of the bed this morning."

Wayne laughed:

"No. I think maybe his eggs were a bit rotten."

Wayne had already noticed that Dean's mood had not improved from breakfast. He couldn't help but feel a huge sense of achievement at having wiped that all too perfect shiny white smile off that glib, permanently tanned face. Natalia had also noticed Dean glowering at Wayne just after the happy couple had been seen off:

"I'd be careful Wayne." She cautioned her husband, "he looks a nasty piece of work."

Wayne nodded:

"Darling, you have simply no idea." He agreed.

The Higginbotham's were due to spend one last night in Los Angeles at a hotel near the airport, before catching the early Sunday afternoon flight back to London.

Wayne checked out of the Rosarito hotel while Natalia and the kids waited by the hire car. The hotel lobby was full of wedding guests saying their goodbyes and hugging and kissing. Wayne had just kissed Marina goodbye and was about to step out of the hotel front door when he was suddenly conscious of a presence behind him. He felt a hand on his shoulder and turned to see Dean's furious face:

"I don't like not having the last word, Michael." The older man spat.

"I didn't like what you said this morning. Someone played a real lousy, dirty trick on me last night and you seem to be well informed about it. Now I have warned you. If you say or do anything to upset things…" He turned to see if anyone was listening, then turned back and whispered:

"You or someone dear to you will end up just like your buddy, Malone."

As far as Wayne Higginbotham was concerned, Dean's provocation was every bit as bad as Baz Thompson's, which had seen Wayne, albeit inadvertently, render him permanently senseless. It was even worse than what the thug had done to him in the Manchester University Union bar, which had ended in a misfortunate fatality.

Wayne Higginbotham, however, was not a kid any more, nor was he an arrogant youth, full of his own self-importance and insuperability. Wayne Higginbotham was now a family man in his forties, so he did what any such man would do. He reached out and grabbed Dean Vitalia's chin in the palm of his right hand and pulled the surprised looking older man's face towards his own. Then he whispered:

"Come and have a go, if you think you're hard enough, Deano, but come yourself, don't get Aurelio to organise some low life punks to fake a robbery. Come and do your worst, Deano. I'll be waiting. You really have no idea who you are messing with."

He pushed Dean away and smiled as the old man opened and closed his mouth, totally lost for words. No one had ever spoken to Dean Vitalia like that. Nobody, not in over sixty years.

Wayne turned to leave but then thought of one other thing. He turned back and smiled again:

"By the way, Deano. I'll wager you a million bucks that the next President of these here United States, will not be not called Vitalia."

With that, Wayne Higginbotham left the Hotel.

Sixteen

The single most anticipated TV show in the history of broadcasting, started off quite unremarkably. The usual opening credits followed by the usual topical Oprah jokes and even a normal opening guest, the celebrated, venerable British stage and screen actor, Sir Ian Mcillvenney. Ever the consummate professional, Oprah betrayed no signs of nervousness, either at the prospect of hosting the most watched show in history, or of meeting the Son of God. The show had been syndicated to be shown live on most TV networks, although China, North Korea and most of the Islamic world had decided not to show it, claiming the material would not be of interest to their viewers, especially at the unsociable time of transmission.

Sir Ian cracked a few self-deprecatory jokes in his deep, sonorous theatrical tones, about his role as history's most celebrated warm up act and how no one would ever remember a single word he said. Then he went on to plug his new movie in which he was to play an evil academic:

"As per usual, I shall play the villain," he quipped, "It seems that the English always get the role of the psychopath in Hollywood. I really don't think you have forgiven us for making you live next door to Canada in revenge for your declaration of Independence."

The specially invited studio audience laughed gently as Sir Ian continued to regale Oprah with anecdotes about his fifty-year career. At last Oprah thanked Sir Ian, turned to the camera and said:

"Ladies and Gentlemen, Sir Ian Mcillvenney! Next, after these few messages, we'll be talking to Luca Vitalia. Actor, musician, Independent prospective Presidential candidate and self proclaimed Son of God. Don't go away."

All over the world power surges hit grid systems as viewers jumped up from their sofas to switch on kettles, or went off to the bathroom, before the main event. Even so, the advertisers who had paid record figures for the commercial break slot prior to Luca's appearance still had more of a captive audience than even they could have dreamed of. Later estimates stated that over two billion people watched the live transmission, over a third of the world's population. Another billion caught edited highlights later.

Finally the moment arrived as the Oprah show recommenced and she announced:

"Ladies and Gentlemen, Luca Vitalia!" The studio audience went crazy, whooping and hollering as Luca strolled towards Oprah's desk, grinning from ear to ear.

"Welcome Luca." The hostess welcomed her guest with a kiss on both cheeks.

Luca waved at the audience, then sat down next to Sir Ian Mcillvenney, who shook the young man's proffered hand politely.

"So Luca!" Oprah had to almost shout to be heard above the raucous audience:

"When did you change your name from Luke Lively?"

Luca laughed:

"As soon as I decided to enter politics, I realised that my stage name would sound too much like a call to action to be taken seriously, plus the press would use any setback to make wisecracks like "Not looking Lively" or, you know, that sort of stuff. Luca Vitalia is my real name, so it seemed the right time to revert to that name."

Oprah nodded:

"Was the move into Politics a recent decision?" She asked pleasantly.

Luca shook his head:

"No. The acting, the pop thing, they were just vehicles to promote me, you know, to get me recognised. I needed a bit more than fifteen minutes of fame to propel me to the launch pad, which is where we are now. Plus, politics is expensive, my earlier careers earned me a few bucks."

The audience chuckled. Oprah nodded sagely:

"What do you say to those who say you are too young and inexperienced to run for President?"

Luca smiled thoughtfully.

"I'd say that I've watched my father be a senator all my life, so I've always been familiar with politics if you like. I'd say that I'm not tainted by past mistakes, you know. I see myself like a breath of fresh air coming to blow away the old, stale GOP versus Democrat stalemate."

The audience applauded and cheered.

Oprah nodded:

"What about the rumour that you were born outside the United States?"

Luca laughed:

"A mere triviality that will soon be considered totally irrelevant."

Oprah nodded again:

"People are saying that you were insane to declare yourself the Son of God. They say it has destroyed the huge amount of credibility you earned as a singer and actor."

Luca grinned his most charming, sparkly toothed, grin.

"Give me their names and addresses." He joked.

Luca eyeballed the nearest camera.

"The last time I came to Earth, I came as the son of a humble carpenter and his wife, at the very edge of the Roman Empire. I could have come as Caesar, but that wasn't the plan. Yet from those humble roots, I started a religion that is now the World's largest. Even so, more than half the World is still in darkness."

"By darkness you mean worshipping in other religions?" Oprah interjected.

Luca nodded:

"Or none at all. This time I decided I would come as Caesar. The President of the United States is as close to that as anything that exists in this day and age. The rest of the world will get the message and the Kingdom of God can begin."

The audience whooped and cheered.

"As simple as that?" Oprah asked.

"As simple as that!" Luca repeated.

"So exactly what will you do when you become President?" Oprah pressed the young man as she leaned towards him.

Luca spread out his arms:

"I will end war, pestilence, poverty and famine. I will obliterate racial and religious intolerance, so ending all terrorism. I will put an end to greed and inequality. I will stop global warming and reverse the impending environmental catastrophe."

He paused theatrically:

"My plans for the second day are not yet fully worked through, but I do intend to have a lie in on the seventh day."

The audience roared with laughter, applauded and cheered.

"Those are all big asks, even for a deity." Oprah opined sceptically.

Luca laughed.

"I'm not just another politician, Oprah. I'm not here to make empty, vacuous political promises. Look, put aside your journalistic scepticism. I am here, quite simply, to save the world. I promised the world proof of my divinity tonight. I promised..." Luca turned and looked straight at the nearest camera.

"I promised all of you sceptics and unbelievers out there nothing less than a miracle."

Luca Vitalia stood up abruptly and flicked some dust off the sleeves of his shiny grey suit.

"Is there a Doctor in the audience?" He asked.

About five hands shot up.

"Would you all come down here, please?" Luca beckoned to the audience members with hands raised. Four men and a woman walked down on to the studio floor.

Luca grinned:

"You may have noticed that Sir Ian has apparently fallen asleep. I didn't realise I was so boring."

Luca waved his left hand in the direction of the previous interviewee who was slumped in his chair before Oprah's desk, his eyes were closed and his head was hanging over his chest. There was nervous laughter from the audience. Oprah stood up with a squeal:

"Oh my God!" She gasped.

"Please keep filming!" Luca demanded of the director and the cameramen, then asked the doctors to check the aged British actor.

The first doctor checked Sir Ian's pulse, shook his head and looked up nervously.

"He's dead." The doctor stated. The others checked for a heartbeat, one felt the artery in his neck. One opened the old actor's eyes.

"We need ECG, quickly," the first doctor yelled as various studio runners and backroom staff began to panic.

"Call 911." One of the other doctors yelled at Oprah.

For two solid minutes the doctors checked for any signs of life, then they all stood back and shook their heads.

Oprah had her hand over mouth:

"I think we need a commercial break." She whispered to the control room.

"No!" Luca shouted. "You must stay on air."

His voice was somehow different and certainly boded no argument.

"Sir Ian is dead. The medical professionals here are of the opinion that his heart failed him. Is that right?"

The five doctors looked at other, shrugged and nodded awkwardly.

Luca grinned:

"And you are quite sure that Sir Ian is dead. Paramedics will be here any second. Will they be able to revive him?"

The doctors looked at one another again and the one who had been the first to examine Sir Ian shook his head.

"I guess it's possible with the ECG, but I doubt it."

Luca turned to the audience and then the nearest camera and shouted:

"Now watch and BELIEVE!"

He walked over to Sir Ian, waved a hand over his head, shouted:

"Rise!" then stood back.

Sir Ian Mcillvenney awoke with a start, coughed and looked extremely surprised and embarrassed:

"Did I fall asleep?" He slurred: "How incredibly rude of me."

The audience stood as one body, whooped, screamed, applauded and cheered as Oprah, open mouthed in shock, sat slowly back on her chair and the doctors scratched their heads and looked at one another in amazement.

Luca Vitalia prowled the stage as though he was the new presenter of the show:

"See, Sir Ian is like Lazarus. He is risen."

The handsome, smiling young man shouted as he approached a camera and stared into the lens.

"Now you must believe!" He implored the watching millions.

"Now here is the real miracle. Anyone who had died in the last five minutes will have awoken just like Sir Ian. I personally closed the gates of heaven and of hell. My name is Luca, short for Lucien. Lucien means light. I am Christ reborn. I bring the gift of light to the world. This is not reality TV, this is the new reality of life."

Across the world millions of people fell to their knees in front of their televisions, while others shook their heads and scoffed at the ridiculous parlour trick that they had just witnessed.

Oprah had by now recovered her composure and with the help of the crew managed to quieten down the audience, many of whom were crying ecstatically. Two of the doctors from the audience escorted the bemused Sir Ian backstage while Luca retook his seat. His grin was wider than ever as he basked in the admiration and prolonged applause of the studio audience.

"Well!" Oprah gasped. "That was, er, something."

Luca nodded:

"There will be no more miracles until after I am elected. What I did on Bannerman and what I have done tonight, I have done to gain attention and to encourage people to believe that I speak the truth. I am not a magician, a cheap conjuror, performing parlour tricks. You will not see me performing in Las Vegas. You will not see me walking across San Francisco bay, or feeding Africa with a loaf and five fishes. I am saving my powers for the new age, the new kingdom that will begin on the day I take office."

Oprah frowned and her eyes misted and her voice cracked as she asked her next question:

"Luca, one thing I know that is worrying people all over the world is, does this mean that judgment day is just around the corner? That the end of the world is nigh?"

Luca laughed:

"All people need to worry about for the moment, especially here in the United States, is making damned sure that I am elected. Judgment day is election-day; which is in just a few short months time. Pretty soon after I am elected, believers will live in God's kingdom for a thousand years."

Oprah scratched her nose:

"And non believers? The one's you haven't managed to convince at that time?"

Luca Vitalia laughed:

"Let's just say I don't think there'll be many of those by the time I'm sworn in."

Oprah took a deep breath:

"Luca Vitalia. There is a rumour that your mother, committed suicide, is that true?

And if so, if you are the Messiah, why couldn't you bring her back to life?"

There was a huge, indignant collective gasp from the studio audience.

Luca stopped smiling, his face clouded as he considered his answer. For a moment his face was thunderous and Oprah swallowed nervously.

"Yes." He muttered after a few long and painful seconds had elapsed.

"Yes, my mother committed suicide when I was a child. I was too late to stop her.

I was on my way back from L.A. with my father when she did it at our home in New England. I tried to bring her back, truly I did, but I was too young, I guess. My Mom thought she wasn't pure enough to be looked upon as the new Madonna. She was so modest, so pious, that such a thought as to be compared to the Blessed Virgin drove her mad. She was a good Catholic. My Momma was a Saint."

A tear ran down Luca's cheek and a million more hearts melted.

Oprah gulped and continued with her aggressive line, however:

"And your father, Senator Aurelio Vitalia has always been dogged by accusations of involvement in organised crime. Isn't that a strange background for the Messiah to be raised in?"

Luca shrugged:

"So last time I was born the son of a carpenter and I hung with fishermen. I was a real person then, I am a real person now. My father has never been found guilty of any involvement with the mafia, or any other criminal organisation for that matter. It is racism, the accusations fly purely because he has an Italian name. Had he been called Rockefeller, or Rothschild, or something like that, none of these rumours would ever have started."

Just off camera, Dean and Aurelio Vitalia grinned. Oprah's hard journalistic questioning was washing over Luca like water off a duck's back.

"He's doing well, real well." Dean whispered. Aurelio nodded:

"He's as good as in the White House already."

Finally the time came for Oprah's last question:

"So Luca. You manage to keep your private life out of the glare of media scrutiny."

Luca nodded, his smile had returned and he looked relaxed and confident as Oprah continued:

"So is there a prospective first lady in the background? And will any kiss and tell stories be coming up in the scandal magazines?"

Luca's bright white shiny teeth lit up millions of TV screens as he grinned and blushed slightly:

"Why? Shucks, is that a proposal, Oprah?" He replied with a cheeky wink, before going on to say how his busy schedule had prevented him from having much fun, but that he would sure like to get married in due course.

Oprah thanked her guest, wished him luck and then admitted that she was now totally convinced about Luca's credibility.

"Sir Ian Mcillvenney really did pass away there." She whispered.

"It's the first time anyone has died on my show, well if one discounts Britney's last appearance. But I tell you, that man brought him back right in front of our eyes, Praise the Lord! I for one, now believe."

Backstage Luca was being slapped on the back by Aurelio and Dean.

"Great job kid!" Deano gushed as Aurelio regarded his son proudly.

Luca rubbed his chin:

"When the reports start flooding in about the dead rising, then most will be convinced."

Then he smiled:

"Who will dare to stand against me now? Father it is time to start the "Brigade of Light.""

Aurelio nodded.

"Dean and I will start the preparations."

The two men left Luca to wipe off the powder, while they talked business.

"Aurelio, I need a favour from you." Dean whispered.

"I don't suppose the preacher is still around?"

Aurelio shook his head furiously as he glanced around to make sure no one could hear:

"He's been dead for years. His son runs the business now."

"Is it an international business?" Dean persisted.

"Sure." Aurelio gasped: "But we've got to be real careful now. We can't afford to be tainted."

Dean laughed sarcastically:

"Avoiding being tainted is exactly why I need the son of the preacher man."

Aurelio's eyes widened as Dean whispered in his ear.

"Little punk!" He whistled through his teeth.

"Grabbed you by the chin huh? Give me the details and consider the matter as good as dealt with."

Seventeen

Monsignor Doyle had pored over Father Abraham Reichmann's journals and notes for days before he found the information he was looking for. Fr Reichmann had been extremely meticulous in his cataloguing of incidents relevant to his investigations of the "Sacred Order of St. Gregory." Yet he had also been shrewd enough to hide any trace of information that might lead a potential enemy towards anyone that Reichmann considered to be on the side of good. His record of the interview with the young English boy that Monsignor Doyle remembered he had made tea for, all those years earlier, was simply referenced as:

"I met a young man today, who could just possibly be the individual referred to in an ancient prophecy. I am shocked that far from the monster that has been alluded to, he seemed a good and honest fellow, displaying a fair degree of courage, integrity, honour and typical British humour. Whether he is the key, or not, I am almost certain he will have an important part to play in pivotal events that are yet to transpire and I am sure that my instincts will not prove to have been mistaken. Yet, it is my sad confession that I rely now more on instinct and faith than on any hard facts."

It was when Doyle was examining a passage in a diary note relating to a visit to California that Doyle noticed another reference that could prove important:

"The Irish Priest may have lost the collar, but he has not lost all faith. He said something this evening that reassured me more than anything I have heard in a long time. His exact words were: "There is someone out there who is our side. All things balance and yes, I do believe the "Order" allowed a power of unimaginable darkness into the world, but maybe God, maybe something else, I don't know, got there first. We have a powerful ally, Father. A very, very powerful ally."

Monsignor Doyle closed the leather bound journal and looked at his watch. It was nearly time for the "Oprah show." Maybe the Church would be given a much more definite hint about Luca Vitalia's claimed divinity within the next hour, but for the moment, Declan Doyle was chewing over his mentor's diary entry.

Who was the ally that James Malone, for the collarless Priest was obviously Malone, had referred to?

Was the British youth truly the "God's assassin" of the prophecy, as Reichmann had anticipated and did that make him good, or evil? Reichmann seemed to err on the side of good.

If, however, Luca Vitalia did prove to be the son of the Sicilian, virgin Nun and was indeed the Son of God resurrected, then Reichmann had been wrong and the British boy must be, by default, evil. If on the other hand, Luca Vitalia did prove to be evil, then the youth, who was probably a man in his forties now, could be mankind's only hope, if, he was still alive. The possibilities were endless and clarity impossible to discern.

Monsignor Declan Doyle began to get a searing headache as he rubbed his forehead. The world was teetering inevitably towards an enormous precipice and the next few hours would be crucial. The entire world was now looking towards Los Angeles, California and to a young ex-actor and pop star.

Monsignor Doyle's mouth dropped open:

"Los Angeles." He gasped: "Malone's widow. Father Reichmann said that she was party to all James Malone's thoughts. Maybe she knows who the boy was?"

Such was Monsignor Doyle's excitement at the brilliance of his brainwave that he almost forgot his appointment to watch the Oprah show in the Pope's private apartment.

He arrived at the Pope's chambers panting and out of breath just as Oprah's interview with Sir Ian Mcillvenney ended. His Holiness Pope Gregory XVII was sat on a sofa, wearing his usual white robes and skullcap. A small portable colour Television had been placed on a carved mahogany coffee table of indeterminate age and incalculable value. Several red robed Cardinals were perched on other chairs while a couple of Bishops in black stood behind the Papal seat. The atmosphere in the room was palpably nervous.

"Declan, come sit down. The Vitalia boy is on next."

The Pope indicated the space on the ornate purple leather sofa next to himself, which Monsignor Doyle took, noting the envious glances cast from several Papal officials as he glanced around the room.

The Priests watched the ensuing events in silence. Furtive glances were cast from one to another when Sir Ian was discovered to be dead and a few gasps permeated the tense atmosphere when Luca Vitalia waved his hand over the deceased actor, commanded him to rise and seemingly brought him miraculously back to life. A couple of Cardinals sitting near one of the Pope's windows started to whisper, glancing at the Pontiff like naughty schoolboys, until he glowered at them admonishingly.

Monsignor Doyle sighed despondently as the credits rolled and the Oprah show came to an end. He for one had not been convinced by Luca Vitalia's performance, although he could see in the eyes of some of the gathered Cardinals that they had seen something that both excited and inspired them.

Pope Gregory XVII had not changed his position during the entire interview, apart from that one glance at the whisperers. He had remained perched on the edge of the sofa with one elbow resting on his knee and his hand slowly stroking his chin. He had stared impassively at the screen as if watching a particularly boring show about cooking or gardening, yet his attention had not wavered. Eventually he raised his eyebrows and looked at the sea of expectant faces surrounding him. Slowly and painfully he climbed to his feet. The small group of high ranking Catholic Churchmen carefully contemplated the Pope's expression, every bit as keenly as an ancient Roman might have studied a pile of sacrificial intestines, searching, probing for any omen of approval, or not. Pope Gregory remained defiantly impassive.

Finally Cardinal Limpoko of Nigeria, an outspoken conservative and traditionalist could stand the silence no longer:

"Well, Your Holiness?" He cried.

"Is our Saviour reborn in your view? Have we reached the most momentous days in the history of the world?"

The Pope scratched his head.

Monsignor Doyle also stood. He waited with baited breath as the Priest who had once been plain Pietr Warzowski began to cough and the cough slowly turned into a laugh.

Cardinal Limpoko looked somewhat offended, while two other Cardinals fell to their knees.

"Do you believe he is Our Lord and Saviour, Your Holiness?" Limpoko barked impatiently.

The two kneeling Cardinals nodded eagerly.

The Pope shook his head:

"If, that is the second coming of Jesus Christ, Our Lord, then He is guilty of the sort of vulgar, uncouth, crass commercialism that permeates almost every single facet of our modern world. Maybe He has adapted. Maybe He wants to grow his new Church at a considerably faster rate then the two thousand years that it has taken us to get to where we are today. Maybe God has become media savvy. The rapture is to be delivered as a TV reality show? I must say, I seriously doubt it. Would Our Lord have stopped Lazarus' heart, just so that he could impress a crowd by starting it again five minutes later? Would Our Lord have arranged for crowds of pilgrims to gather on the shore, just to watch him calm the storm on the Sea of Galilee? I doubt it. Would He have demanded a host of witnesses to gather and watch him walk on the waves? No, He would not, nor would he have asked Pilate and all the Roman officials and the Pharisees in Jerusalem, to come to the tomb so that they could see him roll the stone aside and step out into the world, resurrected. If nothing else, Our Lord taught us that we must have faith. He did not use ostentatious showmanship to publicise his miracles. He used the word of mouth of just a few disciples. Did he not chastise Thomas for doubting what he was told? If he had wanted to do what this boy seems to want to do then he would have marched here, to Rome and performed his miracles at the court of Caesar himself. He would have performed his tricks in the Colosseum. I ask you my friends, do the tricks of this cheap, conjuring, popinjay not fly in the face of everything that you have ever believed about Our Lord, Jesus Christ?"

The Pope took a deep breath and shook his head:

"Yes, what I have just seen does defy belief, but it does not necessarily mean that Luca Vitalia is the embodiment of all that is good. The Church line will be that I shall reserve my judgment until I have met this, this person. Television is a medium that is vulnerable to any manner of technological deceit and visual lies. I will use my own eyes to see what goodness is in his soul and I will use my own ears to judge the veracity of his words. If he is truly the Son of God, then I expect that he will soon be paying his representative on Earth a visit. Until then, the official word from the Holy See, is that we shall all have to wait and see!"

Once the assorted Cardinals and Bishops had filed out, the Pope asked Monsignor Doyle what his thoughts were on the matter. Doyle raised his eyebrows:

"Like you, Your Holiness, I thought it was wonderful theatre, but I sincerely doubt that Our Lord Jesus Christ would have resorted to such cheap party tricks."

The Pope smiled:

"You are a sceptical old cynic Declan, but then, I'm afraid, so am I. In many ways I would love for this boy Luca Vitalia to be who he says he is. Yes, I do fear the Day of Judgment, but the second coming of Our

Lord would be the most glorious thing and is it not what we are all waiting for? Yet, I really do now fear that the "Sacred Order of Saint Gregory" raised a demon in our midst and this Luca is possibly that very demon. I fear poor Cardinal D'Abruzzo made what we might now call, the mother of all mistakes.

The question is; how do we prove it, one way or the other? The boy has started an avalanche and I fear that we may all be swept away by it. We must try to stage manage public expectation, especially in the Roman Catholic Church, but we must do it without sounding churlish and lacking faith."

Monsignor Doyle nodded his agreement.

Pope Gregory shook his head:

"Many years ago Father Abraham refused to divulge to me the identity of an individual that he believed could save the world, if D'Abruzzo's protégé did indeed turn out to be the spawn of Satan. He said such secrecy was necessary, just like the Pharaoh's killing of the tomb builders."

The Pope laughed sadly.

"Ah, Abraham, if only you were here now."

Monsignor Doyle coughed politely:

"Your Eminence, I believe I once met the person that Abraham was referring to. The "Order" referred to him as "God's assassin" as he was the only one powerful enough to slay their "second coming." They, of course, took that as being for ill. He was no more than a youth when I met him, if I am correct that it was he, of course, he was a typical English teenager. I would ask for leave to go to California next week. I believe from Abraham's notes that someone there might be able to identify this "God's Assassin."

If I can find this man, if he still lives, then I can definitively judge Luca Vitalia. For they are as light and darkness and if the British boy's soul is evil, then we know that Vitalia is who he claims to be."

Pope Gregory XVII nodded his ascent.

"You have three months, Declan. I will ensure that this Vitalia does not get an audience until then. If this person does prove to be the evil one, then be careful. Get word to me in any way you can, as soon as you can. May God be with you."

Eighteen

Jonathan T. Sherman was in turmoil. He had never experienced such all consuming, overwhelming stress. He had been a happily married family man, with two perfect children and the perfect wife. He had enjoyed the perfect career, had received fantastic rewards as well as having unlimited prospects and he and his family had enjoyed the perfect lifestyle. Jonathan T Sherman had lived the ultimate American dream. From preppy rich student to fabulously wealthy lawyer, his life had been the quintessential success story. Four little words, however, had sent Jonathan T. Sherman's Ivory tower crumbling and crashing to the ground.

In the glare of the studio lights, as he stood just behind the cameras of the Oprah show, waiting for Luca's guest appearance, Jonathan's mind replayed Aurelio's words from the previous evening at the Beverley Hills Four Seasons Hotel over and over again:

"Get rid of her!"

Aurelio had made his statement as soon as he had stepped outside the Hotel into the sultry heat parking area with Jonathan.

"Luca don't like your wife, get rid of her."

Jonathan had been dumbfounded:

"What?" He had asked, stupidly.

Aurelio had looked around to make sure that none of the parking valets or porters could hear as he took Jonathan by the arm further away from the brightly lit lobby, into the shadows of the grounds. His eyes darted from left to right, nervously. His face was obscured in the darkness. Jonathan could hardly hear the Senator's voice above the sound of crickets and traffic in the background.

"Luca don't like your wife. You know, he's got sensitivities. He's the Messiah for Christ's sake. He can read people at first glance and he don't like your wife."

Jonathan had grimaced and shook his head as though he couldn't believe what he was hearing:

"So he doesn't want Lucy working for him? I mean she's a key player in Sherman General especially in Los Angeles, she's............."

Aurelio had held up his hand to silence Jonathan:

"Buddy, you ain't listening to me. It's not just that he don't want her working for him. He said: "Get rid of her." I think that's pretty explicit, don't you?"

Jonathan had frowned. He was now totally confused:

"You don't mean............."

Aurelio grinned wolfishly.

"Yes, that's exactly what I do mean."

"Divorce the mother of my children?" Jonathan had bleated incredulously.

Aurelio had sighed:

"Yeah, that would be a start." He had muttered as he turned back towards the hotel entrance.

"I'm sorry to hit you between the eyes with this Sherman, but when Luca speaks you gotta learn to jump. I don't know what he didn't like about your wife, but he was sure as hell adamant that she had to go."

Jonathan nodded:

"I understand." He had whispered.

Now, stood in the studio, waiting for Luca Vitalia's much anticipated guest appearance, Jonathan T. Sherman wasn't sure if he'd understood at all. Was Aurelio alluding to divorce, or was he actually talking about murder?

Maybe those whispered allegations about the Senator's past were not without foundation.

Jonathan scratched his head. The instruction had come directly from Luca Vitalia, however. Aurelio had merely been the messenger boy.

Jonathan shook his head. He was just confused and totally stressed. Aurelio must have exaggerated Luca's intent. The message had been made harsher simply in the way that Aurelio had interpreted and conveyed it.

That wasn't the only thing that had stressed Jonathan. Just a few minutes before he had walked out on to the studio floor, to watch his celebrated client's historic interview, Carol Anne Riley, Luca's new press secretary, had made it quite obvious that she was extremely attracted by him. Jonathan had been extremely embarrassed by the woman's less than subtle approach. In the space of a five-minute conversation she had continually run her fingers through her lustrous long blonde hair, licked her lips provocatively as she had stared longingly into his eyes and touched his hand several times. As if he hadn't made it clear enough in the way she had behaved physically, her sycophantic praise of Jonathan's case work in Sherman General, which she had meticulously researched, almost amounted to hero worship. She had then straightened his tie and ran a long, slender, blood-red nailed finger slowly down his lapel:

"We must get to know each other better, Jonathan." She had murmured, huskily.

"Luca thinks we are going to be such an awesome team. He wants us to work real close."

Jonathan took a deep breath as he reflected on Carol Anne's last sentence:

"Luca thinks we are going to be such an awesome team." And "work real close."

Luca had instructed Aurelio to tell Jonathan to "get rid" of his wife and then the stunning Carol Anne Riley states that Luca thinks we are going to be such an awesome team.

Jonathan's thought process was stymied by the explosion of noise that erupted in the studio as Luca Vitalia emerged. The reception the studio audience gave the young man was almost akin to rapture. Jonathan couldn't help but forget the concerns that had plagued his mind only seconds earlier and was bowled along in the euphoric atmosphere that prevailed in the studio. The apparent death of Sir Ian Mcillvenney caused a huge amount of concern for several minutes, but the cough that marked Sir Ian's resurrection was greeted with an ecstatic response that was loud enough to numb the senses.

Jonathan was mesmerised. Luca truly was the Saviour and the proof had just been aptly demonstrated to an immense global TV audience. As he walked off the studio floor, Luca grabbed Jonathan's hand:

"How did I do, buddy? " He asked. Jonathan, tears rolling down his face, grinned:

"Just fine. I think you did, just fine."

Luca grinned:

"I'm sorry about my message. I believe it was delivered in a form that might be described as, you know, a bit curt."

Jonathan shrugged:

"It was certainly, er unexpected."

Luca grinned again as he enthusiastically pumped the hands of studio staff along the corridor to his dressing room. Aurelio and Dean Vitalia were waiting at the dressing room door, both grinning like idiots.

Just before he turned to enter the dressing room, having gestured for the older Vitalias to enter, Luca turned to Jonathan and looked straight into his eyes.

Jonathan T. Sherman's eyes widened and his face went pale:

"She has demon blood, Jonathan, that's not good. I think you'll enjoy the replacement I've provided." Luca chuckled as he patted Jonathan's cheek and entered his dressing room, leaving his new attorney standing dumbfounded in the corridor. Jonathan felt an arm slip low around his waist and he turned, half expecting to see Lucy, but he knew that she'd stayed behind in the hotel.

His eyes met the vivid blues of Carol Anne Riley's as she smiled beatifically at him:

Luca's words reverberated in his mind: "The replacement I've provided."

Jonathan smiled back at the beautiful press secretary.

"Wasn't that just sooooo awesome." She gushed.

Jonathan nodded:

"Yes, it just sort of leaves you feeling so high." He stammered.

Carol Anne nodded eagerly:

"I know what you mean. I feel sort of, you know, drunk." She giggled.

"I feel so..........wheeeee." She laughed.

Jonathan laughed too. He laughed like he hadn't laughed in years.

As the laughter began to subside, Jonathan T. Sherman and Carol Anne Riley realised they were looking into each other's eyes. A mutual understanding and longing seemed to be being communicated without words.

Before he knew what had happened, Jonathan T. Sherman felt Carol Anne's lips meeting his own and the sense of elated euphoria was complete.

Terri Thorne had been determined to ignore the Oprah show. She had a million things to do in the wake of her son's wedding and watching her ex-husband's relatives being eulogised on chat shows was certainly not on top of her agenda. Marina had persuaded her to watch the show eventually, by producing a box of Cadbury's chocolates that Wayne had brought over from England.

Marina was a huge fan of Luca Vitalia. Not only was she related to him, but she considered that they had a special bond because she had been his co-star on "The Amishers" and she had loved his material during his brief but incredibly successful Pop career as Luke Lively. Luke had been awarded five Grammy awards and two Brits in the space of three years, so no one could accuse him of being a talent-less jerk, who had used his celebratory status and his angelic good looks to milk a few bucks with bubble gum pop. His movies had also been well received and had garnered much critical acclaim. Indeed, according to the celebratory gossip columns, he had supposedly been in the running for an Oscar, until he had announced his proposed Presidential candidacy.

Now, here he was, really running for President.

As far as Marina was concerned, Terri's scepticism about him was wholly attributable to her malaise with everything relating to the Vitalia family. It was time to grow above such churlish nonsense. Terri should now forgive and forget her ex-husband's minor misdemeanours. Marina had taken her parents divorce much harder than her brother Marco. He had seemed relatively impervious to the trauma that had befallen the Vitalia family in that house on Coldwater Canyon. Marina had reacted by rebelling, a "spirited" little girl soon seemed to change into a rebellious teenager and Terri had been hard pressed to keep her daughter from going totally off the rails. High School had been a nightmare. At least she now seemed to have settled down.

The fact that she was "between boyfriends" at the moment meant that she was spending more time at home.

Mother and daughter snuggled up on the sofa in front of the TV. Terri poured two glasses of a very palatable Californian Merlot, Marina opened the chocolates and the show began.

Terri tried very hard not to snort with derision when Luca made his entrance. His grin would have made an Osmond look dentally challenged, while the studio audience reaction made her feel a touch nauseous. As far as she was concerned, Luke had been a brat in his younger days and was now over-rated beyond belief. She couldn't help but feel slightly irritated by the way Marina leaned forward to afford herself a better view of the TV and then sat perched on the edge of the sofa as though hanging on every word. Terri was also slightly dismayed to see her daughter nodding eagerly at almost everything Luca said. There was no doubt, however, that she was disgusted by her daughter's reaction when Luca brought Sir Ian back from the "dead." Marina Vitalia prostrated herself on the ground before the TV and then started to writhe while crying "Alleluia."

Terri stood up, her hands on her hips:

"I've seen better in Vegas." She hissed:

"Does he really expect us to fall for that?"

Marina continued to lie on the rug, but her "Alleluias" had now turned to tears of enraptured joy.

"Praise him, for he is Our Lord." She gushed.

"He is not our Lord!" Terri stated with more than an edge of contempt. She couldn't help herself quoting from an old Monty Python movie:

"He's not the Messiah; he's a very naughty boy."

Marina leapt to her feet.

"Why can't you give Dad's family any slack, Mom. You are lucky enough to have been married to someone who just happens to be related to the new Messiah and you are still so bitter and twisted that you can't find any warmth in your heart, even for the Son of God!"

She stormed out of the living room and grabbed a light jacket.

"I believe in Luca." She yelled:

"And if I were you, I would too, because believe me, before long he's going to be judging you and I would like my Mom to be with me in his Kingdom. You're either with him, or you're against him and I guarantee the devil will take the latter."

Marina Vitalia stormed out of her mother's house and slammed the door behind her.

Terri sighed, walked back into her living room and picked up the phone.

Carrie Vasquez was alone. Her husband, Miguel, had taken the opportunity after the wedding to go off to visit a relative in Mexico. Aoibheall was with Marco in Acapulco on their honeymoon. Carrie had just wanted to get home. The pressure of being the mother of the bride, especially one marrying into the family of her husband's killer, had been immense. She felt physically and emotionally exhausted. She also felt incredibly lonely. For over twenty years she had dedicated her life to Aoibheall. Her daughter was all that she had left of James and now she had gone. Yes, she had been through several marriages, but none of them had matched James in any way. Miguel was a good man, but James had been the love of her life. Carrie's altercation with Dean and her confrontation with Michael, or Wayne, or whatever name he was using now, had also upset her. In Dean's case she wished that she had gone further and hit him or something. Her attack on Wayne had just made her feel guilty. She couldn't blame him for James' death, but he was supposed to have special powers, so why hadn't he used them to save his buddy?

One thing was for sure, Box Canyon was going to seem a whole lot lonelier from now on.

She switched on the TV and settled down in front of it, falling asleep as soon as her head hit the leather padded back of her armchair.

Carrie awoke to the sound of tumultuous applause. Luca Vitalia was just walking out on to the Oprah show. Carrie picked up her remote control to switch off the TV, but some compulsion stayed her hand. She watched Luca run through his interview with a gathering sense of abhorrence. Here was a member of her new son in law's family, espousing that he was the "Son Of God" on TV when the Vitalias were no more than mobsters. Carrie regarded Marco as Terri's son, as

103

opposed to Dean's, so she did not have a problem with him, but as for the rest of them.

The resurrection of Sir Ian was the final straw. Carrie switched the TV off and stormed out into the yard. The vista of the entire San Fernando Valley in its nightly illuminated form stretched out before her. The light had only just faded and it was still baking hot.

A lumbering passenger jet roared as it passed directly overhead.

Looking out over the view Carrie wondered just how many people had been taken in by the consummate showman: 20%, 50%, 75%, everyone?

How could people be so dumb as to believe such nonsense?

One thing was for sure. If Wayne, or Michael, whatever, was going to be the one destined to stop Luca, then he had better get moving.

At that moment the phone indoors rang. Carrie closed her eyes and inhaled the heat and the perfume of the bougainvillea. She went in and picked up the phone:

"Hi Terri!" She cried: "You got back Ok?"

She listened intently for a moment then said simply.

"No I think he's a charlatan, but whether he is, or not, a lot of folk out there are only too willing to believe. They have waited for this all their lives, as did their parents and their grandparents and every generation all the way back to Jesus himself. One thing is for sure, the World is never going to be the same again after that show. Nothing!"

Carrie and Terri agreed to get together for a coffee. Both women were outraged at what they had just seen and both expressed their indignation that so many in the studio audience seemed to have been taken in by what seemed such an easy trick to prearrange and to manipulate. They agreed that they had both seen much more convincing magic on regular TV shows. Yet, privately, if either one of them had cared to admit it, they were both absolutely terrified. They were both far too close to the centre of a maelstrom that was threatening to sweep away and swallow up everything they knew.

As the mother in law of a Vitalia and as someone who had lost the love of her life at their hands, or so she believed, Carrie Vasquez was the most afraid. Yet, deep in her heart she remembered what James had said about the young kid that she now knew as Wayne Higginbotham and what Wayne himself had promised her at the wedding.

All she could do now was hope that James had been right about him and that Wayne would prove as good as his word.

Terri Thorne, the mother of two Vitalia children was more afraid for them, than for herself, but her major concern was for Wayne. She had heard about his confrontation with Dean and couldn't help but feel that such actions could prove fatal, even in normal circumstances. Yet, she too now knew that Wayne wasn't quite the normal down-home guy he pretended to be. She thought back to a distant hillside in Ireland and a supposed down-home boy from Tupelo, Mississippi, turning into something from out of a child's fairy storybook. She had always believed that it had been a nightmare, a living nightmare that had given her a nervous breakdown, but now she knew better.

The children she had borne for that "Tupelo" boy were probably both just as magical as he had been. She certainly believed now that Wayne had some sort of special "power" that she didn't understand. Yet, was he a match for Luke Lively? If Luca really could bring people back from the dead, then he was very a powerful entity indeed.

Terri Thorne's mind flitted back to Ireland, this time just a few years ago. Her father had been dying in a hospital in Westport. She had travelled over with Marco and Marina to see him for one last time. She remembered Daideo grabbing her hand and gripping it for all he was worth:

"He's the one, Theresa, your Michaeleen is the one. Look after him, for I have seen him cross into the green mists of Tir Na Nog. He is a sidh, I told you and you wouldn't be believing me. I have seen it with my own eyes. He lives between Worlds and legend says that one like him will..........."

The old man's eyes had closed before he could elaborate and his words had stuck in his throat. Terri had put it down to an old man raving in the last throes of death. Yet with what she had learned over the past few weeks, combined with what she had always known, but had been unable to believe, maybe there was a chance that her son had a significant role to play in everything that was happening.

Or then again, maybe she really was just a crazy bitch, like Dean had always suspected.

Nineteen

Wayne Higginbotham had never experienced a "sixth sense" before. Indeed, had you asked him he would have professed a profound disbelief in such things, yet he had a very bad feeling about the police car that he had noticed parked just down the leafy lane from his house. There was nothing in particular he could put his finger on, it just sort of felt wrong, in some way.

He had first noticed the car, complete with two uniformed officers several weeks after the family had got back from the States. In the media storm that followed the Oprah show, however, he had initially disregarded the vehicle. The Higginbothams hadn't actually watched the show. They had been too busy getting their luggage sorted for the flight home. Yet once they had arrived at Heathrow, they found that no one seemed to be talking about anything else but Luke Lively. Reaction to Luca's performance had differed massively around the world.

In the United States, the South and Mid-West had reacted to the show with an immediate, unprecedented hysteria that dwarfed the pop cults in the past. The press in the homelands had been almost universally sycophantic and had all heralded the Second Coming as the dawn of a new age, where a good ol' American boy would lead the entire world onto a new path of righteousness. An organisation called "The Brigade of Light" appeared overnight, organising mass rallies in major cities in support of the new Messiah. Brigade members took to wearing white arm-bands bearing an image of a yellow sun shining. A few older commentators noted the eerie similarity to the red swastika armbands of the Nazis and the Rising Sun emblem of Imperial Japan. "Luca mania" became a phenomenon that threatened to sweep away all the conventional Christian denominations as well as any other religious grouping overnight.

The more sceptical, liberal and secular elements on the coasts were not as swept away as the heartlands, but there was a general "lets wait and see" attitude, which tacitly leaned towards approval, yet refrained from getting involved.

The President himself had been asked for his comments:

"The only President I will comment on is the current President of the United States," he had said: "As for Religious matters you better ask Church Leaders."

Naturally, Western European reaction had initially been much more sceptical to say the least, while the notorious British tabloid press had mercilessly ridiculed the young Presidential hopeful. Headlines appeared like: "Hoodwinked, America falls for magician." "And for my next trick," "Just like that!" and "Americadabra."

Even the serious press had found the spectacle of a renowned British actor being "used" on the show as a vehicle for Luca's "magic," as having been tasteless at best.

Members of the Magic Circle were wheeled out on TV news bulletins to explain how such a trick could be carried out and still appear legitimate.

Australia and New Zealand were similarly scathing, using the studio audience reaction to Luca's miracle as evidence of the superior Oceanic intellect:

"Can you imagine a group of Aussie's reacting to a conjuring trick by throwing themselves to the floor and prostrating themselves?"

The mass hysteria in the States was observed with a wry Aussie smile and a shake of the head.

South America saw mass rallies in support of Luca, but traditional Catholic elements rejected the notion of the new Messiah and street battles erupted in most major cities.

Riots had also broken out in most Islamic countries, especially Pakistan and Iran, where militants whipped up the fervour of the crowds by declaring that Luca was simply an attempt by America, "the Great Satan," to hijack the great monotheistic, Abrahamic religions. The mullahs declared that Luca was a mere Presidential stooge, who would be used by the American military to legitimise a new crusade against non-Christian countries, especially in the Middle East.

Israel maintained a dignified silence, although some extreme Orthodox Jewish groups did throw a few rocks in Jerusalem and Tel Aviv.

The Far East maintained a keen interest in the events that had transpired on their TV screens. In Japan, where Luke Lively had been extremely popular, teenagers started to gather in larger and larger groups to "worship" Luca.

In China there had initially been an awful lot of internet activity that showed far more interest in the event than the government was comfortable with, but that soon snowballed into mass hysteria, even as the internet was blocked. Crowds marched through cities holding aloft portraits of the one time pop star and chanting his name. Water cannons and tear gas were deployed against the crowds but they simply regrouped elsewhere.

In India, the news was greeted with an almost surprising equanimity, but the word grew and suddenly internet sites were jammed with people watching the "miracle."

Church leaders around the world, from Istanbul to Canterbury, from Moscow to Rome, were questioned almost continually about the significance of the events. All maintained that they would have to wait and see what happened in the coming weeks.

Over the following weeks, as news slowly seeped out about other people who had mysteriously risen from the dead when Luca had commanded Sir Ian to rise, even traditional British scepticism began to succumb to a grudging acceptance.

Australian branches of the "Brigade of Light" sprang up and the question on everyone's lips soon became the same across five continents: Was Luca Vitalia, truly the Son of God?

Wayne had tried to ignore the media hoopla. He was probably the only man in the world who knew who Luca Vitalia was. His first concern, however, was to get through the weeks until his Christmas vacation, juggling work and school runs and being the kids number one taxi driver. He fully intended to plan his campaign against the Vitalias, during the Christmas break. To be truthful, he didn't have a clue how he was going to approach the inevitable showdown. Twenty years earlier, it would have been a simple case of child murder. Something that Wayne had known he wasn't capable of. The current situation, however, presented him with a whole new ball game. The only certainty was that Wayne would have to face Luca before he was elected President. Once he had achieved office, he would be the best-protected man in the world.

Wayne began to wonder if he had already left it too late.

It was just before the kids broke up for the Christmas holidays, that events were unexpectedly taken out of Wayne's hands. The knock on the door at 7:30 am was totally unanticipated. It was a Tuesday morning and Natalia had decided to work from home while Wayne had intended to drop Katie and Frankie off at school on his way to the office:

"Who is that at this time of the morning?" An infuriated Natalia had asked.

Wayne, who was already dressed, stomped downstairs to open the door. He was greeted by the sight of two uniformed policemen standing on the doorstep.

"Good morning, Sir." The bigger and heavier of the two greeted him. Wayne had the same bad feeling that he had about the police car he had observed weeks earlier:

"Mister Higginbotham?" The smaller, swarthier policeman asked, pleasantly.

"Yes, er can I help you?" Wayne stammered, wondering what on earth the police could possibly want with him.

"We'd like you to accompany us to the station, if you don't mind, Sir?"

The large policeman spoke again.

Wayne wondered if it was just him, or did policeman usually have tattoos on their necks.

He had noticed the black mark just above the big fellow's collar.

"Can I ask what it's about?" Wayne asked.

"It's a very delicate matter Sir, probably best discussed away from the family, if you get my meaning." The smaller Cop whispered.

The policeman's High visibility jackets were dazzling in the glare of the porch light.

"Am I being arrested?" Wayne demanded testily.

The smaller Cop shook his head:

"No Sir, we just need your help."

"Ok." Wayne muttered. "I'll get my coat." He turned back into the house.

"Can you take the kids?" He asked Natalia who had emerged in her dressing gown.

"What's going on?" She demanded.

"I don't know, I think someone may have died." Wayne whispered, remembering when two officers had arrived to tell him that Doris had passed away.

"It's probably an identification job."

Natalia frowned: "Does it have to be done now?" She groaned: "I've a ton of work to do."

Wayne shrugged.

"I don't think it'll be long." He gave his wife a reassuring peck on the cheek then picked his coat off a hook behind the door and stepped out onto the drive.

"This way, Sir." The smaller policeman pointed to a Ford patrol car. Wayne climbed into the rear as the two officers jumped into the front seats. It was the car that Wayne had noticed parked down the lane weeks earlier. The one he'd had the bad feeling about.

"This won't take long, Sir." The smaller policeman in the passenger seat turned and grinned at Wayne as the car sped off through the predawn winter gloom.

"Can you tell me what it's about?" Wayne asked as he racked his brain for any possible traffic offences he might have committed, or who might possibly have died?

The small officer turned back toward him and grinned:

"You'll see in a minute."

Wayne scowled. What had he meant by that? The more he looked at the smaller officer, the more Wayne wondered about falling standards in the police force. The man's hair was far too long for a start.

Suddenly the car turned into an old farm track and bumped and rattled through a series of puddles, ruts and mud.

"I thought we were going to the police station?" Wayne asked, his voice now betraying his anxiety.

"Did I say that?" The smaller officer laughed.

"Nah, I might have though." The driver shouted as the car stopped with a jerk:

"OUT!" The smaller Cop barked and for the first time Wayne noticed a gun in his hand, which the cop waved at him menacingly.

An old Jaguar was parked in the derelict farmyard and in the darkness Wayne saw three men standing by it: one white man of medium build and two huge black men.

"You got him then?" The white man grinned at the officers.

"Yeah, sweet as a nut. Came along quite willingly, didn't you, sir?" The larger policeman exclaimed ironically.

The white man standing by the Jaguar was, probably in his early fifties. He was dressed in a smart, expensive looking business suit. His hair was grey, neat and slicked back. He blew a ring of cigar smoke towards Wayne. Wayne glanced around nervously. He knew his bad feeling about the police car had been warranted. He also knew that this was all likely to end in tears. The last time he had been threatened with physical violence in any way, someone had died. The smaller Cop was now just behind him to his left, the larger cop just behind to his right. The two leather jacketed black men moved up and flanked the businessman.

"You guys aren't really cops, are you?" Wayne asked as he grinned sheepishly.

"You catch on fast. Don't you?" The businessman grinned back as he appraised Wayne Higginbotham in the slowly improving light. Wayne noticed that he had a conspicuous gold tooth and that his accent was possibly of Eastern European origin.

"So what's this all about?" Wayne demanded; trying his best not to sound in the slightest bit intimidated.

"Let's just say a friend of ours has asked us to teach you a lesson, my friend."

The businessman smiled.

"Our friend said we deal with you this time and if you ever upset him again, we deal with your pretty wife and your pretty daughter. My boys here want you to upset him again, don't you boys?"

The two "cops" and the two black men, who, Wayne had decided, both looked like boxers, laughed.

For the first time in many years Wayne felt the heat surging through his body. He had quite forgotten what it felt like. Yes, he had been angry with Dean and had been involved in road rage arguments over the years and had been furious with various people, but he had not experienced the full force of his magic since that fatal accident in the student Union building. He had to admit, it felt good.

"So, who was it I supposedly upset?" Wayne asked, folding his arms defiantly.

The businessman laughed.

"Why? Upset a lot of people do you, Mr. Higgybottom?"

Another plume of smoke followed the question.

Wayne smiled:

"There's only one person I can think of, but that was a long way from here. The name's Higginbotham by the way."

The man in the suit shook his head:

"We all live in a very small world now, my friend."

He nodded to one of the thugs wearing a police uniform.

Wayne tensed; he felt every muscle in his body contract.

"Look guys, you don't know who you're dealing with, you…….."

Wayne heard the mocking laughter as he felt the pain of the first thump in the small of his back. He staggered forward, stars appeared in his eyes as an excruciating pain filled his senses, only to be caught by one of the black men who promptly turned him and pinned his arms to his side all in one movement.

Wayne heard sarcastic laughter coming from all around him.

The "businessman" strolled round to face him.

"It don't matter who we're dealing with, Mr Higgybottom. We have our orders, don't we boys?"

The second huge black man moved in front of Wayne. He grinned, his teeth were white, clean and bright, his sadistic grin shining in the gloom like a Cheshire cat's. The black man swung his fist to punch Wayne in the stomach. Wayne was now viewing the scene in slow motion and through a strange red mist. His blood was surging through his veins as though pushed by some huge mechanical pump instead of a

111

heart. He could hear the slow, deep, rhythmic thud, thud, thud as it forced the life giving liquid around his body. The pain of the enormous fist ramming into his stomach was colossal, but it was the catalyst that spurred him into action. He had bent forward when his assailant had hit him, despite having contracted his stomach muscles as much as he could, he could still feel all the breath leaving his body, but despite the tight grip on his arms, Wayne threw his head back and felt a satisfying crunching sensation as his skull made contact with something behind him.

Wayne heard a grunt of surprise as his arms were released, just enabling him to catch the black man's fist in his right hand before it rammed into his stomach a second time. Wayne raised his left hand, opened his palm and the surprised looking black man flew across the farmyard as though a bomb had exploded underneath him.

Wayne turned quickly and put his hand flat on to the other black man's chest. Even in the half-light, Wayne noticed dark blood pouring over the man's ebony skin from his nose. Wayne concentrated and the second black man blew away as though he had been made of paper caught up in a gale.

Wayne turned back to the three other thugs facing him and smiled unpleasantly:

"Did you boys really think this was going to be easy?"

He noticed the businessman looking somewhat bemused as the larger of the "cops" rushed towards him, his face a contorted mask of anger.

Wayne simply raised his hand again and the thug flew about twenty feet into the air, landing in a crumpled heap next to the first black man, who was just beginning to pick himself up, slowly and painfully.

The smaller cop pointed the gun at Wayne. His face belied his fear, however. He had just seen his mate tossed aside as though hit by a speeding car. Wayne forced a blast of power from the palm of his right hand and the man's pistol was blown out of his hand just as it coughed a burst of flame. Wayne felt the draught and heard the hiss of a bullet as it passed millimetres from his ear.

"That was a bit too close." He muttered to himself as he gleefully blasted the fake "cop" in the middle of his chest knocking him to the ground.

Wayne turned to the "businessman," who was now looking around the yard, open mouthed, at his four colleagues, two of whom were now unconscious. Both of the black men were back on their feet, the whites of their eyes betraying their fear and confusion.

Wayne walked slowly towards the first member of the gang that he'd blasted. The larger of the two black boxers. He snarled and tried to run at Wayne, but another raised palm and the man was once again was tossed through the air like a discarded rag doll.

"Stop!" The businessman shouted.

Wayne turned. While he had been distracted, the gang leader had picked up the fake "cops" pistol and was pointing it at Wayne.

Wayne shook his head:

"And you had the audacity to call me slow on the uptake?" Wayne disappeared into thin air. The businessman's mouth dropped open as he fired the pistol once, then again. Wayne reappeared behind him, raised his hand and blasted the gang boss face down into the mud.

Wayne walked over to him, grabbed the gun out of his hand and hurled it as far as he could. The gun disappeared over a shed roof. Wayne picked the businessman up by the lapels of his muddied designer suit:

"Who sent you?" He demanded, with a curl of the lip that made him look every bit as mean as any one of the thugs.

The businessman laughed nervously:

"Like, I'm going to tell you." He coughed.

Wayne smiled.

"We'll see." He said as he dropped the man back into the farmyard mud.

Wayne opened both palms over the businessman's body.

The businessman's eyes opened wide in horror as pure energy emanated from Wayne's hands and pain like an electric shock ran through every nerve in his body:

"You will tell me." Wayne stated quietly, his voice oozing menace.

"Nooooo!" The businessman screamed as pain like he had never felt before filled every corner of his mind.

"Giametti!" He cried. "Paolo Giametti."

Wayne pulled the gangster to his feet by his lapels again.

"Where do I find this Mr Giametti?" Wayne hissed.

The businessman was now crying like a child:

"He'll kill me." He wailed pathetically.

Wayne gave him another jolt of energy:

"So will I!" He sneered.

The businessman tried to roll in the mud, but Wayne blasted him again:

"And now, Jedi, you WILL die!" Wayne couldn't help but impersonate the evil Emperor from Star Wars, as he watched the man writhing in pain below him.

"I'll tell you, I'll tell you." The businessman squealed. "But please stop, I'll tell you, I swear."

Wayne stepped back and the businessman whispered an address.

Wayne nodded then he leant forward and stared into the man's wide terrified eyes, as he placed his right hand flat on his forehead:

"Forget!" He commanded. The businessman slumped back into the mud, unconscious.

Wayne turned and surveyed the farmyard. It was now almost bathed in full daylight.

The two white men who had imitated policemen were sat on the ground shaking their heads disbelievingly as he approached and removed their memories. The black man who had hit him in the stomach was conscious, but was rolling on the ground in agony.

"Don't kill me, I gotta wife and kids." He cried as Wayne approached him, his face cold and emotionless.

Wayne put his hand on the black man's forehead and took his memory at the same time as he numbed his pain. The final gang member, the black guy who had held Wayne's arms was still unconscious. Wayne knelt and slapped his face to wake him. The black man groaned as he began to wake up, his eyes widened in terror as soon as he saw Wayne kneeling over him:

"What the hell are you? You a Djinn, man." He groaned.

Wayne put his hand on the black man's forehead:

"I am a Tuatha, like my father before me." Wayne smiled as he continued to paraphrase his favourite Star Wars movie.

"And you will remember nothing, my friend."

The policeman scratched his head. He had seen some strange sights in his time, but this had to beat them all. The anonymous phone call had lead him and his colleagues to a farmyard in rural Berkshire, where they found a badly mocked up copy of a Panda car, a Jaguar, two unconscious men in fake police uniforms and two huge black men who couldn't even remember their own names, all four of them had at least one broken limb.

The weirdest sight of all, however, was the expensively attired, grey haired businessman who was sat in the middle of a puddle of mud, splashing like a three year old and singing what later proved to be an Albanian translation of Norman Wisdom's ancient hit song:

"Don't laugh at me 'cos I'm a fool."

Twenty

Lucy Sherman sat on the bed, her mouth dropped open in disbelief and amazement.

"Jonathan, you really cannot be serious." She gasped, incredulous at what she had just heard her husband say.

She thought back to when Jonathan had first declared his belief that Luca was the "Son of God" and his implied threat that she would have to be as fervent an admirer of the new Messiah as he was:

"I would hate to have to consider a future without you." He had said in all seriousness.

Now here he was in their Los Angeles hotel room, just days later, telling her that Luca did not want her around and that therefore she was being fired from Sherman General Law Inc. Her own husband was firing her from his family Legal firm:

"But, why? What did I say? What did I do?" She asked as calmly as she could manage, given the circumstances.

Jonathan shrugged:

"He said there was just something about you that he didn't like."

"What?" She screamed: "My face? My hair? ....My boobs?"

Jonathan shook his head and frowned. Lucy found his apparent emotional detachment almost as hard to bear as the news itself:

"Well what?" She yelled.

"It was something about your eyes. I think." Jonathan shrugged again.

"My eyes? What the colour? The size?" Lucy gesticulated wildly.

"I mean, God Damn it! What the hell is going on here Jonathan? You don't like or dislike someone just because there is something about their eyes that you disapprove of. What sort of freak is this guy?"

"He's the Messiah." Jonathan stated as easily as if he'd just said: "he's male."

"Yeah and I'm Joan of Arc." Lucy spat venomously.

Jonathan looked more saddened by his wife's comments about Luca than by her reaction to his sacking her.

"How can you not believe?" Jonathan T Sherman asked pleadingly.

"You saw the TV."

Lucy smirked:

"I've seen David Copperfield on the TV, Jonathan. In fact I've even seen Paul Daniels do better." She whispered as she scurrilously mentioned a once popular British magician.

Jonathan pursed his lips.

"How can you not see his divinity?" He asked, sadly.

"How can it be that after so long together and agreeing on most things, we now see things so differently?"

This time it was Lucy's turn to shrug.

"It's not me who's fallen in love with someone else." She stated simply.

Jonathan looked totally taken aback.

"How do you know?" He gasped.

Lucy walked over to the window and looked out at the twinkling lights of Beverley Hills.

How many other people out there were being torn apart right now? She wondered.

"It's pretty obvious Jonathan. I mean you talk about nothing else. It's been Luca this, Luca that, ever since we got the contract."

Jonathan looked confused. He sat on the bed and shook his head:

"You think I'm in love with Luca?"

Lucy laughed:

"Well just how would you describe it then? Infatuation? Hero worship?"

Jonathan rubbed his forehead:

"He's the Son of God. Can you not get that into your thick skull? I am not in love with him, but I do worship him and I will follow him to the very ends of the Earth."

Lucy frowned:

"So if you're not in love with Luca Vitalia, who were you referring too?"

Jonathan closed his eyes:

"Carol Anne Riley, I guess." He whispered.

"The press secretary bimbo?" Lucy actually laughed.

Jonathan took on an affronted look.

"She's not a bimbo." He grumbled. "She believes in Luca too. We have a lot in common. Maybe more than you and me at this moment in time. At least she is not part demon."

Lucy gasped uncomprehendingly.

"What? Nearly twenty years of marriage? Two beautiful children? A successful business? Oh no, correction there. I've just been fired haven't I? Oh and now I'm a demon? What the hell makes me a demon?"

Jonathan's blank stare told Lucy all she needed to know.

"OK" She said, calmly as her husband sat implacably on the bed.

"Have it your way, Jonathan. I resign from Sherman General Legal Inc. I will, of course, be in touch to negotiate a suitable settlement. I guess I will also be filing for divorce. Now would you please leave me alone. Go join your blonde floozy! Get out while I pack."

Jonathan T. Sherman stood and fiddled with his tie.

"It wasn't meant to be like this Lucy. I…………..."

He carefully considered what he was about to say, then seemed to change his mind. He shook his head sadly, sighed and walked out of the room, his head hanging forlornly. He closed the door gently behind him.

Lucy sat on the bed and heaved a huge sigh. She felt far too cross to cry.

One thing was for sure. The children would be staying in Europe over the impending Christmas Vacation. Jonathan could keep his family business, as long as she got a share commensurate with the value that she had added over the years. Plus, he could keep his blonde Californian bimbo and they could worship the Second Coming together to their hearts' content. The children, however, were hers and she would fight tooth and nail to ensure that they didn't end up in the clutches of some ridiculous, insane religious cult.

She would die before she would let that happen.

Twenty-One

Carrie Vasquez found herself quite unprepared for the knock on the door. Unexpected visitors were rare at her home in Box Canyon. Miguel had just left the house for a round of golf with some of his buddies from the office and Carrie had put up the Christmas tree and decorated it alone for the first time she could remember. She was just stood by the stone fireplace admiring her handiwork when she heard the sharp knock. She was even more surprised to see a Priest standing on the threshold, when she opened the door.

"Hello, can I help you?" She asked pleasantly, although she still maintained a mistrust of clergymen, especially Catholic Priests, due to James' experiences with the "Order."

"Ah, erm, would you be, by any chance, Carrie Malone?" The Priest asked, his accent clearly betraying his Irish origins.

Carrie twisted her face:

"I used to be, my, that was a long, long time ago."

"Ah!" The priest exclaimed:

"I am Monsignor Declan Doyle. I have come all the way from Rome, very much in the hope that you can help me, madam."

Carrie appraised the Priest at her door. She wasn't too happy about inviting him in, but he didn't look evil. In a curious way, he reminded her of maybe what James would have looked like if he'd stayed a Priest, gotten older and shorn his hair.

"Come in, Father." She beckoned the Priest into her home.

"Can I get you a coffee, or tea, maybe?" She asked as the Priest walked into her living room.

"Tea would be great." The Irishman called as he sat in a comfortable armchair.

"White, but no sugar, thank you."

Several minutes later, after a small amount of innocuous conversation and with a reviving cup of tea inside him, Monsignor Doyle cut to the chase:

"I really don't know if you'll be able to help me with this, but many years ago, my predecessor and mentor, Father Abraham Reichmann came here to speak to your late husband, James."

Carrie nodded.

"Yes, I remember. We were terrified. We really thought the "Order" had come to finally eliminate James."

Monsignor Doyle laughed, although Carrie could see the embarrassment in his eyes.

"Father Reichmann was operating on the side of good, er, Mrs Malone."

Carrie smiled patiently:

"I'm Mrs Vasquez now, Father, but call me Carrie."

Monsignor Malone nodded:

"I see." He smiled reassuringly.

"Well, Mrs Vasquez, er Carrie. It seems your husband at that time, James Malone, told Fr. Reichmann that there was someone out there. Someone he knew, who could counter what he called "the enemy of God." Considering recent events, it is now urgent that we find out who that person is."

Carrie was confused:

"Why? Are you going to kill him?"

Monsignor Doyle looked shocked, amazed and insulted in equal measure.

"I am a priest, not an assassin, madam." He stated indignantly.

Carrie took a deep breath:

"Is this all to do with this Luke Lively guy? I mean do you guys believe he is really the Son of God?"

Monsignor Doyle grimaced and held his hands in the air:

"We are not sure about this Luke Lively character. We are not sure at all. His Holiness wishes to reserve judgment until he has had a chance to meet him."

Carrie shrugged.

"I can't believe the CIA, or the FBI hasn't rubbed him out already. The Government agencies must be terrified at the prospect of being run by a lunatic. I mean let's face it, he could be this "enemy of God" that you have just mentioned."

Monsignor Doyle blanched and took a deep breath:

"The problem is, none of us know the truth of the matter at the moment. As far as we are concerned there are three distinct possibilities. The first is that Luca Vitalia could very well be the Second Coming of Our Blessed Lord, Jesus Christ. If so, then we shall embrace him and welcome with open arms and look forward to the blessed hegemony of Heaven that his return shall bring.

It is also, perhaps, possible that he is no more than a simple con man, adept at conjuring tricks and adapting technological wizardry and that he really is currently managing to fool just about all of the people all of the time. If that is the case then I am sure the secular authorities will find out in due course and will duly bring an end to his ambitions.

The third possibility, of course, and the one that concerns the Holy See most, is that Luca Vitalia really is a being with supernatural powers, whose purpose is perhaps much more malevolent than any of us can possibly imagine. It was a secret organisation operating within the Holy Church of Rome that brought Luca Vitalia into this world, in the true and honest belief that he was the Saviour. Subsequent events, however, have cast serious doubts upon the legitimacy of that claim."

"You're talking about the "Order."" Carrie interrupted the Priest.

"Those schmucks were pure evil. They certainly tried to kill James on more than one occasion."

Monsignor Declan Doyle grimaced again.

"I would not say they were necessarily evil." He stated uncomfortably, as he screwed up his face and tried to find the right words to justify what he was about to say:

"But I would say that they were probably, misguided. I suppose it's like the old saying, isn't it? They were very well intentioned and the road to hell itself is paved with good intentions."

Carrie snorted derisively.

"And those guys were sure on the road to hell."

Monsignor Doyle winced. Carrie Vasquez's mouth dropped open:

"That's what this is all about isn't it? You think Luke Lively is taking us all down that road to hell, don't you? You guys are terrified that the "Order" brought the devil to earth?"

Monsignor Declan Doyle gulped.

"It is as I said Mrs. Vasquez. We really do not know and we must reserve judgment. Father Reichmann certainly believed that Luca would prove to be at best a demon, at worst, Satan himself. If he was right then this person that your husband had so much faith in, may be our only hope. The "Sacred Order of St. Gregory" was responsible for bringing Luca to this earth. His Holiness has created a new "Order" of which I am the head, I suppose, to make sure that the mistake, if it does prove to be a mistake, is corrected. If there is someone out there who could put things right, then we would like to know if he is alive and if he would be willing to help us."

Carrie closed her eyes and thought about James. What would he have done?

There was really only one answer.

"I think I know who you are referring too." She murmured, "and he is still alive. But you know what? I'm not going to tell you who he is. I do not trust you guys enough. James never trusted Priests after what happened in Ireland. He told me you never knew which ones were in the "Order." Leave me a contact number and I promise I will tell you, if this Luke Lively does start showing evil tendencies. In the mean time, trust me. The guy you are referring to has promised me that he has been biding his time and is going to act very soon. Vitalia's agent was responsible for the death of my husband. He managed to do what your "Order" couldn't. My friend, James' friend, has promised me vengeance."

Monsignor Declan Doyle nodded empathetically.

"I understand your reluctance to divulge the person's name, Mrs Vasquez, but I beg you, however, to urge him to contact me. If Luca is as evil as Father Reichmann believed, your friend may just need our help."

Carrie smiled:

"I'll tell him the next time I see him, I promise. I don't think anyone who can blast lightening from the palms of their hands will need help."

Doyle's eyebrows shot up his forehead.

Carrie nodded enthusiastically:

"Oh yeah, he can change his shape into whatever he wants, go invisible, all that stuff. I don't know if he can fly or if he's indestructible, but James saw him do all the other stuff. He said it was like, just so totally awesome. It lived with him for the rest of his life. I mean. Wow, imagine seeing someone do that?"

Monsignor Doyle placed a card on the coffee table and rose to leave.

"We are certainly living through some very strange times, Mrs Vasquez. May the good Lord protect and keep you." He sighed.

Carrie nodded and showed the Priest to the door.

Just before he left, Monsignor Doyle turned back to Carrie:

"He didn't have dark curly hair, a leather jacket and a habit of wearing make up when he was younger, did he?"

Carrie laughed:

"A long, long time ago, yes, he did."

Doyle pondered for a moment:

"And he is definitely British, isn't he?"

Carrie put her hands on her hips defiantly:

"Yes, he is English, but you're not getting his name. Not yet anyway."

The Priest nodded.

"I understand. I just hope he is as powerful as you say and as good as Father Reichmann seemed to think. If, the old man was right about Luca Vitalia being evil, of course."

He shuffled off across the yard to his car and Carrie shut the door behind her.

So the Roman Catholic Church didn't believe in Luca Vitalia's divinity, yet.

There was some hope then. A fool's hope, maybe, but any hope was better than none.

Monsignor Doyle rubbed his forehead as he drove down the steep twisting lane that was Box Canyon.

"So he can shoot lightening from the palms of his hands. He can change his shape into whatever he wants, go invisible and do "all that stuff". She doesn't know if he can fly, or if he's indestructible. That's the problem with California. They get life mixed up with the movies. Maybe I should be looking for a mister Clark Kent." The Priest muttered as the car's tyres squealed in protest at the speed way he was throwing the car around the narrow S bends.

Yet, somehow, Carrie's words, as utterly absurd as they were, made him feel just a little bit better.

Declan Doyle had already made his mind up about Luke Lively, or whatever he wanted to call himself and if there was any chance that a comic book super hero was waiting out there to deliver Truth, Justice and the American way, then maybe, just maybe mankind had a chance. If he chose to wear make-up, a suit, jeans, or bright red underpants outside a pair of fetching blue tights and a cloak, well, that was up to him, just as long as he was capable of matching anything Luca Vitalia could throw at him.

Twenty-Two

If there was one common criticism that had recurred in all of Wayne Higginbotham's appraisals throughout his marketing career in fast moving consumer goods, it was that he lacked subtlety. Wayne's style could only really be described as direct. So direct, that on occasion it verged on being rude:

"Kelton's Corn Flakes: Only a moron would buy any other brand."

"Kelton's Bran Cereal: Clean up your act, clean out your intestines"

"Comptons Diet-Cola drink: Drink a British Cola for that great British Smile."

"Melton Light Cigarettes: You know they're killing you, but you'll die cool."

Of course, Wayne always blamed the advertising agencies for the brutality of his brand positioning, but no matter which company he worked for, or agency he used, Wayne's brand management was always about as subtle as an Australian chat up line. Wayne's junior brand manager position had, by now, become an embarrassment to him. Indeed, by the time he had hit forty, Wayne had been by far the oldest "junior" brand manager that he knew of. Wayne Higginbotham hated his job and it seemed that his job hated him. He was, however, fortunate on two accounts. His first piece of good fortune had been the discovery of Aillen's horde. A couple of shrewd investments when his trust funds had been released when he had hit twenty-one, had meant that the Higginbotham's would never starve, although the millionaire lifestyle was not a possibility, due to the fact that Wayne had inadvertently given the most valuable items away.

Fortunately for him, Wayne's second piece of good fortune came in the delectable shape of his wife. Natalia had achieved a great deal more career success in her own field of Information Technology than Wayne had ever achieved, or could ever hope to achieve in marketing. By the time she had hit thirty-five, Natalia had been appointed the I.T. director of a huge multinational company. Not only was Natalia much more successful than Wayne, she was also very beautiful, so although his career had turned out to be something of a disappointment, his marriage had turned out to be a great success.

This was especially true when Wayne considered his and Natalia's children: Katie and young Frankie Higginbotham. They were probably two of the nicest kids imaginable.

Overall, Wayne Higginbotham was quite happy with his domestic situation, so when something threatened his family idyll, he was bound to react with the same degree of subtlety that he employed in his approach to work.

Wayne's direct approach to the attack on his person and the implicit threat to his family saw him ring his office, take a week's emergency holiday, much to his boss' chagrin and drive straight into London, to face the man who had despatched the gang of thugs to hurt him and his family.

The Albanian "businessman" had told Wayne that Paolo Giametti had an office in London's Canary Wharf, indeed he must have been doing well, because it was almost at the top of one of the newest and most prestigious skyscrapers. Wayne had not planned much about his attack on Giametti, but he had set off with a rough idea of what he was going to do and what he was going to say. All he had to do was to find out if Deano had been behind the attack. If Dean had arranged it, Wayne planned to be on one of the earliest available flights to Los Angeles to extract revenge on his erstwhile Father in Law and his entire crooked clan.

The farmyard on the Buckledon road, would be Wayne Higginbotham's private Pearl Harbour and the ripple caused there would turn into a tidal wave that would sweep the Vitalias and the "Order's" gift to the world: Luca Vitalia, right off the face of the earth.

War had been declared and Wayne's finger was on the nuke button.

Wayne parked his car in a public car park near Tower Bridge and St Katherine's Dock and used the Docklands Light Railway to get him to the place the Albanian had sworn that Giametti was based.

The building where Giametti's office was located, on the old Isle of Dogs, overlooked the dockland loop of the Thames. Wayne was impressed by the sheer size of the steel and glass tower. Had he not been so angry, he would have been intimidated. He found a quiet corner near the skyscraper, looked around to make sure no CCTV cameras could be seen and then changed his shape into that of someone much younger.

The new Wayne strolled confidently into the huge open atrium through the revolving glass doors. The atrium was light and airy, potted palm trees were located strategically around the white marble floor and the back wall was almost entirely taken up by a huge stainless steel waterfall that filled the atrium with the sound of tinkling water.

Wayne walked up to a wide reception desk and announced himself as Mr Michael Finn, here to see Mr Giametti, of Giametti and Associates; the Theatrical Agency.

The pretty blonde receptionist looked at him, then at his bag.

"And you are here to meet, Mr Giametti?" She queried, doubtfully.

Wayne smiled his sweetest smile.

"Yes." He replied.

The girl picked up a receiver:

"There's a Mr. Finn here, to see Mr.Giametti. No, I'll ask. Do you have an appointment?"

She asked Wayne, the look on her face, dismissive at best.

"I think you'll find that I don't need one." Wayne whispered threateningly as he glared into the girl's pretty, but vacant, blue eyes.

"I think you'll find that he doesn't need one." The girl informed the person on the other end of the line, before thanking her and replacing the receiver.

"Floor Forty two." She informed Wayne in an emotionless monotone.

"Thank you." Wayne smiled sweetly, then turned and walked to the row of lift doors. He glanced around, again looking for cameras. He couldn't see any, but the atrium was so immense that he wouldn't have been able to see them if he had searched for an hour.

Fortunately, Wayne was able to enter a lift alone and it was a very different individual who emerged on the forty-second floor, than the one who had just left the atrium.

Wayne had changed his shape into that of a tall, well built man, dressed entirely in black leather, complete with heavy motor cycle boots. He had brought his wrap-around shades especially and had placed them carefully onto his nose just before the lift doors opened.

A small reception desk was located just to the right of the lift, from where another blonde, glanced at him and then allowed her mouth to drop wide open:

"Mr Finn? Are you a courier?" She asked in a timorous little voice.

"No, I am not a courier. I am a terminator." Wayne replied robotically but with a soft Germanic accent. Keeping a straight face was proving to be far more difficult than a terminator face:

"Where do I find: Giametti?"

The girl gulped nervously and pointed towards an office door on the other side of a wide-open space carpeted entirely in white.

"That's his office." She stammered. "Shall I tell him you're coming?"

Wayne turned his head slowly and looked at the receptionist:

"If you ring him, you will be sorry!"

He informed the girl in the same flat robotic voice, before marching across the open space, his boots clumping noisily on the wooden flooring. Once in front of the door bearing a small brass nameplate engraved with the name Mr P. Giametti, Wayne held up the palm of his hand and blew the office door off its hinges.

A few individuals standing at he far end of the open office space gasped and began to edge quickly towards the lifts.

The door fell with a loud thud on to the thick white carpet of Paulo Giametti's opulent office. Had he had time to look, Wayne would have been impressed by the view behind the large central desk, a complete panorama of central London was spread out before him, but he had other things on his mind at this particular moment. Three men were stood in front of the desk and one small, dark man was sat behind it. All four looked totally shocked and horrified.

"Which one of you punks is Paulo Giametti?" Wayne asked, moving his head in short jerky mechanical movements:

The three standing men all tensed and clenched their fists. They were all well built and had the look of men who were used to handling themselves. Wayne realised that he might have to take much more drastic action than he had intended, if his mission was to succeed.

"I'm Paulo Giametti." The man behind the desk spoke slowly as he rose from his large black leather chair and gestured to the three men to move back, away from the black clad figure standing in the ruined doorway:

"I presume that this is some sort of a joke." Giametti hissed through clenched teeth and tight, thin lips.

"Because, even if it is; it's going to be a very expensive joke for somebody. Know what I mean? As you can see I am not laughing. I am not even smiling. I am not finding this funny at all. I am, in fact, in the middle of a very important meeting and you are disturbing it."

Wayne cocked his head to one side as if he had not quite understood.

"The meeting is now over, ass hole. You three will leave, immediately!"

Wayne jerked a thumb back through the blasted doorway.

The robotic drawl, the unsmiling face, the authority of the command and the fact that Wayne had stepped forward on to the broken door as he spoke seemed to dispel any notion that a practical joke was taking place.

Wayne noticed Giametti nod, almost imperceptibly, to the largest of the three men standing by his desk. The man, a huge shaven headed beast, with a dark five o clock shadow, grinned and pulled his hand from his black leather jacket pocket. Wayne noticed, as the man stepped forward, that his fist was encased in a brass knuckle-duster.

Wayne raised his hand and the man flew backwards straight across the office, slamming into a wall by the side of the incredible picture window. He slowly slid down the wall into a sitting position, leaving a huge indent in the plasterboard, his eyes closed; the grin fading from his lips.

From the corner of his eye, Wayne noticed a second man pull something from his pocket. Having nearly lost an ear, or worse, in the farmyard, Wayne was not going to take any chances. He used as much energy as he could in the two handed blast that hit the man squarely in the chest and violently hurled him up against the huge picture window. He had not even had time to raise the pistol he had pulled from the pocket. The sound of exploding glass filled the office, Giametti wrapped his arms over his head as splinters and shards flew into the room, the third man ducked, as the man with the gun disappeared out through the shattered window and, as though in slow motion, tumbled backwards into the void beyond.

Wayne would remember the look of shock and surprise on the man's face for as long as he lived. The sound of a long piercing scream filtered through the huge hole, then there was a dull thump and an eerie silence, before a great deal more screaming emanated from somewhere far below and filtered through the gaping, draughty hole in the window. Papers blew around the office as Giametti uncovered his head, his eyes now wide and terrified.

Wayne had not flinched despite his internal horror at the look on the man's face. He knew that it had been a case of "him or me." For Wayne Higginbotham, this really was now a war. The knuckle-duster and the gun pointed squarely to the fact that Giametti was a gangster and was probably working for the Vitalias. He turned mechanically to the third of Giametti's henchmen, as the man hesitated, obviously unsure as to whether to attack the intruder or not.

"You! Out! Now!" Wayne intoned loudly, jerking his thumb in the direction of the exit.

The man did not telling twice. He ran over the pieces of the broken office door and headed for the lifts as fast as his legs could carry him.

"W, W, What do you want?" Giametti stammered. He had fallen back into his seat and had now lost the defiant, imperious look, replacing it with an aura of undiluted terror. He was probably about forty, with slicked back, jet-black, hair. Like his Albanian henchman at the farmyard, Giametti was wearing an incredibly expensive suit.

Wayne moved slowly and deliberately towards the desk. His time spent in the lift on the way up to the forty-second floor had been extremely productive. Not only had he managed to morph into a terminator that even Arnold Schwarzenegger would have been proud of, but he had been able to quickly practice a stunning party piece.

Wayne took off the shades to reveal one normal eye and one surrounded by what looked like exposed metal, the pupil shining bright red:

"Who arranged for the Albanian to attack Wayne Higginbotham?" He asked, looking directly into Giametti's eyes.

"I don't know." Giametti mumbled pathetically.

Wayne remained totally expressionless but cocked his head to one side. He slowly raised his hand, palm out towards the seedy little man sitting quaking in front of him.

Through the broken glass, from somewhere way down below, he could now hear the clamour of multiple sirens.

Giametti squealed:

"Please, no. It was Aurelio Vitalia. I work for Aurelio. Don't kill me. Please don't kill me. I have a family. It was Aurelio Vitalia who told me to deal with Higginbotham. He wanted him hurt and frightened, so that he wouldn't ruin things for Luca. The schmuck had insulted Aurelio's cousin and threatened to de-rail Luca's Presidential campaign."

Wayne straightened his head.

"And if he had refused to be intimidated?"

Giametti's chin trembled.

"Aurelio told me that he would be, that he was a nobody."

Wayne repeated the question, this time moving the palm of his hand to just in front of the gangster's face:

Giametti held up his hands:

"Ok, Yalov, the Albanian was told to kill his family one by one. They were told to make sure he was the last."

Wayne gave one curt nod.

"Thank you. Hasta la vista."

Wayne replaced the glasses and with one quick motion grabbed Giametti's greased hair and slammed the slimy looking gangsters face into the desk. When Wayne pulled his head back up, the man's nose was pouring blood.

Wayne removed his glasses again. The sound of wailing sirens now filled the room, even on the forty-second floor. This time the eyes were Wayne's own and as he glared into Giametti's dark brown orbs, he whispered:

"You will remember a fight. Nothing more!"

Giametti's head fell forward, unconscious. The gangster who he had slammed against the wall was still out cold. Wayne found it amusing to think that he and the gangster who had run would be reporting that a terminator had blasted their colleague out of the window and done all the damage, but that there would be no trace of such a figure entering or leaving the building. He clumped over the broken doorway and left Giametti's office. The open space beyond was deserted. Everyone must have fled when he had made his somewhat unsubtle entrance through Giametti's door.

All the lifts were engaged and seemed to be coming up to the forty-second floor. It was probably the building's internal security and police already.

He looked around for cameras; one was located just above the lift doors. Wayne raised a palm and blew it to pieces. He walked over to the emergency stairwell and stepped through the heavy fire door, just as he heard the swoosh of the lift doors opening. He could hear multiple feet rushing up the stairs. Wayne Higginbotham had one last trick up his sleeve. First of all he morphed back into the familiar shape of Wayne Higginbotham, blew a sigh of relief and then promptly disappeared.

As he climbed back into his car about an hour later, Wayne Higginbotham had to admit that he did feel a bit sick. That was now two people that he had killed in his lifetime. Both incidents had been accidental in the respect that he had not intended to kill either of his victims, but accident or not, both were now dead and he couldn't do a Luke Lively and bring either of them back to life. Wayne sat, gripped his steering wheel and wondered how many more people would die before he had eventually fulfilled his destiny and how many of them would be innocent, unlike the two that he had accidentally despatched so far.

Giametti had pointed the finger at the Vitalias and so everything had fallen into place. Wayne Higginbotham had tried to deny his destiny. He had managed to deny that he even had a destiny for more than two decades. Maybe it had been for the best. In his teens and early twenties he had not been capable of killing a child, no matter how evil that child might have turned out to be. That child was now in danger of becoming the most powerful individual on the planet, complete with the World's only superpower military arsenal and a huge stockpile of nuclear weapons.

Despite trying to hide behind a normal career and a normal family life, Wayne's destiny had come back and bitten him squarely on the backside. There was no hiding place any more and no escaping the facts. Fate had determined that by dint of extraordinary co-incidence, or by devious and possibly Divine intervention, his birth mother had, for a while, been married into the family that the "Sacred Order of St. Gregory's" pet demon had chosen to raise him to adulthood.

Wayne's own brother and sister were related to the demon for goodness sake.

"Of all the families, in all the world, she had to walk into that one." Wayne muttered in his best Humphrey Bogart voice.

Well, he had enjoyed his normal life and was grateful for all the good things he had enjoyed in the time that had been allotted him.

Wayne turned the key in the Audi's ignition and his head filled with a song that he had sung many times. The voice of Edwin Starr:

"War, huh, what is it good for.....................»

Twenty-Three

Jack Baring, the United States Secretary of Homeland Security, twiddled his expensive Mont Blanc Fountain pen between his fingers as he listened to Director Marshall Williams of the FBI explain his department's progress to the incumbent President, Elmer Ford over the telephone.

"Yes, Sir. We know what he what he's going to have for breakfast long before he does, Sir. We know when he goes to the bathroom, when he goes to….. Yes Sir, I guess even the Son of God needs to take a leak now and again. We will stick close to it, twenty-four, seven, Sir."

Williams replaced the receiver and blew out a relieved sigh:

"Hell, he's in a bad mood today." He informed his colleague who was sat on the other side of his desk. Jack Baring shook his head:

"He's bound to be. He's already a lame duck, yet he's got over a year left of his Presidency. Who is going to remember the guy who served a four year term before Jesus H. Christ came along?"

Marshall Williams laughed:

"If this guy is Jesus, then I'm Bugs Bunny and the President is Elmer Fudd."

He stood and pulled a file out of a steel grey metal filing cabinet:

"The Vitalias both had interesting histories in the Seventies and Eighties. A journalist was murdered and two disappeared on the West Coast. Common factor: they were all doing stories at the time, supposedly exposing Dean Vitalia's one time mafia involvement. The local Feds checked everything; there was nothing to link Vitalia with the murder, or either of the disappearances, nothing!

Five people involved in some way with Aurelio Vitalia had disappeared on the East Coast, including two journalists and a cop. The funny thing is we haven't gotten a single shred of evidence that he was involved either. He always played the race card: The poor Italian victim of a white Anglo Saxon conspiracy. Sure, there were lots of whispers but never any proof. No rap has ever stuck on either of these guys, hence why Aurelio Teflonia has been sat on his ass in the Senate for so long. They're either very smart or they have the luck of the devil himself. It seems they've both been clean as a whistle for over twenty years now, not even the slightest whisper of scandal."

Baring stood and put his hands on his hips as he stared out of the window. He could see the White House in the distance,

"So what did you find on the kid?"

Williams shrugged. "He was born in Italy, but legally adopted here in the United States when Aurelio married his mother. He was born in Rome and raised in the Vatican City 'till the age of five, when Aurelio met his mother. Funny thing is, no one in the Vatican seems to know anything about him. His career since then has been peachy clean: Actor, singer, movie star and billionaire. I mean the kid is the ultimate embodiment of the American dream."

Baring sucked his teeth and whistled:

"Why here? Why now?"

Marshall Williams shrugged:

"They always said he moved in mysterious ways." He laughed at his own little joke but stopped as soon as he saw that Baring was not seeing the funny side.

Baring grimaced painfully, removed his spectacles and rubbed his chin.

"You know Marshall. This guy is going to let himself down soon. We have to be ready."

Williams nodded:

"I just informed the President that we now have him under strict observation."

Williams grimaced as Assistant Director Amanda Thomas brought a new file in.

"You may want to take a look at that."

The attractive, slim brunette informed Williams, before turning and walking straight back out of his office, casting an enigmatic smile in Secretary Baring's direction.

Williams opened the file eagerly:

"Well?" Baring barked. "Do we have any dirt on the little sucker yet?"

Williams shook his head:

"No, but take a look at this. It's the transcript of a call made on a cell phone registered to an employee of Aurelio Vitalia's. It was made to a cousin of Aurelio's based in England a few days ago:

Vitalia Employee: Hey Paulo, How's it going?"
Paulo Giametti: Hey Franco, good, what about you?
Vitalia Employee: Good. Listen I have one for you. A code grey silencio.
  Name: Michael O'Brien
  Address: Mill House, Pangfield Road, Upper Buckledon.
Paulo: Code grey? You sure?

Vitalia Employee: Yes, no sale or return, if offer not accepted: code black on the entire house.
Paulo: For Auro? or Deano?
Vitalia Employee: All of us.
Paulo: Understood.

Baring shrugged:
"What the hell is that all about?"
Williams grinned as he hitched up his pants and read the rest of the file:
"Code grey, it seems, is a punishment beating. The silencio means that whoever is taking the beating is to be sworn to silence. Sale or return means if the terms are accepted or not...."
Baring nodded as he interrupted:
"Code black means execution."
Williams grinned:
"You got it."
Baring grimaced:
"So who's the O'Brien guy? The one taking the beating?"
Williams shook his head and slumped back into his chair, crossing his legs and putting his hands behind his head as he spoke:
"Here's the strange thing. There's no Michael O'Brien at that address. Now it may or may not be linked, but two days ago, Scotland Yard found five well known crooks beaten up in a farmyard, only five miles from downtown Upper Buckledon. One of the guys they found is an Albanian associate of Paulo Giametti, Aurelio Vitalia's cousin from that transcript. He had suffered a nervous breakdown. It seems now he can't remember a single word of English. Convenient huh? Two of these guys were ex-heavyweight boxers.
Yet, they'd been beaten to a pulp. Later the same day, now get this; it seems a guy dressed up as Arnold Schwarzenegger broke into Giametti's office in London, England and threw one of his men right out of a reinforced security glass window, on the forty second floor. Giametti and the other guy in the office are still hospitalised. Seems they can't remember a thing, not even their own names."
Jack Baring stroked his chin.
"Arnold Schwarzenegger?" He asked incredulously. "You've gotta be kidding me."
Williams shrugged his shoulders.
"Dressed as the terminator! The Brits say the likeness on the CCTV is incredible."
Baring nodded.

"Keep an eye on that one for me, Marshall. I'll inform the Secretary of State, we may need CIA involvement. I wouldn't trust the Brits to pin a tail on the donkey even without the blindfold. Sounds like Giametti might have bitten off more than he could chew when he followed the Vitalia's instructions."

Baring stood up again and looked out of the window towards the Whitehouse.

"We need to know who really does live at that address and why Giametti was given the name O'Brien. Why did they want this guy beaten?"

Marshall Williams sat back in his chair again:

"You speak to the Secretary, Jack. I'll get my people to see if there are any links to an O'Brien in the Vitalia file."

Baring grinned as he shook his head again:

"Arnold Schwarzenegger, man, don't that just beat all!"

Detective Chief Inspector Archie Knox was perplexed and the thick set, Lancashire born career policeman, with twenty-four years service, was very rarely perplexed. He paced up and down the incident room in Millwall's police station and scratched his head.

"So, let me get this straight." He muttered to Detective Inspector Ratchett, a tall, grey haired Londoner with twenty years experience in the C.I.D.

"CCTV did not pick up this Schwarzenegger lookalike entering the lifts, but picked him up at the top coming out?"

Ratchett nodded.

"The receptionist downstairs doesn't remember anyone coming in dressed in leather, but the girl upstairs registered a Mr. Finn going to see Giametti, at round about the same time as this guy walked out of the lift, Sir."

Knox pursed his lips.

"And there was no CCTV footage of this "terminator" leaving the building?"

Ratchett shook his head.

"None. The camera upstairs went dead just as he was preparing to get into the lift. The cameras in the atrium were working but he simply did not come out of the lift."

Knox slumped into a chair behind an untidy desk. He picked up an empty takeaway Burger box with a look of disdain and tossed it into a waste paper bin.

134

"And from what your men tell us, no firearms were used. Giametti and his surviving sidekick are just very badly bruised, both externally and internally?"

Ratchett leaned forward in his own chair.

"The injuries are exactly the same as those suffered by the gang the Thames Valley boys found, out in the sticks, near Reading. The bruises look like a giant fist has smashed each of them slap bang in the middle of the chest. At the autopsy on Finch, the guy who fell from Giametti's window, they found that the blow he had suffered on the chest was equivalent to a kick from a full-grown stallion. His ribcage was smashed before he hit the ground."

"What the hell could do that?" Knox wondered out-loud, before turning back to his colleague.

"And you say this Albanian bloke that they found in Berkshire, often worked for Giametti?"

"Yes, Sir." Ratchett nodded enthusiastically.

"Then there has to be some sort of connection between the two incidents."

Detective Chief Inspector Archie Knox stood up again and walked over to a flipchart board. He picked up a pen and started scribbling.

"I don't suppose the Albanian has said anything useful yet?" He asked his colleague as he dumped his thoughts on the flip chart pad.

Ratchett laughed.

"He hasn't said anything, not in English anyway."

Knox turned and looked at Ratchett quizzically.

The Detective Inspector shrugged: "He was going on and on in some obscure Eastern European vernacular, so we got an Alabanian speaker in, to see if she could understand what he was jabbering on about."

"Well?" Knox demanded impatiently.

Ratchett grimaced.

"Well according to this translator woman, your man is singing Norman Wisdom songs and repeating dialogue from the movies. It seems Norman Wisdom was extremely popular in Albania when it was run by the commies."

Knox put a pencil in his mouth and started to suck the end.

"So let's see what we've got shall we? What I've written down here is:

1) Who is this terminator?
2) Was he involved in both incidents? London and the sticks?
2) How did he just go and disappear from the lift?

3) Why did he attack Giametti?

4) How did he, on his own, take out two well known London hard cases, with more form than a Pentonville prison roll call and if it's the same bloke, another five in Berkshire, including two heavyweight boxers?

5) What caused the horrific injuries to the gang members?

Whoever he is, he's a one-man army. Any sign of Burns, yet?"

Knox asked, referring to Giametti's bodyguard who had escaped when Wayne had commanded him to leave Giametti's office.

Ratchet shook his head.

"No, Sir. The receptionist on the forty-second floor said she'd never seen anyone look so terrified. We saw CCTV footage of him running through the atrium as though he was being chased by the devil himself."

Detective Chief Inspector Archie Knox scratched his head again.

"I think this one is a case for Mulder and Scully. We have a six foot, six inch shape shifting alien, doing what seems like a superhero crime fighting job all around the South of England."

Detective Inspector Ratchett laughed.

"There's one thing that will make you laugh, Sir.

Detective Chief Inspector Archie Knox looked up at his colleague expectantly.

Ratchett grinned:

"Well Sir, you know this nutter in America who reckons he's the Son of God?"

Knox nodded:

"Giametti is related to him. He's a distant cousin of the wannabe Messiah's father."

Detective Chief Inspector Archie Knox frowned.

A faint warning bell was tinkling at the back of his skull. He had seen Luke Lively on the Oprah show. He had seen the "miracle." Now here, on his own manor, someone related to the guy performing "miracles" was getting turned over by somebody who seemed to have the ability to just disappear into thin air. Detective Chief Inspector Archie Knox did not believe in the occult, but he had a gut feeling, borne of experience, that told him that this case wasn't going to be very straightforward, or simple.

"Ratchett!" He declared:

"This is probably going to turn out to be the tip of a very sharp and pointy iceberg. Something big is happening here and I don't think it's going to be pleasant. I don't think it's going to be pleasant at all."

Twenty-Four

Terri Thorne was chewing on what had once been a beautifully manicured fingernail.

Marina was late again. She had promised her Mom that she would be in by midnight, but that hour had long since passed. Terri looked at her watch: 2:30am. What annoyed Terri more than anything else was the fact that Marina had a cell phone, but seemed to be just too damn thoughtless to use it. It had been like this ever since her father, Dean Vitalia, had stepped back into her life and had encouraged her to join the Brigade of Light. Dean's bribe had been the opportunity to "hang" with Luca for an evening. The same offer had been made to Marcus and Aoibheall, but they had turned it down citing prior commitments. Dean was well aware of Aoibheall's antipathy towards him and had laughed off his son's rejection of the opportunity of meeting the Messiah as the first signs of marital manipulation. Marina had joined Luca's evening soiree, along with about twenty other distant relatives and had immediately fallen under his spell. Terri had been devastated when Marina had told her that she was going to be a senior officer in the Brigade of Light:

"They disgust me!" Terri had complained.

"They remind me of the Nazis in Germany in the early days of Hitler's rise to power. They have been beating people up in some States, just for expressing doubts about Luca's divinity. The little armbands with the sun motif are just so like the Nazi swastikas."

Marina had sighed heavily and complained that Terri was wrong to believe the sceptical liberal press and TV channels rather than her own heart and her own family.

"Luca is a great force for good, Mom." She had exclaimed.

"He intends to eradicate religious divisions and has a plan to resolve the problem of world poverty. He should be given a chance, after all, the Republicans and Democrats have been letting America down for years."

Terri had found arguing with Marina as being as useful as trying to convert a devout Jehovah's Witness to the cause of atheism. It was almost like Marina had been brainwashed. Her eyes had seemed glazed and unfocussed at times and her depth of conviction hadn't seemed that great. As far as Terri was concerned, Marina's conversion to the cause of Luca Vitalia had been based on a limited number of repeated sound bites and a giant dollop of hero worship.

On this particular night, Marina had told Terri that she was going to a Brigade of Light convention in Hollywood. She had told her mother that many famous Hollywood stars would be turning out to profess their admiration and support for Luca.

"It's like the new scientology." Marina had declared:

"Anybody who is anybody is climbing on the bandwagon. It's just all so awesome."

Terri checked her watch again: 2:45 am

"Right, that's it. I'm going to bed." She muttered as she stood and placed her water glass in the sink. Just at that moment she heard the metallic clunk of a car door outside. Seconds later an extremely embarrassed Marina bowled through Terri's front door:

"Mom, I am sooooo sorry, I'm sooo late." Marina gushed: "But Mom, you should have been there. I mean it was really just like sooo awesome. It was like the Oscars. Luca was there and really, I just can't even begin to tell you how many big movie stars and musicians and TV people."

Terri nodded:

"That's great, honey. Why didn't you call me and tell me you were going to be so late?"

Marina shrugged.

"I guess I was just so overwhelmed. Dad introduced me to soooo many famous people. It was just so awesome, so like "wow," all night."

Terri smiled.

"I'm glad you had a great time honey. I'm going to bed. Goodnight."

Marina glowered at her mother's apparent lack of interest.

"Mom, I've got something to tell you." Marina called as Terri opened her bedroom door.

Terri turned,

"I'm going to move in with Dad and Silene for a while, if you don't mind. You know it will be easier with all the Brigade stuff I'm doing now. I'll still come and see you and stuff."

Terri nodded:

"Silene?" She asked, unfamiliar with the name Marina had mentioned:

"Yeah, she's Dad's new girlfriend. I guess she's about thirty. She's really beautiful and sooooo cool. He dumped Cindy soon after Marco's wedding."

Terri shook her head.

"She's young enough to be his daughter, but then they all are."

Marina pouted sulkily.

138

"Do you mind me moving out?"

Terri shook her head:

"No honey. Your life is your own. I'm tired, we'll talk tomorrow." Terri turned and closed her bedroom door behind her.

Marina Vitalia grinned. At least two A list movie stars had taken her cell phone number as soon as Dean had introduced her as a cousin of Luca Vitalia. She had lost count of the number of minor celebrities who had tried to impress her.

Marina pirouetted around the kitchen. Life was going to get soooo awesome now that Luca was going to rule the world.

Not too far away, Marco Vitalia was lying awake in bed. His back was turned on his beautiful young wife, who he presumed was also still awake. They had just had their first major row and it was all to do with Luca. Marco sighed. He could hear crickets chirping outside and in the distance a train hooted like a mechanical owl.

All he had wanted Aoibheall to do was to give his cousin a chance. Luca seemed a really nice guy and although Marco was somewhat sceptical about his claim to be the Son of God, he did seem like he would make a good President. He was young, his ideas were idealistic, but they were what people wanted to hear. Marco thought it would be pretty cool to have a relative as the President of the United States of America.

Aoibheall had been adamant, however. As far as she was concerned, Luca was evil.

Aoibheall was always an excellent judge of character and even Marco had to admit that she was never wrong about people.

The discussion had originally started off with Marco asking Aoibheall if he would be allowed to join Marina at an upcoming rally. Aoibheall had been appalled that he had even considered such an action. The discussion had turned into an argument with each of them attacking their in-laws, then taking each attack as a personal insult. The argument had grown into a full-blown row, which had continued when the newlyweds had gone to bed.

Marco felt Aoibheall's warmth in the bed next to him. Luca might be the Messiah, the Second Coming, or whatever, but Aoibheall was his wife and she would always come first. He turned and whispered:

"I'm sorry, honey." Then he put his arms around her and held her tight.

Luca could wait. After all, it was still weeks off the Iowa Caucasus and well over a year until Luca would take office.

Marco was sure he would join Marina in the Brigade of Light, but not yet. Aoibheall would come round. Marco was sure of it. He would just have to convince his father to swear to Aoibheall beyond any doubt that he had not been responsible for the death of Aoibheall's father; then everything would be OK.

If Luca could bring peace into his Mom's heart too, maybe she would forgive Dean his silly infidelities and the family could be reunited. Even Michael could truly be part of the family.

Twenty-Five

Luca Vitalia was feeling totally elated. His Hollywood rally had been a spectacular success. He hugged Dean and thanked him for all his hard work in getting so many celebrities to attend the function that had taken place in the Beverley Hills Four Seasons Hotel. Even Sir Ian Mcillvenney had made a public appearance and had thanked Luca for saving his life. Of course, the media had been out in force and Newspapers and celebrity gossip magazines all over the world would be full of photographs from the event and the many ringing endorsements that Luca had received from the many famous faces who had attended. Luca walked along the hotel corridor and opened the door into his bedroom.

A beautiful blonde girl was lying, naked on his bed, smiling up at him. Luca didn't even look at her:

"Please get dressed and leave." He commanded, gently but firmly, "I will not be tainted by any scandal. The pleasures of the flesh can wait."

The girl sniffed haughtily, quickly pulled on her clothes and left.

Luca slumped onto his bed and grinned. It was all going so well. Even he had not expected everything to fall into place so quickly. The Press were trying everything to tempt him away from the path of righteousness. The naked girl had probably been sent by a newspaper in a weak attempt to prove that he was not as perfect as his image suggested. Government Agencies were trying their best to dig into his past. Luca knew that at least four FBI agents had been employed full time for more than three months in trying to dig up incriminating evidence on him. They would fail. The incumbent President would be made to bow down to him and to lick his shoes as soon as he became the leader of the free world.

Luca began to laugh. He would have the President, the Pope and the Queen of England, all grovelling at his feet and apologising for their refusal to recognise him as the Son of God as soon as he had made his original announcement.

His only short-term problem was reigning in the Brigade of Light. He did not want bad publicity and many of his more enthusiastic followers were already taking things a little too far. Luca would speak to his press secretary, Carol Anne, first thing in the morning and get her to release a statement that would forbid any violent action by the

Brigade of Light, no matter what provocation they might face from unbelievers.

They would be allowed to take their revenge later. He would allow them to indulge themselves in an orgy of violence and retribution, once he was in power. Then, once their usefulness had ended, he would incinerate them.

Luca walked over to the dressing table mirror. He put his hand under it and pulled out a small camera device.

"Tut tut." He whispered as he crushed it in his fist.

He looked in the mirror.

Luca Vitalia was as handsome a product as the human race could possibly produce. He ran his hand through his blonde curls and tousled his hair. Soon he would be able to indulge in every single fantasy that he had ever envisaged. He would have absolute command over every single living thing.

He would keep all the really beautiful people to be his slaves and the most devoted of his followers would be allowed to survive, for a while. All the rest of humanity would be disposed of and the irony was that they were going to willingly give him the power to destroy them all. Luca stared at his reflection and posed imperiously. He would soon be a God with all the powers of life and death. Luca grinned, a mad, psychotic leer. He wanted blood, he wanted to taste his power, but he could not afford a scandal. Luca pondered for a second, who could he kill slowly and maliciously, savouring every moment of his unbridled power?

He had not liked the lawyer's woman, the one who had looked at him disdainfully in this very hotel. There had been something in her eyes that he had hated the moment he had seen her. Something he couldn't explain. She had had something in her that he half recognised as dangerous. He had commanded her husband to "get rid of her" and he, Luca, the light of the world had been benevolent enough to provide a younger, more beauteous replacement for that miserable sop. He was too wet, Aurelio had been mistaken in hiring him, but he was adequate for the moment. Luca would deal with him later.

Since he had arrived in the realm of mortal men he had been so good and it had been so boring. Now that he could almost taste victory, he would allow himself a little fun. No one would ever know. It wouldn't damage his campaign. He would kill the lawyer's wife. He would watch her die, slowly.

Because he didn't like her eyes.

Because he could.

Oh, so much power and so little time to use it.

Was there no one on this miserable rock of a planet who was capable of opposing him?

Luca Vitalia closed his eyes and thought about the course of his human life, from angelic cherub to prospective President, via acting and pop music. It had all been so incredibly easy.

Then, suddenly, a small dark thought crossed his mind.

He had faced opposition on one occasion. Someone had once stood up to him.

Luca jumped up and racked his brain:

Who? Where? When?

Then he remembered.

Whatever had happened to that voice that had invaded his mind when he had been but a boy? Luca's reflection suddenly looked concerned and the elation he had been feeling quickly evaporated as he remembered the voice that had once filled his consciousness and had terrified him.

Luca thought back to his campaign against the "Order." How he had invaded the minds of the "Order's" Priests, getting each one to name his associates and then filling their minds with such images of horror that they had gone insane and killed themselves rather than face seeing any such imagery again. While he had been seeking out the minds of his opponents, he had come across a skinny young whelp, who seemed to have some sort of destined role to play in future events. Nothing of what Luca had seen had been clear, but he knew that he had been attempting to terrify the whelp, when suddenly and without warning the whelp had turned on him:

"I KNOW WHO YOU ARE, LITTLE MASTER VITALIA. I KNOW WHERE YOU ARE, YOU SPOILED LITTLE TANTRUMING BRAT AND I KNOW HOW TO DESTROY YOU AND TRUST ME, WHELP, I AM GOING TO DESTROY YOU!"

The words flooded back into Luca's mind as though they had been uttered yesterday, yet he knew that it been well over twenty years since he had destroyed the last vestiges of the pathetic "Sacred Order of St Gregory" and had stumbled on the whelp.

"How do you know me?" Luca had asked.

"That's for me to know and for you to fear."

The voice had said.

Luca shivered.

For over twenty years he had covered up that memory. He had built up his image of infallibility. Now, however, just as he had been feeling totally and utterly insuperable, the memory had come back to haunt him.

Why had the voice not carried out its threat?

Why had it lain dormant for so long?

Maybe there had been someone capable of opposing him and that individual had come to grief.

Luca stroked his chin as he paced up and down the floor of his suite.

He would seek out that mind again, if it still lived and this time he would destroy it just as he destroyed the entire rat pack that called itself "The Sacred Order of St. Gregory."

He would destroy his opponent slowly and in the cruellest manner imaginable to punish it for its impudence all those years ago.

Luca ripped off his clothes and jumped into his bed.

It would soon be time for Luca Vitalia to have some fun.

Twenty-Six

Performing magic without the "Stone of Falias" had proven to be much harder work than Wayne had anticipated. He felt as though every last ounce of energy had been drained from his body after his exertions in Giametti's office.

The next day it felt like he had run the London marathon; even getting out of bed proved a struggle. If he was going to go after the Vitalia clan, including Luke Lively, who was now likely to be a demon of considerable power, Wayne would need to equip himself properly.

His first priority would have to be the retrieval of the two treasures of the Tuatha de Danaan that he had abandoned so many years earlier. The Stone of Destiny: the "Lia Fail" that amplified Wayne's powers. He had no idea how much, because he had not used it, since it had magically reformed in his bedroom in Shepton all those years earlier.

It would definitely be necessary if he were to have any chance in the fight against Luca.

The Spear of Finias would be needed as well. He had retrieved that from the cliffs of Moher at great risk to life and limb, so he might as well use it. The legend was, that once thrown, it never missed its target. The other treasure that he would need was the Sword of Gorias that Nuada had wielded in the distant days of myth. That was a weapon that supposedly rendered its wielder unbeatable.

As far as he had been able to ascertain from his attempt to gather the treasures in his student days, before the Union fight disaster, that particular sword was now in the possession of the Getty museum in California.

As soon as he got up the day after the Canary Wharf incident, Wayne, despite his aching body, picked up the phone and made his travel arrangements. The incident with the Albanian and his gang had persuaded Wayne that Natalia and the kids should be moved somewhere safe until he had finally defeated the Vitalias. The fact that they knew where he lived was worrying and Wayne had no idea whether Aurelio had any more thugs in Britain that he could let loose to intimidate the Higginbotham family.

Of course, getting Natalia to co-operate in her self-protection was going to prove difficult without telling her about the dangers that the entire family faced. So, that evening, Wayne sat Natalia down on the sofa with a full glass of wine and started to explain:

"I'm afraid we are all in danger." He mumbled as a way of starting the conversation.

Natalia thought he was joking at first.

"What?" She laughed, "Why? No, don't tell me. You are not in marketing at all. You actually work for the "government."" She made a little gesture with both hands that indicated quotation marks.

"You don't drive an Audi, you actually have an Aston Martin complete with an ejector seat and machine guns. Your favourite drink is not a New World Syrah, or a smooth Merlot, but a Vodka Martini, shaken not stirred."

Wayne listened to Natalia's mickey-taking with an embarrassed sickly smile and when she finished with a girlish giggle, he shrugged:

"You are far closer than I would like you to be, or, believe me, you would like to be."

Natalia slowly stopped giggling and cleared her throat in an effort to be serious.

Wayne stood up from the sofa and walked over to the piano that was the main feature of the Higginbotham living room. He rested a hand on the keyboard cover:

"You know I was adopted, and you know my Mom and that she came from Ireland."

Natalia nodded, a faintly sardonic smile still playing on the edges of her lips.

Wayne desperately wanted to tell his beautiful wife the truth. He really wanted her to know that he had powers that were the stuff of legend and fantasy. He was bursting to tell her that her children were the descendents of an immortal race and the grandchildren of a King. He felt that he would explode if he didn't tell her that Katie and Frankie belonged to a Royal Line that was already ancient when the Pharaohs ruled Egypt.

Yet, at the last minute, courage failed him.

"It goes right back to an old IRA feud." He blurted, trying desperately to recall the pertinent details of the yarn that James Malone had used to explain events to Wayne's adoptive mother, Doris Higginbotham and his Aunt Margaret, way back when the psychotic Pierre De Feren had been trying to kill Wayne on behalf of the "Order." Malone had invented an entire history of a complex IRA feud going right back to the Nineteen Fifties. He had explained that Wayne's birth father, Mickey Finn, was a senior IRA man who after years of active service had turned informer and had been eventually caught and executed by the IRA. The demise of Mickey Finn had not been enough for some families, Malone had patiently explained to the terrified

Yorkshire women, a blood feud had been sworn on the entire Finn line and De Feren had been an assassin working to kill Finn's illegitimate son, Michael Sean O Brien. Doris and Margaret had swallowed every line, as had the police when Malone repeated the story to them after he had rescued Wayne from the fire at Cavendish Street. Wayne repeated the story to Natalia and then added all the recent events in the farmyard and in Canary Wharf, although he had conveniently "forgotten" to mention the use of magic.

Instead of looking horrified, Natalia Higginbotham, looked, not surprisingly, totally perplexed.

"So after all these years, these people have found out where you are again and are trying to kill you, again?"

Wayne nodded eagerly.

"So, let me get this straight." Natalia put her glass down on the coffee table and sat up straight on the sofa. Her eyes bored into Wayne's.

"Nothing has happened with this IRA feud since you were sixteen years old and still living on Cavendish Street?"

Wayne nodded.

Natalia pursed her lips:

"Then, out of the blue, yesterday, you were abducted by a gang, some of whom were dressed as policemen. You were taken to a farmyard where you managed to beat up five members of this gang, all on your own and then off you went into London to take out the boss who had sent these guys to get you?"

Wayne slowly nodded again and pursed his lips. Even with the element of magic taken out and the addition of James' IRA scenario, Wayne realised his story did lack a certain degree of credibility.

Natalia licked her lips, patiently:

"So, once you got to London, you beat up three thugs and identified that the main man, behind this attempted abduction, now lives in Los Angeles and you are going off to America, tomorrow, to deal with him?"

Natalia brushed some fluff off her knee as she perused her husband's increasingly red face:

"And you are going via Ireland, where you need to liaise with your field manager. Wayne, are you sure you're not going to tell the police about any of this?" Natalia asked with a look that almost incinerated Wayne on the spot.

Wayne gulped: "No, now you see that's the funny bit in the story."

Natalia raised an eyebrow.

"Go on Wayne, make me laugh."

Wayne knew that his story couldn't get much more ridiculous so he decided to go for it:

"The thing is…." He coughed.

"I really am a secret agent, trained in martial arts, survival techniques and assassination. I really do have a licence to kill. I've effectively been a sleeper for many years, but now I'm afraid I've been reactivated as it were. If the police get to know, it will hit the public domain and the whole Irish peace process could be put in jeopardy."

He tried to smile reassuringly.

Natalia cocked her head to one side:

"Have you been drinking?" She asked, shaking her head.

Wayne scratched his head.

"You don't believe me, do you?"

Natalia stood up and strolled over to the sink and placed her glass on the draining board:

"Wayne." She laughed:

"I have known you since you were a student with corkscrew hair, pimples and a ridiculous penchant for wearing too much black eye liner.

I knew your adoptive Mum, Doris and I have met Terri. I know you better than you probably know yourself."

She put her hands on her hips:

"Now, you tell me that you are actually James Bond, Jason Bourne and Jack Bauer, all rolled into one. You tell me that I have to go into hiding with the children and that you are going to Los Angeles, via Ireland, to carry out an assassination that relates to a situation that was supposedly resolved in 1998 with the Good Friday Agreement?"

Wayne's mouth opened and closed but nothing came out.

"Please tell me the truth, Wayne. Are you having an affair?" Natalia asked plaintively, her eyes trying to dig deep into Wayne's to see if there was any sincerity in there at all.

Wayne opened his mouth again but before he could utter a single word, Natalia blew out an exasperated sigh:

"I mean why invent all this absolute rubbish? If you're going to leave, for goodness sake just have the guts to tell me."

Wayne took a deep breath as Natalia shook her head despondently.

"I'm going to bed." She sighed:

"Maybe I drunk too much wine and this will all turn out to have been a joke, or maybe I'm dreaming and I'll wake up in a minute. Wait until I tell you the story you've just told me. You ought to write it all down, you know. You could make it into a book. No, having said that, the plot is just too ridiculous. It must be a dream. That's the thing with dreams, they're so ridiculous, you couldn't even make it up."

She started to walk past Wayne on her way to the hall and then the stairs. Wayne grabbed her arm just above the elbow. She turned to him, her eyes full of fury:

"Don't you bloody dare!" She started to shout, but the look in Wayne's eyes took the breath right out of her body.

"I am not having an affair and what I have told you is absolutely true, in so far as what happened yesterday." He spoke slowly and clearly, his voice steady and controlled:

"You already know that what happened on Cavendish Street is true, Doris told you that story many times. I can assure you I have told you a sanitised version of what is going on. If I told you the whole truth about what is behind all this madness, then you would not believe a word of it. I swear this to you though, on my life, on my mother's life and on Katie and Frankie's lives. I am not doing anything illegal and I am most certainly not having an affair. When it is all over, I will tell you absolutely everything."

The intensity of Wayne's stare shocked Natalia. She knew now he was telling the truth, in as much as he could.

"So do you really think we are in danger?" She asked.

Wayne shook his head:

"Not right now, I think I've dealt with the local connection, if that's what you want to call them. But if anything goes wrong you could be in a lot of danger. I would call the police tomorrow evening and tell them that there have been some suspicious characters hanging around and that I'm away in Ireland. Don't mention the America bit."

Natalia nodded:

"I'll set the alarm at nights. I mean the drive is securely gated and you installed that CCTV camera and security light."

Wayne touched her cheek gently.

"I'm sorry to lay all this on you. When I get back, I really promise I will tell you the absolute whole truth and nothing but the truth and I promise you it's even more incredible than what you've heard so far. Trust me!"

Natalia's eyes filled with tears.

"Oh my God. Something really is going on, isn't it?"

Wayne nodded and tried to smile reassuringly.

Natalia kissed his lips then put her hands on the sides of his head, covering his ears.

"It's Dean you're going to see isn't it? I saw some of what happened in Mexico and I heard about Carrie losing it with him. She blames him for James' death, doesn't she?"

Wayne kissed his wife's hand as she drew it away from his head.

"Like I said. I'll tell you the full story when I get back."

"Make sure you do." Natalia whispered:

"Get back, that is."

Wayne Higginbotham closed his eyes to go to sleep. He felt much better having unburdened some of the weight on his shoulders. When he did get back from the States and the demon had been destroyed and the last legacy of "The Sacred Order of St. Gregory" had been consigned to the dustbin of history, then he would tell Natalia everything. Absolutely everything.

Twenty-Seven

Monsignor Declan Doyle had paced up and down the corridor for what seemed like hours. He had not slept since he had got back to the Catholic hostel from Carrie's house. James Malone's widow had provided some encouragement for the Irish Priest, but her refusal to divulge a name had left him powerless. The more he had thought about Luca Vitalia and the way he was operating: the manipulation of the media, the formation of the Brigade of Light and his use of a family suspected of involvement in organised crime, the more he thought it much less likely that he was the Messiah. So who was he? What did he want?

Monsignor Doyle turned, as he approached the white panelled door at the end of the corridor and walked slowly back along the passage with his hands behind his back. He had not informed the Pope of his failure to find the English man that he had once seen in Father Reichmann's office. He was not prepared to admit failure. He clenched his fist. There must be a way of identifying the boy, as he was then. Surely Father Reichmann would have left some sort of a clue, somewhere. Yet the more he racked his brains, the less inspired Monsignor Doyle became. He had examined all of Reichmann's notes, all of his files and even his personal journal. Yet, he had found nothing at all.

Finally Declan Doyle opened the door to his room and took himself off to bed.

"Maybe I'll find inspiration tomorrow." He muttered before he settled on to his knees to pray.

Even in bed, sleep still eluded him. He decided to take one more look at Father Abraham Reichmann's small red leather bound journal. He placed his spectacles on the end of his nose and settled back on to his pillow. The journal fell open right at the back page. Doyle was about to turn to the main body of the extensive hand written tome, when he noticed a small scribble at the bottom of the page. It was almost illegible, yet had been underscored with a thick scribbled line. The Irish Priest peered hard at the spidery scrawl, moving his glasses up and down his nose to try and focus the words, which he finally deciphered as: "Warren Higginbutton."

Was that the name of the English youth he had been looking for?

Monsignor Doyle thanked God for answering his prayers and jumped out of bed.

It was now late at night in Los Angeles, but it was the middle of the day in Rome.

He picked up his cell phone and started to dial excitedly.

"Father Lessi?" He asked as his call was answered.

An Italian accent confirmed that he was in fact Father Lessi, the young Italian Priest who had been acting as Doyle's secretary.

Doyle was so excited he could hardly get his words out:

"Check for me, please, the name: Warren Higginbutton. I think it may be very relevant.

Particularly check around the dates that we discussed Abraham seeing the English boy, he must have passed through security."

When he had finished the call, Monsignor Declan Doyle collapsed back on to the bed and almost immediately fell into a deep sleep, comfortable in the knowledge that he had made a breakthrough, he could feel it in his bones.

Mac Brown handed the file to Secretary Jack Baring with a grin.

"The CIA boys have been busy, Sir" His Deep South origins identifying themselves in every spoken vowel.

Baring opened the file and took out an envelope marked "Top Secret"

"Thanks Mac." He intoned as he ripped open the envelope and quickly scanned the contents.

Marshall's boys had been working flat out with their colleagues in the CIA and all the information had been compiled on this one report:

Michael O'Brien: age 43, Landlord of the Mucky Duck, Towcester, England

Michael O'Brien: age 25, Painter and Decorator, Lewisham, London

Michael O'Brien: age 56, bank robber serving time in HMP Wormwood scrubs.

Michael O'Brien: age 29, jockey, Upper Lambourne, Berks

Michael O'Brien: age 14, student, Old Swan, Liverpool

The list went on and on.

Baring looked up at Mac Brown and sighed:

"There are over 300 Michael O'Briens on this list. Has no one narrowed it down? Has no one found one with connections to Giametti, or Vitalia?

Mac Brown shook his head.

"No, not yet. The name seems mainly blue collar. There's a couple geographically near Giametti, but nothing with any link to Vitalia. The

152

CIA are checking out the two guys near Giametti with the Brit security services."

Baring turned the page:

Occupier of Mill House, Pangfield Road, Upper Buckledon

Wayne Higginbotham: Married, Natalia Robson, two Children:
                              Katherine, Frank.
                              Parents Frank and Doris Higginbotham,
                              deceased.

Schools: Gas Street Junior, middle and infant, Shepton
                              Wormysted's Grammar School, Shepton
                              University of Manchester

                              Career Marketing Brand Management

                              Employers: The Kelton Cereal Co. GB Ltd

The list went on looking like Wayne's personal CV.

Jack Baring scanned it quickly:

"So does this guy have any connection with Giametti, or Vitalia?"

Mac Brown gulped:

"We don't think so, Sir. He's as normal and boring as you could possibly imagine.

Blue collar background in Northern England, wife has a successful career, kids at Private school near his home village. He's as white as a lily. The only strange thing was that we couldn't find a birth certificate."

Baring tossed the report on to his desk.

"This isn't good enough Brown. No wonder Williams sent you instead of showing up himself. I want your people to dig deeper. I want to know everything about these O'Briens and I want to know if there is any connection with this schmuck Higginbotham."

Mac Brown nodded nervously:

"Yes, sir." He turned to leave but a thought suddenly sprung into his mind:

"Oh, by the way, Sir. Dean Vitalia used to be married to a young actress called Terri Thorne, she was in………"

"Yes, what of it?" A clearly irritated Jack Baring interrupted him.

"Well, sir, her real name was Theresa O'Brien."

"Have you got people checking out that angle?"

Mac Brown grinned as he left the office:

"You bet, Sir."

Jack Baring sighed as he stood up and stretched his aching limbs. The President and the Secretary of State had both telephoned him that afternoon and asked if he had any updates on the possible dirt on Aurelio Vitalia. It had been embarrassing to say that he couldn't update them, but that he had people working on it.

He leaned against the Venetian blind covering his office window and keeping the Washington winter gloom out:

"If only………" He murmured.

As far as Jack Baring was concerned, if he could prove that Senator Aurelio Vitalia was a gangster and had always been a gangster, then Luke Lively would be finished before he had ever really gotten off the starting block.

However, he only had a matter of weeks to make a solid case before the first Primaries and Caucuses began. If the self proclaimed "Son of God" continued to build the huge momentum that had already started, in the year leading up to the election, then maybe not even a scandal about his adoptive father being a crook would prove enough to stop him. The general feeling across the entire United States, as more and more verifiable reports came in about supposedly "dead" people coming back to life during that Oprah show, was that Luca was the real deal. Even some of the more sceptical columnists and talk show hosts were now hedging their bets and declaring that they had "open minds," instead of being openly hostile.

Jack Baring was damn sure that Luca Vitalia was not the Messiah. All he needed was some incriminating evidence that would finish Aurelio Vitalia and his spooky son.

Detective Chief Inspector Archie Knox ran his hands through what was left of his hair as Detective Inspector Ratchett briefed him on the latest developments in the Peter Finch murder case.

"Any sign of Burns yet?"

Ratchett shook his head.

"Don't worry Sir, he won't get far."

Knox snorted.

"He's already had enough time to walk to Argentina. What about Giametti? Has his memory come back?"

DI Ratchett shrugged.

"Giametti reckons he can't remember what happened. Not a thing. We've even had to remind him of his name and the fact that he's married. It's almost like his memory's been totally erased."

154

DCI Knox laughed sarcastically:

"So a bloke who's practically indistinguishable from Arnold bloody Schwarzenegger, walks into his office and he can't remember a thing? He's having a laugh!"

Ratchett shrugged again.

"What about the other geezer in the office: Larcombe?"

Knox persisted.

Again Ratchett shook his head.

"Says he can't remember a thing, either."

Knox heaved a huge sigh:

"And I don't suppose the Albanian and his motley crew have all suddenly decided to sing like canaries?"

DI Ratchett shook his head:

"No, although the Albanian has actually stopped singing now."

Knox raised his eyebrows:

"Oh good." He exclaimed, a hint of sarcasm in the tone of voice:

"Real progress there then!"

DI Ratchett grimaced painfully.

"There is certainly something weird going on though."

Knox folded his arms across his chest.

"Weird? So what's weird? Arnold bloody Schwarzenegger walks totally undetected into a lift, throws a guy out of an office window on the forty second floor, beats up two other guys, letting one scarper, then he goes and promptly disappears into thin air. Meanwhile only the receptionist on that floor and a handful of witnesses remember anything about it. You call that weird?"

DI Ratchett sucked on his teeth and acknowledged that the whole thing was not exactly routine.

"Oh I haven't finished yet." Knox almost shouted.

"So while Arnie is knocking eight bells out of the boss in old London town, somebody else is kicking seven shades out of five of his best villains in some bloody farmyard, and once again, surprise, surprise, no one seems able to remember a single bloody thing. I think that's a bit more than weird, don't you?"

Ratchett nodded.

DCI Archie Knox blew his nose into a grubby handkerchief:

"And just to put the icing on the bleeding cake, we've had spooks and Yanks sniffing around, because Giametti is some relation to this Jesus Christ Mark two bloke. Oh well, it's Christmas in a few weeks. Maybe Santa will turn himself in, as he seems to be the only other geezer I've heard of that can be invisible and disappear at will."

DI Ratchett took a deep breath:

"I better go and carry on, Sir."

DCI Knox nodded while heaving a huge sigh.

"Be careful Ratchett. If it is Arnie out there: He'll be back."

Twenty-Eight

Lucy Sherman had been looking forward to her trip back to England to collect the kids for the Christmas vacation. Now of course, the trip had taken on a whole new significance. She had been effectively sacked from her job, she had lost her husband and if she was entirely logical about what had happened, she had lost her home too. Lucy Sherman had been in America for nearly half her life. Yet now she had no real reason to stay in New York. Thank goodness she had arranged for the kids to be schooled in England.

Lucy carefully folded the blue silk blouse on her bed and placed it carefully in her suitcase. It was as she placed a piece of tissue paper over the blouse that the emotions began to flood out. Jonathan had bought her that blouse in Macy's during the summer.

Barely six months had passed and yet she was now living in a different world. Lucy Hetherington had ceased to exist as a person while she was still at Oxford. Even as she had graduated, Lucy was thinking of herself as Lucy Sherman. She had completely submerged herself in Jonathan's world and although she had maintained her own independent career for much of their marriage, apart from when the kids were very young, and had maintained a few of her old friends, she was as much a part of Jonathan as one of his own limbs. The speed of events had also been shocking, from one moment being the dorky, but happy go lucky Jonathan, to being a religious freak within days and an adulterer hours after that. Lucy had tapped into her massive reserves of British upper middle class stiff upper lip fuel to get by, but now, all of a sudden, the emotions broke through the dam wall she had built.

What will the children say? She wondered. How will they react?

Jemima would be resilient, she had a classic stoical female personality that seemed to thrive in adversity, but Jonathan Junior would freak. He idolised his father and was prone to emotional hysteria at the best of times. It was certainly not the time for them to be 3000 miles away from both parents. Lucy stumbled into the bathroom to pick up a tissue to wipe her eyes and blow her nose. She gazed at the wonderful blue tiled en-suite with its golden taps and double vanity unit. She wiped her finger along a marble tile. They had been so fortunate, Jonathan and her, to have both been born into such wealth and to have had such privileged lifestyles. Well, not born, exactly, but fate had decreed that her early life with the Hetheringtons on Jersey had been luxurious to say the least and marrying into the incredibly wealthy

Sherman dynasty had meant that her lifestyle had been opulent beyond her wildest aspirations.

For a brief moment, Lucy wondered what her life would have been like had she been raised by the woman who had surrendered her for adoption. Where would she have lived? What was her twin brother actually like, if he was still alive?

Lucy shook her head:

"Pull yourself together, old girl!" She said out loud. "This is not the time for wallowing in self pity."

Lucy had left Los Angeles the same evening that Jonathan had walked out of their hotel room to join his blonde floozy, as Lucy had referred to her. She hadn't seen or heard from him since and that had been weeks ago. Lucy had used the time well. Mummy had already found her a little bolthole, in St. Helier, so that Lucy and the children didn't have to stay in the old family home while Rupert was so ill. Mummy had been ever so diplomatic as both she and Lucy knew that the children got on Rupert's nerves.

"What's the matter with them, Lucy?" He had barked during her last visit

"Children should be seen and not heard, the amount of noise these two are making can probably be heard on the mainland. No Manners, no decorum, no bloody class, Lucy. I am surprised, given your upbringing that you've allowed your own children to turn into, into bloody yahoos!"

Melinda hadn't told her husband about the impending divorce yet. He was too ill to bear such news at the moment, according to Melinda. Lucy couldn't help thinking that her mother was covertly revelling in the news. Of course, she had sounded devastated when Lucy had informed her about recent events over the phone, but Lucy knew her mother too well. Melinda Hetherington was never happier than when there was an enormous crisis and she could take centre stage and play mother hen for all she was worth. Not only would her daughter be returning home to Jersey, but she would also be getting the children every school holiday for the foreseeable future. Mummy was in heaven!

Lucy had had no idea how long she would be staying on the island. Of course she would have to find another job, but for the moment, all she needed to do was to get back to Jersey, get the kids home safely and then she could plan the rest of her life.

Naturally, a huge settlement was inevitable. Lucy had already decided that her contribution to Sherman Legal had been far beyond even that of her husband. Her Los Angeles unit had been responsible for over sixty percent of the company's profits in the last two fiscals.

"I am going to squeeze him until the pips burst, let alone squeak!" Lucy had hissed to her mother.

"Well do be careful dear, don't strangle the goose that lays the golden egg." Melinda had whispered. "He will need a good income to pay adequate maintenance. Jonju and Jemima have a lifestyle to maintain."

"And what about me?" Lucy had demanded indignantly.

"Don't worry darling, I'm sure with your legal skills you'll be able to make something of a living." Melinda had giggled before she had assured her daughter that she was only joking as she heard the splutters of outrage from the other side of the Atlantic Ocean.

"Poor Daddy, this will be the death of him." Lucy had whispered as she thought about the way he would react to the news of the divorce.

Melinda had laughed again:

"Darling, I'm sure he'll be upset, but a part of him will be delighted. As far as he is concerned at least you'll be able to get those children properly disciplined now."

Lucy laughed as she remembered the phone call. Mummy had been quite a tonic.

Rupert and Melinda had been wonderful parents to her; she really couldn't have been adopted by nicer people.

She walked back into the bedroom, glanced at her case and decided that she would pack later. She walked over to the Penthouse apartments' window and looked out over the view of New York that the bedroom afforded. She could just see Central Park down the long straight boulevard. She was certainly going to miss New York City and when she thought about what she spent on her shopping forays, New York was going to miss her.

Oh well, she had wished for the quiet life at times and compared to New York, St. Helier, Jersey would certainly be quiet.

Lucy strolled into her drawing room and picked a Silver framed photograph off the top of the Grand Piano. It was a black and white portrait of all of them, taken just before Christmas last year. The Sherman family had used it as their Christmas card.

"Happy days." Lucy sighed as she carefully replaced the photo back on the piano.

"They sure were." Jonathan's voice emerged from the doorway.

Lucy gasped.

"Jonathan? How long have you been here? When did you get back?"

Jonathan was wearing his familiar cream mackintosh and carrying his brown leather briefcase.

"I just got in." He murmured, looking down at the carpet.

159

"I guess I just didn't think hollering: Hi Honey, I'm home, was appropriate, given the circumstances."

Lucy took a deep breath.

"No, no I guess not." She said, her voice strained and hoarse.

"I'm leaving, tomorrow. I've already packed and despatched some of my stuff. It's just a few clothes now."

Jonathan stood stupidly in the doorway and nodded.

"OK right." He whispered: "I'll er, book a room nearby for tonight then. You, er, don't want to talk about things, I guess?"

Lucy sniffed.

"What's to say?" She couldn't help but smile.

"I think we've both heard you'll be hearing from my lawyers too often, not to know what's going to happen. It's just that this time, we aren't the lawyers."

Jonathan smiled.

"Guess not. I do need to talk to you though, Luce. I haven't been myself lately. It's been like, I dunno. It's been like somebody else has been inside my head."

Lucy sighed.

"It's a little late for apologies, if that's what you're intending."

Jonathan edged into the drawing room and put his briefcase down by a sumptuous red, leather armchair.

"I know, I know." He mumbled, "but I'd like to try and explain some stuff and I need to talk about the children, our children."

Lucy walked around to the front of a matching armchair and perched primly on the edge, her hands around her knees.

Jonathan slumped into his chair, still wearing the Mac.

"Go on." Lucy prompted him.

Jonathan nodded and seemed to take an age to lubricate the inside of his mouth.

"I really can't explain, what's been going on," he began.

"When I first met the Vitalias, I just thought it would be a good, lucrative contract.

I had no idea that Luca would be for real. I mean, you know me, Luce, when have I ever fallen for a charlatan before?"

Lucy bristled at the mention of the name, but her husband didn't notice.

"I knew from the moment I met him that he is the Messiah. I don't know how, or why, but take it from me, I just do. I had no idea how all consuming it is to be utterly devoted to some one without it involving love and sex. Even so, I wanted you all with me. I wanted you to represent Luca on the West Coast, while I took the East. I wanted my family to be committed to the New World. I wanted to enter the Garden of Eden together. I sure had no intention of sacking you or of going off with Carol Anne. I don't know what has happened and it has all happened so fast."

Jonathan T Sherman started to cry. The great wracking sobs of a distraught man.

Lucy tried to stay implacable, but couldn't. You just can't turn love off like a tap she thought to herself, as she hugged her husband's head, pressing it into her chest.

"I am truly sorry, honey." He sobbed.

"It's OK." Lucy whispered.

"I asked Luca on the flight over why he didn't like you." Jonathan mumbled.

"He said it wasn't that he didn't like you. He just knew immediately that you would not be chosen. He said there is a part of you that is his enemy."

Lucy shushed her husband.

"Shhhh. Let's just forget about Luca Vitalia for a moment." She whispered.

Jonathan sobbed loudly: "I told him you are a wonderful person and that if he got to know you he would love you too. I told him how good you are."

Lucy grimaced but continued to hug Jonathan's head.

"So that's why I came along." The smooth voice came from the doorway and Lucy froze as she turned.

Luca Vitalia was stood, casually leaning on the white wooden frame of the door.

"Your husband said I should come and see just how good you are." Luca leered.

Lucy stepped back and glanced down at Jonathan who slumped back in the chair. His eyes were closed as if he were already in a deep comatose sleep.

"Don't worry. He is just sleeping." Luca grinned as he strolled into the drawing room.

"How did you get in?" Lucy demanded.

Luca was looking around the room:

"Nice place, very tasteful." He whistled as he saw a painting on the far wall:

"Oh yes, very tasteful. An original Warhol."

"Where's your entourage?" Lucy asked as she visibly shook with fright.

Luca turned to her and smiled.

"As for your first question, I came in with your husband. It's still his place too, isn't it? He invited me. I was polite enough to wait out in the corridor while you two got reacquainted, as it were."

He wiped a finger along an ornate French antique cabinet.

"You really need better cleaners, honey." He uttered with a disgusted curl of the mouth.

"As for my entourage, my staff and the trailing pack of press and fanatics who seem to think that the sun shines out of my cute little butt, they think I'm in a hotel downtown.

It's simple to avoid them."

Lucy gasped as Luca Vitalia changed his face into that of someone she didn't recognise.

"It was quite nice being a nobody for a while."

Luca grinned as his features slowly melted back into the familiar face that millions still knew as Luke Lively.

"Do you have anything nice to eat?" He asked, smacking his lips.

"I'm starving. I always get so hungry when I'm anticipating fun." He laughed.

"Just think, you're the envy of every woman on Earth. You've got me all to yourself."

"Jonathan." Lucy screamed at her comatose spouse, still slumped in the armchair.

Luca laughed again.

"Oh don't trouble yourself, sweetheart. He's out for the count. He's out forever, unless you're nice to me. That was a touching reunion by the way. I almost had a tear in my eye."

Lucy gulped, took a deep breath, steeled herself and marched over to her phone.

"I don't know who you are in reality, Luca Vitalia, but you're certainly not the Son of God. Now get out before I ring the police."

Luca smiled and sat down on a beautiful Eighteenth Century, English, Chippendale chair.

"Feel free to call whomsoever you like and then do please get me something to eat. I promise I'm a much nicer boy when my tummy is full." He used his old Amisher character, Hans Kirsche's voice.

No matter what she tried, Lucy's phone just emitted a horrid buzzing noise.

"Looks like nobody is answering." Luca sighed.

"I think you'll find your cell phone is similarly disabled. I hate relying on technology, don't you? Have you got Rye bread? Now I'm in New York I could kill for a nice New York pastrami on Rye sandwich and a Coke. People like you do have Coke, don't you? Oh! Nice children."

He exclaimed as he jumped up and picked up the photograph that Lucy had been admiring earlier. She edged around the piano. Luca looked up at her:

"Off to the kitchen with you, woman, or I might start getting cross and breaking things."

He slowly and deliberately dropped the picture frame, the glass shattered on the wooden floor.

Lucy screamed and ran out of the drawing room door. She hurtled down the corridor to the apartment's front door.

No matter how hard she turned the key or the handle, the door remained resolutely locked.

"Help! Help!" She screamed at the top of her voice as she banged her fists on the panels.

"No one can hear you, you silly girl." Luca was leaning against the drawing room door again, this time shaking his head as he watched her futile attempts to open the front door.

"Everyone on this floor has gone sleepy byes, just like your limp husband. It's a little trick I learned a long time ago. Now, I would like my sandwich and my Coke, or do you want me to start my little fun thing now?"

Lucy shook her head as she slowly walked down the corridor towards the kitchen. Luke patted her bottom as she walked past:

"A little bit of pickle would be nice, oh and hold the mayo. I'll wait in here."

He turned and walked back into the drawing room:

"Don't be long. I really am starving!" He shouted as he disappeared.

Lucy could hardly breathe as she walked into the kitchen. She was shaking like a leaf.

She edged over to the window.

"You'll find all the windows are locked. It's a long way down and we don't want any nasty accidents, do we?" Luca's disembodied voice emanated from somewhere in the drawing room.

Lucy could hardly stand she was so terrified. She pulled open a drawer and quietly pulled out her sharpest and largest kitchen knife.

"If you try to stab me with a knife, by the way, I will disarm you, you know, and then I will be really cross and when I'm cross, I'm nasty. Just use it on the sandwich, there's a good girl."

Luca's voice piped up again.

Lucy dropped the knife back into the drawer as she tried to stifle a scream.

She racked her brain. What could she do?

If only Jonathan had possessed a gun.

It was all "if only" now. If onlys and might have beens.

Lucy closed her eyes as she felt the tears welling up.

Lucy Sherman, nee Hetherington, knew she was about to die and there was nothing, absolutely nothing, she could do about it.

Twenty-Nine

"Wait!"

The voice of Aillen Mac Fionnbharr echoed across the bare mountain top as Wayne Higginbotham started the steep descent back down to his late Grandfather's cottage, two of the ancient and magical treasures of the Tuatha de Danaan in his possession.

Wayne stopped and turned back, breathing heavily as he quickly clambered back onto the plateau on the summit of Binnaw.

The mist that surrounded the spectral figure of Aillen Mac Fionnbharr swirled in the early morning breeze.

"Father?" Wayne gasped, his face glowing with perspiration.

The shade of the last true blood Prince of the Tuatha de Danaan grinned.

"It looks like you need to, how do they put it now?"

He paused as Wayne took in several gulps of the fresh mountain air.

"Work out a little?" The spectre suggested mischievously.

Wayne blew out a long plume of hot breath.

"Maybe." He grinned. "When this is all over, I'll walk up here every morning for a couple of weeks, that'll soon have me fighting fit. I have a plane to catch, father. I can't stand here talking to you, though. There's a war on you know!"

Aillen Mac Fionnbharr laughed and put his spectral hand on to Wayne's shoulder.

"It is good to have you back, Michaeleen." He whispered.

"But how can you defeat the "Order's" demon, with the physique of an old man?"

Wayne puffed out his chest.

"Old man?" He spluttered indignantly.

"I'll have you know……"

Aillen held up his ghostly hand to quieten his son.

"In my younger days, mortals of your age were usually dead, or regarded as ancient and venerable elders. You are no longer a boy, or even a youth, my son. You are no longer even a man in his full prime."

Wayne snorted:

"I'm fit enough to…….."

"To fight a man twelve years younger than you? To fight the strongest, most evil, most powerful being, that has ever set foot upon this world?"

Aillen raised his chin so that he looked down his nose at his son.

"Michael Sean O'Brien. Are you up to that task?"

Wayne laughed and immediately morphed into the shape of Mohammed Ali.

"Up to it? Man, I am fast, I'm so fast I can handcuff lightening. Look at me, man, I ain't just still fast, I'm still pretty. I sting like a butterfly, float like a bee, that's why my name is Mohammed Ali."

The shade of Aillen Mac Fionnbharr sighed.

"It is unfortunate that your quotation may in your case be accurate, however, you will find that Mohammed Ali floated like a butterfly and stung like a bee, not vice-versa."

Wayne morphed back into his own shape.

"Oh." He said, blushing.

Aillen smiled and put his hand on Wayne's shoulder:

"There is something you should know my son.

The reason we wanted you, nay, I wanted you to kill this demon long ago, when he was no more than a child, is that he is not just any demon. He is, what some would call, a demi-God. His true name is Lucifer.

Jews and Christians believe he was once God's favourite angel, but that his vanity and lust for power caused him to be cast out of heaven.

This is your third and final great challenge my son. You accounted for Pizarro, you accounted for De Feren. Now you must account for Lucifer himself. I never said it was going to be easy."

Wayne sighed and a sense of despondency grew in his mind. He was an old man. An old man with incredible powers, but an old man all the same.

Then a figure flashed into his mind. A brave but simple human being, another who could have been called an old man, vaulting over a stone wall and landing a haymaker of a punch squarely on the chin of an immortal killer and then delivering the decisive blow with the assassin's own blade before the immortal had time to react. That man had been oblivious to the risks he had faced, just as he had been thirty years before that when he had taken on a German tank. Frank Higginbotham hadn't raised Wayne to be a coward. He had set his adopted son an example that even his immortal Prince of a father couldn't replicate.

Wayne pursed his lips and turned to look at the view over Lough Mask.

"I am scared. No, I'm terrified. Yet I have a job to do. You know, had I attempted to kill this Lucifer when I was a student and if I'd failed, I wouldn't have had a life. Millions of soldiers die in war, mere boys who have never had a proper life. Yet, at least now, I have had a life, a good life. When Frank Higginbotham took on that German tank, he didn't think about everything he might miss out on if he failed. When he killed Pizarro, he never thought about the risks, he did it for me. He did it because he loved me. Well, Father, well Frank, I'm going to do this for the people I love."

Wayne turned back to the spectre of his father.

"And do you know what the best thing of all is?"

Aillen shook his head.

"What you have just told me about this demon being Lucifer. Well, I suppose it means I am definitely the good guy. I had a dream, no, a nightmare, where I was responsible for millions and millions of people being dead. I was literally drowning in gore. I know you might say that might happen if I fail, but I had been worried that, well, you know, because that guy died back when I was a student, I actually thought that I might be the bad guy that the "Order" always said I'd be. Well, they were wrong!"

Aillen nodded.

"My son, I would have killed you myself, had I thought that you had been evil." He stated in all seriousness.

Wayne let a wry smile crease his lips, a great weight had been lifted from his shoulders.

Now all he had to do was to destroy the demon, Lucifer.

Wayne Higginbotham looked at the lake for one last time.

"I will be back here, soon. I will look out on this view again. Now, I have to catch that plane."

Thirty

Monsignor Doyle closed his eyes. Yet another day had passed and there was still no news of the elusive Warren Higginbutton. He had flown back to Rome from Los Angeles two weeks earlier, extremely disappointed that he was no nearer finding the individual who might constitute the balance of power, if the potential President of the United States did prove to be a demon, rather than Christ reborn.

He did, however, carry a small degree of comfort in his heart from what James Malone's widow, Carrie had said:

"The guy you are referring to has promised me that he has been biding his time and is going to act very soon."

"Well he better move quickly," Monsignor Doyle muttered as he picked up Fr Reichmann's journal again. He sat down at his desk, a twinge of rheumatism made him wince as he sat down. If the youth he had seen in Reichmann's office all those years ago had been eighteen then, he would be in his forties now. Doyle hoped that he would be up the job of defeating Vitalia, if it came to that.

The ancient black telephone rattled in its cradle as it rang, furiously. Doyle picked up the receiver:

"I'm on my way, now, Your Holiness." He jumped up straight away, pulled a cloak over his cassock and headed off towards the Papal apartments.

A grim faced Pope Gregory XII was waiting for him:

"Ah Declan," he cried as soon as the Irishman was shown into his private office by Lambardi, the Pope's personal assistant.

He stood and held out his hand so that Declan could kiss the ring.

"I presume you have still not identified the Englishman?"

His voice was calm and measured.

Monsignor Doyle shook his head nervously.

"I found a clue in Abraham's notes, but it seems to have been a red herring, so far. We are doing everything we can to ascertain the validity of the name."

The Pope nodded sympathetically.

"We have but little over one week left, Declan." He declared sadly.

"The Holy See has maintained a diplomatic distance from what is, politically, an American domestic issue, despite the obvious theological ramifications of Luca Vitalia's announcements. However, while we have absolutely no wish to interfere in American internal affairs, Luca Vitalia has made statements and claims that have now forced us to

168

abandon our laissez faire attitude. It is my wish that all Christians, particularly the Roman Catholic Congregation in the United States, should know whether they will be voting for a Saviour, or a charlatan. He has already met some senior religious leaders in the United States and it appears all have been swayed, so far. The Iowa caucus takes place in January; therefore I have called for a Synod here in Rome on the 21st of December. It will be the greatest Ecumenical Council meeting since Constantine made Christianity the religion of the Empire of Rome. I have already invited the most important figures in Christendom and beyond to be here:

The Archbishop of Canterbury, the Ecumenical Patriarch of Constantinople, The Patriarch of Athens and the Patriarch of Moscow. I have also asked members of the American National Council of Churches and a number of recognised Television evangelists as well as several senior figures from other denominations. I have also asked representatives of the Jewish, Islamic, Buddhist, Sikh and Hindu faiths, to attend.

Most importantly, I asked Luca Vitalia and his Father Aurelio to be here. I have received their acceptance today."

Father Doyle had been quite shocked to see how much older the Pope had looked when he had first seen him upon his return from L.A. It had always been said that the Pope's youthful features belied his almost eighty years, now he looked to have suffered through every single one of them. His shock of grey hair had turned almost white and the wrinkles on his forehead had increased fourfold.

"Following our meeting, with the Vitalias, the Ecumenical Council shall spend three days in conference, discussing what we have seen and heard. On December 25th, Christ's birthday, we shall announce to the World, what we have decided. If we feel he is genuine, I shall personally endorse his candidacy for the most powerful political office on earth and ask all secular and religious authorities to subjugate themselves to his decree."

The Pope sat back on his chair, an air of resignation hung over him like a personal dark cloud.

"Do you know what I fear most, Declan?" The aged Pontiff asked as he fiddled nervously with his rosary.

"No, Your Holiness." Declan answered, honestly.

The Pope smirked.

"I fear that he will bewitch us all, just as he bewitched every American housewife when he was an actor and every teenage girl when he was a singer. I fear that we will all hail him the Messiah, when he is nothing of the sort."

Declan Doyle nodded empathetically.

"If you endorse him, Your Holiness, President Ford will be bound to acknowledge him. No one would dare stand against him in the American Elections."

There was a long silence as the two men pondered the possibilities.

Eventually Declan spoke again:

"Why would he need to be the President of the United States, if he is generally acknowledged to be the "Son Of God?" Surely he would have all the power he would need?"

Pope Gregory XVII chuckled.

"I am regarded as being the representative of Christ on Earth, a direct lineage that goes all the way back to Saint Peter. Yes, the schisms in the body of the Christian Church have reduced Papal authority over the many centuries since Peter graced this City with his presence, yet still, billions of people regard my word as the word of God himself. Christ will not need a representative on Earth, if he is here in person. If Vitalia is Our Lord, he will not only become the ruler of the most powerful secular authorities, but he will also be the head of his own Church. Imagine, if the Borgias had controlled the most powerful army and navy in the world. As the President, even those who do not accept his divinity will have to accept the military power of the United States. I did read one magazine interview where he said that he would invite all Christian Nations to join a United States of Christendom, if he was elected. Then he would invite other faiths. A democratic vote would give him secular, religious and spiritual legitimacy and authority."

Declan Doyle stroked his chin thoughtfully.

"But, surely Jesus Christ would not want to back up his word with force of arms. I don't understand it."

The Pope scratched his head.

"The Lord moves in mysterious ways Declan. There is now more urgency than ever, if we are to endorse this thing, or to nip it in the bud. On the 25th of December, the Holy See shall issue that joint communiqué. We will need to know for sure by then whether this Luca Vitalia is truly our Saviour, or our destroyer."

Declan Doyle kissed the Pope's ring and left his chambers.

For a December day in Rome the weather was positively balmy. The sky was blue and as he looked up at the imposing dome of St. Peter's, Monsignor Doyle could not help but marvel at how bright and clean it looked. He wondered how many people over the years had walked past the dome and wondered at its magnificence. All over the Christian World, people had lived and died over nearly two millennia, building soaring spires and magnificent domes, reaching heavenwards in reverence and praise for a being that might, or might not, have come back to earth. Would they have been as dedicated had they heard Luke Lively's worldwide number one single called: "Hot for you!"

Declan looked at the throngs of people, tourists, patiently stood in the long queues to see the Cistine Chapel and inside St Peter's, or those who were just wandering, enjoying the unseasonal good weather. Many, particularly the young, were wearing the bright yellow armband with its red sun logo, of the Brigade of Light.

A chill crept up Declan's spine. The Brigade of Light was spreading like a particularly virulent virus. Millions of people all over the world now sported the armband that displayed their adherence to Luca Vitalia. At the end of the day, "The Sacred Order of St Gregory" had created and succoured Luca Vitalia. As the head of the reformed "Order" it was his job to sort out the mess. The problem was, he didn't have a clue where to go or what to do anymore.

The tourists watched as the black robed Priest slowly and painfully sank to his knees in the middle of the Piazza.

Some took photographs. Some sniggered. Some pointed. Most pointedly ignored him.

Monsignor Declan Doyle prayed for all of their souls and particularly for that of Warren Higgimbutton, whosoever, or wherever he was.

"Please, God. Grant him success. Amen." Monsignor Doyle pleaded.

This time God granted him no favours. There was no flash of light, no miracle. Not even a simple gesture like a book falling open just at the right page.

Monsignor Doyle suddenly became aware of all the attention he had attracted. He blushed, rose slowly and disappeared as fast as he could, back into the darkness and the safe anonymity of the Vatican's corridors.

Thirty-One

The call had wakened Terri Thorne almost as soon as she had gone to bed. Her first thought had been for Marina, who was still living with Terri, due to her father's total disinterest. Once again she was late home, having gone out on "Brigade" business. This time, however, Terri had been determined not to stay up until the early hours of the morning waiting for her daughter. She had given her a key and told her not to wake her when she came in. That didn't stop her worrying of course.

Terri was relieved therefore, to hear Wayne's deep sonorous English tones on the other end of the line.

"Hi Mom, I hope I haven't woken you up." He sounded slightly out of breath.

"I know it's getting late there, so I am sorry, but I'll be calling in tomorrow."

Terri jolted awake:

"What, you're coming to L.A. again. My goodness, it's not that long since you were here."

Wayne had laughed.

"I know, let's just say I've some unfinished business to deal with. Look Mom, I've got to rush, I've been at Daideo's, I've already been up the mountain this morning and now I'm at Shannon catching the plane. I'll see you tomorrow. Byeeee."

With that, he was gone.

Terri shook her head, turned out her bedside light and tried to settle back down. She would ring her youngest sister Katie in the morning to find out what was going on. Katie lived in the house that had been the family home, where Tom O'Brien, known to all and sundry as Daideo, had raised Terri and her sisters Molly, Siobhan, Annie and Katie and brothers Colm, Sean and Liam. Terri's Mom, Maria had died when Katie had been two, so until she was sixteen, Theresa had acted as mother to the younger children. Then she had met Danny from America, or so he told her and life was never the same again. It was strange that her father had sworn until the day he died that Michael, as Wayne had been named before adoption was of the sidh.

"You can tell by the ears." He had said.

What had he been trying to tell her on his deathbed when he had said that Michaeleen was the one?

172

Of course, Terri had always insisted that Michaels father had been Danny Finn from Tupelo Mississippi, despite the fact that Danny had revealed himself to be Aillen Mac Fionnbharr. Terri had just presumed she'd had a nervous breakdown.

Now, through Carrie Malone of Los Angeles California, she had found out at her second son's wedding, that her father had been right all along. Not only that but Michael, or Wayne, as she was still getting used to calling him was the very last of the little people.

Wayne wasn't coming back so quickly, just for the scenery or just to visit family.

Could "unfinished" business be related to his altercation with Dean at the wedding?

Terri fell into a very uneasy sleep, punctuated by dreams of men in robes like Princes in fairytales, telling her that everything would be OK.

She didn't hear Marina creep in at 4 a.m.

Nor did she feel the minor earth tremor that shook the entire west side of the San Fernando Valley.

Carrie Vasquez almost fell out of bed when the earth tremor hit Box Canyon. It had sounded like a truck had hit the house. Miguel had opened his eyes, farted loudly, then turned over and gone back to sleep, only to start snoring even more loudly than he had before the tremor. Carrie sighed and climbed stiffly out of bed. She pulled on a robe then walked out of the bedroom and crept into the darkness of the yard.

By the standards of Southern California, even for December, it was quite cold. The benefit was that the cool air was clear and Carrie gasped as she looked out over the twinkling multicoloured lights of the San Fernando Valley capped by a panopoly of stars. She had always loved her house high up in Canyon Country. She thought about a similar night, a long, long time ago when an Irish ex-Priest had been similarly amazed at the spectacular panorama before him. Poor old James.

Carrie's mind wandered back to the other Irish Priest who had visited her. He had seemed like a nice guy. Maybe she should check with Wayne and see if he wanted his name given to the Priest. It seemed to her that unless somebody kicked Wayne's butt into action, then Luke Lively would walk right into the Presidency and life on Earth as we know it would end pretty soon after.

James had referred to Wayne as the "Slanaitheoir." So why wasn't he doing something about Luke Lively. James would have roused him. James would have spurred him into action. James would have, but James wasn't around any more.

Somewhere high up in the rocks behind the house, Carrie heard the yip, yip of a coyote.

She was feeling cold so she decided to go back inside.

She took one long last look at the Valley and then turned to go back inside.

Tomorrow she would get Wayne's phone number off Terri and she would bully him into shaking off the shackles of disinterest. He had promised her action at Aoibheall's wedding. Now that seemed to have been just so many glib words.

When Terri Thorne had telephoned her the next morning therefore, Carrie Vasquez had burst into tears. Terri's words had been like music to her ears. At last, over twenty years had passed since James Malone had been brutally murdered and now retribution seemed possibly at hand.

"Yes, he rang me in the middle of the night. I was like so worried that Marina had had an accident or something and it was Michael, I'm sorry, Wayne saying that he was on his way over and would arrive later this afternoon."

Terri had reported with an undisguised frisson of excitement.

Carrie had tried to calm herself.

"And you're sure he's come over, to, you know....."

Terri had shrugged at the other end of the line:

"He said he had unfinished business to attend to and it was the way he said it. I spoke to my little sister back in Ireland this morning. She says he went up the mountain yesterday and brought a bag down from the top. She had no idea what was in the bag, but she thinks that Daideo might have had a gun hidden up there from when he was a young man in the IRA, fighting the Black and Tans."

"The what?" Carrie had asked, bemused by the thought of a man fighting her late first husband's favourite drink.

"They were like British troops that were sent to crush the Irish after the First World War, a sort of British S.S." Terri informed her friend. Carrie contemplated the possibility for a moment as she wandered out into the pleasant winter sunshine of the yard:

"But Terri, honey, why would a dude who can, like, do awesome magic and stuff, need a gun?"

Terri hadn't thought of that:

"Maybe it's just in case, you know, the magic runs out." She had hypothesised with a shrug:

"Anyway, when he gets here I'll ask him. One thing was for sure. He sure sounded like a man on a mission."

Thirty-Two

The flight from Shannon Airport to Los Angeles had been quite uneventful. The only sticking point had been getting his ancient rusty spearhead through Shannon Airport Security. Eventually Wayne had been forced to pack it in his hold baggage, despite his claim that it was a priceless historic relic on its way to the prestigious Getty Museum.

Wayne had watched an awful movie on the tiny screen, drank two small bottles of wine and eaten a spectacularly, tasteless airline meal.

He thought back to his last trip to L.A. when Frankie had asked him, on average, about four questions a minute. The cabin staff had dimmed the lights and people were snuggling down as best they could to try and grab a little sleep. Even though it was a daytime flight, the extension of the day by a full eight hours meant that people usually ended up asleep by the early evening and awake again by the early hours of the morning. Wayne closed his eyes, dropped his seat back a couple of inches and settled down for a quick snooze.

The droning sound of the engines, the vibrations and the constant background chatter provided a surprisingly somnambulistic soundtrack to Wayne's attempt to rest, despite how uncomfortable he felt. Slowly he began to feel as if he was drifting peacefully over a deep silver sea like an albatross in flight.

"BROTHER!"

The female voice filled his mind as though someone had actually shouted inside his head. Wayne's eyes shot open as he jumped up in his seat and looked around to see who had bellowed into his ear. The rotund male passenger in the middle seat had his headphones on and was staring moronically at a Simpson's episode on his movie screen. The aisle seat next to him was empty. The woman who had been sat there must have gone to the toilet.

Wayne settled back and closed his eyes again.

"BROTHER!"

The voice sounded more desperate this time, more insistent. In fact it sounded scared.

Wayne opened his eyes and looked around again.

The slow realisation began to creep over him; the voice really was inside his head. He settled back again. Wayne wondered if he was dreaming, then the voice came again:

"My Brother. I am your sister, Lucy. Lucy Hetherington. You once told me that you existed, that you are real. Please tell me that I didn't imagine it all. Many years ago, you got me to ring the police, the fire brigade and a man in a hotel. You said you were in appalling danger. I am now about to be murdered and possibly even worse. Please help me, if you do exist. BROTHER! You are my only hope."

Wayne Higginbotham gulped as the words in his head stirred long forgotten memories. The voice continued:

"I am in my apartment, number 423 Kennedy Suites Building, West 72nd Street, New York City. I have maybe five minutes to live, if I'm lucky. HELP ME PLEASE."

Wayne felt the hairs on his neck rise and every cell in his body seemed to freeze. He snapped open his seatbelt, jumped up and climbed over the man sat next to him who humphed and grumbled, but hardly took his eyes off the screen. He staggered into the aisle and rushed past the queue waiting by the washrooms:

"Excuse me sir. You can't go in there." A young stewardess chirped as he pulled back the curtain to enter the first class cabin.

Wayne glanced at her.

"I'm sorry, but this is a matter of life and death. I must speak to the Captain, now. Don't worry, I'm not a terrorist, or a hijacker, but I do need to save a life and very, very, quickly."

Whether it was the wild look in his eyes, the tone of his voice or whether he had involuntarily used magic, Wayne didn't know, but the stewardess immediately rushed off towards the cockpit door. She knocked on it twice and shouted for a nearby male steward who Wayne remembered had been introduced as the cabin director to help her. The smart young cabin director introduced himself to Wayne.

"I'm Sean, sir. Jackie there is getting the Captain, how can we help?"

Wayne gulped:

"I'm sorry I forgot to turn my mobile off. You're not going to believe this, but my sister just texted me. She's about to be murdered. We need to contact the New York City Police Department, right now!"

Sean's eyes widened. He suddenly took on the air of a rampaging hero. He nodded.

"Right Sir, come with me, quickly."

Sean shouted into the cockpit: "Code green, passenger emergency."

The cockpit door swung open and Wayne was quickly escorted in. The stewardess had already told the Captain that a passenger needed to contact JFK ground staff urgently. Sean, the cabin director repeated Wayne's story in an Irish accent so thick and so quickly that Wayne hardly understood. The Captain glanced at him.

"Give me the name and address. I've got an ATC on the line now with pen and paper."

Wayne closed his eyes: "Number 423 Kennedy Suites Building, West 72nd Street, New York."

The Captain relayed the information then turned back to Wayne.

"I hope they get there in time, Sir. Now if you'd like to re take your seat. Sean will get you something to help you relax. Oh and please make sure your mobile is switched to flight safe mode."

Wayne smiled weakly and thanked the Captain and the cabin crew. Sean and the stewardess both shook his hand before he wandered forlornly off back down the cabin to his seat.

He clambered over the Simpsons fan again and tried to close his eyes, but there was no way he could sleep now. He tried to re-establish contact with the voice in his head, but to no avail. For the second time in his life, Wayne had been in contact with his twin sibling.

The first time, he had contacted her and she had saved his life. Wayne Higginbotham did not believe in God, so praying was pointless, but Wayne was now praying, he was praying for all he was worth.

Sean arrived with a very welcome Cognac, which Wayne accepted gratefully.

Wayne swigged the liquid and closed his eyes again. The Cognac burned in his throat, but it did seem to be working. He was slowly drifting off to sleep.

"BROTHER, PLEASE, PLEASE FOR GOD'S SAKE HELP ME!"

Wayne's eyes shot open once again, but this time he knew that the voice was coming from his own mind. The voice now sounded beyond desperate.

He closed his eyes and concentrated as hard as he could:

"Lucy, my sister. I am your brother, Wayne. Can you hear me?"

Instead of a voice, Wayne actually heard a female gasp in his head.

"Oh my God! Oh my God! Wayne did you say? You're real. I can really hear you."

Wayne actually stopped breathing he was so overcome with emotion.

"Wayne you have to help me. Please help me. Get the police."

Wayne took a deep breath:

"Lucy the police should already be on their way. What is happening?"

Wayne could sense his sister's fear. He could actually feel her panic.

"Oh my God, he's banging on the bathroom door. It's Luca Vitalia, he's not the Son of God. He's evil. He's going to kill me. Oh my God."

Wayne wanted to scream:

"Lucy. You must fight him. Tell him that the whelp he fears is coming. Tell him the whelp is coming to get him. Then, if you can, get to O'Brien's Irish pub on West 54th. The owner is your Uncle. Lucy can you hear me?"

Wayne could feel the Simpson's fan staring at him as he writhed and sweated in his seat. For whatever reason, contact had been broken.

For all Wayne knew, the twin sister he had never met was already dead.

Tears welled up in his eyes. The greatest irony was that she had mentioned Luca Vitalia.

If he had harmed one single hair on her head..............

Thirty-Three

Lucy desperately tried to calm her nerves as she placed the sandwich and the can of coke on the small tray. She took a deep breath, picked up the tray and turned to walk towards the drawing room. She jumped with shock when she noticed Luca standing in the kitchen doorway watching her and only just managed to hold on to the tray.

"I was wondering what was taking you so long." He sneered while his mouth twisted in an insidious grin.

Lucy gulped and handed Luca the tray. He took it and walked slowly into the drawing room, placing the tray on an antique Italian coffee table. He made a great show of examining the sandwich, lifting one of the pieces of bread with a suspicious glance at Lucy:

"Just checking you haven't laced it with poison." He laughed, then sniffed the sandwich:

"Mmmm, Smells good. I'll eat it here."

Luca sat in the same chair that he had occupied previously. He took a huge bite out of the sandwich and then opened the can of soda.

"I can't think of the best way of doing this." He mumbled, spitting food from his mouth as he spoke with his mouth full.

"You're very well preserved for a woman of your age, what are you, mid-forties now?"

Lucy nodded as she instinctively folded her arms protectively over her chest.

Luca looked her up and down lecherously.

"It's been very hard trying to be so good." He informed her, sounding for all the world like a friend simply enjoying a pleasant and convivial conversation.

"You know, all those years acting and singing. Sure, I've had girlfriends and stuff, but I've never done anything that could later be held up and used as proof that I am not divine. That sort of thing I've had to do privately, ensuring that the people I've had fun with, never get to tell."

Lucy tried to swallow, but her mouth was too dry.

"You mean you've murdered them?" She croaked.

Luca took another bite from the sandwich.

"Let's say, silenced them. Delicious sandwich!" He exclaimed as he picked up the Coke:

"Now, why was it that I decided that I didn't like you?"

Lucy gulped again and shook her head. Her stomach was churning and she desperately wanted to scream, but she knew that it would be to no avail.

Luca grinned as he wiped the corners of his mouth with the napkin Lucy had provided. He placed the Coke can back on the tray on the coffee table.

"It is because I think I saw something in your eyes, Lucy Sherman. You did not believe in me, in my claim to divinity and do you know why you did not believe in me?"

Lucy shook her head again:

"I don't know." She whispered.

Luca pursed his lips:

"It is because, you are like me. You are not quite fully human either."

Lucy frowned.

"What on earth do you mean?" She whispered.

Luca shrugged. He had just taken the last bite of the sandwich. He took the tray off the table and placed it carefully on the floor.

"Come now, are you trying to tell me that you don't know?"

Lucy closed her eyes and shook her head.

"I really don't know what you're talking about. You're insane!" She hissed.

Luca scowled and scratched his head.

"I find that hard to believe. Someone, one of your recent ancestors, probably one of your parents was one of my old enemies, an immortal. Show me your ears."

Lucy nervously reached up and pulled her shoulder length hair back to expose her elfin pointed ears.

"Mmm, just as I expected. I knew as soon as I saw you, Lucy Sherman. You are at least part-sidh, one of the Irish "little people." So the "Order" didn't quite complete their task, did they? Never mind, I will correct that anomaly."

Luca took a swig of coke, as Lucy shivered nervously.

"I really, really don't understand what are you talking about?" She gasped.

"What do you mean an immortal? What is the "Order?"

Luca laughed.

"Oh, don't worry. It's irrelevant, now. Your heritage is wasted. We are going to have some fun, well, I am anyway. Take off your clothes."

Lucy's eyes widened like a rabbit caught in the glare of a car's headlamps as she saw the twisted leer on Luca Vitalia's usually cherubically handsome face.

"What?" She whispered timorously.

"Oh, Mrs Sherman, please don't be so shy. We can't have any fun with you having your clothes on now, can we?" Luca chided her like a parent reprimanding a recalcitrant child.

Lucy reached up and slowly opened the top two buttons of her blouse. Her mind was racing, trying to think of a delaying tactic.

"I need the bathroom." She managed to gasp as she bordered on the edge of fainting.

Luca sighed.

"A delaying tactic? How pointless, no one is going to come to your rescue, Lucy, dear, no matter how long you delay the inevitable. Very well. I suppose I don't want you making a mess. Do be quick though. I have some important meetings to attend. I haven't got all day."

Lucy fled into her bathroom and locked the door. She slumped down in a corner, tears flooded from her eyes. She knew that Luca would be able to break down the door without too much effort, so she really had only a few minutes to live. She closed her eyes and concentrated on trying to contact her brother again, as she had in the kitchen. She knew it would be a total waste of time, but it seemed more useful than praying.

Several seconds passed, then a minute, Luca knocked on the bathroom door:

"Come on now Lucy." He shouted. "You can't stay in there all day. I could break this door down in a second."

Lucy screamed in her mind: "I am in my apartment, Number 423 Kennedy Suites Building West 72nd Street, New York City. I have maybe five minutes to live, if I'm lucky. HELP ME PLEASE."

The knocking on the bathroom door continued:

"Lucy, let me in. OK bitch, I'm going to break down the door."

Lucy screamed.

What she wasn't expecting was the sudden male voice that seemed to appear in the middle of her head, just like it had in that dream she'd had when she was a schoolgirl:

"Lucy, my sister. I am your brother, Wayne. Can you hear me?"

Lucy felt a sudden surge of hope as she answered:

"Oh my God! Oh my God! Wayne did you say? You're real. I can really hear you."

Luca's voice suddenly emanated from the other side of the bathroom door:

"Lucy, Lucy, open the door, little pig. I'm going to count to five and then I'm going to blow the door down."

Lucy concentrated as hard as could, her thoughts pleading:

"Wayne you have to help me. Please help me. Get the police."

She knew deep down that she was going mad. No one could talk telepathically. It was the stuff of science fiction. Even if she had communicated with her supposed brother, it would make no difference to her inevitable fate, but the thought that she was not totally alone did provide her with a small degree of comfort.

The disembodied voice appeared in Lucy's head again:

"Lucy the police should be on their way. What is happening?"

"Right that's it." Luca's voice shouted from the other side of the bathroom door.

"Oh my God, he's banging on the bathroom door. It's Luca Vitalia, he's not the Son of God. He's evil. He's going to kill me. Oh my God."

Lucy rolled herself into a foetal ball on the floor as she heard the door hinges breaking.

The voice was in her head again.

"Lucy. You must fight him. Tell him the whelp is coming. Tell him the whelp is coming to get him. Then, if you can, run to O'Briens Irish pub on West 54th. The owner is your Uncle. Lucy can you hear me?"

She was about to try to answer when suddenly there was more banging in addition to that against her bathroom door. This time, she could tell it was coming from her front door:

"Police, open up in there."

Luca stopped trying to break the door. Lucy could hear the wail of sirens.

"Help!" She screamed as loudly as she could manage.

There was more banging on the front door and more shouting then Lucy heard the sound of her apartment's front door being smashed open.

Luca's voice hissed through the gap that he had forced in the bathroom door

"You're a lucky lady, but this is not over, my dear. Don't bother telling anyone, they won't believe you anyway and it'll only be the worse for you. I swear I'll make your death last an eternity." He laughed manically.

Through her racking sobs Lucy managed to shout:

"The whelp is coming, Vitalia, I've been told to tell you that the whelp is coming to get you. He's on his way, right now."

She heard a sharp intake of breath from just beyond her bathroom door, then a loud bang as the front door collapsed.

"Police! Don't move!" A man's voice shouted. Lucy heard another voice that didn't sound anything like Luca's:

"Out of my way." It boomed. There was a noise like an explosion. Lucy screamed and covered her head. There was silence for what seemed like an eternity and then the sound of more voices and scrambling feet. There was a gentle knock on the bathroom door:

"Police, is anyone in there?"

Lucy couldn't help but burst into floods of tears. She had never felt so relieved in her life:

"Yes." She shouted. "Yes, I'm in here. I'm OK."

She climbed to her feet, which wasn't an easy task as she felt as weak as a kitten. She staggered to the partly broken bathroom door. Her hand was shaking like a leaf as she twisted open the lock.

Two policemen were standing just outside her bathroom, pointing guns at her. Two more were inching over the broken front door.

Then Lucy noticed the two uniformed bodies lying on the red carpet in the corridor just beyond her front door.

The cops lowered their guns:

"You OK, lady?"

Lucy nodded.

"Did, did he get away?" She stammered.

The first Cop put his pistol back into its holster:

"Yeah, took out two of our guys on his way out. Fortunately we weren't far behind."

"Did you get a good look at him?" The second cop asked, his voice urgent.

"Oh yes." Lucy stated:

"I got a real good look at him."

The air was now thick with the sound of sirens from the street, way down below.

Jonathan was still comatose in the chair when Lucy, supported by one of the policemen, was escorted into the drawing room.

Yet, her biggest shock was still to come:

"Yeah, we've got two men down right outside the apartment." She heard one of the cops speaking into his radio:

"The assailant must have used some sort of stun weapon. The Lady got a good look, but first description is of an Afro-Caribbean male, must be all of 6 foot six, about 350 pounds."

Lucy screwed up her face incredulously:

"He wasn't black. Luca Vitalia is not black."

The first Cop cast a cursory glance in her direction.

"Luca Vitalia? The Jesus dude?" He asked sceptically.

"We saw the guy, Ma'am. Are you saying it was not the big black guy? Are you saying that Luca Vitalia was actually in here?"

Lucy closed her eyes.

"No, no, I'm sorry. I guess I'm sort of all confused at the moment."

Luca had been right. No one would believe her testimony. He must have had an accomplice, or Lucy thought, although it was much less likely, he must have been able to change his race and size, as well as his shape. What had all that nonsense been about immortals?

The woman who had always lived a perfectly normal, albeit gilded life, had somehow, suddenly been thrust into the middle of indescribable events that defied every ounce of her common sense, logic, rationality and wisdom: Strange voices in her head?

Evil Messiahs?

Immortals?

Shape shifting?

Maybe Lucy Sherman was going mad. She certainly had recent cause to flip out.

"Excuse me." She gestured to the first policeman who had helped her from the bathroom."

"Yes, Lady?" He answered.

"How did you know?" She asked him politely.

"How did you know, what was going on here? How did you know, I was about to be murdered?"

The cop took off his hat and scratched his head:

"Well Lady, this is downright weird. One of the other boys told me that the station got a message from JFK. Seems like somebody on an airplane said you was in danger. Sounds like rubbish to me, but hey. What do I know?"

Lucy nodded.

"By the way, do you know if there is there an Irish pub on West 54th Street?"

The cop nodded:

"Yeah, sure Ma'am, O'Brien's, fine place. Best Guinness on the island. Oh, here's the paramedics. We'll need to take a statement from you when these guys have fixed you up. We'll need a good description of your assailant."

Lucy smiled.

"Thanks." She said gratefully.

She could see that Jonathan was awake again and looking incredibly perplexed to be surrounded by policemen and paramedics.

"What on earth is going on?" He whispered to Lucy.

Lucy smiled weakly:

"Your client is what is going on, Jonathan, your precious Messiah. We need to talk, Jonathan. If he's the Messiah, then I'm Imelda bloody Marcos."

Thirty-Four

Gaily coloured Christmas lights twinkled optimistically in shop windows, as the icy sleet seemed to plummet almost sideways from the heavy grey winter skies. Jack Baring stared out of his window on the seventeenth floor of the unassuming steel and glass tower just outside the main political area of Washington D.C.

Christmas? It sure didn't feel like Christmas. Jack sighed then turned from the window and slumped forlornly back into his black leather chair and glanced at his watch for what must have been the fiftieth time in just under an hour. The phone trilled on his sparse desk, he picked it up and leaned back.

"Baring!" He snapped.

His chair back reclined comfortably as he sighed heavily.

"Send him in." He blustered, as he almost threw the receiver back on to its cradle.

There was a polite knock on his office door.

"Come." Baring shouted.

A young man of no more than thirty walked in nervously.

"Mr Secretary, Sir." He stammered, his eyes wide, almost fearful.

"Jack'll do. So even Mac Brown can't make it now huh? So he sends along a sacrificial victim, a lamb to the slaughter." Baring snapped.

The young man's mouth dropped open.

"Sir?"

Jack Baring glowered at him.

"Next he'll be sending me a kid right out of training school. I hear you've got something for me?" Baring suggested patiently, then he paused, waiting for the young man to tender his name.

The young man froze for a second, as if he had forgotten why he was in the United States Secretary of Homeland Security's office.

"Oh, yes." He spluttered: "We've been working with the British Security Agencies, Sir and they've tied up a link between, erm."

He looked nervously at the file in his hand: "Erm Wayne Higginbotham and Michael O'Brien."

"Well, what is it?" Baring snapped impatiently.

The young man stared at Jack momentarily before emitting a nervous cough and blurting:

"It's the same person, sir."

Jack Baring picked up a pen and put it in his mouth.

"What's your name, son?"

The young man considered the question for what seemed like an eternity:

"Erm Walter, sir. Walter J. Wickert, Walter J. Wickert the third."

Jack Baring nodded, knowingly.

"Alma Mater?"

Walter hesitated.

"Erm, oh, yes, er, Harvard, Sir."

Jack Baring nodded.

"Well, Walter, tell me exactly how this anonymous nobody living in the backwoods of merry olde England can be two people at the same time and why does somebody want him dead?"

Walter Wickert the third looked at his file.

"Adoption, Sir. Michael Sean O'Brien was born in London in 1963. His mother was one Theresa O'Brien, a native of Ireland, Sir. He was one of twins. The British haven't found the other child, a girl, yet. He was then subsequently adopted by the Higginbotham family of Yorkshire, Sir. His name was changed to Wayne Higginbotham."

Jack Baring frowned.

"Theresa O'Brien?"

Walter Wickert the third almost smiled:

"She, erm came to the United States in 1964, Sir. She became an actress, renamed herself Terri Thorne and erm married Dean Vitalia. They were divorced in........"

Jack Baring held up his hand and stood up abruptly.

"Just wait a moment Son. Are you telling me that this guy Higginbotham." He chewed over the word, deliberately emphasising every syllable:

"You are, in fact, telling me that a British Cornflake Salesman, is actually Dean Vitalia's stepson?"

Walter Wickert the third took a timorous step back.

"Why Yes, Yes Sir. It sure looks like it."

Jack Baring picked up the phone and pressed several buttons.

"Get me Marshall Williams. Yeah, in my office at two pm. Thanks."

Jack Baring walked around his desk and slapped young Wickert on the shoulder:

"Let's take a seat son. I want to hear chapter and verse on the subject of the man with two names. Do we have men watching him? Just in case Vitalia tries to finish the job. We need to know how he did what he did to those gangsters."

Walter Wickert gulped.

"Erm, We don't know much more than I've already told you, Sir. He has no police record, not even a speeding ticket. We have no idea why the Vitalias would want to hurt a family member, even if he's not very close family."

Jack Baring took a deep breath:

"The mother may know. The actress, Terri O'Brien or Thorne, or whatever she's called."

Wickert's cell phone erupted in his pocket. He took it out and checked to see who was calling:

"Yep, yep." He repeated several times before closing the clamshell unit.

He looked up at Jack Baring and a faint smile creased his lips.

"You're not going to believe this, Sir, but Wayne Higginbotham, or Michael Sean O'Brien, has just landed at LAX. He's right here in the USA, Sir."

Baring thumped his fist down on his desk triumphantly.

"God dammit, there may be a chink of light appearing in this whole damn dark cloud. Find him, tail him. Whatever you do make sure that someone gets as close to this guy as I ever get to my wife. Something dirty is happening and if it involves the Vitalias it could be exactly what we need."

Walter Wickert the third, grinned.

"We've already got one of our best men on the case, Sir."

Detective Chief Inspector Archie Knox slowly shook his head and grimaced as Detective Inspector Ratchett briefed him once again.

"So Robbie Burns told you that it really was Arnie who walked into Giametti's office?"

Ratchett shrugged.

"Swears it, Sir. Ever since we picked him up he's been blabbing on about how Arnie the bloody Terminator blew the bloody door off, walked in and blasted Finch straight out through the window."

Knox rubbed his forehead as though trying to relieve himself of an awful migraine,

"So, it's quite simple then. We put out an arrest warrant for one of the most recognisable actors and politicians in the world, who has obviously dressed up to replicate one of his most iconic roles, just so that he can take out a petty East London gangster. I do not think so!"

DI Ratchett blew out an exasperated sigh.

"The thing is, Sir. He believes it. He even took a polygraph test."

Detective Constable Fletcher who was stood just behind his boss, decided to add his opinion to the conversation.

"Sir, we could be looking at a piece of brilliant theatrical make up. You know, prosthetic features and all that."

DCI Knox twisted his mouth while DI Ratchett made a sarcastic snorting noise in his throat:

"Swallowed a dictionary, have we, Fletch? What the hell are pathetics?"

"Prosthetics, you moron!" Knox corrected his immediate subordinate before he blew out a long exasperated sigh.

"We'd thought of that, Fletcher. It's just that all the witnesses are totally convinced that it was the real thing. Do we have anything more?"

Ratchett glanced at Fletcher and the embarrassing silence was enough for DCI Knox to declare the end of the meeting.

"Keep working on Burns." He muttered by way of a closing statement as he slammed the file shut.

"There is a very dangerous individual somewhere out there. It is my belief that this is all related to Giametti's illicit activities. It wouldn't surprise me if it was the Chinese Triads moving in, or the Russians, or the Romanians.

The Arnie disguise is an attempt to throw us off the trail, but they don't realise we are made of sterner stuff."

Thirty-Six

Aurelio Vitalia slapped Luca's back as he walked out of his hotel to take part in yet another radio station interview in New York City.

"How ya feelin, Luca? Two more candidates have dropped out of the race. That just leaves two Democrats and one Republican to stand against you. You're a Goddamn shoe-in, buddy." He gushed as he glanced at his son's sombre face.

Luca had rested for a couple of hours during the afternoon after his meeting with his lawyer, but his mood seemed to have deteriorated in the intervening period.

"I need some time to myself." He had hissed at Aurelio as they had left the Hotel foyer.

Scores of flashbulbs illuminated the early evening twilight as the Senator and the prospective Presidential candidate crossed the sidewalk to climb into a waiting black limo.

"I want some time to be able to think. When we get back from Rome, I need a couple of weeks off."

"Luca, there's no chance of that now." Aurelio grunted as he slumped wearily into the limo's back seat.

"You're in the public eye. You're a star. We've got Iowa in January and then a whole series of caucuses, Primaries and debates. That is if anyone has the guts to stand against you. Even so, every move you take, every word you say, will be taken and analysed a million times over. They'll chew on it, savour it and if it ain't exactly what they want to hear, they'll spit it right back you. You're public property now, my son."

Luca smiled and waved as the limo pulled into the stream of traffic.

"Yeah, I guess you're right." He hissed through a clenched grin.

"I'm theirs for now, but soon they'll be mine. Maybe then I'll complete unfinished business."

"What was that?" Aurelio barked, "I'm sorry son, I couldn't hear what you were saying."

Luca turned and appraised the man that he had called "father" since he had been five years old. Aurelio Vitalia was looking his age. His forehead was wrinkled and his olive skin was covered in liver spots, especially his hands. He had also put on a lot of weight. His chin bulged above his collar and his eyes were almost lost in the pudgy flesh, which sagged around his cheekbones. Aurelio was still gasping for breath after the dash to the car.

Luca smiled.

"It's OK, I was just muttering to myself."

He pulled a tranche of paper from his briefcase.

"You've made sure the interviewer is going to stick to the script?" Luca asked his father as he reverted to the smooth, practised political persona.

"Yes, they've been fully briefed. The guy who owns the station, KYNY, is a fully committed Christian, so he's just delighted to have you on the show. He reckons this is the biggest thing since nine-eleven."

Luca laughed.

"Are we ready for Rome?"

Aurelio shrugged.

"Only you can call that one, son."

Luca smiled and nodded as the car came to rest outside a non-descript office block and the driver jumped out to open Luca's door. Flash bulbs went off like lightening as the young man rushed into the reception area without waiting for Aurelio.

"Luca, Luca, over here." Voices bellowed as the paparazzi begged for pleasing shots of the man of the moment. Luca had ignored them all. Aurelio grinned and waved as he wobbled across the sidewalk in his son's wake.

Luca was greeted by a crowd of executives and celebrity guests, as he entered the radio station. The owner got down on his knees and kissed Luca's hand.

"My Lord." He gasped, over and over. Some of the others fell to their knees as the feverish atmosphere began to overcome them.

"Stand, please." Luca commanded, authoritatively.

The radio station owner, John L. Lacey, a bookish looking man in his early thirties, complied.

Luca smiled at him.

"Thank you." He said, placing a hand on the man's shoulder.

The interview didn't last long. Luca answered the standard questions about his plans for the American economy and about his future foreign policy, issuing the same bland responses that he had used many times before. It was when he was asked about his impending visit to Rome, however, that he caused a minor sensation.

The interviewer, D.J. "Big Shot" Cannon asked him how he was going to convince the Pope and all the gathered religious leaders that he was truly, The "Son of God."

Luca had laughed and nodded.

"Yes, I guess I'll be dealing with a great deal of scepticism there. I think some of those guys will be trying to protect their vested interests. That's why there will be another miracle there. One that will leave no doubt in the minds of all those present."

"Big Shot" Cannon blew out a surprised whistle.

"Hey folks, you heard it right here first from the Biggest Gun on the airwaves, yes indeedee, right here on the "Big Shot" Cannon show on New York's rockingest radio station, KYNY. Mister Luca Vitalia just said he is going to perform another miracle in Rome, on December the 21st. This one'll blow 'em all away. Just like we do. So what exactly are you going to be doing Mr. Luca, Sir?"

Luca Vitalia grimaced.

"If I tell you, it won't be a surprise now, will it? Let's just say it'll be," He paused as he searched for the correct word:

".... spectacular."

D.J.Cannon howled like a dog in pain.

"Just remember where you heard it first. Coming at you like a speeding cannon ball on 98.4. KYNY. The explosive sound in the Big Apple. Thank you Mister Luca Vitalia. The next President of the United States and the Son of our Lord, Jesus Christ."

"No, thank you." Luca replied as he slowly removed his headphones.

"Yep, I'm really gonna blow their minds." He whispered inaudibly.

Aurelio looked flustered as Luca approached him.

"You never mentioned no new miracle to me before."

Luca patted the older man's shoulder and whispered in his ear.

"There are still too many doubters. I have failed to convince as many people as I expected by this stage. I expect people to be more like Mr Lacey. I do not necessarily want people to grovel before me, or to worship me, yet, like him and the sheep he has gathered around him, I do want respect, a due amount of deference.

After Rome, I will have all the deference I can cope with. I can assure you of that. I guarantee that only Parvez will stand against me next year. The others, as good Christians, will see that to continue their campaigns would constitute blasphemy." He grinned at Aurelio and slapped his back.

The two men said their goodbyes and after braving the light storm, courtesy of the press corps photographers outside, and sped away in the long black limousine.

Aurelio wiped his forehead with a clean white handkerchief. Hassan Parvez was one of the two remaining Democratic candidates in the race for the White House. A lapsed Moslem, born to Indian immigrants, he had declared himself the only totally secular candidate and had stated that he was extremely sceptical about Luca Vitalia's claim to divinity on several occasions. Luca had not taken part in any of the televised debates that the prospective candidates had already engaged in, so the two had never met, but the media had regarded Vitalia versus Parvez as being the only show in town for some weeks, even though Parvez trailed Janet Regan, the only other Democratic candidate by a mile. Aurelio smiled as the Limo bore him and his son back to their hotel. Luca would absolutely slaughter Parvez in an election. He was going to be the father of the President of the United States and the "Son of God." Life really didn't get much better than this. He turned to smile reassuringly at Luca. Luca Vitalia was staring straight ahead, through the Limo's windshield. His eyes were clear and focused. For the first time Aurelio noticed how devoid of emotion Luca could look. He shivered; well at least he was on the good side of Luca Vitalia, even if he did turn out to be an imposter.

As far as Aurelio Vitalia was concerned, Luca Vitalia could be the devil himself as long as he profited from Luca's success. Suddenly he noticed that Luca's stare had moved on to him.

"You OK, kid?" Aurelio asked.

Luca smiled beatifically as a lock of golden hair tumbled carelessly on to his forehead:

"Oh yes, I'm fine. Just fine and dandy. Actually, you know, I don't think Parvez will be much of a problem. I believe he has just had a nervous breakdown."

Aurelio's mouth dropped open.

"A nervous breakdown?"

Luca nodded:

"I am bored of Politics." He declared with a wave of his hand. "It is my opinion, Father, that my main challenger will not be one of my American Presidential rivals."

Aurelio gazed at his son incredulously. Luca grinned.

"My only true rival is a kid that I have known about since I was small. I have been aware of his existence for many years. It seems that he believes he has the power to destroy me. He was no more than a whelp when I first invaded his dreams and he is no more than a whelp now. He will be happy to die when we show him the very many ways we can destroy a human being. The supposed saviour will save nothing at all, least of all, himself."

Thirty-Seven

Wayne Higginbotham could not remember ever having felt so tense. The last four hours of the flight to Los Angeles seemed to take an eternity. He still couldn't quite believe it. Had he really been contacted, by his long lost sister? Or had he dreamt the whole damn thing? Maybe the airline wine had been stronger than he had anticipated.

Maybe he should have stuck to just one glass.

When he had been sixteen and had been tied up and left to burn in the blazing basement of 18 Cavendish Street, in total desperation, he had attempted to make telepathic contact with her. It had seemed to work for him. Had she really just done the same thing in her own time of desperate need?

Wayne stared out of the small porthole and shook his head. Way down below vast mountain ranges and untamed empty valleys, raging rivers and icy lakes passed by, as the plane traversed Northern Canada. Fluffy white cotton candy clouds drifted far below the Boeing as it cruised at a leisurely 550 miles per hour.

The strangest thing of all was that his sister had said that it was Luca Vitalia that was attacking her. Surely he wouldn't be so stupid as to attack a woman while he was trying to prove to the world that not only would he make a great President, but that he was also the Second Coming of Jesus Christ. It was that thought that made Wayne wonder whether he had actually dreamed, or imagined the whole thing. Here he was, travelling to America to face down a demon of unparalled evil, while, just coincidentally, his sister was trying to fight off a physical attack by the very same monster. Now, that had to be beyond the range of even the wildest of random possibilities.

Wayne's mind just kept running over his sister's last words in his head:

"Oh my God, he's banging on the bathroom door. It's Luca Vitalia, he's not the Son of God. He's evil. He's going to kill me. Oh my God."

If he was a demon of unimaginable power, then Wayne had to accept that his sister was now dead. Yet some faint hope lingered deep in his heart, inexplicably, irrationally and downright illogically.

In a vain attempt to keep his mind from dwelling on the subject, Wayne checked his documents and his planning. His first mission upon landing in Los Angeles had been to get hold of the fabled sword of Gorias from the Getty Museum. He realised that in the light of subsequent events that might have to be delayed, however, he did have everything he needed to pull off the heist that would give him the three treasures of his ancestors that he would need in the inevitable confrontation.

Finally, Sean, the cabin director informed passengers that the plane would be landing at LAX and that everyone should return to their seats. Wayne closed his eyes tight and tried to re-establish contact with his sister, but still to no avail. He cursed silently under his breath and tried to be patient. He looked around the cabin. Hundreds of men, women and children of different nationalities and races, all packed together in one long metal tube. Some were going home, some were going on vacation. Some were travelling with dreams of fame and fortune, some had no dreams at all. Some people would be meeting loved ones for the Holiday season, others had left their loved ones behind. One thing was for sure; he was the only one who was on his way to try to save the world.

"Are you alright Mr Higginbotham?" Sean, the cabin director's voice jerked him out of his reverie.

"I hope everything is OK with your sister and that the cops got there in time. You must let us know. Now if you don't mind would you please fasten your seat-belt. Oh, by the way, I've just been told that you were very lucky to get any sort of mobile signal over the Atlantic."

Wayne grinned, shrugged and nodded his acknowledgement and promised he would let the crew know what had happened for good or evil.

Some two hours later, as he drove his rental car along the Interstate 405 away from the airport, Wayne was still wondering whether the call from the aircraft had got to New York in time. He had tried to ring his mother on his cell phone as soon as the plane had landed. She must have been out as her line went straight on to her answering machine. He sighed for probably the millionth time as the freeway began to climb the first set of mountains to cross into the valley. On his left he could see the white tram slowly ascending to the Getty museum. He would get the sword the next day, right now he had other priorities.

Eventually his Ford pulled up outside Terri's house and he jumped out, ran up her short driveway and knocked on the door. The door opened and he was greeted by a huge hug.

"Hi Mom!" he laughed as she threatened to squeeze the breath from his body.

"You haven't heard from Colm in New York, have you?"

His mother grabbed his shoulders and looked at him as if he had just announced that he was a Martian.

"Now, why on earth would the first thing you want to know is, if I've spoken to Colm?" Terri grimaced, totally taken aback by the random nature of the question.

"I spoke to him last weekend and he was fine."

Wayne shrugged as he hauled his suitcase into his mother's house:

"Look Mom, something really weird happened on the plane. Something very similar happened when I was sixteen. I'll tell you when I've got all my stuff in."

The sun was slowly sinking off to the west as Wayne explained about his experience on the flight and about his telepathy with his sister. Terri Thorne's mouth had hung open since Wayne had started to tell her about what had happened on the plane and about how he believed that he had been in touch with his sister once before, when he was sixteen.

"So, you think you can only contact each other in times of incredible stress?" Terri asked, tremulously.

Wayne shrugged:

"The only time I've managed it was when I was absolutely certain that I was going to die and it looks like it's been exactly the same for her."

Terri closed her eyes.

"Oh my God, Charlotte. Do you think she's dead? My little Charlotte?"

Wayne smiled:

"Was that what you named her? She's called Lucy now. She's still alive. I'm sure of it."

Wayne held both of his mother's hands as she convulsed in tears.

"My other little girl." She wailed. "It's been so long…."

Wayne stood and walked around Terri's kitchen table and hugged his mother.

"Mom, she'll be fine. She's like me. We are survivors."

Wayne Higginbotham bit his lip. If Lucy was dead, then Luca Vitalia would pay.

Wayne had planned to be merciful and quick in despatching his prey. He wasn't a natural killer. The man who had died in the student union bar in Manchester all those years ago, had died accidently and Wayne had never forgiven himself for his actions. The gangster he had blown through Giametti's window had died as a result of his own stupidity. Yet now, things were different. Dean Vitalia would pay first for threatening Wayne's family. Wayne had no intention of killing him. Dean didn't deserve to die. After all, he was Marco and Marina's father and Terri had loved him, once. No, Wayne could think of something far worse than death for Deano Vitalia.

As for Luca Vitalia, he would pay for everything the "Order" had ever done to Wayne's ancestors. They had existed as an organisation with the sole objective of clearing the way for the demon's arrival on earth. The fact that they had been expecting someone rather different was immaterial. The Tuatha de Danaan had been wiped out. It had been genocide on a massive scale. There were now just two half-breed survivors of an entire race, Wayne and his sister and she might already be dead for all he knew. Luca would pay if he had harmed Wayne's sister, he would pay very slowly.

A strange red light flashed momentarily in Wayne's eyes as he contemplated what he would do to Luca Vitalia. He could feel his mother's racking sobs as he held her tight.

Then, without warning, Terri pushed away from her son. She took a deep breath, composed herself and looked into his eyes.

"Have you come to deal with the Vitalias?" She asked, her voice sounding strained but strong.

"I take it your unfinished business is with Dean, but you are going to deal with Luca, aren't you?"

Wayne nodded.

"Especially if he's done anything to harm Lucy, sorry Charlotte."

Terri nodded.

"Let's stick with Lucy. I've still not gotten used to calling you Wayne, instead of Michael."

Wayne smiled.

"I don't mind. I'm both people, I guess."

Then the phone rang.

Thirty-Eight

The man in the raincoat had carefully watched the multitude of travellers as they had emerged from international arrivals into the vast, crowded and noisy terminal area. Loved ones and taxi drivers holding up names scribbled on cards had stood in lines, waiting for the fatigued looking passengers, who had just flown in from Ireland, to appear at the top of the ramp leading from the lower baggage hall.

Families hugged and kissed and lovers entwined as squeals and shouted greetings had echoed around the cavernous ceiling.

The man sipped patiently at his coffee. He had been waiting for over an hour for a single middle-aged, white Caucasian male to emerge. He glanced at the photo in his hand. If the guy had arrived and had slipped through unnoticed, there would be hell to pay, but that wouldn't happen. The man was too good for anything to be able to slip past him.

Three teenagers emerged around the corner of the barrier and rushed up to greet a woman that the man presumed was their Mom. Just behind them a middle-aged male with dark, albeit greying hair, pushed his trolley swiftly towards the terminal exit. He had a cell phone clamped to his ear.

The man in the raincoat glanced at the middle-aged man, then at the photo. That had to be him, he thought as adrenalin surged through his system.

The man in the raincoat dropped his empty coffee cup in a trash-can and followed the other man at a comfortable distance. The middle-aged traveller headed out through the doors and then took up a position in the line for a bus to the hire car lot. The man in the mac ran across to the car park, having made a note of the hire car company that the bus belonged too. This was going to be a piece of cake. He climbed two flights of stairs, jumped into his Pontiac and hurtled down to the car park exit, his tyres squealing. Once on the airport circuit road he drove much more sedately, the last thing he wanted was to attract attention. He soon caught up with the shiny green bus that transported travellers from the airport terminals to the huge rental car lot. The sun gleamed on the bus' bright chrome and on the Pontiac's bonnet. The man sighed. Just another gorgeous winter's day in Southern California, it felt good to be out of the frigidly cold madhouse that the Terminal had presented. Once the bus had passed out of the airport, the man drove straight to the rental car exit. He was going to have to be patient again, but that was his job. There was a football game on the radio and the sky was blue, plus the heat of the day had passed, so sitting in the car wasn't going to be too uncomfortable. It was going to be just like hunting up in the mountains, or one of his fishing trips to Tahoe. Patience was all that was required.

He waited and waited and waited. Two hours passed, the football game finished and there was still no sign of the Englishman driving out of the lot.

"Man, they must be busy in there." The man spoke out loud. He was glad that he hadn't just flown for twelve hours and then been forced to suffer the ignominy of immigration control, customs and the baggage carousel, before standing in line for two hours for a rental car.

Two hours became three and the man began to wonder if he had been given the slip. The afternoon shadows were getting very long as the sun began to slip below the buildings to his left. He had watched every car leave the lot. Small hatchbacks, medium and large sedans, wagons and SUVs had all been leaving the yard at regular intervals and he had watched every single driver. There was no way the Higginbotham dude could have slipped out past him.

He swore and got out of his car, crossing the busy road at a run. He stepped round the barrier and over the cruel looking teeth that would shred the tyre of any driver trying to steal a car. He flashed his FBI badge at the African-American security woman on the gate. She nodded with a due degree of disinterest. The man in the mac strode over to the rental office and peered through the window. There was no sign of the Higginbotham dude. The man scowled. How on earth had he got out past him? He entered the office, his mood deteriorating by the second. He approached one of the assistants who had just handed the keys of a car over to a customer and had been in the process of beckoning the next in line. He flashed his badge again. The people in line glanced at the man with unveiled contempt. Who the hell did he think he was? The line was moving slowly enough without some buck in a raincoat pushing in.

"Hey buddy!" The large black man who had been at the head of the line shouted. The man looked round:

"FBI." He stated quietly and succinctly.

The large black man swore under his breath and raised his eyebrows sardonically at the next in line.

Five minutes later the man was running back across the road to his Pontiac. A uniformed Highway Patrolman was just in the process of putting a ticket on his windshield.

"You can't do that!" The man bellowed:

"I'm FBI." He reached into his pocket for his card.

199

"Hands away from your body!" The cop shouted back, his gun already in his hand.

"I don't care if you're President Elmer Ford himself. This car is parked illegally. Now put your hands on the hood!"

The man sighed and reluctantly obeyed. Somehow the Higginbotham guy had managed to rent a car and get past him. He was going to be in such deep doo-doo when his boss found out. At least he had the rental car details and it was almost certain that Higginbotham would be heading for his mother's place. As the Highway patrolman patted down his pockets, the man smiled. He would pay his fine and get on up into the Valley. He had Terri Thorne's address. He would soon be back on Higginbotham's tail and he sure wouldn't let the little sucker give him the slip again.

The Highway Patrol man grinned as he examined the man's FBI badge:

"Looks like you should know better, buddy." He drawled in an accent that clearly wasn't local. The Cop's companion sauntered leisurely up and handed him a credit card machine.

The man presented his credit card without so much as a word and two minutes later and a hundred bucks worse off, he was driving up the 405 Interstate North.

"I wonder what this guy has done?" He asked himself as he drove past the Getty museum high up on a hillside by the Freeway.

Whatever it was, he hadn't been told. His instructions had been to follow him and watch him and let his boss know everybody he came into contact with. The man whistled:

"Must be a drug dealer, or a terrorist. I'll teach him to go sneaking past Henry T. Burgermeister. Goddamn Punk!"

It was about an hour later when he pulled up outside a pleasant row of houses in the San Fernando Valley suburb of Chatsworth. He squinted in the early evening twilight as he examined the house numbers. He had memorised Terri Thorne's address and sure enough, there it was and right outside was the red Ford rental car that Higginbotham had hired. He double-checked the details he had written down in the rental office, before finding a convenient, legal, parking spot just up the street.

Yep, nobody outsmarted Henry T. Burgermeister, especially not a Limey schmuck with a name like Higginbotham.

"I mean who the hell has a name like Higginbotham?" He laughed to himself as he settled down to watch the house and the car.

Special Agent Henry T. Burgermeister was not going to get fooled again.

Thirty-Nine

"Can I help you?" The handsome, young barman asked the extremely confused looking woman who had just walked into O'Brien's Irish Pub. She was not the usual type of clientele who used the bar, especially in the early afternoon. Smartly dressed in an expensive grey business suit, she looked as though she had just stepped out of a boardroom meeting. She looked around the bar, nervously examining the nicotine stained décor on the walls, memorabilia of football, baseball, basketball and soccer teams.

"We don't bite you know." The barman tried to reassure the woman. It was quite clear she had suffered some sort of upset. Her mascara was smudged black around her eyes, where tears had been wiped clean.

"Erm, this is going to sound so utterly ridiculous." She intimated to the barman. Her distinctive, perfectly pronounced British accent sounded quite out of place in the rough looking drinking den.

"You are going to think I'm crazy, but……." She hesitated.

"Everybody's crazy here, Ma'am. It's the rule, it's a goddam Irish pub." The barman stated, his face remaining deadpan and expressionless.

"Well, I'd like to speak to the owner, please." Lucy Sherman whispered.

The barman leaned down towards her.

"That'd me, now, I suppose." He said as he shrugged and picked up a glass to wipe.

"But, you're not old enough to be my Uncle." Lucy gasped and then shook her head as she realised how stupid she sounded. She began to turn to walk out of the bar.

"I'm sorry, I'm making a fool of myself." She muttered.

It had been a ridiculous notion that she could have been given the details of her Uncle's pub in an imaginary telepathic conversation with a brother that she had never met. She had obviously panicked in a moment of extreme crisis and had imagined the whole thing. The brain can do funny things under extreme duress and she had certainly suffered great duress that day. She had spent more than six hours in the local police station since her rescue, going over and over the events that had led to the police arriving at her apartment. She had decided even before her interviews that it was pointless mentioning Luca Vitalia. Especially after the police had mentioned that the man suspected of stunning the first policeman to arrive on the scene had been a big, black man.

"Hold on, Lady! Your Uncle? Would it, maybe, be me dad, Colm, you're looking for?" The barman shouted after the retreating woman.

Lucy stopped dead and turned back towards the young man.

"I'm sorry, but that's what's so stupid. I really don't know, but I was told in good faith that this bar belonged to my Uncle. I'm adopted, you see." She made a gesture that showed how crazy the whole thing sounded.

"Are you an O'Brien?" The barman asked.

Lucy laughed:

"Again, I really don't know." She shrugged.

The barman laughed and stroked his chin.

"Well, this is all a bit strange, to be sure. Whose would you be then? Let me guess, You don't sound like an Aussie so your not Siobhan's, anyway, I've met all her kids. I've never met Sean's, but you're not a Kiwi. Katie's kids are too young and not you're a paddy. Our Liam's kids are all as American as apple pie. You are English, aren't you?"

Lucy nodded.

"The thing is," She began before pausing to find the right words:

"The thing is I don't know whose child I am. I am supposedly one half of a pair of twins. I supposedly have a brother. We were born in London, in 1963."

The barman put the glass down and he studied the woman's face.

"I'm Tom." He whispered holding out his hand.

"I'm Colm's eldest. He's semi retired now and he's sorta handed the bar over to me."

Tom walked around the side of the bar towards the traumatised looking woman.

"Tell me…" he gulped.

"Was your brother also raised in England?"

Lucy started to shrug, but then the memory a trip to a small Yorkshire market town when she had been a student flooded back into her mind.

"Yes," she gasped excitedly:

"Yes, he was raised in, now where was it? A town called Shepton, Yorkshire, I think."

Tom nodded knowingly and then shook his head.

"Holy Mother of Jaysus. I think I better go up and get me dad down here. Can I get you a drink? I sure as hell need one."

"You know something, don't you?" Lucy gasped,

"You know who I am, don't you?"

Tom held up his hands:

"Whoa lady, let's not jump to conclusions, but I think I might have a good idea who you are. I'll need me dad to confirm it. He's just upstairs. Now before I get him, will you be having that drink, it's on the house."

Lucy decided that a stiff brandy would be useful. Tom duly poured her a large one and knocked one back himself, then ran upstairs as fast as his legs would carry him, to bring Colm O'Brien down into the bar.

Minutes later a slightly dishevelled looking old man with a shock of grey hair entered the bar from a door behind the counter.

"Now what's this nonsense all about?" he grumbled grumpily.

Tom pointed at the professional looking woman sitting at a table nearby.

"I have a feeling that that lady, might be your niece. She was certainly told that you are her Uncle. She sounds like the feckin' Queen of England."

Colm screwed up his eyes as he peered myopically at the woman, as she sipped the large brandy.

"I've never seen her before in me life." He muttered. "And I know all me nieces and nephews."

Tom leaned towards the old man:

"I think she might be Aunty Theresa's?"

Colm O'Brien pondered for a moment.

"You don't mean that this could be the boy Michael's sister?"

Tom nodded.

"He was adopted in England wasn't he? And Aunt Theresa always said that she'd had twins, a boy and a girl."

Colm's mouth dropped open.

"Holy Mary, Mother of Jaysus."

He murmured before slowly leaving the counter and approaching the woman.

"Hello Ma'am, I'm Colm O'Brien." He nervously introduced himself.

The woman stood and held out her hand:

"Hello Colm. Tom has probably told you that I'm an appalling mad woman who came in from the street with some wild goose story that you are my Uncle." She laughed.

"I know it's probably crazy and quite simply quite untrue, but I really was told on good authority, so I thought I ought to check it out. I'll leave, I'm so sorry to have troubled you. Tom was just humouring me, wasn't he?"

Colm stared into the woman's eyes. They were so like Theresa's.

"Wait." He suggested gently as the woman turned to leave again.

The woman looked extremely embarrassed.

"No really, I think it's better if I leave." She was almost babbling, she was feeling so humiliated.

Colm held out his hand and gently grabbed her arm.

"Please, wait a moment. Ma'am. I think Tom is right. I think we know who you are."

Lucy Sherman closed her eyes.

"This is all so surreal. I'm going to wake up in a moment."

Colm beckoned for her to retake her seat. Will you let me make one single phone call?"

He let the question hang for a second.

"I'm Lucy!" the woman stated: "Lucy Sher, no, Lucy Hetherington."

She shook Colm's hand.

"Will you be passing me the phone there, Tom?" The old man asked his son, who duly obliged. Colm dialled a number into a cell phone and waited.

Lucy stared at the old man and at Tom in turn. Could it be possible that these two scruffy New York Irish men were the first real members of her birth family that she had met?

Was there a physical resemblance? Not that she could see, neither of them had her awfully pointed ears.

Tom was busily drying glasses as he watched his Dad and "cousin" talk.

He had only met Michael once, at Daideo's funeral, but he had seemed a pleasant guy and he had heard the family legend of Michael's return to the family all those years earlier.

Tom hoped that he was going to pick up a new cousin, but it was all a bit fanciful. She didn't seem to have many facts to corroborate her story. He wondered exactly who had told her that Colm was her Uncle.

Then he saw Colm hand her the phone and her hand flew to her mouth. No more than a couple of minutes later she gave Colm back his phone and then she threw her arms around him and hugged him. Tom raised his eyebrows. Well Goddammit, maybe he did have a new cousin after all.

Forty

Wayne Higginbotham climbed on board the gleaming white tram and took a seat by the window. By the standards of Los Angeles the day was cool, with a chill wind sweeping down from the Sierra Nevada. The advantage of such a breeze, however, was that it cleared the air and allowed the entire city to bathe in bright sunshine, under clear blue skies.

The view from the top of the Bel Air Mountain where the Getty museum was based, promised to be spectacular. Wayne was already impressed by the time the tram got halfway up the hill. He caught sight of his refection in the glass and couldn't help but catch his breath in surprise. The white haired old man staring back at him was certainly not the reflection he was used to. A mop of white frizzy hair exploded from the old man's head, framing his wrinkled face. A pair of half moon glasses perched on the end of his nose, whilst good-humoured intelligence could be perceived from the old man's large, watery blue eyes. Wayne had tried the disguise once before. At the rental car lot he had popped into the washroom as Wayne Higginbotham, mid forties nobody and re-emerged as the venerable Professor Michael Finnegan of the University of Galway, expert in ancient Irish archaeology and artefacts. He had stayed in role all the way from the airport to Terri's, only changing back into his normal shape once his rental car had stopped and parked outside his mother's house.

Wayne couldn't help but grin. He had written to the Getty museum weeks earlier, asking if the esteemed Professor Finnegan might be allowed to authenticate some of the ancient Irish artefacts that the Getty Museum had in storage. Wayne had received a curt rebuttal at the time, but the Museum had changed its mind just the week before Wayne had set out for the USA, citing cultural cooperation as the reason for the volte-face. Wayne wondered if that had been anything to do with his second letter, which had threatened legal action and an investigation by the Garda into the sale of the weapon to the American museum in the first place.

Wayne had, of course, been delighted. He had not wanted to rob the Getty Museum, but he had been quite prepared to, to get his hands on the Sword of Gorias. It had been well over twenty years since he had risked life and limb in his efforts to rescue the Spear of Finias from its precarious hiding place in the Cliffs of Moher. Now he was within touching distance of having three of the four great treasures of the

Tuatha de Danaan in his possession. The tram rumbled to a stop and the occupants, mainly tourists and students tumbled out to gasps of amazement at the pristine white building, its sumptuous well-ordered gardens and divine panoramic views.

Wayne pulled a card out of his wallet:

Professor Angela Ryan
Director of Celtic, Germanic and Scandinavian Studies.

Wayne hurried to the reception and enquiry desk and coughed politely to let the pretty, young, Californian blonde receptionist know that he was there. She looked up and smiled pleasantly, almost blinding Wayne with teeth so even, straight and white that they took the breath away.

"I have an appointment with Professor Ryan, young lady." Wayne mumbled in his best Galway accent, whilst wondering when he would see the pretty receptionist in some blockbuster movie, as she just had to be an actress in waiting.

"Why sure, I'll call her for you and let her know that you're here, mister......?"

She gushed.

"Finnegan." Wayne lied. "Professor Finnegan."

The girl smiled, flashing her atomic teeth again:

"If you'd just like to wait over there, Professor, I'm sure she'll be along in a moment. Be sure to have a nice day now."

Wayne nodded courteously:

"Oh I intend to, miss, I intend to."

He stepped over towards a huge glass window and looked out at the sun soaked vista. When the Americans built museums they certainly do a good job, he thought. Even more impressive was the fact that there was another museum in Malibu that had been built to resemble a Roman Villa in Herculaneum and that was where all the Graeco-Roman treasures were housed. He shook his head in awe.

"Incredible isn't it?" The soft woman's voice took Wayne by surprise.

"Ah, it is, so it is to be sure." He stammered as he turned to face a handsome red haired woman of around fifty, her eyes were as green as polished emeralds. She held out her hand:

"Angela Ryan. You must be Professor Finnegan."

Wayne was almost lost for words. The woman's striking good looks had caught him totally off guard. Like the receptionist, her teeth were whiter than fresh mountain snow:

"Call me Michael." He blurted, almost forgetting his accent.

The woman grinned:

"It's good to hear someone from the old country."

She gently touched Wayne's elbow.

" Come, we'll go and see the swords that you were interested in and I've a few other little surprises for you. Did you have a good trip over, Professor?"

Wayne raised his bushy white eyebrows and allowed his imagination to race.

"Oh, wonderful." He stated dreamily. "Just wonderful."

Wayne followed Angela Ryan down a long well lit corridor and into a laboratory that seemed cleaner than the average operating theatre. Two assistants in white lab coats were busy peering down microscopes.

"I might have misheard you, Professor." Wayne did his best to sound like a bumbling stuffy, Irish academic, "but you referred to swords in the plural. It was my belief that it was just the one sword that the Getty museum obtained from Dublin."

Professor Ryan laughed:

"Goodness me no. We bought ten from the National Museum in Dublin. Some were in an awful state and we have done what we can to preserve the fabric of what remains, but there are three that are in quite remarkable condition considering their antiquity. Lenny, if you don't mind?"

One of the lab-coated technicians pulled a tray out from a drawer in front of Professor Ryan and placed it carefully on a table. The tray had a glass cover and below it, Wayne could see the rusty remnants of what had been three iron swords. Professor Ryan handed Wayne a pair of clear thin rubber surgical gloves and pulled a pair over her own hands.

"These are the best three. As you can see, no disrespect, but we are doing a much better job of looking after them than the previous owners."

Her voice was edged in sarcasm as she gave Wayne an admonishing glance, which melted into a smile:

"And we did acquire them totally legitimately, professor. I have all the relevant paperwork, if you would care to see it."

Wayne shook his head as the Professor, aided by the technician, lifted the lid off the tray.

"No, that won't be necessary." He muttered as his eyes widened at the sight of the barely recognisable strips of pitted orange metal.

He had no idea which of the three, if any, was the sword of Gorias.

"Mmmm." He mumbled as he carefully lifted and examined each sword in turn. He could feel professor Ryan flinch every time he touched the swords, even though he was trying to be extremely careful.

"They are very, very fragile." She whispered. Wayne nodded:

"I know." He stated simply. "I have a great deal of experience in handling such weapons."

There was no magical reaction to his touch as there had been with the Spear of Finias. He placed each sword carefully back on the soft plastic base, then quickly glanced around the room to see if there were any cameras. There was nothing to suggest a security system in view. Wayne heaved a covert sigh of relief. He knew he needed to touch each sword with his bare skin as he suspected that the rubber gloves were preventing any magical energy from his body getting to the weapon to restore it.

Professor Ryan laughed. It was a lovely sound, like a tiny tinkling bell.

"Sometimes, I like to fantasise, in my wilder moments, that one of these is the Sword of Gorias." She giggled self consciously, like a little girl.

"I mean wouldn't that be just so awesome though?"

Wayne smiled indulgently.

"You know of the treasured weapons of the Tuatha de Danaan?"

Professor Ryan looked slightly hurt:

"Of course I do. I read Lady Gregory and Yeats when I was still at school in Ennis."

Wayne raised his eyebrows:

"So you are actually Irish yourself, then?"

Professor Angela Ryan scowled at him:

"Red hair, green eyes and Ryan as a surname. You don't think I'd be German now, do you?"

Wayne gulped:

"No I'm sorry, I just thought, you know, you might have Irish ancestry, but that you might have been born here."

He surreptitiously pulled off one glove then slipped a ring off his finger and allowed it to fall to the ground.

"Oh bother!" he exclaimed loudly. Both Professor Ryan and the technician bent down to pick up the aged academic's ring, while Wayne with his free hand quickly touched each of the three swords with a naked finger. Nothing happened.

"Why, thank you. That's very kind." He gasped as professor Ryan handed him his ring.

"And the other swords?" Wayne suggested.

Professor Ryan nodded at the technician who walked over to his colleague and the two of them pulled another tray out of drawer adjacent to where he was working.

Professor Ryan strolled over to the tray:

"These are not such good specimens, in fact some are hardly discernible as swords at all."

Wayne shrugged.

"It is not the current condition that interests me, so it's not."

The technicians lifted the lid off the tray. Wayne peered in. The professor had been right to say that some were hardly discernible as swords. Two looked like little more than rust stains on the white silk. Wayne sighed.

"Excuse me, but do I have something in my eye?" he cried as though something had just hit him on the eyeball.

Professor Ryan and the two technicians all turned as a single body to look at him and Wayne's eyes caught all three of them in a fraction of a second:

"You will not remember this. You will sleep until I ask you to wake." He commanded, in a voice that seemed to come from someone else entirely.

Wayne touched each sword quickly with the end of his index finger. By the time he got to the fifth of the seven, he was beginning to despair. The fifth sword was little more than a thin rusted strip of iron no more than a foot long, with an unrecognisable lump of metal where the pommel had been and a fragile black stick where there had once been a hilt.

It was therefore with more than a little shock that Wayne recoiled as though an electric current had just passed through him as soon as he touched the pommel. He instinctively rushed his finger to his lips.

"Jumping Jehoshaphat." Wayne exclaimed with a whistle as he reached down and gently picked up the remnants of the sword. The light in the room suddenly seemed to grow incredibly intense and Wayne could feel energy flowing down his arm and out through his hand. He watched open mouthed as the sword slowly reformed, section, by section, from the edge of the pommel to the tip of the blade. The two foot long blade now shone like freshly burnished glass and the handle had recovered and reformed itself in thick brown leather. The hand guard and the pommel were both leafed in gold. The mighty sword of Gorias looked as though it had just come off the blacksmith's anvil, fresh, new and hungry for the blood of its enemies.

Wayne, suddenly feeling quite exhausted, morphed back into his own shape. He clicked his fingers and asked Professor Ryan alone to wake.

Professor Ryan regained consciousness with a start:

Wayne spun the sword in his hand:

"Behold, the sword of Gorias is whole again." He shouted and held sword above his head.

It was the turn of Professor Angela Ryan's mouth to drop open.

"Who the hell are you?" She demanded.

Wayne grinned.

"Angela, I am he who you saw as Professor Michael Finnegan. We are living in strange times, Professor. I'm afraid I need to borrow this. I already have the spear of Gorias and the stone of Falias. Now my collection is complete, for I have no need of a magical cauldron."

Professor Ryan rubbed her eyes in disbelief.

"Either you're kidding, I'm dreaming, or I've gone stark raving mad."

She glanced at the tray of ancient swords and noticed that the fifth was missing.

"How......how did you? How did it?"

Her mouth began to move but no sound came out.

Wayne smiled.

"No, you are not dreaming nor are you mad and I am not kidding. This is real. I am Michael, son of Aillen Mac Fionnbharr. I am the last of the mighty Tuatha de Danaan. I am the "Slanaitheoir Mor.""

Professor Angela Ryan stepped back and took a deep breath.

"Get outta here." She gasped.

Wayne swung the sword as though in imaginary combat.

"This is weird." He exclaimed.

"I can feel the sword. I can feel it as though it is a part of my arm. It feels so light."

Professor Ryan shook her head.

"May I ask why you need to borrow a three thousand year old sword?" She asked.

"I mean aren't there better swords out there, or is it just a rarity kick that you're acting on. Are you going to hold the sword to ransom?"

Wayne shrugged:

"No, I will be returning it. If I succeed, that is. If I don't, you probably won't care too much about swords and archaeology any more."

Angela looked confused.

"Are you going to fight someone with it?" She asked.

Wayne laughed for a moment:

"Indeed! I have a bone to pick with a certain would be Messiah."

Professor Angel Ryan closed her eyes:

"Maybe if I click my heels together three times."

"You'd only end up in Kansas." Wayne laughed.

He put the sword in his battered old leather briefcase:

"I swear I will return it before next year's first new moon. If I succeed, that is. Good-bye Angela Ryan. I just had to tell you all this stuff because you're Irish, but that's it, I'm afraid."

The two technicians had not even blinked. Professor Ryan shook her head. Wayne touched her forehead.

"Forget." He commanded then he stepped back and clicked his fingers, you will all awake in five minutes and you will not remember the fifth sword. I bid you all a nice day and thank you very much."

Wayne Higginbotham bowed and disappeared into thin air.

A couple of minutes later one of the metal detecting security devices went off for no apparent reason and a couple of minutes after that, a middle aged man climbed on the tram to return to the parking lot. He patted the battered old briefcase that he clutched on his knee. A brown leather hilt was sticking out of the open case.

Wayne Higginbotham was now fully armed and that wasn't all.

In a few hours he was due to meet his twin sister for the very first time in his life. She was alive and well and on her way to Los Angeles. Colm had rung Terri the previous evening, saying that a strange woman had just wandered into his bar claiming to be Terri's missing baby.

Terri had been rendered speechless, so Wayne had asked to speak to the woman knowing that his telepathic conversation must have worked and that she had followed his instructions to get to Colm's pub. He had saved her life just as she had once saved his.

It was all coming together.

Wayne Higginbotham had known such elation before, however. He remembered the euphoria he had felt when his Uther plan had succeeded and Sabine had made him the happiest man on the planet.

This time Wayne would not allow success to go to his head. There was much to do and greater challenges to face than he had ever faced before.

Wayne Higginbotham's third and final trial was going to be the greatest challenge of them all and given his age, it was more than likely that he would fail.

Luca Vitalia was a hundred times more dangerous than Francisco Pizarro and a thousand times more evil than Pierre de Feren. Even so, he would savour his current success and enjoy the moment.

Forty-One

Luca Vitalia was not in a good mood. In fact he was in what could only be described as a totally vile mood. He had managed the interview brilliantly, but his demeanour with Dean and Aurelio was in marked contrast to the charm he had displayed to the host of the D.J Cannon show.

"He don't wanna go to Rome." Aurelio worriedly whispered to his cousin Dean.

"It reminds him of when he was a kid and his Momma and all that stuff."

Dean shrugged:

"If the Pope anoints him as the "Son of God," then the election is a shoe in. Who's gonna stand against Our Lord Jesus Christ, for God's sake?"

The cousins and the disgruntled Presidential candidate were standing in the VIP lounge at JFK airport in New York City, waiting for the flight to Los Angeles. Dean was flying home for a brief visit, while Aurelio and Luca were just seeing him off.

Luca poured himself a glass of red wine, wandered off and sat down sulkily. Neither Dean, nor Aurelio had the courage to ask him what the matter was. They assumed that he'd just had a bad day and that he would soon be his normal arrogant, confident self again.

Luca stared at the wine and brooded miserably. He should have killed the woman. He could have just blown the bathroom door aside and killed her long before the cops arrived. He could have blown up the whole damned block. Yet for some unfathomable reason, he had waited and his vacillation had resulted in her survival. He could, of course, have killed all the cops and then taken care of the woman, but that would have incurred unnecessary risk.

Luca snorted, he had already incurred more than enough unnecessary risk by allowing himself to indulge in his personal fantasies. How stupidly weak had he been?

All he had to do was to wait until he had been accepted as the Messiah and had taken the Presidency, then he would be able to indulge in his secret sadistic whims to his heart's content. But oh no, he had decided to have a little bit of fun with the wife of one of his acolytes and managed to put his lifetime's work in jeopardy.

He had always been so good, so careful to maintain his good image, why had that woman intrigued him so much, that he had been prepared to risk everything to humiliate and destroy her? She was just the middle-aged wife of a stupid lawyer. Why did he have such a desire to subjugate her and then eliminate her and any evidence that she had ever existed?

Luca pondered on the fact that the woman was of Irish fairy stock, although she had clearly appeared ignorant of the fact. Could his feelings towards her be the result of a natural warning system, deep within his psyche? Maybe this woman was the enemy that had been sent to destroy him? Luca had been totally convinced that the person he had terrorised years ago had been a male. Maybe he had been wrong. If this woman was the supposed "Saviour" that had been prophesied, then that would explain his reactions. It would explain why he hadn't just wanted to kill her, but had been determined to torture and humiliate her.

As he sat and railed at himself over his own lack of foresight and discipline, Luca failed to notice the concerned glances of his adoptive father and uncle and the various members of his team.

Jonathan T. Sherman was not amongst them. He had stayed at home after his wife had stormed out when he had declared his disbelief in her accusation that Luca had tried to rape and murder her.

Luca half smiled when he recalled Sherman's anguished phone call:

"I think my wife's had a breakdown." He had moaned, "she's hallucinating."

Luca shook his head. Sherman hadn't even remembered that Luca had accompanied him home that morning.

Luca frowned.

Luca had made sure none of the phones in the apartment had worked, even the cells. So how had the cops found out that something untoward was happening?

The more Luca thought about it, the angrier he got.

Angry with himself, angry with Lucy Sherman, angry with the NYPD.

"You OK, Luca?" Dean's voice disrupted Luca's train of thought.

He looked up at his Uncle and glowered.

Dean Vitalia nearly wet himself when Luca looked up at him. He had never seen his cherubic, handsome nephew look so menacing. In fact he had never seen anyone look so menacing:

"I'm going to get my flight, I'll see you in Rome. Take care, Luca." Dean stammered before turning and scurrying off to the departure gate as fast as his legs would carry him.

Luca stared at Dean's back until he had disappeared.

Why were his people such losers? Luca wondered.

Except for his father, of course.

He had chosen Aurelio Vitalia to be his guardian long before his "human" birth. The Vitalias were good at what they did. Aurelio was as slippery and devious, as he was evil.

That was all Luca had needed, someone who, quite simply, did not get caught. Someone who could protect him far better than the pious sanctimonious bores of the "Sacred Order of St. Gregory."

Luca allowed himself a moment of inner triumphalism as he recalled the way he had hunted down even the most covert members of the "Order," simply by invading their minds. That was what he would do to the Sherman woman and she would not shut him out this time. He smirked as he remembered how easy he had found it to kill off O'Leary and D'Abruzzo and all the rest. He would invade her mind, just like he had theirs and ensure that she killed herself before she could convince anyone that maybe Luca Vitalia was not what he was purported to be.

Aurelio looked at his adopted son as he re entered the lounge having just seen off his cousin. Luca was actually smiling again. Aurelio sighed contentedly. In a few days the Pope himself would join those who had recognised Luca as being the second coming. His adopted son would then go on, take the Presidency and would eventually rule the world. Aurelio Vitalia would be at his side all the way and would savour every moment of having absolute power over mankind. Aurelio licked his podgy lips as he contemplated some of the indulgencies that he could engage in. He mopped his brow with a handkerchief. He was going to have so much so much fun when his adopted son ruled the entire world.

Luca waited until the following day to make his move on Lucy Sherman. Luca, Aurelio and their core group had gone back to the house in New England to prepare for the trip to Rome. Luca had said that he needed some time alone, so he went off for a rest in his old room. He lay back on his bed, closed his eyes and concentrated. He was aware of billions of life forces, he skimmed over them until he could feel her presence, her individuality. It was so much easier than seeking the Priests had ever been. At least he had met Lucy Sherman and did not have to delve into her thoughts to identify her. He just knew where she was. Ah, yes, she was on a plane, he could feel that. Where was she going, he wondered, before attempting to enter her mind? Oh yes, this was going to be so easy. He would make her have a fit and attempt to hi-jack the plane and hopefully he could kill everyone on board. That would be such fun.

Now he could visualise her in his mind's eye. He could feel her terror:

214

"Hello Lucy." He grinned.

Forty-Two

Special Agent Henry T. Burgermeister drummed his fingers on the steering wheel of his car as he sat on the suburban street watching the house. He had been sat there all night and had not slept a wink. Special Agent Henry T. Burgermeister was a professional.

He always worked alone and like the Mounties up in Canada, he always got his man.

Usually, however, he knew what they'd done, how dangerous they were and what risks he was undergoing in tailing and nailing them. He knew diddley squat about this Higginbotham guy, other than that he had been ordered to stay on his tail and let his boss know who he met and what he did, especially if anything suspicious happened.

The sun was quite high in the sky by the time a little old man with a shock of white hair emerged from the house. Burgermeister slipped a pair of binoculars from his door pocket and peered through them. The old man looked to be at least seventy as he arthritically struggled into Higginbotham's Ford rental car.

"Huh, bet he hasn't paid for extra users." Burgermeister sneered under his breath.

He didn't like Europeans. The Brits were all either hooligans with shaven heads, or toffee nosed snobs who looked down on Americans as though they were culturally and aesthetically bereft. The French were rude, smelly and cowardly. The Germans, arrogant and bombastic. The Poles were stupid, Russians and Italians were all crooks in Armani suits and the Irish were drunkards. They were all damned communists and atheists and none of them were capable of obeying the law.

The old man drove off down the street towards the Topanga Canyon Boulevard. Burgermeister put his binoculars away as a young mother walked past pushing a stroller. She cast the Special Agent a wary glance as one of her toddlers pointed at a huge Christmas Santa on one of the rooftops.

It looked like Higginbotham was catching up on his sleep. Burgermeister pursed his lips. He could wait. He waited when he fished. He waited when he hunted. At least he didn't have to ring his wife and explain why he hadn't been home or why he would be late for dinner. She'd left him years ago.

The hours passed. The sun climbed high in the sky and Burgermeister began to doze as the car got uncomfortably warm.

Suddenly, however, he snapped back into full alertness as the woman he presumed to be Mrs Terri Thorne left the house.

Burgermeister's research had said that she had been a movie star and it was apparent that she still had the look of a beautiful woman. The Special Agent waited until her car had disappeared before he climbed out of his own car. He placed his Ray-Bans carefully on his nose and looked around. The street seemed empty so he quickly crossed the road to the house he had seen Higginbotham enter so may hours earlier. He pressed the doorbell and waited. He would just act when the limey answered the door. He would just claim he was looking for someone in the area, but Special Agent Henry T. Burgermeister wanted to get a feel for the man who had almost escaped him the previous day. He wanted to look him in the eye and see what made him tick.

There was no sound of movement inside the house.

Burgermeister frowned, stepped back and looked up at the dormer windows of the second storey. The drapes were all open.

The Special Agent looked around again and then slipped through a gate at the side of the house, pulling his black leather gloves on as he sneaked quietly down the side of the yard.

The house appeared comfortable, but modest, for someone who had once been a movie star. Burgermeister peered through a window that looked into a modern stainless steel kitchen, with its typical huge American fridge and a shiny hooded range. There was no sign of anyone in the house.

The back door was locked but Burgermeister pulled a tool from his pocket, slipped it into the lock and turned the handle. The door opened quietly and easily. He had no idea how he was going to explain himself if he bumped into the Brit, but he knew he would think of something. The FBI man tiptoed silently across the kitchen floor and then through into the hall, peeking into each room as he passed to the stairs. All the rooms were tidy and well furnished, but there was absolutely no sign of the Brit.

A quick inspection of the three bedrooms and their en suite bathrooms, proved that Higginbotham had managed to leave the house without being noticed. Burgermeister examined the Brit's bag. Nothing but underwear, socks and shirts. What the hell was going on?

How had he gotten out of the house without Special Agent Henry T. Burgermeister noticing?

Burgermeister shook his head and carefully replaced everything as he had found it. Within seconds he was back out in the yard, sneaking quietly up the gate and meticulously checking to see if anyone had noticed him, before he nonchalantly crossed the road back to his car.

Special Agent Henry T. Burgermeister bit his lip as he pulled his cell from his pocket.

This was the second time that he'd lost Higginbotham and there was no way he could disguise his failure this time. He had absolutely no idea how he been given the slip or where the Brit might now be. As he dialled the number, he just hoped that the guy wasn't a terrorist, or whatever. If half of L.A. blew up because he'd let some British nobody outsmart him, well he'd, he'd.......

"Whaddya mean your man lost him?" Walter Wickert the Third barked down the phone as he heard his immediate subordinate try to explain what had happened.

"When Baring hears about this, he's gonna roast my ass." He moaned as he waved his secretary away before she had even passed through the glass-panelled door.

"So I thought you were gonna put your best man on this job?"

Wickert listened carefully as the FBI officer explained how his best man: Special Agent Henry T. Burgermeister had carefully stalked the British guy, Higginbotham, all the way from the airport to his mother's house in the valley and had then spent endless hours watching the property. The Brit had not emerged at any point. Burgermeister had reported that an old man with a shock of white hair had taken Higginbotham's rental car and had not returned it, but he had insisted that there was absolutely no way that he could have been Higginbotham in disguise.

Wickert sighed: "And what makes him so damn sure?"

The FBI officer explained that Burgermeister had gotten a good look at the old man and even the best prosthetic make up could not have achieved such convincing results.

"Does this Burgerjoint dude not watch movies?" Wickert demanded angrily.

"They can do anything these days. His mother was in the movies for Christ's sake. Has he taken any action to establish whether Higginbotham is still in the house?"

There was a momentary embarrassed silence.

"Well?" Wickert shouted.

Burgermeister's superior coughed and then related how his best Special agent had approached the house as soon as Mrs. Thorne had left. He had knocked on the door, to no avail, and had then checked through some of the windows. There had been no sign of anyone in the house. Eventually, despite a lack of a warrant, he had gained entrance and checked the entire home. It had been totally devoid of renegade Brits, or anything else of note.

"So is he still there? Who is on the case now?" Wickert asked as patiently as he could manage, which still came out as little more than an angry growl.

The FBI man explained that Burgermeister had left the scene to rest and had been replaced by two Special agents, who had been briefed to maintain a 24/7 vigil and let Burgermeister and his boss know as soon as Higginbotham turned up back at the house.

"Do we pull the mother in when she returns?" The subordinate asked hopefully.

"On what grounds?" Wickert snapped: "For having a Brit as a son?

No leave them be for now. Just watch them. In fact just watch him. As far as Baring is concerned there is no proven link yet between this Higginbotham guy and Vitalia's Presidential campaign. That is very much an as yet, though."

Wickert put the phone back on its receiver. Higginbotham hadn't committed any crime in the US, indeed as far as the British authorities were aware he hadn't even committed any crimes in his homeland. There was still no progress on the Giametti incident. So why was Jack Baring so keen to keep tabs on him? Walter Wickert stared out of his window at the sun soaked street below. Even in December, L.A. was still one of the finest places to be.

Wickert scratched his head and shrugged. He had more pressing matters, than worrying about some schmuck that Baring seemed to have taken a disliking too, like getting his wife a Christmas present. Whatever they suspected this Higginbotham of, he was in far more danger from his wife than from Baring, or a Brit.

Forty-Three

Wayne had been extremely disappointed to find that Dean was not home when he had called. He had driven to the old house, 2145 Coldwater Canyon Boulevard, straight from the Getty Museum. His intention had been to "strike while the iron was hot and exact swift retribution for the attack on Wayne and his family that Deano had instigated.

According to Dean's obscenely young new girlfriend, he was only due back that evening, having been in New York with Luca.

"They're going to Rome, that's Rome, Italy, on Friday." She had informed the supposed young swimming pool salesman with the cute English accent at the door.

"Really?" Wayne had answered with more than an edge of sarcasm.

"Italy, as opposed to?"

The girl had chewed thoughtfully on her gum, sleek blonde hair shining magnificently in the afternoon sunshine, pneumatic boobs trying to push out of her tight, white Tee shirt.

"I think there's a Rome in Georgia." She pontificated, then beamed triumphantly and widely at Wayne, who had almost been blinded by her perfect straight dazzling white teeth.

"Ah." Wayne replied: "I'll, er pop back tomorrow then."

The girl pushed a tanned hand back through her hair.

"Ah'm looking forward to it already." She breathed huskily, before breaking into laughter.

"Though I guess you won't have much luck. Dean's already got a real nice pool."

Wayne smiled patiently.

"I know, but I've got the latest in fashionable European pools. I'll be back."

With that Wayne strolled back to the Ford and slumped into the driver's seat.

His thoughts turned to the impending arrival of his sister.

"My God, how weird did that sound?" Wayne muttered to himself.

"My Sister and I'm not referring to Marina."

The Ford wound its way up Coldwater Canyon, back towards the Valley and eventually Wayne stopped by the side of the road.

He climbed out of the rental car and ambled across the tarmac to a fence that overlooked a small drop to a tinkling stream. It was weird to see water in one the canyons. It had usually been summer when he had visited his mother and the Canyons had always been brown and parched, the streambeds dusty and dry. Now the canyon was bathed in glorious shades of green and the stream twinkled gaily in the sunlight.

Wayne loved the Californian climate. At home right now it would be a freezing grey morning. The trees would be skeletal and bare and the roads filthy from yesterday's freezing, slushy rain.

The kids were about to finish school for the Christmas holidays and everything would be winding up towards Christmas. Wayne had hardly thought of Christmas since the supposed policemen had called at the house and galvanised him into action. He hoped that he would be able to make it home for the festivities, but a nagging doubt seemed to be telling him that he would not be there. He missed Natalia and the kids and hoped that if anything untoward did happen to him then they would be OK.

He looked up at the brown canyon walls and to the brilliant blue sky above, criss-crossed by the vapour trails of planes taking loved ones home to their families for the holidays.

Wayne strolled along the roadside and then sat on a large rock to enjoy the sunshine.

He wondered about his sister, what she would be like, whether he would like her and vice versa.

It was hard to conceive that they had shared the same womb for nine months and had not seen each other in the more than forty years since they had exploded into the world.

Wayne smiled. When he had been reunited with his birth mother he had been shocked to find her stunningly beautiful. That was one compliment he had never been able to pay Doris Higginbotham.

Doris had raised him well, he owed her and Frank just about everything, but she could never, ever have been described as beautiful. Wayne wondered if his sister would resemble Terri. He wondered if she had the ears and laughed, covering his mouth so that the occupants of a passing car didn't think he was mad.

Wayne wondered what her life had been like. She had sounded very posh when he had spoken to her the previous evening on the phone. He sort of remembered thinking that the voice he had heard in his head, when De Feren had been trying to murder him in Cavendish Street, had been very southern and posh, but that had been different to a real voice. Well one thing was for sure, he had no regrets about his life. Doris and Frank had done their best for him. They hadn't had much, as Doris had always moaned, but what they'd had was his. He had had a distant relationship with his real Mom, not surprising since they lived on opposite sides of the Atlantic Ocean, but they got on extremely well and had the same sense of humour. The fact that they had been reunited when he was still a young boy had helped Terri to get over the fact that the child she had surrendered as a tiny baby was no longer cute and cuddly. Wayne wondered how Lucy and Terri would bond. Was it possible for a forty odd year old woman to bond with a woman over sixty?

Wayne smiled again when he thought of the risks that he and Frank had taken in ensuring that his reunion with Terri remained a secret as far as Doris was concerned. Letters were hidden, the rare phone call arranged weeks in advance. Wayne's old headmistress had colluded in the conspiracy and Doris had never found out about the reunion, although she had had her suspicions. When Frank had died, Wayne had really struggled to keep the secret and little Katie had once almost totally blown things when she had asked Doris why daddy had two (Wayne and Natalia's eyes had grown as wide as saucers as they imagined her next word, fortunately the child had been smarter than they had credited)........bunnies?

Doris would have hated Terri on sight and the jealousy would have been unimaginable. Doris had been unbelievably envious of her sister, Margaret Houghton-Hughes, just because she was a bank manager's wife, so the glamorous, young Hollywood actress would have been her ultimate anathema. Poor old Doris.

Wayne wondered if Lucy's adoptive parents were still alive and how they would react to the reunion, if she ever told them. If they were very old and opposed to her knowing her roots, such a shock could be fatal.

He watched an enormous buzzard drift lazily on the breeze. It reminded him of the Red Kites at home. It was a magnificent sight as it wheeled over the rocks and disappeared.

Wayne grimaced. He was probably more nervous about meeting Lucy than he was about dealing with the Vitalias. He had had thirty odd years to prepare for the latter. Lucy, he had deemed to be little more than a figment of his adolescent imagination and someone he would never see or hear from again, until the flight over to L.A.

Now he was going to meet her at last and it scared him out of his wits.

He climbed into the Ford and set off back up the Canyon. The next few hours and days were going to be nothing if not spectacular.

Forty-Four

Lucy felt more confused than she had ever felt in her life. She was sat in an aeroplane that was travelling in totally the wrong direction. Before the events in Los Angeles and then the subsequent horror of the previous day in New York, she had fully been expecting to be on a London bound flight, looking forward to an emotional reunion with her twins. Now, instead, she found herself sitting on a westbound flight, hurtling towards a meeting with her natural mother and her own twin brother.

Lucy had rung her mother from the New York airport hotel, that she had spent the night in and arranged for Melinda to pick up Jon Junior and Jemima from Pangfield College and to take them back to Jersey until she arrived. Melinda had readily agreed. She was always desperate to help in any way she could with her Grandchildren, despite Rupert's all too evident grumpiness and general state of irritation, whenever his American Grandbrats, as he contemptuously referred to them, arrived.

Lucy's mind was in turmoil. In the space of what seemed little more than a few weeks, she had lost her husband to a cult, she had lost her job because of her husband and she had lost her peace of mind, having almost been raped and murdered. The one good thing, at least potentially, was that she had found her birth family. Not that she had been actively looking for them, of course. That would have been far too scary.

She had taken that one journey to some market town in Yorkshire, while she had been up at Oxford, in the vain hope of finding something relating to her supposed brother. She thought back to a student from up North, Martin Berenger was it?

Whatever, the whole thing had proven to be a total waste of time and she had gone on to forget all about the small market town in the Dales, with its splendid wide cobbled boulevard of a main street, its castle and medieval church. She had also forgotten about her dream of the boy in the burning building, until Luca Vitalia tried to assault her in her own apartment.

Lucy sipped on her Diet Cola as she stared out of the airplane window. Far below a solid bank of cloud obscured the immense flat prairies of the mid-west. The clouds looked like an immense sea of cotton wool with huge waves rising and falling. Lucy loved the sea. She had been so lucky to be raised by the Hetheringtons. Jersey was such a lovely place, especially St. Ouen and Rupert and Melinda had been the most splendid parents. Their circumstances could best have been described as comfortable, perhaps even reasonably opulent. The family had been lucky enough to have a cook, Ginny, a chauffer, Brown and a gardener, Mr Le Clerc. They had had a Bentley when she had been small, which had proven to be far too big for the island's narrow roads, but had come into its own when they had crossed to Britain or France. They had then gone on to have several Range Rovers and a rather lovely yacht that daddy kept in St. Helier.

Lucy had been quite spoiled, even she would have admitted to that. She had always had everything she had wanted. A smile crossed her face when she thought back to her stumpy little first pony, Norbert and then her favourite: Flick. God, she had loved that horse. She could see the paddock with its white picket fencing and the row of weeping willows by the little brook, where she had spent endless days in long forgotten summer vacations, simply riding all day. She remembered sunny afternoons on the beach and copious amounts of fresh Jersey ice cream.

Then there had been that awful night in Roedean, when she had been caught on the phone long after lights out. She had been quite unable to provide any sort of credible explanation and the house-mistress had assumed that she had been on the phone to a boyfriend and was, to put it crudely, lying through her teeth.

That little incident had, of course, led to the revelation about the circumstances of her birth.

She thought back to the day when daddy had first told her that she had been adopted. She had been sixteen and had been at home in Jersey for an exeunt weekend. The family had just sat down to dinner when Rupert had coughed apprehensively:

"Mummy and I have something terribly important that we've been meaning to tell you poppet. We were going to wait until you were eighteen." Rupert had blathered on, stammering and spluttering nervously. He had mentioned the recent incident at school, when Lucy had initially insisted to her house-mistress that she had been telepathically contacted by "a twin brother" in the middle of the night, to explain why she had been caught making a telephone call after lights out. Eventually, he had finally admitted that Lucy had been adopted and might therefore have a brother and that she had been specially chosen because "Mummy couldn't have babies." Lucy had fainted on the spot.

It had not been until just before she had gone up to Oxford that Rupert had finally admitted that she did indeed have a twin brother. She smirked wistfully as she remembered the scene in Claridges:

"Look poppet." Rupert had whispered as he had held her hand:

"No time is a good time for this sort of thing, but we really did mean to tell you this when we told you about the adoption, but I suppose I lost courage when the news seemed to hit you so terribly hard."

Lucy remembered Melinda disappearing off to the powder room clutching a tissue.

"I do have a brother, don't I, daddy?" Lucy remembered interrupting her Father.

He had smiled sympathetically:

"Yes poppet, you do, in fact, ahem, the fact is, well, yes, you have a twin brother."

Well here she was, finally on her way to meet him and her birth mother. This time it was for real. That trip to Shepton, or whatever it was called, had been a token gesture that she thought she ought to make when she had found out from Martin Berenger that a town called Shepton really did exist.

Lucy remembered her fears at the time.

Was she the product of rape?

Would her birth mother remember having had her?

Would her birth mother want to see her?

Was her mother poor? An alcoholic? A criminal?

Was her brother a skinhead, or something similarly frightfully working class?

Would they like her?

Would she like them?

Did she look like mother, physically?

Would her brother resemble her?

Did they have the pointed ears?

Here she was, all these years later and despite the fact that she had talked briefly to both her natural mother and her twin, the previous evening and both had sounded quite articulate and pleasant, she still had most of the same fears. O'Brien's pub hadn't exactly made her feel confident about her birth family background.

The blanket of cloud below began to break up and the rolling brown hills of Nevada began to appear. Lucy accepted a glass of wine from a stewardess. She wondered how Jonju and Jemima would react to having new cousins. Her brother, Wayne, had mentioned that he had two children. Lucy grimaced: Wayne was not a particularly auspicious name.

Slowly her thoughts turned round to Jonathan. She wondered what he'd do now. He would probably go on and marry that P.R. tart, once the divorce was finalised. One thing was for sure, she would be damned if she would allow Jonju and Jemima to go to stay with them over vacations, not with that vile Luca Vitalia in the vicinity.

Lucy's eyes began to feel heavy. Fluffy white clouds passed rapidly by as Lucy began to drift off to sleep.

She was back home on Jersey. The sun was shining, a slight sea scented breeze was rustling the weeping willows and Flick was gambolling in the nearby paddock. She could see Brown washing the Range Rover. The sea was shining silver in the distance.

Why did she feel so cold?

Lucy turned and started to walk back towards the house. The sun faded and all of a sudden it went dark, as though a huge thundercloud had just blotted out the sun.

Lucy tried to run, but her legs felt like they had been cemented into iron blocks. That was when she noticed the dark figure walking purposefully towards her across the ornamental garden. As the figure got closer, the trees, which seconds before had been full of emerald green, luscious leaves waving in the breeze, were now empty, dark and skeletal. The flowers, that she had been able to see and smell just seconds earlier, had disappeared.

Lucy felt panic rising from the pit of her stomach.

The figure was now much closer, totally draped in black robes with a huge hood, so obscuring that no face could be seen. The figure stopped just yards away from her:

"Hello Lucy." It leered.

Lucy knew that voice.

"You!" She gasped.

"Surprised are you?" The faceless figure asked, his voice sounded pleasant.

Lucy didn't answer.

"I think we have unfinished business, you and I." The robed figure gloated:

"Don't you?"

Lucy gulped. Somewhere in the background of her dream, Lucy could hear the hum of the plane:

"This isn't real." She thought to herself. "This is a dream. I am on a plane, not at home, this is not real."

She gritted her teeth and breathed deeply, forcing the panic to subside as she had been taught in her yoga sessions.

"So where did we get to?" The faceless figure queried before adding rapidly:

"Ah yes, the unwrapping of the sacrifice."

"Bugger off, you freak." Lucy shouted at the top of her voice and she charged at the figure that she knew was Luca Vitalia.

Somehow, knowing that he wasn't there physically, made her much more courageous.

She flung herself at the figure and screamed. The noise she emitted was a horrible, piercing wail. She had never heard anything like it. It was as though something left her body, a huge blast, as though all her insides had just blown a hole right through her chest. The figure gasped and then just crumpled, leaving nothing more than a pile of steaming black material on the ground.

Lucy awoke with a start. Her neighbouring passenger glanced over:

"Are you OK?" He asked:

"You look like you've just seen a ghost."

Lucy smiled weakly as she gasped for breath:

"Yes, I'm fine thank you." Her breath came in short bursts. She felt like she'd just run the New York City marathon. Down below she could see the vast bright sunlit expanse of the Mojave Desert. She could almost feel the warmth.

Lucy Hetherington felt much happier than she had in days. She had a strange feeling that somehow, inexplicably, she had just secured a second victory over Luca Vitalia.

After several weeks that Lucy would describe as the worst days of her life, Lucy Hetherington had just turned a corner and was beginning the long climb back to happiness.

The kids would be fine about the divorce.

Mummy and Daddy would rally round as they always did and her birth family would be just fine, she was sure of it.

Far away, in a grand house in New England, Luca Vitalia found himself lying on his bedroom carpet. He opened his eyes and gasped for breath. Overcome by acute embarrassment and rage.

So the Sherman woman was more powerful than he had expected. His instincts had been right the first time he had seen her. Twice now she had defied him.

No matter, he would deal with Lucy Sherman when he returned from Rome. He had not yet called upon anything like his true power. Many would pay for ridiculing Luca Vitalia, the doubters, the agnostics, the self-proclaimed atheists.

Only those who surrendered to his will and his every whim would survive the coming conflagration. Lucy Sherman would be one of the first to die and she would die slowly and horribly.

Forty-Five

"It'll be Ok! I swear." Carrie Vasquez patted her friend Terri's shoulder as the pair sat at the dining table in Carrie's house. She poured another glass of Pinot Noir for Terri, who was clearly as nervous as could be.

"Let's go outside. It's cool but pleasant." Carrie insisted:

"One thing about December, up here, at least it's clear."

Terri looked out over the San Fernando Valley. The snow capped mountains in the distance looked like they were auditioning for a picture postcard. Charlotte would be impressed, Terri hoped. She shook her head.

"I am definitely going to end up calling her Charlotte, Carrie, I just can't think of her as Lucy."

Carrie laughed:

"I am sure Lucy won't mind what you call her. You still call Wayne, Michael, when you're not thinking."

Terri looked indignant:

"Do I?" She asked and then laughed.

"Guess I do."

The two women looked out over the wonderful vista that Carrie's house provided.

"Do you miss him?" Carrie asked her friend.

Terri looked surprised:

"Who?"

"Wayne." Carrie whispered.

"You've never really seen that much of each other, you know, since you got back together."

Terri shrugged.

"I was always very careful not to try and take over. He had a mum and dad in England who loved him and were raising him well. I met his dad, he was a wonderful gentle man. I never met the mother, but I always thought of her as his mother. I don't really know how I thought of myself, at first. I guess I was still young and full of career ambition and I still wasn't quite ready to be his Mom. He was already a very grown up, articulate, well-spoken young Englishman, not the tiny baby that I'd given birth to."

She laughed, an ironic little snort of a laugh.

"Funny isn't it? Here I am about to meet my daughter who is in her forties and I still haven't totally bonded with her twin after nearly thirty years. I love him, don't get me wrong, you know. He's awesome as I'm sure Char…Lucy will be. It's just that I was there when Marco took his first step and I kissed his first bloody knee better and wiped his little butt. I saw Marina's first smile, her first word, her first giggle. I was there for them twenty-four seven. When they were ill, well, naughty or good. I was there.

When I first saw Michael…"

She snorted again.

"When I first saw Wayne, back at Daideo's. He was a stranger, somebody else's kid. No worse than that, he looked like his father, especially with those ears. Don't forget, I thought I'd had a nervous breakdown over that guy. I loved him immediately, as I'm sure I'll love Charlotte, Lucy, oh whatever!"

Carrie laughed.

"Keep practicing, you've got a few hours yet. What did she sound like on the phone?"

Terri sighed and took a sip of the wine:

"I guess that's another thing. When I first heard Michael's voice, Wayne's voice."

She slowly and calmly corrected herself:

"It was so alien. I mean I'm an Irish girl, but by then I considered myself almost a native New Yorker and this kid sounded like, you know, a Yorkshireman, a northerner. Char, Lucy sounds like the bloody Queen of England."

Carrie laughed so much she bent over and almost spilled her wine:

"Guess she went to a good home then."

Terri and Carrie laughed for a while and then Terri's face retook its previous pallor:

"What if she's hated me all these years? What if she's never forgiven me?"

Carrie pursed her lips and nodded.

"It's possible I guess. There are always those perfect paragons of virtue who swear that they could never surrender a child, whatever the circumstances. If she's had kids of her own I guess she could be one, but I doubt it, she wouldn't be coming if she was such a Goddamn prig. When I hear anyone say that I always think: yeah right, lady!"

Terri grimaced:

"I've never forgiven myself really, I guess. There isn't a day that goes by when I don't think I could have kept them?"

Carrie hugged herself.

"It's getting chilly out here. The sun's going down."

She turned to walk back into the house but Terri ignored the suggestion and walked to the yard wall. She leaned against it and watched the orange light and the lengthening shadows in the valley below.

"So many lives down there." She said almost mournfully.

"You know, for eleven years I looked at every baby, then every toddler and then every little boy, always wondering if, by some strange chance, that could be my son. I've done the same thing every day for more than four decades wondering if that baby, that girl , that woman could be my first daughter. It never, ever got any easier. That's the thing with adoption. You have a huge gaping hole in your life, someone called it the primal wound and no matter what happens it can never be truly healed."

Carrie nodded thoughtfully and sympathetically.

"Not even when you're reunited?"

Terri shook her head.

"No, not even then."

She turned away from the panorama spread out before her and looked her friend in the eyes:

"You know, when you give a baby away, you lose a big part of yourself. Even if you meet them again years later, you can never regain the time lost. It's like I said about Marcus and Marina, I was there for the first smiles, the steps, the words, the bloody knees. I cuddled them when they couldn't sleep, I hugged them when they did well at school and yes, I yelled at them when they were naughty. Someone else did that for Michael and for Charlotte. The people that you get back, whether it's after a year, eleven years or approaching fifty years are not the same people. They even have different names, so the wound is covered with a sort of sticking plaster, I guess, but it can never heal.

You get to see the photos and hear the stories but it's not like you were there."

Terri began to sob as she said the last few words and Carrie stepped over and hugged her.

Terri composed herself and laughed.

"Hey, this won't do. I'm crying and I haven't even met her yet."

Carrie smiled reassuringly.

"You are sort of lucky, you know, Terri. I know a couple of women who surrendered their babies and they've never seen them again. One woman actually found her daughter, but she just didn't want to know. They both told me that it was as bad for them as it was for me losing Jimmy. At least Jimmy and me had some good times and I have Aoibheall to remember him by. I guess I sort of got closure, but they can't do that. They know their babies are out there, every day, like you said they could be passing them in the street and they wouldn't even know. They can't mourn the living and they can't count them as dead."

Terri nodded:

"Yeah, at least I know that both of mine are alive and I guess I'm going to know what happened to Charlotte, just like I know what happened to Michael."

She shivered violently.

"You were right, it's getting real chilly out here, let's go inside."

The car headlights illuminated the kitchen window soon after Carrie and Terri had retreated into the warmth of the house. Both women knew that Miguel was away on business and that Marcus and Aoibheall were working late. So the anticipation and expectation built swiftly. Terri's eyes were wide and she felt nauseous. Carrie couldn't help feel almost as worried as her friend, the possible what if scenarios were innumerable. It was with an equal amount of relief and disappointment therefore, that both women sighed when Wayne walked through the door.

"Hi Mom, Carrie." He shouted.

He poked his head around the doorway into Carrie's living room, the two women were giggling like teenagers.

"She's not here yet, then?" Wayne enquired, his eyebrows raised expectantly. Terri stood to hug and greet her son as Carrie took a sip from her glass. Before she had completed her hugging, Terri started to laugh, Carrie spluttered her wine as she laughed out-loud.

Wayne looked bemused.

"Is it something I said?" He asked, hands raised in supplication.

Terri shook her head, her giggling was infectious and even Wayne cracked a smile.

"Your Mom just said as you walked through the door: Bloody hell, she looks exactly like Michael." Carrie informed him before both women dissolved into fits of laughter again.

More car headlights appeared in the kitchen window, beams of light illuminating the room in the gathering gloom. Wayne turned and looked out:

"Well, it seems we're going to find out what she looks like any second now. I guess that's her."

Outside a Buick rental car ground to a halt, a woman of average height climbed out and looked timorously towards the house. Wayne walked out of the door and approached her.

She was immaculately groomed considering she had just flown across the continental United States and had then driven for an hour.

Her hair was brown, fashionably cut to shoulder length. Even in the gathering darkness Wayne could see that her face was almost unlined. It was absolutely amazing; she looked so familiar, yet he knew he had never set eyes on her before. The shape of her face was reminiscent of his own and while her eyebrows had been perfectly shaped, her forehead and nose were like his had been in his teens. Even in the darkness Wayne could see that his sister was still beautiful.

"Lucy?" he asked timorously, in his best, poshest, "the name's Bond," telephone voice.

"Wayne?" She responded equally apprehensively. Then they began to walk slowly towards one another, slowly at first but then breaking almost simultaneously into a run that propelled them into each others arms and an embrace that both had dreamed about for many, many years. Lucy pushed Wayne back and stared into his eyes, just as their mother had so many years earlier.

"Oh my God, you have my eyes." She gushed, tears pouring from her own.

Wayne smiled:

"Ah, but have you got my ears?"

Lucy grinned and pulled her hair back. In the light pouring from the house, Wayne could see the dramatic points on the tips of her much smaller ears."

"They don't stick out like mine!" He moaned, pretending to pout his bottom lip sulkily.

"Daddy paid to have them pinned back when I was much younger." Lucy laughed.

"My nickname at school was Pixie."

The twins could see instantly that even after almost half a century of being apart that they were going to get along. Wayne offered to grab Lucy's bags.

"I guess I better introduce you to our Mom." He whispered.

He heard Lucy take a sharp intake of breath.

"I think you're going to be very surprised." He continued.

"Oh, by the way. Thanks for saving my life when I was sixteen."

Lucy shook her head:

"Until what happened with Luca Vitalia, I really thought that I'd dreamed that episode."

She said as she glanced at her brother.

"Thanks for saving my life too."

Wayne grinned sheepishly and walked to the trunk of the car to pick up his sister's bags. Natalia had been right about one thing; genetic sexual attraction was a very powerful force. Wayne Higginbotham had fallen head over heels in love with his sister the moment he'd clapped eyes on her.

"Must gain control." He muttered to himself as he slammed the trunk on Lucy's car.

"This isn't backwoods Alabama and falling in love with ones own genes is unutterably narcissistic and ten steps down the path to madness. Plus, Natalia would slap me!"

As he walked back round the car he could hear sobbing and there in the framed light of the doorway he saw that Terri Thorne had been reunited with her second and last missing child.

Wayne smiled and felt the warmth of a happy tear rolling down his cheek.

For one night at least, he could afford to relax and be the happiest man alive.

Forty-Six

Dean Vitalia had not given any thought to his girlfriend's report of the English Swimming pool salesman. If some limey schmuck wanted to waste his time trying to sell pools to people who already had them, then that was his problem. He had gone to bed almost as soon as he had got home and had slept like a log.

He had just one full day in Los Angeles before he was due back in Boston to link up with Luca and Aurelio for the trip to Rome and he intended to make the most of that day.

What was concerning Dean as he drove towards his office the next morning was his mid morning appointment. Luca had demanded that Dean forego his agency business so that he could dedicate his time to the presidential campaign.

Dean, however, had no such intentions. As far as he was concerned his business was his hobby. Sure, Luca would get a fair share of his time, but what he did as a Hollywood agent was fun, not work and right now he was going to be late because of the traffic on the Santa Monica Freeway. Dean Vitalia did not want to be late because he was scheduled to interview probably the hottest chick he had ever seen in his life and she had approached him to represent her interests.

Dean Vitalia lived to help out any Lady who needed him.

Dean's radio blasted out one of the latest hit sounds which he sang along too tunelessly as his car crawled along in the pool car lane, suddenly there was a break in the traffic and Dean accelerated away gleefully.

He pulled his new black Cadillac Escalade into the parking lot and strolled through the entrance doors whistling happily. Mason Rock, the new security guard greeted his boss with a smart salute and the pretty young receptionist smiled sheepishly as she remembered Dean's demands of her when she had had the gall to ask for a raise.

Dean took the elevator to his office and then spent almost half an hour with his Personal assistant reviewing his schedule and appointments. He glanced at his watch. It was nearly eleven, the aspiring actress was due any second.

"OK Jenn, that's enough." Dean purred as his P.A. poured him a small Scotch.

"Send Miss Beta in as soon as she arrives."

"Of course, Mr Vitalia." Jennifer Borne agreed as she replaced the cap on the bottle of Scotch and left Dean's office. Jennifer was the best

P.A. he had ever had and there had been seven since his previous best: Suzi. She had been a useless secretary, but a wonderful girl Friday.

"And I think to myself, what a wonderful world." Dean crooned as he gazed out of his window at the sun soaked cityscape outside. His desk intercom buzzed:

"Miss Beta, to see you sir." Jenn's calm voice informed her boss as he shimmied back to his desk.

"Send her right in, honey." Dean leered, then he sprayed his mouth with breath freshener.

The confident looking blonde strode into his office.

"Thanks for seeing me, Mister Vitalia. " She gushed.

"No problem, Miss Beta, in fact it's a pleasure." Dean responded, grinning from ear to ear: " Now, what can I get you to drink?"

The Ford rental car pulled into the parking lot and parked next to the black Escalade.

The door opened and Luca Vitalia climbed out. He pulled at the waist of his shirt to straighten it, tightened his tie, pulled his jacket on and marched briskly into the Vitalia Agency offices. Mason Rock, who's grandfather, Earl had worked for Mister Vitalia, almost fell off his chair:

"Mister Vitalia, m, m, Mister President, I mean sir." He stammered as the receptionist stared open mouthed.

"Top floor, I presume." Luca spoke without looking at either Mason or the receptionist.

"Yes, Sir, shall I inform Mr Vitalia?...."

"No, definitely not." Luca interrupted the young security man. He marched up the elevator pressed the button and disappeared without so much as another word.

"Wow, did you see that?" Mason Rock shook his head.

"That's what I love about L.A. You get to see everybody who is anybody, yes sir!"

Dean Vitalia was breathing very deeply and his tongue flicked across his thin, dry lips.

"Yes, please remove the rest. I need to see if you have any flaws." He instructed Alpha Beta as the young would-be actress stood confidently in front of his desk wearing nothing but her bra, pants and stiletto high-heeled shoes. She had just unclipped her bra strap when the door to Vitalia's office burst wide open and an extremely flustered Jennifer Borne rushed into the office followed by a very annoyed looking Luca Vitalia.

"I'm sorry Mr Vitalia but Mr Vitalia was very insistent."

The young secretary bumbled nervously as she caught sight of the semi-naked girl standing before Dean's desk. Luca pushed past her and glowered at Dean.

"So this is how you avoid scandal is it?"

He turned his gaze on to the budding actress who was clutching her unfastened bra to her chest. She looked at Luca, then Dean, nervously.

"Luca, I....." Dean, his face ashen, held up his hands as his mouth moved wordlessly.

Luca looked back at Miss Alpha Beta.

"Get out!" He whispered menacingly to the girl.

Alpha Beta urgently picked up her discarded clothes and scurried to the door, conveniently being held open by Jennifer, which she hurriedly slammed behind her as she left.

Dean shook his head:

"Luca, I just...."

Luca Vitalia held up his hand to silence his father's cousin.

"Do you think that by getting girls to take off their clothes in your office that you are respecting me?"

Before Dean could even begin to think of an answer, Luca continued:

"Do you think that by arranging hit men to go kill someone you had a domestic argument with, that you are respecting me?"

Luca watched Dean gulp nervously.

"So do you think that when some girl speaks to the tabloid press about the President elect's perverted second cousin, or whatever, that it isn't going to do me any harm?"

Dean shook his head:

"It was just one girl Luca, one girl, that's all and as for the other thing it wasn't a hit. I told Aurelio that our contact in London should just, you know, teach the guy a lesson. He's the son of my ex-wife and he really embarrassed me in Mexico at my own son's wedding. I mean really disrespected me."

Luca put his fists on his hips.

"So you did arrange, albeit via Aurelio, for Paulo Giametti to take revenge on Wayne Higginbotham."

Dean looked stunned.

"Who?" he asked before suddenly remembering Michael's adopted name.

"Oh yeah, well it wasn't meant to be a big deal. Anyway, how did you find out about it?"

Luca grinned:

"I am the Son of God, remember?"

Dean licked his lips again, this time out of nervousness, as opposed to pure, unadulterated lust.

" Oh yeah." He echoed: "I guess that means, you like, see everything."

Luca nodded as he walked around Dean's office to a carafe of wine and two crystal glasses on a tray:

"Everything I need to see." He muttered just loud enough for Dean to hear.

He poured himself a glass of white.

"So will you go after him again?"

Dean coughed: "I won't have time, we go to Rome tomorrow."

Luca Vitalia nodded.

"Oh no you're not."

Deano looked flabbergasted.

"What?"

Luca smiled at the older man sitting behind his huge desk.

"I just needed the confirmation that you were the source of the attack, my dear old step-Dad."

With that, Luca Vitalia's features slowly melted and changed into those of Wayne Higginbotham.

"Wh, who are, wh, wh, what are you?" Dean stammered as his ashen face turned even whiter.

Wayne Higginbotham shrugged:

"I am your deepest, darkest nightmare. I am James Malone." Wayne morphed into the form of his late friend.

"Remember Rosarito, Dean, old boy? Your confession in Mexico was most enlightening. I'll be betting that you told the thugs who murdered me "to just teach the guy a lesson" didn't you?"

James' Irish brogue assaulted Dean's memory as he recalled the visitation of the Irishman's ghost at the hotel in Mexico. James Malone's face merged back into that of Wayne Higginbotham.

"As for your question: what am I? I am the son of the last Prince of the immortal Tuatha de Danaan. I am the Slanaitheoir Mor, that's the great saviour to you and I am prophesied to bring down a Messiah, so they say. The "Sacred Order of St. Gregory" called me "God's Assassin." Funny, because we seem to have one, all of a sudden, don't we?"

Wayne watched as Dean's right hand slipped down towards a desk drawer.

"If you are thinking of pulling a gun out of that drawer, Dean, I have to say that I wouldn't recommend it. The last guy who pulled a gun on me now sleeps with the fishes as you gangster dudes say. Well no, actually that's wrong he fell forty storeys, or something and he missed the river, unfortunately, so I presume he sleeps with the dead pigeons."

Dean raised both hands above the surface of his desk so that Wayne could see them.

Wayne shook his head:

"You know Dean, I haven't liked you since you first married mom and tried to persuade her that having had a son adopted would be bad for her career and that she should forget that I ever existed. That really upset me."

Dean didn't say anything. His mouth was hanging open and his hands were still raised.

Wayne stroked his chin.

"So what now? You confessed to James' murder. You've as good as confessed to the attempt on my life. What am I going to do with you?"

He deliberately turned towards Dean's office window. From the corner of his eye he saw Dean quickly reach down and pull the gun from the drawer. Dean stood, his eyes wide:

"I don't know who you are, or what you are, but I will not allow you to interfere with Luca."

Before he had a chance to raise the gun, however, Wayne half turned, raised his hand and a bolt of pure energy lifted the man, who had once been Wayne's step-father off his feet.

"Oops." Wayne put a mocking finger to his mouth as he walked past the humungous desk to find Dean lying on his back gasping for breath. The gun was lying on the plush carpet just by Dean's hand. Wayne kicked it away.

"Tsk tsk. Silly old man." Wayne hissed.

"Come on, stand up. You have a call to make: A very important phone call. I have an early Christmas present for your little Protégé: Mister future President."

Wayne put his hand over Dean's forehead and closed his eyes. It had been over thirty years since Wayne had received the letter from his Mom, Terri, saying that Dean had advised her to stop seeing her son. If revenge was a dish best served cold then this was very cold indeed.

Some five minutes later, Dean Vitalia was sat at his desk holding the phone to his ear.

"You must come now. It is very urgent. Life or death." He droned in a peculiar robotic monotone.

"You and Luca must come, Aurelio. I need help."

He replaced the phone on the receiver as Wayne sat in a corner of his office and watched.

"Excellent!" Wayne declared.

"And those will be the last words you will ever utter. From now, from this moment henceforth, Dean Vitalia, you shall remain silent and your forked tongue shall speak no more lies. In one hour you will drive home and take to your bed. You will not remember my visit!"

Dean's eyes did not flicker nor did they register any emotion at all. Wayne had stripped his mind of all memory and knowledge just as Dean had stripped scores of aspiring actresses of their clothes and their dignity over several decades.

Wayne resumed the form of Luca Vitalia and marched confidently out of the office, whistling.

"One down." He muttered as walked out of the elevator and left the building. Mason Rock held the door open for him as he left.

"Good luck, Sir. I sure hopes you gets to be Mister President and brings the whole World Salvation."

Wayne turned and smiled.

"I'll do my best, my son. I'll do my best."

Forty-Seven

Monsignor Declan Doyle followed the snaking line of dignitaries in their incredibly ornate robes into St. Peter's. Rome was in a state of total turmoil. The City had not seen such activity since it had been the centre of the greatest Empire in the known world. With just three days to go before Luca Vitalia was due to have his audience with the Pope, in the presence of every major religious leader on earth, rehearsals were taking place to ensure that every piece of ceremonial choreography was timed to perfection. Vatican officials were determined to ensure that whether Luca was going to be proved the Son of God, or not, the Holy See was going to be presented as the most professional and awe inspiring religious institution on Earth.

Security was incredibly tight. The Italian authorities were sparing no expense in ensuring that the Vatican City was turned into a fortress. Several high-ranking Muslim clerics had unexpectedly flown in to peruse the supposedly reborn prophet, including the most senior theologian in Iran, Ayatollah Kameli. That alone had presented a security nightmare, but in addition to that, there had been several clashes between thousands of members of the Brigade of Light and gangs of what were now referred to as scepticals on the streets of Rome.

Declan Doyle shook his head as he heard the distant chanting of Brigade supporters. They sounded more like football hooligans than religious pilgrims and the racket was ruining the dignity of the dress rehearsal, even though the crowd was massed beyond the walls of the Vatican City. The Carabinieri were ensuring that only vetted ticket holders were being granted access to St. Peter's Square and the Basilica in the run up to the audience and airport style security checks had been installed in front of the great Cathedral.

Declan Doyle blew out an exasperated sigh. The new "Order" had failed to find any incriminating evidence that might have proved that Luca was not what he claimed to be and there had been absolutely no trace of the Englishman, who Fr. Reichmann had believed could be the true saviour, despite months of effort. Now it was almost too late. In less than a week, the world would know whether it had a new Messiah, or not and there was very little that Declan Doyle or his little "Order" could do about it.

The fanfare snapped the priest out of his reverie as several trumpets heralded the arrival of the procession of clerics into their allotted places under the dome of St. Peter's. For this particular rehearsal, some lesser clergy were acting in the roles that their superiors would fulfil on the big day.

Monsignor Doyle as a confidante and advisor to the Pope was one of the few present who would actually sit in the same place on the day itself.

He took his place on the front row of seats before where Luca would be "tried" by His Holiness and Cardinal Rinaldi, a former lawyer and the Vatican's foremost expert on Christian doctrine. Rinaldi had been appointed Chief Inquisitor, by Pope Gregory, with this one task in mind. The catechism he would face would test Luca Vitalia's knowledge of religious lore, more than any other possible test.

Doyle glanced around. Cardinals, Bishops, Imams, Rabbi's and representatives of just about every denomination and faith on Earth would fill the same aisles in three days. The most important Ecumenical Council meeting since Nicea under the Emperor Constantine, would pass judgment upon the man who seemed destined to grab the most powerful political position on the planet, as the President of the United States. It seemed almost absurd that he would attempt to pre-empt that with the seizure of absolute global spiritual authority in this very building.

The Monsignor gazed up at the dome above his head. Thousands of faithful Christians had laboured their entire lives to construct and decorate the marvellous church in which he sat and in which, if he was right, a demon would fool the cream of the world's spiritual leaders into believing that he was the second coming of Jesus Christ. Doyle sighed morosely and grimaced as he speculated what the possible consequences might be of a world ruled by a demon from hell.

A shaft of sunlight penetrated a high window near the dome and clearly illuminated a medieval image of St Sebastian high on the wall, his body pierced by several arrows. Declan Doyle gasped, suddenly he knew what he had to do. He had heard the term flash of inspiration but this was beyond that. This was divine intervention.

If the English boy that Father Reichmann had believed to be the saviour had died in the intervening twenty years, or had fallen victim to the dark powers that propelled the young Italian American forward, towards what seemed to be his inevitable destiny, then there was simply no one who could stop Luca Vitalia from subjugating the world under his own spiritual and secular hegemony. Not unless he, Monsignor Declan Doyle, intervened.

God had finally spoken to the middle aged Irish Priest in a way he never had before. Declan Doyle had to become a martyr like Saint Sebastian.

He had to act with the same mindless devotion to his faith that Islamic terrorists used to justify their atrocities and in the same moment Declan knew that was why he had become the embodiment of the "Sacred Order Of St. Gregory."

It was suddenly all so clear and obvious to him. He had been raised in Northern Ireland and had known many Catholic militants, who had given their succour and support to the IRA. He even knew one or two men who had seen active service. He could use them to access the resources he needed. Here he was, occupying a key role in the most important event to have taken place in Christendom since the time of the Emperor Constantine and he just happened to be able to get hold of the weaponry of deliverance from evil. God certainly moved in mysterious ways.

The new Pope was also a Gregory and he had recreated the "Sacred Order of St. Gregory", under Declan Doyle, to stop the powers of evil from assassinating the true saviour. Well maybe they had already done that, but he, Declan Doyle could thwart them in the very hour of their ultimate triumph.

The droning Cardinal who was describing the order of ceremony finally finished and sat down, it still seemed like an eternity to Monsignor Doyle until the rehearsal was over and he was able to scurry back to his apartment. Within the hour Declan Doyle was in a taxi on its way to the airport. The Monsignor was on his way back to Ireland for a brief visit.

God had spoken to him and he had understood. The "Sacred Order" would succeed in their mission after all those centuries and he would be the key to that victory.

Declan Doyle closed his eyes and smiled as the taxi sped through the streets of Rome. He felt strangely calm, serene even. Now he understood why martyrs always seemed to possess a bizarre insouciance to their fate. He believed in heaven and now knew that he would get there. Declan Doyle would be the most celebrated of all martyrs.

Why, they might even make him a saint.

Forty-Eight

FBI Director Marshall Williams handed the tape of the phone call to Jack Baring:

"You must come now. It is very urgent, Life, or death. You and Luca must come, Aurelio. I need help."

Baring stubbed out his illicit cigar and scowled.

"So what the hell is going on?" he growled.

"Why is Deano Vitalia calling for help?"

Marshall Williams shrugged.

"No idea, Sir. It's the voice that gets me. It's so flat, monotone, almost robotic. He doesn't sound like a man in danger of losing his life or anything, yet the words he uses are so like, desperate."

Jack Baring stood and strolled over to his window.

"Have your boys found the limey yet?"

Williams shook his head.

"No, sorry Sir. Wickert is on the case. He tells me the Brit hasn't used his cell in a couple of days and we haven't seen the car yet. We'll get him though, you can be sure of that sir."

"Get him?" Baring growled again. "I don't want you to "get him." He hasn't done anything yet as far as I am aware. I want your boys to watch him, that's all. If he is here to take some sort of revenge on the Vitalias, then this call from Dean could be related. I want Dean's house watched. I want a man at his office. We know that the Vitalias wanted this guy beaten for some reason. It seems they took on more than they bargained for. Maybe he's an ex spy or something because they way those guys in London were dealt with is beyond the capabilities of just any plain old John Doe. Our boys over there tell me the Brits haven't got a single word out of any of the guys that were found in London, or near O'Brien's, or Higginbotham's home, whatever you wanna call him."

Baring grinned wolfishly:

"Say, if this Brit deals with the Vitalias, it could save us a job."

Marshall Williams gulped.

"With all due respect, Sir, what if Luca Vitalia is Jesus Christ?"

Jack Baring's forehead creased slightly and he stared, silently, at the slightly younger man for several seconds, his face inscrutable.

"What?" he finally asked, incredulously.

"Surely you don't believe all this B.S?"

The FBI director shrugged.

"I was always taught to keep an open mind Sir, I mean it would be kinda wonderful if…"

His voice trailed off as he noticed the expression on Jack Baring's face.

"I'll, er get on the case, Sir."

Jack Baring sat back down in his black leather chair, still staring at the visibly squirming Williams.

"Yeah, you get on the case, Marshall. Like I say, just watch!"

Marshall Williams turned and left the office, licking his lips nervously. Baring's door had hardly closed before the United States Secretary of Homeland Security picked up his phone and barked:

"Get me the President would you and Mac Brown. I want Mac in my office as soon as possible."

Special Agent Henry T. Burgermeister was chewing his lip nervously when his cell phone began to vibrate angrily in his vest pocket. The partner Wickert had forced him to accept, a green young buck, fresh out of the academy was asleep on the passenger seat, his head bent back uncomfortably, loud snores punctuating the early morning silence of the Chatsworth street where the one time movie star Terri Thorne lived.

Burgermeister glanced at the screen on his cell. The caller did not display an identity.

"Wickert." The embittered FBI man muttered under his breath. He pressed the key to accept the call and put the phone to his ear with a roll of his eyes.

The rookie stirred, stretched and opened his eyes as Burgermeister whispered:

"Yes Sir." For about the seventh time. As he switched off his cell and put it back into his vest pocket, the older man shook his head disdainfully.

"Damn, I wish they'd make their minds up." He muttered.

The rookie straightened his back and gulped, he had not expected to see such cynicism in an agent with a reputation like Burgermeister's.

"What have we got to do now?" He asked, as he examined his partners face to try and ascertain just how annoyed he was. He had found Henry T. Burgermeister incredibly difficult to get along with. The irascible older man had worked without a partner for years and was not happy at having to share responsibilities once again and had made that abundantly clear to the rookie.

"Wickert wants us to seize the Brit, or his mother, whoever happens to show up first. Director Marshall Williams, himself wants answers. He says that Luca Vitalia could be in serious danger."

Burgermeister laughed sardonically.

"I mean Luca Vitalia? That's the biggest con since Bush told us there were Weapons of Mass Destruction in Iraq."

The rookie shifted uncomfortably in the passenger seat. Burgermeister shook his head.

"They say this "Brigade of Light" now has more members than the Catholic Church. Can you believe that?"

The rookie shook his head unconvincingly.

"There's gonna be a lotta red faces when this Vitalia guy is exposed as a cheap two bit con man." Burgermeister continued, warming to his theme.

"I mean the audacity of the man, claiming to be the Prince of Peace and a third part of the Goddam Holy Trinity when he hangs out with known mobsters."

The rookie grinned a humourless grin.

Henry T. Burgermeister grimaced.

"It's a damned strange world kid, and it just keeps on getting stranger."

Before the rookie had time to reply, Terri Thorne's red Pontiac turned into the street.

Burgermeister moved with a speed that belied his age and before the rookie's feet had even touched the sidewalk, the older man was flashing his I.D. card at Terri Thorne as she climbed out of her car on her driveway.

By the time the rookie reached Burgermeister, an initial exchange had already taken place that had led to Terri looking extremely defiant.

Burgermeister sighed.

"OK Ma'am, if you don't want to protect your son voluntarily, then I guess we'll just have to damn well do it the hard way." He declared routinely.

"Terri Vitalia also known as Terri Thorne, ma'am, you are under arrest, anything you say may be used as evidence against you at a later date."

Terri Thorne looked confused at first, then her expression turned into one of amazement and then she did something that Burgermeister had not expected. She started to laugh.

"You have just got to be kidding."

She gasped through peels of laughter:

"I mean what the hell am I being charged with?"

Burgermeister shrugged:

"It's a matter of National Security ma'am."

Terri shook her head, her expression still one of incredulous amusement.

"National Security?" She queried. "Are you sure you've got the right person here?"

Burgermeister nodded:

"Would you accompany us, please, Ma'am?"

Terri nodded as the smile slowly slipped from her lips.

"Just let me check those I.Ds again." She demanded as the two agents compliantly held out their cards.

"You sure this isn't Candid Camera, or something?" She asked as the FBI agents bundled her across the street and into Burgermeister's car.

"I mean where are the cameras? This is a joke isn't it?"

The rookie shook his head.

"No ma'am." He declared:

"We're here on the highest authority, Homeland security. We have reason to believe your son may be a terrorist."

Special Agent Henry T. Burgermeister's mouth dropped open in surprise. It was the first time the rookie had spoken more than two or three words. At about the same moment he noticed the small "Brigade of Light" pin badge, a cross with a lightning flash passing through it, in the rookie's lapel. The rookie glanced at the older agent and flashed a wide toothy smile.

"We'd better make sure the house is covered while we take Ms Thorne downtown. The Brit could show up anytime."

Burgermeister glowered at the young man.

"Sure thing Sherlock." He growled.

"I'll radio them right away, boss."

The rookie cast his eyes down into the foot-well of the car.

"Sorry." He murmured demurely.

Back in Washington D.C. Director Marshall Williams took the call from Walter Wickert the Third as soon as he got back from lunch.

"You got her? Excellent. What about her boy?"

He fingered his lapel badge nervously.

"Keep pressing her. We have to find out what is going on between him and the Vitalias."

A small pin badge bearing a cross and a lightening bolt fell onto his desk.

"And you have Dean Vitalia covered?" He asked as he placed the pin back in his lapel.

"Luca and Aurelio boarded the early flight from Boston to L.A. this morning. What? He didn't go into his office this morning? Are you sure? Try and find out if he's OK. If anything happens to Luca while he's under your watch, I'll have you fried! Wickert, do you understand? No I didn't say fired, I said fried!"

The FBI director slammed down his receiver.

"Something big is going on here. I can goddam smell it." He muttered to no one in particular.

Forty-Nine

Lucy Hetherington stood in Carrie's yard. The sun was just rising over the mountains away to the east. She shivered in the fresh morning chill and pulled her arms tight around her body for warmth. Nothing could have prepared her for what she had heard the previous night and the sense of unreality that had descended around her like the grey-green mists of Tir na Nog that Wayne had described.

The night of her arrival had been beyond amazing. To finally meet the woman in whose womb she had grown and whose likeness she bore had been incredible enough, but to also finally meet the twin brother who she had talked too, telepathically, twice in her life was the icing on the cake. Why had it taken nearly half a century to finally close the circle and answer the questions that she had carried like wounds for so long?

She smiled as she recalled her fruitless journey from Oxford to Shepton, when she had been a young, innocent undergraduate. Then the smile turned into a grin as she remembered the absolute incredulity of her headmistress at Roedean when she had professed to having had a dream about a twin brother in desperate peril and that was why she had been caught out of bounds after lights out.

"Lucy Hetherington, do you think that I was born yesterday?" She had screeched.

"If you do not tell me the truth I shall jolly well be forced to suspend you. Dreams and twin brothers indeed! Wait until your father hears about this!"

Lucy shook her head:

"Well Ma'am, if I had told you half of what I heard yesterday, then you really would have thought that I was a liar. In fact you'd have had me committed."

After all the pleasantries and overwhelming emotional reactions of the first evening, the previous day had been a time to really try and catch up on the missing years. Wayne had left Terri alone with Lucy for most of the day, so that mother and daughter could connect and get to know one another.

Lucy had been spell bound by Terri's tale of her childhood in the West of Ireland, about Daideo and her siblings and about her own mother, Lucy's grandma. Terri had been careful to moderate the description of her seduction by Danny Finn from Tupelo and her subsequent flight to London and then New York. She had not deemed it wise to relate the tale of Danny's morphing into one of the fairy folk at such an early stage in their relationship. It had been Wayne who had told Lucy the truth much later in the evening. Terri had gone on to tell her about the pain of having to surrender the twins and how the Nuns had told her that both children had gone to live in luxurious circumstances, way beyond a poor Irish girl's wildest dreams.

She had told Lucy about how she had started to model in London and that had led to some TV work and eventually she had chanced her arm in New York and eventually Hollywood. That was when she had told Lucy about her other two siblings Marco and Marina and their father, Dean.

The hairs on the back of Lucy's neck had pricked up when the name Vitalia was mentioned, even so, her mother's story had been incredible enough to deflect Lucy's rage at the name and her own mother's connection to her nemesis.

Lucy, of course, had been careful not to overplay her love for her adoptive parents. As much as she did love Rupert and Melinda, she did not want to make her Mom unhappy by making her envious almost as soon as they'd met. She did, however, tell Terri all about the opulent circumstances in which she had been raised on the Channel Island of Jersey.

By the time Wayne had returned from his short meeting with Dean Vitalia, the two women had managed to cover most of the most important events in their lives. Terri was basking in the knowledge that her daughter had had an affluent childhood, an Oxford degree and had had a successful career as a lawyer, while Lucy had been proud to hear that her mother had been a Hollywood movie star.

The sun had risen quite a way into the clear blue sky by the time Lucy began to reflect on her conversation with Wayne. She had gathered the most basic facts about his working class upbringing in Yorkshire the previous evening and he had been amazed that she had actually visited 18 Cavendish Street Shepton and The Junction Inn. The two had been equally amazed to discover that they had both known Martin Berenger and it had only been through him that Lucy had even begun to believe that a town called Shepton really did exist.

Terri had left Carrie's house eventually, in order to visit Marco and Aoibheall and tell them the good news, she had already called Marina and asked her to be at her brother's apartment. Carrie had stayed with her daughter and new son in law, to allow the reunited family some space.

Terri had informed Lucy that Carrie's husband was now away in Guatemala on business. In fact, Terri had laughed, Carrie was beginning to wonder if he was ever going to come home. Terri told her long lost daughter that Carrie had insisted that their family reunion should take place on neutral ground and that her house in Box Canyon was the ideal venue. She had even arranged proceedings in deciding that Terri and Wayne should be the first to meet Lucy and that Marco and Marina should follow on later. Terri had readily agreed. Lucy had to agree as she looked out over the San Fernando Valley, that the view was certainly impressive.

Her thoughts soon flew back to the previous two day's conversations.

It was only after Terri had left to go to Marcus' place that Wayne had told Lucy about the true circumstances of their conception and the part played by Mickey, or as he was known to Theresa O'Brien, Danny Finn. He told her all about Aillen Mac Fionnbharr and the Tuatha de Danaan.

Lucy had been curious to know how he had discovered the family history and the circumstances of his own reunion. So, Wayne had told her about his discovery of his magical abilities at the tender age of eleven. How a local thug had assaulted him and how, even though his magic had defeated the much older boy, he had ended up being hospitalised. He told her how it had been a doctor's careless whisper that had initially informed him of his adoption and his resulting anguish and confusion.

He had amused her with a rollicking rendition of his adventure in running away to London and his subsequent journey to Ireland. How he had met various members of their family, like their Aunt Molly, before his fateful meeting with their biological grandfather and eventually their magical forebear, Mickey Finn, also known as Aillen Mac Fionnbharr.

He told her all about the treasures of the Tuatha, the way the Stone of Falias amplified their magical powers and how the Spear of Finias and the Sword of Gorias had helped the Tuatha de Danaan in their victories.

She had been astounded when he had told her that all three of the treasures that he had described were in his possession. He related the story of the night that their father had died at the hand of Father Francisco Pizarro, chief assassin of the "Sacred Order of Saint Gregory."

She had been astonished and horrified in equal measure when she had heard how that had merely been the culmination of nearly two millennia of genocide.

Then, when he had achieved a level of confidence, he had demonstrated the art of shape shifting and achieving invisibility before her very eyes. Her amusement at his morphing into a perfect facsimile of Rowan Atkinson's Mr Bean character had been tempered by the shattering of all of her previous preconceptions about the world in which she lived. Everything she had ever known, everything she had learned in her extensive and expensive education seemed to have been rendered almost irrelevant.

Whether it was natural law, science or philosophy, the existence of magic seemed to challenge everything she had believed. To suddenly find that one's assumptions about the world had been wildly off the mark did have a certain destabilising element.

Wayne had opened a bottle of wine and the anaesthetising effect of the alcohol helped her to deal with the shock of what she was hearing.

She had laughed when she had heard Wayne tell her about how he had once got progressively drunk, whilst trying to impress some girl called Stephanie and how his shape shifted persona had slowly begun to unravel, under the effects of the alcohol.

She had heard with horror his story about Pierre de Feren and the demise of Aoibheall, the Banshee in that house she had once visited in Shepton.

She had beamed with pride when he had told her that it had only been her timely intervention that had saved his life, with just seconds to spare.

Her mouth had been hanging open when he had related the tale of his showdown with the Bishop, who had been the head of the "Order" in Ireland and how De Feren had killed his own boss, before attempting to murder the young Priest James Malone and Wayne.

Wayne told her about how the "Order" had thought that they were defending the Second coming and had allowed a baby to be born that they were convinced was the reincarnation of the baby Jesus, but that he believed they had been duped and the baby that had eventually become Lucy's nemesis, Luca Vitalia, was much more likely to be a demon than the new messiah.

Lucy had responded by telling Wayne the full story about Jonathan, how he had fallen under the spell of Luca Vitalia, when he had been appointed his legal representative and how Luca had attempted to assault her in her own New York apartment. This time it was her turn to thank Wayne for his timely intervention.

Lucy had cried when she had heard about how Wayne's friend, James Malone had been killed in the very house where they were now sitting, by people that Dean Vitalia had admitted hiring and how he had even admitted to the attack on Wayne in England. The most impressive part was how Wayne had extracted both confessions, simply by assuming the shape of another person.

Lucy had suddenly felt that she had become disoriented and detached from most of what she was hearing. It was simply just all too much to take in. Now that probably was partly due to the wine. Even so it had been a hell of a twenty-four hours. Not only had she been reunited with her natural mother and her twin brother, events that were totally cataclysmic in themselves, but also she had entered an entirely new world.

A world where magic sat comfortably alongside science, technology, rationality, logic and reason.

A world where fairy tale characters, at least of the Irish kind, not only existed, but had intercourse, in every sense of the word, with human kind.

It just all sounded so far fetched, despite Wayne's physical demonstrations of his powers.

Such major events could have caused severe trauma and possibly a nervous breakdown in even the strongest minded of individuals and after what had happened to her in recent weeks, Lucy certainly didn't feel that strong.

Lucy took a deep breath of the clear morning air. Normal people were getting out of their normal beds down in the valley. Ready to start another normal day in their normal jobs with their normal colleagues and families.

Yet here she was in what had really become La-La land.

She had listened to more of Wayne's stories and he to hers and although she had initially felt guilty about the disparate circumstances of their upbringing, it had all turned out right in the end. The disclosure that Lucy's children and Wayne's daughter just happened to attend the same private school in Berkshire blew even the Martin Berenger co-incidence into a cocked hat.

"Small world, eh?" Wayne had whistled through his teeth, shaking his head in bewilderment.

Lucy had left Wayne at a reasonably early hour, claiming tiredness. In reality, she had just wanted some time to clear her head and to consider her options.

In one way, part of her just wanted to walk away from it all. She had found out the true circumstances of her birth and subsequent adoption, that had been her main objective in finding any of her birth relatives and now she knew everything.

She could have just taken her rental car down the freeway to the airport, gone back to England and then Jersey and forgotten all about the O'Briens and the Tuatha de Danaan and magic. She could have submerged herself in helping Melinda to look after Rupert and bringing up Jonju and Jemima in the best way she could.

She could have gone back to a normal life, just like all those people down there in the Valley.

Yet, as she had tried to rationalise her situation and consider her alternatives, she had realised that there was no such thing as a normal life for her any more.

Luca Vitalia could shape shift just as well as Wayne Higginbotham and he was almost on the verge of becoming the most powerful man in the World.

After New York one thing was for sure, he hated Lucy Sherman, nee Hetherington. If he did become President of the United States, he could get to her any time he wanted.

Magic had irrevocably entered her life, whether she wanted it to, or not.

Lucy Hetherington had to admit that she could now never really have a normal life, having seen what she had seen and heard what she had heard.

Lucy took in another lungful of air and watched the shadows in the Valley below shorten as the sun climbed higher in the sky and the wide boulevards, streets and freeways sprang to life.

Wayne had told her that he was supposedly the "Slanatheoir Mor." The great saviour, whatever that meant. He had told her that his only nemesis now was Luca Vitalia and the sole purpose of his life was to destroy him, well, so was hers now, so at least they were on the same side.

Lucy was also nervous about meeting Marco and Marina. How would they react to her? How would she react to them?

Lucy turned from the view of the wide San Fernando Valley and walked back into the house and into Carrie's daughter Aoibheall's bedroom.

She sat down in front of the dressing table mirror, took a deep breath and did exactly what Wayne had said he did. She thought about Melinda Hetherington, about every single facet of her adoptive mother's facial features. She concentrated; she concentrated as hard as she ever had in her life. When she opened her eyes again, Melinda Hetherington was staring quizzically back at her from the mirror. Lucy squealed and clapped her hand over her mouth and watched as her face quickly sank back into her own familiar features.

Lucy's breathing was now hard and fast. She could feel her heart pounding violently against her breast. Lucy Hetherington could shape shift!

Wayne had described how he had always been able to get inside people's minds and influence them, although he had been quick to qualify himself and declare that he only did it when absolutely necessary.

Lucy thought back to the times she had inwardly pleaded with people, like her headmistress when she had been on the verge of suspension. If she was honest, Lucy had to admit that she had always got what she wanted. She thought about the way she had manipulated Jonathan at times and how she had managed to bend him to her will even when he had seemed absolutely adamant about an issue. That was until Luca Vitalia had entered Jonathan T. Sherman's life, anyway.

Now she knew why her life had seemed almost charmed. She had always had the power to impose her will on people.

Lucy concentrated again and watched herself slowly disappear from the mirror, like a ghost, or a character beaming up in one of those science fiction TV shows.

Lucy began to laugh, quietly at first but then louder and then uncontrollably.

It was just all really just too insane. Lucy Hetherington really, really could do magic.

She was a one hundred per-cent fully paid up member of the union of the Tuatha de Danaan and she had never even realised. She pulled back her hair and carefully examined her neat pointed ears. Why had she never realised?

Lucy Hetherington could perform real magic. Not pier end, variety show conjuring tricks, not even the vast, spectacular illusions performed in Las Vegas, but real, bona-fide, fantasy story magic. Wait until Jonju and Jem saw this. She didn't even need a wand!

The pang of guilt that she felt when she thought about her children was almost overwhelming. She would ensure she was back with them by Christmas, whatever happened and would she have some stories for them.

With a sigh Lucy wiped her eyes and fell back on to the bed and into an immediate deep sleep, haunted by shape shifting clowns and raving knife-wielding clerics. When she awoke, sweating in the heat of the mid morning, Lucy wondered momentarily if it had all been a dream, but the sight of her-self morphed into the approximate shape of Michelle Pfeiffer in the mirror, convinced her for once and for all that there was a new Lucy Hetherington in town. She pursed her lips and pouted at the reflection of the beautiful movie star. Lucy Hetherington laughed; maybe she was beginning to enjoy being able to perform magic. At least she'd never have wrinkles again, just think of the money saved on cosmetics.

Fifty

Wayne Higginbotham ended his call to Natalia. He had just told her all about his reunion with his sister over the course of the previous day and the evening before that.

Of course Natalia had had a million questions about her new sister–in-law, which Wayne had answered as patiently as possible.

"What's she like?

Is she pretty?

Is she rich?

Is she fat?

Is she posh?

Does she have the ears?"

Wayne had told Natalia everything he could about his sister, but it still didn't seem to fully satiate her curiosity. She had been amazed that Lucy just happened to have two children at the same school as Katie, the odds against such an eventuality must have been enormous, especially as Lucy had been resident in the United States for many years.

By the time Wayne put the phone down, he felt like he had repeated the previous day's entire conversation. He shook his head and laughed as he climbed into the shower.

As the refreshing cool water exploded powerfully over his head, he wondered if he had gone too far in relating his life story. Lucy had looked decidedly uncomfortable at times, yet he had avoided telling her about his mistakes at University and why he had given up using magic for over twenty years. He didn't tell her about the drink-driving episode, the seduction and "rape" of Sabine, or about the men he had killed.

"Oh well!" He shrugged as he shampooed his hair. "I'll get round to it."

Wayne had always believed that honesty was the best policy, except when he had been trying to have his wicked way with Stephanie Fleming, or Sabine, or indeed in his denial of his magical abilities to his wife, his children and his wider family throughout his married life.

As Wayne climbed out of the shower he came to the realisation that maybe he wasn't quite the man he imagined himself to be.

Wayne Higginbotham's life had been based on lies since he had been eleven-years-old and had run away to find his roots. He had lied to

Doris about finding his birth mother and had been forced to influence her thoughts on the issue on more than one occasion.

He had lived that lie for almost a quarter of a century, until Doris had died.

He had never told Natalia about his magical abilities.

Admittedly, he had never used magic to influence her, or seduce her, but he did feel guilty that he had been keeping something from her for so many years.

He had never told his children about his abilities.

That too caused him a degree of guilt.. He often wondered if either Katie, or Frankie had inherited any of his abilities and whether he should try to help guide them if they did have magical powers. People who could do magic were potentially dangerous, not only to other people, but to themselves as well. He was more than aware of that.

As he pulled on his tee-shirt, Wayne sighed. At least now his Mom knew about his powers, even if it had been Carrie who had told her. He had to admit that it seemed to lift some of the weight from his shoulders, knowing that someone else knew.

He wondered if that had been why he had been so keen to blurt out his adventures to Lucy. She was his twin for goodness sake. She was as close to him as any human being could be. They had communicated telepathically long before they had ever met. So if he couldn't tell her; exactly whom could he tell?

Wayne lifted the Stone of Falias out of his bag and placed it on the bed in Carrie's guesthouse. The guesthouse was a self-contained bedroom and bathroom about ten yards from the main house. The stone glowed with a pale green light emanating from the very centre of the sphere.

Next, Wayne placed the Sword of Gorias on the bed. It looked brand new, every etching on the shining blade seemed as if it had been done days before, not thousands of years and the golden pommel shone like a tiny star. The miracle that had happened as soon as he had touched the ancient rusted metal relic did not seem as though it was ready to fade any time soon.

Finally Wayne reached into the bag and took out the Spear of Finias. In the corner of the guesthouse bathroom, Wayne had found a plastic broom. It seemed rather demeaning to ram the ancient spearhead onto a blue plastic broom handle, but a spearhead needs a shaft and the broom handle felt heavy enough to allow Wayne to throw the spear should the need arise.

Wayne stepped back and admired the three treasures lying on his bed. Thousands of years of history, encapsulated in the three items that, at first sight, looked so innocuous.

Wayne shook his head and blew out a nervous sigh.

He looked at his watch.

What Wayne had failed to tell his sister, along with all the other stuff he hadn't wanted her to hear, was that he intended to kill Luca Vitalia.

Before his shower Wayne had checked the breakfast news to see if Luca had taken the bait and was coming back to L.A. in response to the call from his Hollywood Agent.

Sure enough, the news anchor announced that Luca Vitalia, the hottest news item in the world was making a surprise visit to Los Angeles, just a day before he was due to fly to Rome. Luca had declined to comment to the masses of reporters at the airport, but his father, Aurelio, simply stated that Luca had a minor family problem that he wanted to resolve before the "Rome gig."

Wayne checked the flight arrival times on the internet. He had a couple of hours or so to kill before Luca would arrive at Dean's house. He carefully picked up the treasures and carried them to the rental car. Then he quietly walked into Carrie's kitchen, having cast an admiring glance over the sunny Valley.

Natalia had informed him that it was cold and wet at home, typical English December weather. He wondered, in passing, why Christmas cards always portrayed snow scenes when it rained every single bloody Christmas. At least it was lovely in Los Angeles.

There was no sign of any life in the house. Wayne knew that Carrie was still at Marco and Aoibheall's place, as was his mom, Terri. Carrie's husband was somewhere in South America. Lucy must have still been sleeping. Wayne smiled. He had a twin sister at last, how weird was that?

He wondered if Lucy had any magical abilities, beyond telepathy. She hadn't said that she possessed any magic the previous evening. In fact her life had been so damn cushy that she'd never needed to use magic.

Wayne climbed into the Ford and reversed out into Box Canyon.

Did he feel jealous about Lucy's good fortune in having been adopted by a wealthy Jersey couple? Wayne pursed his lips as he glanced in the car's rear view mirror.

In a way, he had to admit he was jealous.

Doris and Frank Higginbotham had certainly done their best for him and Wayne had never felt deprived, not in the way poor children in

Africa were deprived. He did remember his shame, however, when he had found out that he was the only boy in his year at Wormysted's Grammar school whose dad did not have a car and who did not have a colour TV, or a phone and he would remember until the day he died one very posh friend's comment that the Higginbotham's little terraced house, 18 Cavendish Street, was so "cosy' in comparison to his own family's humungous, but draughty, Dales village Manor House.

So yes, Wayne did have to admit to a little pang of jealousy about Lucy's opulent upbringing. Her life had been one of horses, Pimms parties, private school and exotic holidays, but he was also glad that she had been happy.

What he had not been happy about had been the way that Jonathan T. Sherman had betrayed his own wife and the mother of his children to serve Luca Vitalia.

Wayne smirked when he thought about how he had yet another reason to enjoy destroying the smug ex-child actor, pop star and self proclaimed messiah.

"That's for my sister, punk!"

As he drove up the snaking canyon road towards the Santa Susanna pass, Wayne noticed how green everything looked. When he had been to L.A. before everything had looked parched and brown, especially when the family had come over for Marco's wedding, but now the bushes and cacti bordering the road were nothing less than lush. Wayne realised that there must have been quite a bit of rain before he had come out to California. He was busily admiring the verdant landscape when he noticed the Highway patrol car hidden in a gateway. Wayne hardly gave it a second thought. His speed was within the limit and he was as sober as any judge. He looked ahead and saw the sign for the 118 Interstate, the Ronald Reagan freeway. Wayne intended to pull off the freeway on his way to his appointment with destiny at Coldwater Canyon, to stop at the Porter Ranch Retail Park and grab an early lunch at the "In n' Out burger" joint. He could almost taste the fries and licked his lips in anticipation.

The ominous wail of the siren brought such fantasising to a brusque end. Wayne pulled over at the sight of the red and blue flashing lights in his mirror, fully expecting the Patrol car to hurtle past on its way to an emergency somewhere. Much to his surprise and dismay, however, the car pulled up behind him, right on the slip road onto the freeway. Wayne watched the policeman climb slowly out of the car from his rear view mirror. His colleague was on the radio. For a brief second, Wayne considered putting his foot down and racing down onto the freeway. Wayne had seen enough cop shows and movies to know that a high-speed chase would be disastrous; he would have a hundred cars and choppers on his tail within minutes. Even so, what would the Cop do when he found a sword and a spear on the back seat of the rental car?

Wayne slowly pressed the switch for the window, which slid away into the door, just as the cop came alongside the Ford:

"Could I see your driver's licence, Sir?"

The Cop drawled as he bent down and stared into Wayne's car.

Once again Wayne's saving inspiration came from Star Wars. Many years earlier he had morphed into the terrifying shape of Darth Vader to intimidate Aoibheall the Banshee when she had tried to assault him in his bedroom. This time Alec Guinness became his saviour as Wayne remembered the scene at the checkpoint when the Storm troopers pulled over Luke Skywalker's speeder.

Wayne pulled off his sunglasses and stared into the Cops eyes.

"This is not the car you're looking for." Wayne droned.

"This is not the car we're looking for." The cop repeated obediently.

"There has been an unfortunate mistake." Wayne intoned solemnly.

"There has been an unfortunate mistake." The Cop repeated verbatim.

"You may go about your business, sorry for the delay."

Wayne could hardly stifle a grin.

"You may go about your business, sorry for the delay."

The Cop nodded politely and walked away from Wayne's car bearing an extremely bemused expression.

Wayne glanced in his mirror as he pulled away. The Cop who had been on the radio had climbed out of the car and was gesturing furiously at his colleague, his finger waving in the general direction of Wayne's car. Wayne sped out onto the main carriageway and checking his mirror carefully to ensure that the patrol car hadn't torn off after him, he pulled off the 118 at the first exit and waited for ten minutes. He then pulled back onto the freeway and carried out his mission to get a burger. A smile crossed his lips as he noticed the same patrol car slipping away from the takeout section of the burger bar, well ahead of him.

Fortunately they turned onto the road in the opposite direction and Wayne blew a sigh of relief. He wondered why he had been pulled over. It was the first time that had happened since the incident on Shepton High Street when the tail-light on his Escort had died.

Once he had devoured the burger and fries, he checked the back of the car. All the lights were working, as they should. Wayne shrugged and climbed back into the car.

It was possible, of course, that someone was on to him. Wayne twisted his face. No, that was totally far fetched. Who could possibly suspect that a respectable English tourist intended to assassinate the prospective President of the United States and the second Coming of Jesus Christ?

Wayne licked his greasy fingers. Whether someone was onto him, or not, he needed to carry out his mission as quickly and efficiently as possible, just in case.

Fifty-One

Terri Thorne folded her arms across her chest and shook her head.

"No, no, no! How many times do I have to tell you guys? I will not tell you where Wayne is. I mean what exactly is it he is supposed to have done anyway?"

The man in the suit crossed his arms defensively.

"I can't tell you that ma'am. As I keep repeating, it's a matter of national security."

Terri Thorne crossed her arms and her legs at the same time and her face hardened.

"And as I keep repeating, ad nauseum. If you cannot, or will not, tell me what it is that you are accusing my son of doing, then I will certainly not tell you where he is. I will not say another word. I have had enough, I want my lawyer, until then I take the Fifth."

Henry T. Burgermeister rolled his eyes.

Terri's declaration that she was not going to say another word in case it incriminated her was the last thing he had expected, especially when he had jogged over to pull Terri in earlier that morning.

"Mrs Vitalia?" Henry had asked as Terri had climbed out of her car.

"Yes." Terri had replied pensively.

Henry had flashed his FBI badge:

"Henry T. Burgermeister, Ma'am, Federal Bureau of Investigations. We have reason to believe your son, Wayne Higginbotham, sometimes known as Michael O'Brien, is in mortal danger. We need to know his whereabouts right now, Ma'am."

Terri had frowned:

"From who?"

Henry had been somewhat taken aback by the direct question.

"From who is he in danger? I can't tell you that Ma'am, National Security."

Terri had shaken her head.

"Then I'm sorry I can't tell you where he is. That is, even if I knew."

That was when the rookie had arrived and Henry T. Burgermeister had arrested Terri Thorne on the spot.

In the hours since then, Burgermeister had gotten increasingly frustrated and Terri infinitely more stubborn and defiant.

Walter Wickert the Third strolled into the interview room. His black hair was slicked back, his designer suit was perfectly pressed and his shirt gleamed white.

"Leave this to me, Henry." He whispered.

He pushed his designer framed spectacles up his nose:

"Ms Thorne. I'm a great admirer of your work. I saw you in "Tornado" when I was a boy. Man, that was some movie. You were awesome, Ma'am."

Terri smiled sardonically, but didn't say a word.

The salacious leer on his face told her that he had actually seen the movie and her character's fate, impaled by a road sign wearing nothing but her underwear.

"I'm Walter Wickert, by the way."

Wickert proffered his hand, which Terri shook with a look of utter contempt written all over her face.

"I also saw you in "Four Days in Vegas" and what was that vampire movie?"

"Bloodlust IV" Terri sighed: "My movie swansong, released straight to video. So Mr Wickert, you have proved that you have seen at least one of my pictures and you can read a movie database. Thank you for attempting to flatter me at least. That is all I am going to say until my lawyer gets here."

Walter Wickert pursed his lips.

"OK, Ma'am let's cut to the quick. You used to be married to Dean Vitalia. Dean's cousin's son, is, as you know, the front running candidate for the Presidency of the United States. Not only that, many people actually believe that he truly is The Son of God, the Redeemer, The Messiah, The Second Coming of Our Lord Jesus Christ, whatever you know Him as. Due to some weird stuff that happened in Great Britain, we believe, that maybe, your son is possibly here to take some sort of revenge against a member, or various members of the Vitalia clan. Revenge for what, we don't know. Obviously as a prospective President, Mr Luca Vitalia is granted the full protection of the State, through the department of Homeland Security. Now we do not know which particular Vitalia your son may be mad at, if any. We were hoping you might have a better idea, you know we need a light shining on what is going on. It could just be all one big misunderstanding."

Terri rolled her eyes.

Wickert cursed under his breath and looked around the room. A bored looking young FBI Special Agent stood in the corner of the bare windowless white walled office, illuminated by a single strip light. Wickert presumed that he was the rookie that he had personally forced onto the reluctant Burgermeister. He certainly didn't know the kid. The only furniture in the room comprised two cheap plastic chairs, one of which he occupied.

Terri was sat on the other.

"You know," Wickert sucked in a deep breath: "Technically you are no longer a United States Citizen, Miss Thorne. You know, as you are no longer married to Mister Vitalia."

We could deport you back to Ireland."

Terri smiled at the much younger man, but her eyes still glared at him.

Wickert rubbed his forehead:

"Ma'am, if your son tries to get to Luca today and yes he is here in Los Angeles, he could get himself shot."

Terri Thorne raised her eyebrows and shrugged.

"I'll ask him when I see him." She said indolently.

"And, by the way, I do have a valid green card. I've had one for nearly thirty years."

It was then that she noticed the "Brigade of Light" pin badge in Wickert's suit lapel.

Terri snorted derisively:

"You can threaten me all you want, Mister Wicked, but I will not say another word until my lawyer arrives."

Wickert stood and bit his lip. He nodded his head towards the door, indicating that the rookie leave the room.

"We'll leave you alone until your lawyer arrives. Just let me know if you change your mind and decide you want us to help you protect your son, ma'am."

Once back in the noise and bustle of the main FBI office in the San Fernando Valley, Walter Wickert shook his head despondently as Henry T. Burgermeister, the local Head of Operations and the Rookie convened around a desk:

"Has Luca arrived yet?" Wickert demanded. The local FBI Chief nodded:

"He's in a small motorcade on his way to Dean's house."

Wickert grimaced.

"Do we know if Dean's OK?"

The local chief coughed:

"We monitored a call from Dean's girlfriend to Aurelio before they left Boston. It seems he's fine, he's just, well not talking, I guess."

Wickert glowered.

"Not talking?" The station chief shrugged:

"All she said was, that Deano had taken to his bed when he had gotten home last night and wouldn't talk to her. I mean it sounds like a domestic to me."

Wickert frowned.

"So why would Luca and Aurelio come racing over because Deano isn't talking to his girlfriend? And what the hell do I tell Mr Williams?"

The small group meeting was interrupted by an attractive young female agent, who looked rather embarrassed. She passed a piece of paper to the station chief. He raised his eyebrows and muttered something to her.

"What's that?" Wickert demanded.

The local Chief sighed.

"We've just had a call from the California Highway Patrol. It seems that one of their cars pulled over a guy matching Wayne Higginbotham's description, this morning, in a car bearing the licence plate of his rental car."

"So where the hell is he? Where are they holding him?" Wickert demanded, his demeanour becoming more and more agitated.

The Chief rolled his eyes and grimaced:

"They let him go." He stated simply.

Walter Wickert's mouth dropped open and he stared at the local Chief with a look of total and utter incredulity. After several elongated seconds, Wickert gasped:

"They let him go. In the name of all that is Holy, why?"

The chief smiled a weak embarrassed smile:

"I asked the same question. The cop's lieutenant told me, and I quote, that the cop thought that there had been some sort of mistake."

Wickert fell into a chair and put his head in his hands.

"If anything happens to Luca Vitalia then my career is just so totally over!"

He looked up at Henry T. Burgermeister and the rookie:

"Get your asses to Deano's house immediately." He looked at the local chief:

"Have you got any more field agents you can send? We need every man and woman we can possibly spare over there."

The older man nodded:

"I'll go myself and I've got three good agents I can send."

Wickert, his face pale, nodded.

"I'll be there too. Excellent. Let's just hope this is one big mountain made out of a tiny goddam mole hill."

Fifty-Two

"What?" Luca had screamed. "We are going to Rome in two days time to convince the World's religious leaders that I am truly the Son of God and you tell me we now have to go to L.A first?"

Aurelio had thrown his hands in the air:

"Deano is in trouble, you heard the message. His broad rang me this morning saying he's giving her the silent treatment. She said he looks like he's suffered some sorta breakdown."

Luca had snorted:

"Why doesn't she get a Doctor to see him?"

Aurelio had glowered at his adopted son but had not replied.

That had been before the Vitalias had boarded the flight, now they were in a black Lincoln Navigator SUV as it rolled up the busy 405 towards Coldwater Canyon.

"I've arranged that we fly direct to Rome from here." Aurelio announced as he closed the clamshell on his cell phone.

Luca affected a measured insouciance.

If Deano was messing him around, then he would be sorry. Luca was mortified at the prospect of a twelve-hour flight to Rome instead of the still tortuous nine-hour leap from Boston. Deano's excuse had better be good. The man had always been more interested in his women than in helping his cousin's son get to the White House.

He should have stayed married to the Irish woman. Luca had quite liked her.

He watched the insignificant ants pass by on the opposite carriageway. The cars on the massively congested freeway were constantly bunching and coming to a halt. Luca smiled. It was all so close now. All he had to do was to convince the Priests and High Priests of the various temples and sects, that modern man loved to consider as advanced religious orders and he was on the home straight. Acceptance of him as the Son of God would make his election a mere formality and then he would re-mould the religious and political maps of the World.

He had already planned his Roman party piece. The Pope would be kissing his feet in less than forty-eight hours and all of the unimportant little people in their stupid little BMWs, Mercedes, Buicks, Toyotas, Chryslers, Hondas and so on and so on, would be celebrating the dawn of a new age.

"Hey Luca, you OK?" Aurelio's annoying voice snapped him back into reality.

"I just spoke to Deano's broad again. She says there is no change in his condition. So I tells her to call a Doctor and she says that Deano shakes his head when she suggests it."

Luca yawned:

"We'll be there inside half an hour. Then we'll see what's going down." He muttered, turning his attention back to the view from his window.

Aurelio took a deep breath. He knew better than to annoy his adopted son. The kid was a deity for God's sake. Aurelio was worried about Deano. They had always been close and Dean's media savvy had been invaluable in promoting Luca's image. Universal acceptance of Luca's divinity was now so close that Aurelio could almost taste it, as well as the promise of the rewards that would flow from such approval.

Aurelio Vitalia would be the second in command of an Empire that would dwarf Rome and all the petty Imperial powers that followed through the Centuries. Luca would be automatically accepted as the leader of the western World on Religious grounds alone. Once he was President, he would have the secular authority and the military muscle to ensure the subjugation of the rest of the Globe, until everyone on Earth accepted his ultimate and eternal hegemony.

Aurelio patted his forehead with his handkerchief and licked his bulbous lips. He wouldn't have too many years to enjoy the fruits of Luca's sovereignty, so he was determined that he would pack in as much unbridled hedonism as soon as possible.

He watched the police outrider indicate to turn off the freeway onto Mulholland. The driver of the SUV followed in turn. Aurelio glanced back. As well as two outriders, a marked patrol car was following them, a car full of Government agents and a posse of press cars. Aurelio shook his head. He found the idea that the Security Services were protecting Luca hilarious. The huge guy sat in the front passenger seat of the Navigator worked for the government. Aurelio stared at the wire coil of the Security man's earpiece and wondered how it was that the Vitalias had been so lucky to get away with all their past misdemeanours. He knew, of course, that it was all down to Luca. Some elements within Government had always been doing their level best to discredit him in particular. He had always suffered from the whispers of those who had believed him to be a crook, but he had always gotten away with it.

Unlike Aurelio, or Dean for that matter, Luca was whiter than white. That was why he had been able to build up such powerful momentum in his twin campaigns. No one could really find a bad word to say about him.

As Dean's gate swung open automatically and the car pressed through the pack of photographers and journalists standing on the road, Luca allowed himself the indulgent thought of how he would finally dispose of Lucy Sherman, once he got back from Rome.

The security staff and police waited by the door as Luca and Aurelio entered Dean's house. His girlfriend was standing in the marble floored hall, hopping from one foot to another as she tried to explain Deans' symptoms to Aurelio.

"The Doctor has absolutely no idea what the matter is." She declared, as she glared at the disinterested face of the supposed Son of God.

Aurelio nodded.

"Let's see him then." He barked at the woman who almost jumped out of her skin.

"Sure, this way." She twittered as she wandered off towards the pool.

Dean Vitalia was sat on a chair by the pool in the warm Southern California December sunshine. His eyes were fixed on some point on the ground, near where the paved area by the pool met the manicured lawn.

"Deano, Hey Deano." Aurelio shouted. "What's happened Dean? Come on talk to me, buddy."

Aurelio clasped his cousin by the shoulders while Luca strolled to the end of the yard where he looked out over Beverley Hills. His face oozed boredom from every pore.

Luca Vitalia just wanted to get on with the conquest of Rome, now.

Aurelio was by now almost shouting at the blank faced Dean.

"Deano, Deano, speak to me." He wailed.

Dean's girlfriend burst into tears:

"He's been like this for nearly two days now. It must be a breakdown." She cried.

"Mr Vitalia, Luca, please. You must be able to do something. Can you not, you know, do one of your miracles?"

Luca sighed and strolled down the side of the pool towards his stricken relative. He placed his expensive sunglasses on his nose to avoid the glare of sunlight on the sparkling water.

"Take the girl inside." Luca commanded Aurelio, who nodded and took Dean's girlfriend by the elbow back towards the house.

"Can he fix him? Can he cure him?"

Luca heard her questioning Aurelio as he took her indoors.

"Sure he can. He's Jesus." Luca heard Aurelio assure her.

Luca smiled:

"Of course I am, father!" He reached out and touched the side of Dean's head.

"Speak to me." He commanded.

Dean's sharp intake of breath accompanied a wide-eyed look of panic in his eyes.

He looked around urgently, as though someone might be watching.

Luca frowned:

"What is it, Dean? What happened?"

Dean glanced up at the younger man. His eyes were wild, terrified even. He opened his mouth to speak, but nothing came out except a strange, plaintive, strangulated wail that even frightened Luca.

Luca put both his hands on to Dean's head and concentrated.

He could now see what Dean had seen. He saw an image of himself in an office. He saw himself laughing at Dean and then the Luca Vitalia figure changed into someone else. Luca gasped. Someone was now walking towards Dean with a look of pure contented satisfaction in his eyes. Someone was reaching out.

A helicopter rattled noisily overhead.

"Who the hell did this?" Luca exclaimed as he released Dean's head and stepped back from his terrified press agent, a look of horror crossing his face as he realised that Dean had not had a breakdown, but had been attacked by powers that could only be magical in origin.

"Me!" Someone said just behind Luca.

The quiet voice that had provided the simple answer had been totally unanticipated.

Luca frowned, unsure if he had really heard anything above the clattering noise of the helicopter overhead and several others nearby.

"I said it was me. I did this to Dean!"

The voice repeated, quietly and insistently.

Luca literally jumped and yelped like a kicked dog as he turned to see the source of the declaration.

"So even Messiahs get surprised?"

The quiet but deep voice exclaimed, with more than a little amusement.

The sight that greeted Luca Vitalia was as unexpected as it was incongruous in the typical opulent Californian back yard, with its pool, lounge chairs, high tech gas barbecue and with police and news channel helicopters hovering nearby.

Standing in front of Luca Vitalia, just in the shadow of a large garden umbrella, was a tall man. His wavy hair was worn long, down over his shoulders. He was wearing a circlet of gold on his head and was dressed in medieval robes that looked best suited to some "Dungeons and Dragons" fantasy movie, or a geekish computer game featuring Elves, dwarves and wizards.

Around his waist the man wore a belt, knotted at the buckle and by his side the golden pommel of a sword glinted in the sunshine, between folds in the man's robes.

The man's face was pale, his eyes blue with hints of green. He bore the same confident expression that Luca had seen in Dean's memory, but it was the ears that most attracted Luca's attention. The large pointed ears that poked out of the man's hair.

Luca smiled as he regained his composure and a glint of recognition flashed in his eyes:

"So, Cardinal D'Abruzzo lied to me. The once mighty and oh so proud "Tuatha de Danaan" were not totally expunged from the face of the Earth. They left a stain behind."

The figure before Luca smiled.

"I am Micheal Mac Aillen, Mac Fionnbharr and I am the last of the once mighty Tuatha De Danaan, Lords of Fine Finias, Glorious Gorias, Fair Falias and the magnificent Murias."

Luca Vitalia smiled again:

"Then it shall be my pleasure to complete the task that my late little friends in the "Order" failed to complete. I would have dealt with them much more severely had I known the extent of their failure. Their deaths would have been much slower and much more painful than the quick suicides I granted them. You, however, will not be so fortunate, oh, last little Princeling of a long forgotten people! I am Lucifer, Light of Heaven and Lord Of all darkness!"

Luca's voice had deepened all the way through his little speech, until by the end it was a little more than an incredibly low rumbling growl.

The furniture around the pool began to shake and the water in the pool became choppy and rough. The Windows in Dean's house began to rattle and vases on tables began to move involuntarily.

The press, police and security staff at Dean's gates and outside his front door looked around frantically, as they believed they were experiencing a major earth tremor.

"Luca, Dean, It's an earthquake!" Aurelio's voice bellowed from just inside the house.

"Stay back. I'm busy!" Luca replied, shouting in in his more familiar tones.

He turned back towards the figure before him and his eyes flashed red.

"I have not waited for several millennia to seize this miserable lump of rock and to be duly served by the miserable primitives who inhabit it, only to be thwarted by a miserable whelp. The last survivor of a race of weaklings, pacifists and cowards, who only fought as a last resort and who all died squealing like the pigs they were!"

He raised his hand in the twinkling of an eye and a massive bolt of pure energy flew out of the middle of his open palm, straight towards Michael Mac Aillen, last of the Tuatha de Danaan.

Fifty-Three

Monsignor Declan Doyle stood on the huge cliff and watched the white foam-flecked Atlantic rollers as they crashed on to the small sandy beach far below. The cold, winter grey sea bubbled and boiled, under an equally sombre sky, heavy with rain. Typical Donegal, typical Ireland. The priest smiled wistfully.

He had not visited his native County of Donegal in more years than he cared to remember and it was ironic that his last ever visit was destined to be so short. He had simply flown in to collect the tools he needed to carry out his planned job of work as quickly as he could and then he intended to get back to Rome as quickly as possible, so as not to miss the testing of the self proclaimed Messiah. Indeed, he had been in Ireland for only some eighteen hours and here he was saying goodbye to his beloved Erin's Isle for the very last time.

He sighed heavily and jumped into his hire car. He had a long drive ahead of him and he wasn't getting any younger.

He could have flown back to Rome, but his tools would have been difficult to get on to a plane, especially given the extensive security checks now in place at even the smallest regional airport. He planned therefore to drive all the way to Cork, where he would take a ferry to Roscoff and then he planned to take a train to Paris and on to Rome.

He had studied the timings and checked the connections, if everything went to plan, he would be back in Rome several hours before the prospective President's Papal audience.

The man he had visited in the village of Gweedore had proven to be every bit as reliable as Monsignor Doyle had dared hope. He had also been extremely co-operative, far more than Doyle had even dared hope.

Doyle had feared that the tools he needed might have been regarded as too valuable to be surrendered to an old Priest on a fool's mission, yet the man had remembered his long-standing debt to the Priest and had given him everything he had needed without any argument whatsoever.

The man's debt to Monsignor Doyle stretched back over thirty years, when Doyle had been a very young Priest over the border in the republican enclave of Derry. He had sheltered a wounded IRA man on the run, providing food warmth and sanctuary when many others were turning their backs on the men of violence. He had lied to the R.U.C men who came to check the Rectory and he had lied to the British troops who had searched the building, but had failed to find the man's secret hiding place.

Even so long after the event, Declan Doyle had remembered the man's passionate belief in a United Ireland and his profound hatred of every manifestation of the British State. He had been confident that when the IRA had "put it's weapons beyond use', in the wake of the Good Friday Agreement, that the man would have kept some of his ordnance, just in case hostilities were ever resumed and he had been proven right.

When Monsignor Doyle told the man exactly what he needed, the man had not even asked him what he wanted it for. The debt of gratitude was so great.

As he drove down towards Sligo, Monsignor Doyle smiled and wondered at the mystery of life. It was, after all, incredibly ironic that something as monumentally evil and as tragic as the troubles in Northern Ireland, should have provided the rare resources that might save the world.

Doyle was under no illusion that his plan was anything like foolproof. There were so many things that could go wrong; it had been a plan that had been constructed in almost undue haste and desperation after all. Yet surely the inspiration, coming as it had from the shaft of light in St. Peter's, had been divine.

Monsignor Doyle had faith. He had faith that should Luca Vitalia be the true Son of God, then he would fail in carrying out his mission and that would only be right and proper.

If, however, as the venerable Father Reichmann had suspected, Luca Vitalia was a demon, introduced into the world by a deluded "Sacred Order of Saint Gregory," then God had indeed provided the necessary inspiration through the image of the martyr Saint Sebastian and He would ensure that either Doyle himself, or maybe even the hitherto conspicuously absent Englishman, would stop Luca.

His Holiness himself had re-activated the "Sacred Order of Saint Gregory" in the shape of Monsignor Doyle, so that he would defend the World from the forces of supernatural evil, so surely that had been instigated by Divine inspiration.

As his car passed the huge Doric columned houses that seemed to have sprung up all over Ireland in the passed age of the Celtic tiger, Monsignor Declan Doyle began to sing. Not a hymn or a piece of religious music, but a song he had sung as a young Liverpool fan on one of the very few occasions he had managed to get to Anfield in the mid-Seventies:

"Que sera, sera, whatever will be, will be" and then instead of eulogising a trip to Wemb-er-ley, Declan Doyle, in a typical piece of gallows humour, sung about being blown to eternity, que sera, sera.

Fifty-Four

"I have just got to tell Wayne that I can do all this stuff too." Lucy muttered to herself as she staggered to the bathroom, still flabbergasted by her ability to do things that she had imagined being totally and absolutely impossible. The late morning sun was high in the sky and light was flooding into Carrie's house from every chink in every blind.

The funny thing was, Lucy would have always have been capable of using magic, but had been totally unaware of her powers, so they had lain dormant and unused for most of her life. Had she never been reunited with her birth family, she might have passed through her entire life in total ignorance of her latent abilities.

Today, her second full day with her birth relatives, she was due to be introduced to her half siblings, Marco and Marina. It was quite a sick co-incidence that they just happened to be related to Luca Vitalia and Marina, it seemed, was a committed member of the "Brigade of Light." Even so, they were her little brother and sister, so she was sure that such issues were no more than minor details.

Lucy grinned as she planned her call to Jonju and Jem. She missed them more than she could ever have imagined and was determined to be on a plane back to Europe the very next day. She had spoken to Melinda and the twins the previous day, but had been coy about her reasons for being in Los Angeles. There was no way she would be able to tell her adoptive mother that she had met her birth relatives, until they were both sat down with large glasses of a decent Brandy.

Lucy was quite certain that she would never be able to tell Rupert. He was so ill that such a shock might kill him. Of course, the twins would have to know about their new relatives as soon as possible. They would be utterly amazed to find out that they had a cousin in the fifth form at their very own school, Pangfield College.

She showered, dressed and made herself as beautiful as was possible for a woman of her age, which was the way she looked at things now. She had become much more aware of her wrinkling skin and the effects of ageing on her once pristine figure since Jonathan had left her life. She was painfully aware that she was "back on the market" as Jem had so adeptly described her situation in one emotionally draining phone call, when Lucy had first announced that she had left Jonathan. Then again if she could shift her shape into that of Michelle Pfieffer, then she could lose a few wrinkles. Who needed plastic surgery when you had magic?

Would she ever tell the twins about the magic?

Like Wayne, Lucy wondered if the twins might have inherited any of the magical inheritance of the Tuatha de Danaan that she shared with her own twin brother. If so it would be far better that they were told and were taught to use magic responsibly, rather than finding out by accident and going off the rails. Lucy laughed to herself. Here she was, one day after discovering that she had "special powers" and she was already planning "use magic responsibly" campaigns.

She stepped out of Carrie's house and strolled across the yard in the pleasant winter sunshine. She looked at her reflection in the window of the guesthouse and decided instantaneously that she would impress Wayne with a quick demonstration of her shape-shifting prowess.

Should she go beautiful, or scary? The latter won.

She concentrated and her features reshaped and remodelled themselves into those of Margaret Thatcher, (who Rupert had idolised.)

She knocked on the door and waited. There was no response. She knocked again and this time tried the door, it was open. Lucy quietly opened it and Margaret Thatcher stepped into the guesthouse only to find it stubbornly empty.

"Oh!" Lucy exclaimed disappointedly as she slowly morphed back into her own shape.

She stepped back out of the guesthouse and wandered to the front of Carrie's house. Wayne's rental car had gone. Lucy wondered why he hadn't woken her, but she guessed that was his business. Even so, she did feel disappointed that she had been left on her own in a strange house. She looked at her watch. It was nearly twelve. Wayne had said that Marco and Marina were going to arrive at about one. Lucy Hetherington shrugged and decided to make a coffee while she waited. She couldn't explain it, but for some reason Lucy felt a creeping sense of trepidation. It was as though she knew something bad was going to happen, but was totally helpless because she had no idea what the threat was.

At about one-fifteen Carrie arrived with Aoibheall and Marco and Marina. Carrie had been totally perplexed by the absence of both Wayne and Terri and after she had introduced Lucy to her two younger siblings and her own daughter and after all the initial hugs and kisses and howls of delight, she asked the younger woman if Wayne had mentioned going out at all.

Lucy had stated that he had not, but that he had obviously left the house at a reasonably early hour. Carrie shook her head. It was most unlike Terri not to call if she had arranged to meet someone. Terri's cell just rang straight to her answering machine.

276

Like Lucy, Carrie began to feel an uneasy nagging sense of doubt deep in the pit of her stomach. As the afternoon wore on the feeling that "something was wrong' just got worse and worse. Neither Lucy, nor Carrie could put their finger on it. Marina, Marco and Aoibheall seemed totally oblivious to it.

Lucy found it much harder to relate to her half siblings. They were so much younger than she was and so very L.A. Marina was obsessed with stardom and fame, while Marco was obsessed with Aoibheall. They were obviously in the first throes of their new marriage and incredibly happy.

It was only when Marina just happened to mention as part of a wider conversation that she had seen on T.V. that Luca Vitalia was in town and as far as she knew, he was at her father's house, that the penny dropped with both Carrie and Lucy.

"Isn't that just, like so awesome." Marina had squealed excitedly.

"I mean he's like God and he's our next President and he is like just so related to us."

Carrie had instinctively looked at Lucy; her eyes betrayed a fear that Lucy understood immediately.

"He's gone in, hasn't he?" Carrie gasped.

"He's gone to get Luca."

Marina's mouth had dropped open and Marco and Aoibheall had looked stunned.

"What do you mean: He's gone to get Luca?"

Marina had gasped.

Carrie shook her head.

"Nothing! I'm sorry, it's just......"

Marina had pulled out her cell phone and urgently began to bash numbers into the keypad.

Lucy shook her head:

"Who are you ringing?"

Marina had looked up at her, her face betraying obvious annoyance.

"My dad, I've got to warn him that my insane brother is on his way to kill Luca. Is that OK with you big-sis?"

Her tone was totally sarcastic.

Lucy smiled sweetly and stared into Marina's eyes:

"That would be silly, don't you think?"

Marina's mouth fell open.

"Yes, it would be silly, wouldn't it?" Marina murmured.

"Look, I'm sorry guys, I'm going to lie down. I think this has all been a bit much. I've got a headache."

Carrie cast Lucy a knowing glance and Lucy smiled weakly, her eyes betraying her embarrassment. She had known her little sister for a little over a couple of hours and she had already used her newly discovered mind influencing powers on her. Oh well, she thought; that proves I really can do that as well.

Suddenly, without warning, Lucy felt the world begin to slip away. She could see the room swirling, spinning. Marco and Aoibheall were talking and then looking at her with concern etched on their features. Carrie was moving towards her, saying something. It was like watching a slowed down movie. Carrie's voice was so deep and slow. Then it was as though a hole in the ground had opened up and swallowed her whole. She was falling, falling into a deep dark abyss. Everything went black and somewhere Lucy heard a scream. Not of pain, but of anguish and frustration.

When she opened her eyes, someone was holding her head up, the warmth of a pair of hands on Lucy's cheeks provided a comfort that brought tears to her eyes.

Carrie's concerned face came slowly into focus:

"Lucy, are you alright, Lucy?" She was asking.

Marco and Aoibheall were both leaning on the table staring intently at her.

"Lucy, are you alright?" Carrie repeated, peering into her eyes.

Lucy nodded and took a sip from a glass of water that Aoibheall had been holding.

"I must have fainted." Lucy stated eventually, her voice strained and weak.

"I've never done that before." She emitted a short laugh and then coughed.

Carrie gave her shoulder an encouraging squeeze:

"After what you've been through over the last few days, I'm not surprised. Meeting three siblings and your natural Mom must have been a real strain. I'll get you a brandy."

Lucy frowned and shook her head:

"It's not that. I've just had this awful feeling all day, that something terrible was going to happen and I can't help thinking that it just has."

Carrie nodded:

"I know. I've had the same feeling, funny but James used to say I was a bit psychic, but it looks like you're closer to it. I just hope Terri is OK. It really isn't like her not to be here."

Lucy took a deep breath:

"Yes, let's hope it is just the pressure of such much emotional overload and that you're not psychic and Terri and Wayne are fine. In fact let's just hope that we're a couple of neurotic women and everything's fine."

Carrie and Lucy both laughed, but for Lucy at least, the laugh was a thin veneer over a belief that something terrible really had happened.

Fifty-Five

Wayne had decided to make his final showdown with Luca even more dramatic than it would otherwise have been. He had sniggered to himself when he remembered how he had changed his shape into that of Clint Eastwood when he had blasted his way through the doors of Bishop Donleavy's office in Dublin Cathedral and how it had been "The Terminator" who had stormed into Giametti's office.

Wayne wondered how he could possibly top those two images. He could don a kilt and wade into Dean's house wielding his sword like Braveheart. Maybe a Roman, like in Spartacus, or Gladiator? He shook his head. He'd been Darth Vader, he didn't want to be Rambo, nor did he want to be Captain Kirk. A Klingon? No, although the thought of cursing Luca in harsh guttural Klingon did have a certain geeky appeal.

It was the thought of his sword, the Sword of Gorias, however, that finally influenced his decision. This time he would not be a movie hero, someone else, he would be himself. At least the version of himself that he would have been had he grown up as a Tuatha warrior. He stretched his mind back to Mickey Finn's cottage in the West of Ireland, when his father had morphed from the rotund Irish farmer Mickey Finn, into his true form, as Aillen Mac Fionnbharr.

Aillen had reminded Wayne of the Vulcan Ambassador from "Star Trek." His hair had been long, his robes ornate. He had worn a circlet of gold on his brow and his belt had been tied in a knot. Wayne nodded in satisfaction as he glanced into his rear view mirror to make sure that no more patrol cars were on his tail.

He turned into Coldwater Canyon and drove slowly along the winding road until he came to a line of parked cars, trucks and vans in the side of the road. He noticed a policeman just down the road and something of a crowd. Overhead he could hear the buzz of a helicopter.

Wayne gasped as he realised that all of this was for Luca. Not only was the press out in force, but the public were also gathering as word had got out that Luca Vitalia was at Dean's house on Coldwater Canyon.

Wayne reversed and carelessly parked the car in the first convenient space. He would have to walk to Dean's.

Wayne sighed and got out of the car. He selected the Sword of Gorias as his weapon of choice and stuck it in his belt. The Stone of Falias could stay in the car, its power would reach him, as it was only a mile or so to what had once been his mother's old house.

The spear could stay in the car too. Frankly, the blue plastic broom handle was a bit embarrassing for such a weapon of note.

Wayne started to walk down the Canyon. He could hear several helicopters buzzing overhead now. Wayne guessed that some would be police, the rest would be for the news channels.

He quickened his pace. He saw the press pack and the Luca fans ahead, so he stepped behind a tall cypress tree and simply disappeared.

Getting through the crowd proved somewhat difficult, even for an invisible man. He squeezed through the throng stepping on toes and barging with his elbows until he eventually got to the front. Although Wayne did enjoy one moment when a beautiful young female reporter, wearing unfeasibly tight jeans, blocked his path. He mischievously pinched her bottom and watched with glee as she turned and punched a slimy looking reporter right on the nose, which exploded in a shower of blood. The look on his face had been absolutely priceless.

Getting through the police and security agents at Dean's gate proved slightly less difficult although the gate itself remained resolutely closed. Wayne whispered something into a Cop's ear. Seconds later the gate opened and an extremely confused-looking police officer stood scratching his head in bewilderment. Wayne wandered through the gate and up the drive of 2145 Coldwater Canyon Boulevard. He could still remember vividly the first time he had seen that address: on a letter from his Mom saying that Dean thought it best that she erase the son that she had been forced to surrender from her life, in the interests of her career. Wayne grimaced at the memory. Deano had gotten what had been coming to him.

Wayne walked straight past two special agents in the dark suits, shades and earpieces and opened the door into the house that he remembered so well from his youth.

One of the agents standing nearby ran up and checked the door:

"Must have been the wind." He shouted to an older colleague nearby.

"What wind?" The other agent asked incredulously.

Wayne grinned. He wondered what had ever happened to Conchita, the sweet old Mexican housekeeper who had been such a help to his Mom when she had been raising Marco and Marina. He had liked her a lot when he had stayed here. He walked past the staircase, where he had once accompanied a young Californian girl and had passed into into adulthood.

"Now what had her name been?" He wondered.

As he walked into the spacious lounge he saw Aurelio sympathising with Dean's young blonde girlfriend. He ushered her to a sofa, patted her head condescendingly and passed her a remote control. She sniffed heavily and started flicking through the channels on a huge flat screen TV on the wall. Aurelio took a cell phone from his pocket and started to yell into it in Italian.

"That didn't used to be there." Wayne whispered as he admired the TV. He looked at the girl as she sniffed again.

"Daughter? She's young enough to be his granddaughter." Wayne thought to himself, disgustedly as he guessed that the girl was still in her twenties.

The girl stopped flicking when she saw an aerial view of Dean's house and all the activity outside in the Canyon.

"Hey look, it's us!" the girl squealed excitedly. Wayne took a deep breath. He had not taken the news helicopters into account; he would have to be careful not to be seen.

He walked into the back yard, where he remembered swimming as a youth and that party where he had been introduced to Dean's cousin's little cherub.

Wayne smiled:

"Talk of the devil!" He whispered again as he noticed Luca near the pool, his hands pressed to Dean's head. Wayne, still invisible, concentrated on his shape and placed his hand on the handle of the Sword of Gorias. The easiest thing to do would be to walk up and simply stab Luca in the back. Job done, he could go home!

Wayne grimaced. That would be dishonourable. He had a tradition to uphold. The Tuatha were not murdering assassins like the "Order." Lug had been a warrior. Nuada had been a warrior, Fionnbharr had been a warrior. Aillen, his own father, had been a warrior.

Wayne tensed his body and silently crept to a garden umbrella. Luca suddenly released Dean's head and took a step back.

Wayne was aware of a helicopter buzzing directly overhead.

"Who the hell did this?" Luca exclaimed.

"Me!" Wayne stated, quietly and succinctly.

Luca frowned, unsure if he had really heard anything above the clattering noise of the helicopter overhead and several others nearby.

"I said it was me. I did this to Dean!"

Wayne repeated, insistently as he emerged from his invisibility.

Luca literally jumped and emitted a yelp as he turned to see where the voice was coming from.

"So even Messiahs get surprised?"

Wayne grinned at his enemy.

Luca smiled as he regained his composure and a glint of recognition flashed in his eyes:

"So, Cardinal D'Abruzzo lied to me. The once mighty and oh so proud "Tuatha de Danaan" were not totally expunged from the face of the Earth. They left a stain behind."

Wayne continued to smile.

"I am Micheal Mac Aillen, Mac Fionnbharr and I am the last of the once mighty Tuatha De Danaan, Lords of Fine Finias, Glorious Gorias, Fair Falias and the magnificent Murias."

Wayne declared, maybe more pompously than he had intended.

Luca Vitalia smiled back:

"Then it shall be my pleasure to complete the task that my late little friends in the "Order" failed to complete. I would have dealt with them much more severely had I known the extent of their failure. Their deaths would have been much slower and much more painful than the quick suicides I granted them. You, however, will not be so fortunate, oh, last little Princeling of a long forgotten people! I am Lucifer, Light of Heaven and Lord Of all darkness!"

Luca's voice had deepened all the way through his little speech, until by the end it was a little more than an incredibly low rumbling growl.

The furniture around the pool began to shake and the water in the pool became choppy and rough. The Windows in Dean's house began to rattle and vases on tables began to move involuntarily.

"Luca, Dean, It's an earthquake!" Aurelio's voice bellowed from just inside the house.

"Stay back. I'm busy!" Luca roared, shouting in in his more familiar tones.

He turned back towards Wayne and his eyes flashed red.

"I have not waited for several millennia to seize this miserable lump of rock and to be duly served by the miserable primitives who inhabit it, only to be thwarted by a miserable whelp. The last survivor of a race of weaklings, pacifists and cowards, who only fought as a last resort and who all died squealing like the pigs they were!"

He raised his hand in the twinkling of an eye and a massive bolt of pure energy flew out of the middle of his open palm, straight towards Michael Mac Aillen, last of the Tuatha de Danaan.

Wayne swotted the bolt aside with a contemptuous wave of his hand.

"Whelp? You have called me that before, when I was much younger and you were no more than a little boy, yourself. We met in this very yard, Luca Vitalia, you and I, long ago. Before you were even a hammy little TV star in that woeful Amish show. I recognised you from your pathetic attempts to intimidate me in my dreams, but you failed to recognise me, Luca. That saved your life. Back then I had too much of a sense of honour to kill a child, although I felt that even as a youth, I dealt with your "Order" slaves pretty well. Your man, Francisco Pizarro and his successor, De Feren. It is not me who was the whelp. It was you, little Luca. It still is!"

Luca snarled and cast a more powerful bolt at Wayne.

Wayne grinned, although the second bolt did stun him slightly and a feeling like a mild electric shock numbed his left arm.

Wayne held up his right hand and responded in kind.

Luca Vitalia laughed as he caught Wayne's bolt of energy like a tennis ball.

"So you do have some power, little princeling. Good for you! Now, we could stand here all day and toss lightning at one another, but really, I don't have the time. I have an appointment in Rome that I simply can't miss. Now you shall see my true power. Die you fool!"

Luca shouted the last words as he contorted his face and pointed his two index fingers at Wayne's head.

Wayne tensed his body expecting more energy to slam into him, instead it was as though he had been hit in the face by a high pressure water hose. Wayne tried not to panic as the new tactic caught him unawares. He concentrated and tried to force whatever power Luca was using back towards him. For a brief moment, it worked. Wayne saw the shock on Luca's face as he pushed back the different energy that Luca was using. In the background he was somehow aware that people were pouring into Dean's house.

His slip in concentration gave Luca his opportunity and he grimaced and pointed again, pouring the dark power into Wayne's mind. Wayne felt himself clutch at the Sword Of Gorias, trying to pull it from his belt. He wondered why he hadn't just stabbed Luca in the back in the first place. He felt his shape shift lose its integrity and then he felt himself falling, falling backwards into an abyss, into a dark void. He tried to clutch at the light evaporating before him, but he was too far away, spinning, tumbling head over heels, falling, falling.

Then he felt nothing.

The two special agents ran up to Luca Vitalia who was standing over the body of a white Caucasion male, probably in his forties. Luca was examining a sword, which he turned over and over in his hands:

"I shall keep this as a souvenir." Luca muttered.

"Er, We'll need that as evidence, Sir."

One of the agents stated, almost apologetically.

"It's OK, let him keep it, Burgermeister." Walter Wickert the Third flashed his badge at Luca Vitalia and nodded deferentially.

"It's OK Sir. I'm so sorry you've been troubled with this. We'll take it from here."

Luca smiled.

"Thank you." He murmured.

Wickert glanced at the body and scowled.

"So Mr Higginbotham, we meet at last."

He then glowered at the senior agent:

"How the hell did this man get in here, Mr Burgermeister?" he barked.

The agent shrugged and scratched his head.

"I sure as hell don't know Sir. We were by the front door and Joe here thought the wind had blown it open, but hell. I just don't know how he did it. It's like when he got out of his mother's house and I didn't see him. Goddam he was as slippery as a bucket of eels."

Aurelio Vitalia ran up to his son, as several uniformed police officers and more agents burst into the yard.

"How did this schmuck get in here?" The Senator bellowed, pointing at Wayne's body, before turning to ask Luca if he was alright.

Luca nodded, his face was drawn and pale:

"I am fine. He got in here because he was an agent of Satan. He had powers that you would find totally unbelievable. It is fortunate for all of us, that, by the Grace of my Heavenly Father, I was the stronger."

Walter Wickert swallowed nervously as Aurelio put his arm around Luca and gave the FBI man a furious glare."

"When Marshall Williams hears about this, boy. You'll be on goddam traffic duty until the day you retire."

Senator Vitalia guided a weak looking Luca past the cops and agents who were now filling the yard. Dean's young girlfriend appeared and helped to guide her aged boyfriend after his cousin, back into the house.

Walter Wickert's cell phone rang angrily. Wickert answered it:

"Yes, Mr Brown. Yes Sir. I know Sir. Earthquakes and lightning bolts, Sir. I know! They saw it live on TV, Sir. An agent of Satan, Sir. Sorry, Sir. It wasn't an excuse, Sir. It was what Mr Vitalia said, Sir. Yes Sir. Tomorrow, first thing."

Wickert gulped folded the phone and put it back in his pocket.

"Seal this all off. It's a crime scene." He barked at a cop standing nearby. "And get those press hounds out of here."

"Yes Sir." The cop snapped to attention.

The local FBI chief walked up to Wickert shaking his head.

"Mr Vitalia and the Senator are leaving immediately, Sir. They said Mr Dean should be taken into a hospital. Mr Vitalia said even he couldn't save his mind."

Wickert nodded ruefully.

"Are you OK, Sir?" The FBI chief asked.

Walter shook his head and sighed.

"I think my career just got fried as effectively as this poor limey schmuck. It sure looks like he got whatever revenge it was he intended on Deano, but it sure wasn't smart of him to take on Jesus."

Wickert wiped the sweat off his face with a clean white handkerchief.

His cell phone rang again:

"Yes, Mr Williams. A full written explanation, Sir. Yes, Sir. You can tell Mr Baring that Wayne Higginbotham is dead, Sir. Yes Sir. Mr Dean Vitalia is being taken to hospital Sir. Yes, Luca Vitalia is fine and unharmed. Yes Sir, it's true Sir, lightning bolts and earthquakes. Yes, Sir. Thank you, Sir."

Wickert blew out his cheeks and put his cell phone back in his pocket.

"Actually, he's alive, Sir."

The younger of the two agents who had been guarding Dean's front door, the rookie who had helped arrest Terri Thorne, was feeling Wayne's pulse on his wrist.

Wickert's mouth dropped open.

"What?"

The agent continued to hold Wayne Higginbotham's wrist.

"There's definitely a pulse there Sir. It's weak, but it's there. This sucker's still alive."

Wickert was tempted to take out his gun and shoot Satan's assassin where he lay, but he knew that probably wasn't a good idea in front of a score of FBI agents and Los Angeles Police Department Cops.

"Get him straight to hospital. Don't let the press know he's alive. That would cause us more trouble than we could deal with. Put guards by his bed, 24/7. If he so much as twitches I want to know about it. In fact, Burgermeister, you and Joe here deal with it." Wickert ordered Henry T. Burgermeister, before turning to Burgermeister's immediate superior:

"Oh and by the way, release his mother. I guess we can safely say we know where Mr Higginbotham is now."

Fifty-Six

Luca Vitalia turned and waved to the gathered ladies and gentlemen of the Press from the stairway as he climbed to board the private plane out of Los Angeles International Airport. His smile was as wide and as white as a toothpaste commercial. The melee of reporters and photographers held out microphones and shouted and bellowed at him for all they were worth.

"OK!" Luca laughed as he turned back towards the baying crowd:

"I think by now you've all seen the film from the helicopter. Yes, I did trade bolts of pure energy with the assassin. Yes, he was an agent of Satan and yes, I did create a minor earthquake to destabilise him."

Luca laughed as more questions were hurled at him:

"One at a time, please, even I have only got two ears."

"Do you know who the assassin was?"

A huge rotund reporter bellowed from the bottom of the stairs.

Luca grinned:

"Yes, I knew him. I have encountered him before, but I did not feel he was significant."

A woman thrust a microphone towards Luca.

"Were you ever in danger, Luca?"

Luca laughed again.

"No, of course not! I was never in danger. The assassin was good in some ways, he got past an awful lot of security without being detected, but I guess I was just a whole lot better."

Luca cupped his ear to listen to the next question, which was shouted from the back of the press pack:

"Will you be accepted in Rome as the new Messiah?"

"Yes, I do believe I will be acknowledged and anointed by His Holiness, The Pope."

Luca leaned forward and cupped his ear again, forehead creased into a frown as he strained to hear another question:

"No, I'm afraid my father's cousin Dean was very severely injured in the assassin's attack. He is alive and I'm sure he will make a very good recovery in time. As for your question?"

He pointed at the attractive young blonde reporter whose bottom Wayne had pinched earlier that day.

"What are you going to do for your next miracle and have you got a girlfriend?"

Her cheeky grin caused a tumult of laughter from the crowd of journalists and TV people.

Luca put his arms on his hips and threw his head back in laughter. He wiped his eyes and composed himself, grinning suggestively at the blonde in the tight jeans.

"I'm afraid you'll just have to wait and see what my next miracle will be and no I do not have a girlfriend. I have been a bit busy lately." There was more laughter:

"The good news for you is that I have no plans to marry anyone yet and will be accepting selected phone numbers later. Thank you all! God bless you and goodbye!"

He turned and scuttled up the last few steps and disappeared into the plane giving just one more wave and cheesy grin.

Aurelio was already sat in the front row of the spacious private Boeing 767, looking extremely miserable. Jonathan T. Sherman was sat just behind him, next to Carol Anne Riley. Two bodyguards occupied the other positions in the section.

Luca grinned at Jonathan and Carol Anne:

"Good to see you two lovebirds found the time to come down to join us."

His legal representative and his press secretary looked embarrassed and mumbled congratulations of his victory over the attempted assassin.

Luca sat down next to Aurelio and slapped him on the shoulder:

"Why so glum, father?"

Aurelio shook his head and raised his hands in a gesture of helplessness.

"It's Deano. Even you couldn't fix him and I now find that the limey schmuck did the same thing to Paulo in London. He's like a moron, like he's got no brain."

Luca laughed:

"Don't worry yourself. They will be fixed in due course. The important thing today is that we should be celebrating."

As if on cue, a stewardess brought a tray out of the galley bearing several bottles of Champagne.

"Would you like a drink before we take off, Sir?"

"Of course." Luca cried:

"We have a great deal to celebrate. Today I destroyed the last vestige of an enemy power that was once incredibly powerful. There is no one who can stop me now!"

He slurped the champagne.

"Did you know about the prophecy, father?"

Aurelio shook his head.

"Prophecy? What prophecy?"

Luca laughed and patted his father's knee:

"Over fifteen hundred years ago, someone showed Pope Gregory the Great a prophecy, written on papyrus, somewhere in the East. It went something like this:

"A child no mortal man shall sire
By mother's blood Royal line acquire,
Shall suckle he no milk white breast,
Shall rise in exile, unwelcome guest,
Shall learn to change his form at will
His shape, his face, his ways to kill
Unseen, unheard, his telling blow,
His doom to lay The Messiah low."

Luca laughed when he saw Aurelio's face:

"Man, that went over your head like an airplane didn't it?"

Aurelio shrugged:

"Who wrote that stuff, Shakespeare? I don't get Shakespeare."

Luca shook his head:

"Father, it is a good job you paid so much for my education. I would hate to be as stupid as you."

Aurelio was about to make a retort when he saw the flash in Luca's eyes. He thought better of it.

Luca smiled condescendingly:

"The prophecy relates to the individual who was supposed to kill the second coming.

He had to be the product of a union between something that was not mortal and a Princess, or some sort of Royal. So Pope Gregory way back in 500 A.D. or whenever, decided to set up an organisation to exterminate anything that wasn't mortal. It became

"The Sacred Order of Saint Gregory" after his death and canonisation."

Luca laughed. "My previous guardian, before you, father dear, Cardinal D'Abruzzo, had assured me that all the none-mortals, of whatever type, especially the immortals, had finally been wiped out. He had forgotten that one of them might have left a seed behind.

It was that seed that I just stamped on."

Aurelio looked confused:

"So this guy who just tried to kill you. He was immortal? So how come he's dead?"

289

Luca smiled patiently:

"He was the last of the Tuatha de Danaan."

"The Toofer day what?" Aurelio gasped.

Luca slurped the rest of his Champagne.

"Father, it really doesn't matter any more. It was such a disappointing fight. I always believed that the champion they would send would at least be a reasonable challenge, but that was like taking candy from a baby."

He stood and took the Sword of Gorias from an overhead locker.

"I mean he tried to kill me with this. He didn't even have a gun."

The blade of the sword looked slightly rusty and the hilt and pommel had lost their golden sheen.

Aurelio laughed:

"He tried to kill YOU with a rusty sword?"

Luca shrugged.

"I really had expected better."

He perused his empty glass.

"And so mankind's fate is sealed, even before I am presented to this overblown Priest and voted for by the unwashed masses of the ignorant Proletariat and their greedy, stupid masters."

Aurelio heard Luca's whispered mutter:

"What?" He gasped.

Luca looked into his adoptive father's eyes:

"Nothing you fat, sweaty, ignorant, bald moron. Nothing at all."

His eyes flashed with a red light and Aurelio grinned:

"More Champagne." He bellowed.

As he cleared the second bottle of Champagne, a tiny figment of doubt began to creep into Luca's mind. He had destroyed the whelp, but that didn't mean he was totally in the clear. There could be traitors in his ranks. How had Sherman's wife known about the whelp and the fact that he would attack Luca?

About two hours into the flight, Luca suddenly stood up and started to walk around the first class cabin. Then he stood at the front of first class and began to visually appraise everyone in his party. His eyes burned into theirs and all felt as though he was stripping them naked and searching their minds. Carol Anne Riley clutched Jonathan's hand as Luca burned into her consciousness, making her feel exposed and violated.

After about half an hour of this "interrogation," Luca stopped glaring at people and smiled, cynically.

"So, you are all on my side, I see. Not a traitor among you. Good. What you will see in Rome, people will be talking about in a hundred, a

290

thousand years time. I needed to test you all because, after what happened in L.A. I do not feel I can trust everyone. The agents of the devil are everywhere. Many years ago a prophecy was made about an assassin who would try to prevent the Second Coming. Maybe that was what I just dealt with, but I prefer to be sure."

He looked at Jonathan T. Sherman:

"I have a question for you Mister Sherman. I do not doubt your integrity, but I want to know more about your estranged wife. How did she know about the assassin?"

Jonathan T.Sherman looked shocked:

"She did? Well, er, I have absolutely no idea, Sir."

Luca shrugged and whispered under his breath as he strolled back to his seat.

"It does not matter. I will deal with her when I get back from Rome. I will find out exactly what she knows and I shall enjoy myself doing it. She will not escape me this time."

When he got to the front of the cabin, Luca turned and smiled benignly:

"Keep celebrating all of you." He shouted.

"Enjoy the fruits of my labours. For today I have defeated my only meaningful enemy."

There was a cheer from his small entourage.

"Tomorrow I shall make the Pope and all the Priests, Rabbis and Imams that spread the word of God, my servants. They will all worship me and those who oppose me shall tremble and start to flee to the dark corners of the world. Then, my friends, we shall march on Washington D.C. with our foot soldiers in the "Brigade of Light" and we shall seize the White House with the largest majority ever gained in the history of American democracy. We will conquer the world, my faithful lieutenants, and you shall bask in the glory of my victory."

There was another cheer and some whooping.

Luca leant over one of the planes small windows and stared out at the twinkling lights of a city somewhere far below.

His mouth slowly creased into another smile.

"No one can stop me now." He whispered.

"No one."

Fifty-Seven

"You're free to go, Ma'am." The female FBI agent informed Terri, her downcast eyes immediately told Wayne's mother that something was wrong.

"Why now? I still haven't told you where Wayne is."

The woman officer sighed.

"Your family is here for you Ma'am. You are free to leave."

Terri glared at the woman as she escorted her through to the police station's lobby, where Marco, Marina, Aoibheall, Carrie and Lucy were waiting.

They all looked crestfallen.

"What's happened? Where's Michael?" She cried as a realisation hit her. It was the first time she had referred to her eldest son a Michael in a long time:

"Where's Wayne?" She wailed as Carrie hugged her.

"He's alive." Carrie gasped.

"He's in the Cedars-Sinai Hospital, under guard."

"Under guard?" Terri asked, bemused.

Marco shrugged:

"It's been on TV all day Mom. Wayne tried to kill Luca Vitalia, at dad's house for Gods sake."

"And Dad's had a stroke, or a breakdown or something." Marina wailed:

"He can't speak. It's like he doesn't know what's going on."

Terri grasped Carrie's arms:

"Can we see Mi... I'm sorry, Wayne?"

Carrie looked embarrassed.

"He's in a coma, Mom." Lucy whispered, conscious that it was the first time she had addressed anyone but Melinda with such a term, yet it had seemed so natural.

"Yeah" Marco chipped in.

"It was like just totally awesome, they were like blasting each other with lightening and stuff. One of the TV helicopters filmed it all. They've been showing it again and again. You couldn't see Wayne, he was under an umbrella near our old pool, but he must have had like a ray gun, or something because he was just like blasting this stuff at Luca, but Luca was like just blasting stuff from his hands like a superhero, or something, then like he fired this black stuff from his eyes and......"

292

"MARCO!" Aoibheall bellowed at her husband:

"Can't you see your Mom's upset?"

Marco gulped and apologised, but he couldn't help mumbling:

"It's awesome Mom, Carrie says Wayne could always do magic. It's almost like having Harry Potter as a big brother."

"I want to see Wayne." Terri gasped.

Carrie nodded:

"I'll take these guys back to the Canyon. Lucy, would you mind taking Terri to the Cedars-Sinai?"

Lucy shook her head.

"No problem. I've delayed my flight."

Marco and a weeping Marina hugged their Mom first, then Carrie and Aoibheall.

Lucy took the weeping mother she had only met little over thirty-six hours earlier by the arm and led her out to her rental car.

"He'll be OK." Lucy reassured her natural mother.

"Wayne told me about some of his adventures yesterday. He's amazing."

Terri nodded.

"I only found out about, well, you know, his magic and all that, this year. Carrie has always known. She was married to James Malone. Did Wayne tell you about him?"

Lucy nodded as she drove out of the parking lot near the police station.

"He was there when Wayne defeated those "Sacred Order" guys wasn't he? It was such a shame he was killed."

Terri sniffed:

"Do you really think Wayne will pull through or are you just being nice?"

Lucy smiled sympathetically:

"I think I have an amazing twin brother and if anyone can come through this, he can."

Terri directed Lucy to the Cedars-Sinai hospital. The women rushed to reception where they were asked to wait until the agents guarding Wayne agreed to let them see him.

Terri was in no mood to be patient:

"He is my son for God's sake and he is in a coma. I don't think he is going to overpower two guards and run down the corridor and escape, do you?"

The receptionist ignored Terri's outburst and waited for the guards to ring back. Some five minutes passed while Terri and Lucy sat in a waiting area, watching the comings and goings of the hospital.

"You can go up now. Ward 7. Second floor." The receptionist strolled over and informed Terri and Lucy who both jumped up and headed off down the corridor towards the elevator.

Terri bit her nail and then looked at Lucy as the elevator began to rise, slowly.

"I'm sorry." She said with a sad smile:

"This must all seem so weird to you. Police stations, hospitals and such. It's weird to us too, please believe me."

Lucy snorted:

"It's fine, Mom. I'm just sorry Wayne didn't blast Vitalia into orbit."

The elevator doors opened and a dark suited man with an earpiece met them as soon as they had stepped out on to the corridor.

"Ms Thorne?" The man asked.

Terri nodded. The man held out his hand:

"Hi Ma'am. I'm Special Agent Henry T. Burgermeister, Federal Bureau of Investigations. And this is.......?"

"I know, we've already met." Terri interrupted the agent, brusquely. "You're the schmuck that arrested me, remember? This is Charlotte.....I'm sorry, Lucy Hetherington. She's my daughter."

"I'm afraid I'm going to have to check for weapons, Ma'am" Burgermeister explained as his face began to flush.

"Feel free!" Terri blustered angrily as she raised her arms. Lucy did the same.

"OK! He's down here."

Burgermeister, now a deep shade of pink, led the girls down a corridor, until they stopped, next to fire exit.

"This is Wayne's room. I'm afraid for the purposes of security, we shall have to be present at all times. This is my colleague, Ramos."

Lucy nodded curtly while Terri made a beeline straight for the comatose figure on the bed.

Ten minutes passed, then half an hour, then an hour. Wayne Higginbotham did not even flinch. Terri and Lucy sat by Wayne's bed in silence, watched by Henry T. Burgermeister and his young colleague.

A nurse popped in and felt Wayne's pulse.

"Are you sure he's alive?" Terri asked.

The nurse nodded and pointed to a cardiograph machine, which pulsed slowly but clearly.

"His pulse is the faintest I've felt, though." The nurse said with a grimace.

"He's hanging on, but we don't know how."

Lucy closed her eyes. Shape shifting and invisibility were great party tricks, but right now a more useful type of magic was needed. The kind of magic that had saved Wayne all those years earlier and had saved Lucy just a few days ago.

Lucy concentrated on finding her twin brother. She had only just met him; she wasn't about to go losing him already. No matter where he was. She would find him.

Fifty-Eight

Natalia Higginbotham couldn't believe her ears as the two policemen and a policewoman sat in a line on her sofa, cradling cups and saucers of tea. One of the policemen and the policewoman were uniformed officers, the other man was wearing a smart business suit.

Natalia was wrapped in a dressing gown, it being the early hours of the morning.

"Could you please repeat everything you have just told me?" She gasped incredulously.

"Because, I'm sorry to say it, but it really did sound like the most incredible tosh I have ever heard. My husband told me he was just going to be in America for a few days."

The man in the suit, Detective Inspector Ratchett, nodded understandingly.

"I would fully agree, Mrs Higginbotham, but that's what our American colleagues have told us, just this morning."

Natalia shook her head:

"So all that stuff on the news about Luca Vitalia killing some assassin, that was my Wayne?"

Ratchett sighed:

"I'm afraid it does look like it, although there was no identification on the body. He did not have his drivers licence, or passport on his person, it seems."

Natalia took a deep breath:

"And you're certain that Wayne's dead?"

D.I. Ratchett rubbed his chin thoughtfully and grimaced.

"The information we have had, suggests that your husband is in a vegetative state, in other words a very deep coma. The medical specialists have stated categorically that recovery is very unlikely indeed. They say he is well, how I do I put it? Brain dead."

Natalia smiled:

"They don't know Wayne then." She paused then bit her lip.

"Have the Americans given any motives for Wayne's fight with Luca Vitalia and what is all this nonsense about lightning bolts?"

Ratchett scratched his head and blew out an exasperated sigh.

"According to the Yanks who spoke to me this morning, Wayne had some sort of dispute with Dean Vitalia, who I believe was his stepfather?"

Natalia nodded.

Ratchett pursed his lips and then continued:

"It could just have been that he was in the wrong place at the wrong time and things got out of hand. You know what family disputes are like. Even so, the Americans are saying that they believe that Wayne did attack Mr Luca Vitalia with some sort of energy weapon, which they haven't found yet and that, you know, in taking on the "Son of God," Wayne took on the wrong guy."

Natalia actually laughed.

"They don't actually believe this "Son of God" thing do they? Wayne told me that Luca Vitalia was no more than a spoiled, supercilious, jumped up little toad."

Ratchett grinned and shrugged:

"Yes, I must admit that I hold similar views, but the Americans do seem to be taking him seriously and they say that if the Pope approves of him after the summit meeting that's been happening today, then he will be declared the spiritual leader of the Western World on Christmas Day."

Natalia shook her head as she desperately tried to hold back the tears:

"Well I suppose I better make plans to go to Los Angeles. I'll ring my mother first thing in the morning, well as soon as it gets light, to arrange for her to come down to look after the kids."

D.I. Ratchett heaved a huge sigh:

"I am very sorry to have to bring you this news Mrs Higginbotham. Constable Terry here has more details of the hospital in Los Angeles where Wayne is being looked after and Constable Louise Jackson is a family liaison officer, who will help you in any way she can."

He paused for a second and looked at the policewoman, who looked back apprehensively. Natalia Higginbotham seemed to be made of quite stern stuff. She had not shed a single tear so far.

It was while the young policewoman was telling Natalia about what support she could provide that the phone rang, despite the unseemly hour.

Natalia excused herself and took the call in her kitchen.

"Sad isn't it?" Ratchett opined.

"Beautiful kids!" The policewoman stated as she perused a family portrait on the wall of the drawing room.

"Nice house." Constable Terry muttered, somewhat enviously before turning to Ratchett.

"Some of the boys down the station are saying there's a link between this Higginbotham guy and the gangsters who were found down on the old Sykes Farm."

D.I. Ratchett stood and peered around the corner of the door into the kitchen. Natalia seemed to be engrossed in conversation on her phone, so Ratchett turned back to Constable Terry:

"Keep it quiet, but that's what we believe. A cousin of this Luca Vitalia's father was found in the same state as the gangsters you are referring to, in London, along with his henchmen, one of whom had taken a forty two storey tumble."

"So is this chap, Higginbotham, involved in criminal activity then?" Louise Jackson asked, obviously somewhat taken aback that someone with such a nice, middle class home and beautiful middle class family could be involved in gang warfare.

DI Ratchett smirked:

"Don't be deluded by the thin veneer of middle class respectability, love. I've seen people with titles involved in stuff you wouldn't believe. The thing is, this bloke is involved with some very heavy geezers. Giametti, that's the bloke that was turned over in London, he supposedly had mafia connections……."

He tailed off as Natalia walked back into the drawing room:

"That was Terri, Wayne's Mom. It is him, he's still clinging on, but only just."

The confirmation that it was Wayne in the hospital seemed to come as a crushing blow to Natalia Higginbotham. She had been clinging to the belief that there must have been some sort of mistake and that Wayne would have rung soon and would have confirmed that it was all just a silly case of mistaken identity.

W.P.C. Jackson put her arm around Natalia's shoulder.

"He's only just been reunited with his twin sister. They were separated at birth."

Natalia sobbed.

D.I. Ratchett nodded sympathetically.

"I'm sure the Docs over there will do everything they can for him."

He murmured.

Natalia nodded:

"I suppose I'd better tell the children in the morning, then pack. I can't leave until my Mam gets here. I'll try and fly out as soon as possible."

D.I.Ratchett and his team all felt very sorry for the wife of the man who'd tried to kill the Son of God.

Fifty-Nine

Wayne's coma had lasted for almost twenty four hours so far, but Terri had insisted on staying at his bedside, until Lucy came back from Carrie's house where she had spent another night, albeit one without sleep.

Lucy was now stood by Wayne's bed, her features lined as the stress of the preceding weeks now began to really catch up with her.

Could it be possible that she really was going to lose her twin brother so soon after being reunited with him? She had delayed her flight another day. The last thing she wanted to do was miss Christmas with her children, but at least she knew that Rupert and Melinda would look after them well, as long as Rupert was up to it.

Every attempt Lucy had made to contact Wayne telepathically so far had failed. Even she was beginning to lose hope.

Two different FBI Special Agents were now sat just outside Wayne's private room. They had relieved Burgermeister and the rookie for the night and were awaiting their return impatiently. Guarding a body that was 99% dead was hardly exciting, or fulfilling work.

The Doctor that bustled into the room along with two nurses did not look, or sound hopeful. A big African American with a naturally cheerful disposition, he shook his head sadly when Terri asked if there had been any change in Wayne's condition.

"I am sorry, ma'am." He stated, peering over the rim of his spectacles:

"His condition has not improved, but on the bright side, nor has it deteriorated. I guess he's clinging on to life with his fingernails, but, lady, he's still there and I've gotta tell you, I never expected that when they brought him in, yesterday. If I was you I'd pray for all I was worth that the Lord forgives, like they say he does in the Good Book."

The Doctor scribbled some notes on a clipboard and smiled reassuringly at Terri:

"We're doing all we can for him Ms Thorne. He'll get the best care possible, no matter what he did."

For the first time Terri realised the opprobrium that Wayne would suffer even if he did recover. The vast majority of people in the United States did now seem to believe in Luca Vitalia's candidacy as the new Messiah and Wayne Higginbotham would be viewed as the man who tried to kill the Son of God: "God's Assassin."

The Doctor left the room whistling contentedly.

"Oh my God." Terri lamented. "They really think he tried to kill the new Jesus Christ."

Lucy grimaced and shook her head.

"Oh, Luca Vitalia is far from that, I can tell you. Let's go get a coffee while these guys are busy."

When Lucy and Terri got back to Wayne's room, they found the nurses were changing Wayne's bedclothes and washing him behind the curtains they'd pulled around his bed.

Terri shook her head:

"Someone will try to kill Wayne as soon as he recovers. All those religious fanatics will do anything in the name of Luca Vitalia. I mean the "Brigade of Light" are like a modern day Ku Klux Klan." She moaned despondently.

"Maybe he'd be better off......"

"Don't even go there, Mom." Lucy snapped.

"Look you're tired, why don't you go home, freshen up, oh and has anyone thought of ringing Wayne's wife?"

Terri nodded: "Yes, I've told her he's alive. I couldn't bring myself to say how bad he is though."

Lucy nodded, smiled and gave her Mom a brief hug.

"See you then, Mom. Are you sure you don't want me to stay with him tonight?"

Terri grimaced:

"No, I guess I've never really been able to look after him as a son. Maybe it's time I did."

She smiled sadly, turned and left the room.

Lucy went to the bathroom and returned to Wayne's room just as the nurses left, now alone with Wayne, she sat down on the chair next to his bed. The ECG machine beeped and blipped away at regular intervals, indicating that Wayne was still clinging to life, just.

A solitary tear rolled down Lucy's face as she thought about her early impressions of Wayne when he had told her about his adventures.

She closed her eyes and reached out a hand, which she placed gently on Wayne's forehead. It felt quite cool to the touch, which was worrying in itself.

How much longer could Wayne hang on? Lucy wondered as she called to him from somewhere deep within her mind.

"Wayne, can you hear me?"

There was no response.

Lucy kept her hand on his forehead:

"Wayne, talk to me?"

There was still no response.

Lucy fought back her tears but couldn't help a loud sob.

As the afternoon turned into evening, Lucy thought about all the years they'd missed. They'd missed out on growing up together, bickering and fighting, taking pleasure in each other's triumphs and consoling each other when things hadn't gone so well. As twins, they would probably have been extremely close. Now it was all being snatched away by Luca bloody Vitalia.

Tears flooded down Lucy's face.

She grabbed Wayne's hand tightly and this time she seemed almost angry as she gritted her teeth determinedly:

"Wayne, you bugger! Please talk to me, don't let that sleaze ball Vitalia beat you, for God's sake. For all our sakes, wake up, you stupid moron!"

This time her telepathic message was shouted from the middle of her mind, her anger at Luca's victory and her distress at the loss of her brother and a million might have beens serving to concentrate her focus.

She watched Wayne's forehead crease into an angry looking frown and felt his fist clench. Somewhere, far away, somebody had heard her.

Sixty

Luca could not resist planning to perform his greatest miracle yet as he was driven towards the Great Cathedral, where he was to be presented to the Pope and the representatives of all the world's major religions. He had been thinking about it for days.

How he was going to impress them all and leave them in no doubt as to his divinity.

The answer had come in a flash of inspiration and Luca knew it would just blow them all away.

The motorcade, from the airport into Rome, had been mobbed by "Brigade" members and by millions of less fanatical, but still faithful supporters, despite the bitter winter chill of the Roman December.

Progress had been slow, but they had finally reached the outskirts of the Vatican City with half an hour to spare and the car was slowly inching through the throng.

The Carabinieri were manfully trying to push the crowd back to allow the motorcade to pass.

"So how's it feel to be back in your old home-town?" Aurelio asked his son with a grin.

Luca's fixed smile didn't waver for a second.

"I hate this place. It reminds me too much of Momma."

Aurelio shrugged.

"Do you still miss her too?"

Luca shrugged:

"I guess, but she betrayed me by doing what she did. For that I will never forgive her."

Aurelio nodded.

"I guess she had her reasons."

There was a long awkward silence as the car edged through the crowd.

"Hard to believe that just a few hours ago you were crushing that schmuck who thought he could kill you."

Luca nodded.

"Pathetic, really, wasn't it?" He whispered, his voice betraying his boredom.

Aurelio sighed. Luca's apparent ebullience on the flight about his victory over the assassin had turned into an impatient determination. Luca wanted to conquer the world now that the only threat to his eventual success had been removed.

302

"I am so totally sick of waving." Luca had moaned eventually.

"Do you think they can see us in here?" He waved mechanically through the blackened privacy glass.

Aurelio shrugged:

"They can't see much, but it's best to be polite and wave. They are your followers now, so much more than the fans you used to have when you were a pop star. These people would die for you."

Luca smiled and then turned back to his adoptive father:

"Did you see all the freaks holding out their pathetic, malformed offspring and the hordes of the disabled, the blind and the diseased, reaching out to the car?"

Luca whispered as he twisted his face in disgust.

"I can't stand that! It freaks me out, man. I mean look, there's more of them!"

He pointed towards a young mother in the front row of the crowd who was desperately thrusting her wailing baby out towards the car. The car's mirror missed the unfortunate child's head by millimetres.

"Ugh!" Luca spat as he continued to wave.

"Disgusting peasants!"

Aurelio shrugged.

"You're going to have to get used to that son, especially after today and especially in poor countries. Everyone needs to believe in...."

There was a sudden shout and a gap opened up in the crowd as a bearded man in black rushed towards the motorcade.

"Allahu Akbar!" He shouted at the top of his voice. Someone in a uniform threw himself at the assailant and knocked him over before he reached Luca's motorcade.

There was a blinding flash of light and then an enormous bang as the assassin exploded just a few metres from the armoured Mercedes, which rocked and swerved violently, but despite receiving huge amounts of shrapnel, stayed intact.

The driver put his foot down hard, knocking people aside indiscriminately as he made a rush through the morass, for the Via della Concilliazione and the sanctuary of the cordoned off Saint Peter's Square.

For Luca and Aurelio, everything seemed to happen in slow motion. Blood and gore had covered the glass in the car windows, as though someone had hurled buckets of offal over the vehicle. The noise had temporarily deafened everyone nearby, including the occupants of the Mercedes, but the sudden silence that descended on the Via Dei Corridori was in marked contrast to the cheering, screaming and shouting that had preceded the explosion.

It was with huge relief all round when the car spun into the intimidating square, followed by police cars with sirens wailing. Because of the speed of the escape, the occupants of the Mercedes had not witnessed the carnage that they had left behind.

Luca grinned.

"They'll have to do much better than that." He almost shouted, his ears still ringing.

Aurelio shrugged his shoulders.

"I can't hear." He shouted.

"The stupid son of a bitch, he's deafened me."

As the car pulled up before the steps of the mighty Cathedral, hundreds of nervous looking security men, identically dressed in dark suits and shades, with curly wires hanging from their ears, rushed to surround the Mercedes and its precious occupants.

Luca and Aurelio were quickly ushered out, from a door on the opposite side to where the gore and pock marked metal were blended in a gruesome, sickening melange.

Cardinal Rinaldi greeted the pair, concern etched into his features:

"I am so sorry about the incident outside the Holy See." He exclaimed waving his hands theatrically as he hurriedly ushered the Americans into the Cathedral. A pair of Swiss Guards snapped to attention.

Aurelio pointed at his ears and shook his head.

Camera flash guns popped everywhere.

"I can't hear a goddam thing." He bellowed.

Luca glowered at his father and put a silencing finger to his lips.

Despite the buzzing in his ears, Luca Vitalia heard the collective sharp intake of breath that accompanied his arrival into St. Peter's. The great Cathedral was jammed to the doors with religious figures of every race, rank, colour, denomination and faith. All eyes were on Luca who smiled beatifically and waved as he walked towards the place prepared for him under the massive dome.

The Pope, His Holiness Gregory XVII, was sat on a simple wooden chair, facing the main body of the Church. A choir was singing a Te Deum, pitch perfectly in Latin.

An empty chair had been placed strategically directly under the Apex of the Dome and Luca was ushered towards it by Cardinal Rinaldi, while Aurelio was escorted off to an aisle on the left, along with the Secret Service men who had accompanied the Presidential hopeful on the plane to Europe.

Luca Vitalia glanced at the front row of dignitaries. He recognised The Archbishop of Canterbury, the Ecumenical Patriarch of Constantinople and The Patriarch of Athens.

He had no idea who the others were, although he did recognise the Jewish, Islamic, Buddhist and Sikhs by their dress.

The Pope stood and greeted Luca with a kiss on both cheeks, before indicating that Luca should sit in the empty chair.

The Pope then began to speak about the horror that had just occurred outside and about how Luca had survived two assassination attempts in as many days.

"This is why we need unity, my brethren." He implored the selected audience.

"The world has reached a cross roads. We are threatened by climate change, by economic uncertainty, religious schism and conflict. People are starving in some parts of the world, while the grain that should serve as food is being used to power so called gas-guzzlers in others. Individualism, secularism and selfishness have grown like a cancer in the West, while militancy, authoritarianism and intolerance have afflicted the East.

One cannot help feel, that we have almost reached the end of man's dominion on this once beautiful planet, which could once truly be seen as a Garden of Eden. We have almost come to the end of days, the end of all things.

It is in such a time of crisis that we need a leader: Someone to take our hands and lead us singing, into the Promised Land. "

The Pope bowed his head momentarily and the voluminous cathedral fell silent, except for the occasional cough and the shuffling of feet and papers. Outside the wail of sirens could be heard in the aftermath of the attempt on Luca's life.

Eventually the Pontiff raised his head:

"Maybe this is the "close of the age". That Our Lord Jesus Christ referred to after his resurrection, Matthew, Chapter 27. It was Jude, brother of James who said:

"in the last time, there will be scoffers, following their own ungodly passions." We have seen that. Maybe this is the dawn of the thousand-year reign of Christ upon earth.

Maybe we have already reached the point when, according to the Book of Revelations: "The first earth had passed away and the sea was no more and a great voice said: "behold the dwelling of God is with men. He will dwell with them they shall be his people and God himself will be with them.""

The Pope bowed his head again and the next time he spoke his voice was so quiet that even those at the front had difficulty hearing him.

"It is for you now and for us to decide if this man who sits before us, is more or less than a man. For two thousand years we have awaited salvation. Does this man bring such redemption? Or is he the serpent who shall leave the mark of Babylon on the foreheads of the unclean? That is the nature of our task this day. We must determine whether Lucien Vitalia, known as Luca, is the Second Coming of Jesus Christ, our Redeemer, or a charlatan who has deceived more people than anyone else in modern history. In the name of Our Lord and by the Grace of the Blessed Virgin, may we reach the correct decision. I ask Cardinal Rinaldi, head of the Holy Inquisition to start the catechism. May God be with him."

The Pope turned and retook his simple chair, while Cardinal Rinaldi stood and walked towards Luca Vitalia.

Luca Vitalia smiled confidently as the elderly Rinaldi fired question after question at him. Luca's Biblical knowledge was tested, as was his familiarity with all manner of Liturgical processes. Classical Philosophy, extended theology and the history of the entire Christian Church were tested until many in the audience fell asleep. Finally, two hours after he had started to question Luke, Cardinal Rinaldi shook his head.

"Luca Vitalia, your knowledge is no less than encyclopaedic. Indeed, I have never known anyone who knows the Holy Book and the entire philosophical underpinnings of Christianity even half as well as you do and I include myself in that equation. However, I open the challenge to some of my colleagues from the other great religions to question you, if that is acceptable."

Luca, looking every bit as fresh as when the questioning had started nodded amenably.

A Rabbi, an Imam and a Guru questioned Luca every bit as aggressively as Cardinal Rinaldi had. Eventually all three had to admit that Luca Vitalia knew their respective religions inside out. Not only that but he showed a due degree of reverence to each questioner and his religion.

Finally, after a short break, the Pope consulted his senior Cardinals, then he stood at the front of the gathered congregation and spoke slowly and clearly.

"We have severely tested Luca Vitalia here today and have found his knowledge far exceeds all expectation. His philosophy matches our own and his demeanour has been beyond reproach. However, none of these facets make him a God. We shall discuss the matter over the next four days and shall make our announcement before midnight, Greenwich Mean Time, on Christmas Day. May God bless you all in the name of the Father, The Son and The Holy Ghost. Amen."

The congregation repeated the Amen, just as Luca Vitalia stood up and faced his audience.

The Pope, somewhat taken aback, pulled back and leaned on a nearby Lectern.

Luca spoke without the help of any microphone, but his voice carried to every corner of St. Peter's and even filled the Square outside:

"Today, my knowledge has been tested. My beliefs have been tested and my intentions queried. Yet any bookworm could have passed these tests. What none of you have grasped is that this IS the beginning of the end of all things. All the things, both material and immaterial, that mattered to you previously. All the beliefs that you held and opinions that you professed."

Luca took a step forward:

"Maybe my words would have more effect, if I looked like this."

The plan that he had been perfecting for days was carried out in seconds.

The be-suited, business like, clean cut, young American Presidential candidate transformed himself into a long-haired, bearded and robed, swarthy figure with unnaturally pale blue eyes. The entire congregation gasped in amazement:

"Is this not the image you have of the Messiah, Your Messiah. Jesus the prophet, Jesus the Christ? Does this not better suit thy preconceptions? Thy expectations?"

He pulled an extremely small Ciabatta loaf from his robe and a small bottle of wine.

"All shall pass by me in thy hunger, which has grown as you have patiently sat and watched me toil before my Inquisitors, you shall eat of this, my flesh and drink of this, my blood. And the last amongst you to pass, shall eat and drink as bountifully as the first."

With that the Christ like figure pointed to the man nearest to him in the front aisle. The Archbishop of Canterbury stood and was presented with a large portion of the loaf and offered a swig of the wine bottle, which he was about to turn down until he looked into Luca's eyes. The venerable Archbishop gulped from the bottle, then wiped his mouth with the back of his hand. The Ecumenical Patriarch of Constantinople followed the Archbishop's example and slowly each member of the congregation looked into the eyes of the new Messiah and ate and drank copiously from what had seemed a tiny piece of bread.

It was a seemingly insignificant, black-robed Irish Monsignor, who had been about the fortieth to stand in line to take Luca Vitalia's mock communion, who provided the biggest surprise of the entire ceremony, eclipsing even Luca's metamorphosis.

Unlike the rest of the Priests and dignitaries, the Monsignor did not look into Luca's eyes. He bowed his head low, crossed himself rather hastily and with the words:

"Forgive me father, for I do know what I do," summarily exploded in a huge flash of light and a ball of flame which engulfed both himself and Luca Vitalia.

Sixty-One

Wayne Higginbotham couldn't understand it. He was not dead. He knew that, because he was too bloody embarrassed to be dead. It hadn't even been a decent fight. He felt like the boxer who after training religiously for years had been knocked out in the first seconds of the first round and that after months of bragging about how he was going to flatten the other guy. So if he wasn't dead, why was he floating around in what he could only describe as nothingness?

Wayne glanced around. There really was nothing to see, just an inky blackness. It was much darker than when he had been stood at the top of the mountain by the cairn in Ireland.

There were no stars, no pinpricks of distant light. In fact, it felt like he was floating in a barrel of tar, yet he could breathe, so that obviously wasn't the case.

In the absence of anything better to do, Wayne had run through what had happened over and over again.

How had Luca defeated him so easily?

His first energy blasts hadn't even been as powerful as Wayne remembered Francisco Pizarro's being. Yet somehow Vitalia had changed his focus and used a different type of energy. Wayne remembered the way Luca had pointed his index fingers and the stream of what he could only describe as dark energy had emerged. It had flooded Wayne's mind and sent him to wherever he was.

Wayne tried not to panic.

Panic was illogical. Fear numbed the brain and neutralised the thought process. That was the last thing he needed. He was not in hell, because it wasn't hot and if this was heaven then it was even more boring than he had imagined. The only answer then, was that he was in limbo. Strict Roman Catholics believed that limbo was where the souls of unbaptized children ended up. Wayne had never been baptized but he was nearing fifty, a bit too old to be considered a child. The fact that his brain was working gave him some hope:

"Cogito ergo sum." He thought.

"I think therefore I am." If he could remember Descartes, then his mind was fully functional, so the only thing he had to do was rationalise his situation and come up with a plan to escape.

Wayne considered and rationalised for what seemed like an eternity. Eventually he couldn't consider, or rationalise any more. He was tired, so tired.

With a start Wayne remembered all those old black and white movies about naval engagements during the Second World War. The plucky Brits always seemed to end up in the water clinging on to driftwood, or lying wounded in a lifeboat and it was always the ones who were tired and went to sleep who died.

"Pull out of it, Higginbotham." An imaginary bosun bellowed.

"So," Wayne wondered. "What do I do now?"

He concentrated on trying to get in touch with his father, given that he must be somewhere between life and death and Tir Na Nog was in a similar plane.

There was no response.

He only had one other hope. His sister. He couldn't die on her so soon after meeting her.

He concentrated and called her name.

There was no response.

"Oh bum!" Wayne thought to himself.

"This really isn't going so well."

Wayne decided the best thing to do was to examine where he'd gone wrong in his failed attempt to destroy Vitalia.

Could it have been his failure to draw the magical Sword of Gorias?

Should he have used the Spear of Finias, with its fetching blue plastic mop shaft?

Maybe he would have fared better had he had the Stone of Falias secreted somewhere on his person?

Wayne pondered what he could have done better. He analysed his every move and everything that he had done. Still he came to the same conclusion. Luca Vitalia had been just too damn powerful.

His father, Aillen Mac Fionnbharr, had been right along. The misguided sense of honour and decency that, in his youth, had prevented him from killing a child, had allowed Luca to grow into something that he could not deal with. He had refused to kill the child, but the man the child had become was much too powerful for Wayne Higginbotham. He had given Luca an easy victory and in so doing had condemned mankind to oblivion.

The thought of his father spurred him into trying to contact Aillen Mac Fionnbharr again.

Once again there was no response.

He concentrated on Lucy again and called her name.

Nothing.

Wayne Higginbotham was beginning to despair.

"Well done Wayne." He said to himself. "I think you've gone and blown it. All those Tuatha de Danaan died for nothing.

Dear old Frank Higginbotham, died for nothing.

Poor old James Malone died for nothing. Natalia, Katie, Frankie, Mom, Lucy, Marco and Marina are all going to die for nothing. Lucy's kids? I haven't even met them yet, and they're going to die for nothing."

Wayne felt his anger build and then it turned to rage.

"It will NOT end like this. I will not be defeated by Luca bloody Vitalia."

Then he heard something. It was the first sound he had heard in what seemed like days.

It was very distant but he could hear a woman's voice.

"Wayne." It shouted, almost angrily.

Wayne turned in the direction of where it seemed to be coming from.

"Doris?" He wondered. The voice sounded like Doris' when she was telling Wayne off for some misdemeanour, or other and as Doris had been dead for many years this must mean that he was passing through the other side of the void.

"Oh great!" Wayne grumbled to himself. "Here I am about to enter the afterlife and the first thing I'm in for is a telling off from Doris."

The voice shouted again:

Wayne concentrated on the sound. That wasn't Doris, the voice didn't have a Yorkshire accent. If anything it was like a BBC newsreader's voice, plummy, very R.P.

Wayne had a sudden flash of recognition.

"Lucy?" he shouted.

Then the voice came as clearly as if she had been standing right next to him.

"Wayne, you bugger! Please talk to me, don't let that sleaze ball Vitalia beat you, for God's sake. For all our sakes, wake up, you stupid moron!"

In the distance he could see a pinprick of light. He started to move towards it, his limbs felt leaden and unresponsive, but he had to get out of this state of limbo.

He felt himself breaking into a jog, then a run, then he sprinted until the pinprick of light was more like a giant frameless window. Although he couldn't see anything beyond the window, Wayne hurled himself at it.

In the hospital bed his eyes snapped open. The first thing he saw was Lucy staring down at him, her eyes watery and tearful and her features lined with worry. She looked older than he remembered.

She clapped her hands to her mouth.

"Oh my God." She squealed:

"You're alive!"

Then she laughed.

"So you only respond to insults?"

Wayne grinned at his twin sister.

"Only the good ones. How long have I been out?"

Lucy glanced round to see if the FBI men had heard Wayne speak. She pressed a finger to her lips to silence her brother and then she walked on tip-toe to the door and peered round it. One agent was standing at the end of the corridor sipping a polystyrene cup of coffee. There was no sign of his colleague.

Lucy turned back into the room.

"I really thought we'd lost you." She gasped as she hugged her brother.

"You've been out for over twenty-four hours. You're under guard here. You've been a very bad boy, trying to kill the next President of the United States of America and the Messiah to boot. All subtly live on a major news network."

Wayne heaved a huge sigh.

"I really blew it then?"

Lucy nodded:

"Big time, I'm afraid. You managed to make Luca look even more like the Messiah, if that was possible."

Wayne slapped his hand to his forehead.

"Have the police moved my car?"

Lucy raised her eyebrows in surprise:

"How would I know?" She asked as she wondered why that would be his first thought.

Wayne looked distraught:

"The Tuatha treasures are in it: The Stone and the Spear. Do you know what happened to the sword?"

Again Lucy shook her head:

"I suppose the cops might have taken it." She guessed out loud.

"If it was left at Dean's house."

Wayne grimaced and closed his eyes despondently.

"How could I have blown it so badly?"

Lucy smiled sympathetically.

"You need rest. Luca's now in Rome trying to persuade the Pope to anoint him as the Messiah. There's nothing you can do now."

Both Wayne and Lucy flinched as the hospital room's door opened.

Terri walked in carrying two coffee cups.

"I'm back." She called cheerily.

Lucy put her finger to her lips to silence Terri before she squealed with elation at her son's sudden recovery.

Terri's mouth dropped open as she noticed her son's open eyes staring at her.

She ran over and hugged Wayne for all she was worth, tears of joy poured down Terri's face.

Lucy told Terri how Wayne had just suddenly come round.

"Have you told the Doctors?"

Terri asked, "I mean there could be complications."

Wayne shook his head.

"I have to get out of here. I need to rescue the treasures." He muttered.

"Just give me a few minutes to pull myself together."

He closed his eyes momentarily.

Lucy flicked on the TV and began to flick through the channels. Something suddenly caught her eye and she stopped flicking.

A sombre looking anchor-woman stared directly into the camera:

"And we go straight back to Rome where the breaking news, is that Presidential hopeful and self proclaimed Messiah, Luca Vitalia has been assassinated in the heart of St. Peter's, in Rome, Italy. Jim Baxter over to you."

Wayne opened his eyes and quickly sat up in bed.

The TV screen moved from the LA studio to a scene just outside the Vatican City, where a news reporter was valiantly trying to describe the scene, as ambulances and police cars with wailing sirens rushed by."

"It still can not be confirmed, but after the earlier carnage on the streets of Rome when an Islamic fanatic tried to assassinate Luca Vitalia, costing over fifty lives, it appears that someone has now actually succeeded inside this mighty Basilica itself. The very home of Roman Catholicism."

The screen panned to a line of police holding back a weeping and wailing mob in the darkness of the early hours of a Roman mid-winter morning.

The ticker across the screen stated that according to Vatican sources, Luca Vitalia and several senior religious leaders had been killed at around two a.m. Rome time, by a suicide bomber in the heart of Saint Peter's Basilica, despite the heaviest security in Roman history.

"Bloody hell!" Wayne exclaimed.

"Some bugger did a better job than me!"

Sixty-Two

Monsignor Declan Doyle was not a violent man, nor had he ever been. No one could ever have described him as a militant, but he knew that he was alone now. He had seen the news reports that were now describing the assassin who had tried to kill Luca Vitalia in Los Angeles, as a British citizen.

Monsignor Doyle knew deep down inside that this was the boy who had been Father Reichmann's last and only hope. He had seen Vitalia brag on the TV about how he had destroyed the "supernatural" agent that Satan had sent to kill him, by directing energy beams at him.

"That was not what Jesus would have done." Monsignor Doyle had declared, as he watched the giant screen in the Paris Gare de Bercy where he was catching the Artesia night train to Rome.

"So what would Jesus have done?" The question preoccupied Monsignor Doyle's thoughts as the train hurtled through the French countryside. The only conclusion he could possibly come to, was that Jesus would have stopped the assassin's attack by reasoning with him. He would most certainly not have thought fire with fire. It was just one more example of how Luca Vitalia was slowly and surely proving that he was not the Messiah.

Yet, much to Declan Doyle's surprise, no one else seemed to be too concerned with Luca's violent reaction to the attack. TV commentators seemed more impressed with the display of "firework s" and the fact that Luca could shoot energy beams from his hands like a comic book superhero. All the conversation that he could hear on the train was about how brilliant Luca had been in facing down his attacker. Doyle even heard one passenger declare:

"This is what we need. No more turning the other bloody cheek. Hit 'em back and hit 'em hard."

Despite sharing a sleeping cabin with six strangers, Monsignor Doyle had spent the entire night in prayer. He had clutched his rosary and said more Hail Mary's than he had probably done in the rest of his life put together. The loud snoring of some of his fellow travellers had more than drowned out the sound of his mumbled prayers, so he hadn't disturbed anybody. It was only when the train had hit a bad piece of track and had rattled and rolled for several seconds that one passenger woke up and had cast him a derisory glance.

Monsignor Doyle had clutched his ancient black leather briefcase to his chest all the way through the journey. Mr O'Malley had given him the tools he needed to save the world and he was determined not to lose them.

It was the same bag that his father had given him when he had gone off to the Seminary in Limerick, so many years earlier. Declan Doyle's mother had died when he had been small and his father had passed during Declan's time in Limerick. He had been an only child and would have been very lonely, had it not been for his faith. The only regret in Declan Doyle's life had been the fact that he had never loved a woman. He had been close to several, but his adherence to his faith and his fidelity to the rules of his calling had prevented him from falling into sin. With an ironic grin he wondered if Christian martyrs got the same deal as Islamic jihadists. Would he get seventy-two virgins in heaven? Knowing his luck, he would and they'd all be harridans determined to hang on to their innocence.

As the dawn light began to filter through the chinks in the blind at the train's window, Monsignor Doyle took some comfort from the fact that he would soon be leaving physical pain and temptation behind, for something much more ethereal and Holy.

Monsignor Declan Doyle had reconciled himself to his fate during his journey and had prayed for forgiveness. He was almost absolutely certain that Luca Vitalia was an imposter, but there was still the tiniest of nagging doubts in his mind. Even so, Declan Doyle had made his mind up to act and only an act of God could now stop him from carrying out his intended task and if that happened, then he would know that it was God's will and that he and Father Reichmann had been wrong.

Monsignor Doyle's journey through Rome, back to the Vatican, had taken him much longer than he had expected, due to the crowds of "Brigade of Light" fanatics and all those who had just come to catch a glimpse of the new Messiah. He had only just had enough time, when he got back to his apartment, to quickly shower and prepare himself for the ceremonial parade into Saint Peter's.

When he had heard the distant flat thud of the distant explosion from his seat in Saint Peter's, Doyle had hoped that it had been an assassination attempt on Luca. The latter's appearance in the Basilica alongside Cardinal Rinaldi, some minutes later, eliminated any such lingering hope. It would have to be him, Monsignor Declan Doyle, originally from Letterkenny, County Donegal, who stopped Luca Vitalia's inexorable rise to being both spiritual and secular leader of the free world.

His sleepless night on the train had left him in no fit state to listen to the interminable questioning of Luca by Cardinal Rinaldi and

Monsignor Doyle had inevitably fallen asleep during the proceedings. It had been the huge collective gasp of awe and amazement that had greeted Luca's metamorphosis from an expensively dressed, well groomed, ambitious looking, young politician, into everybody's image of Jesus Christ, that had woken Doyle.

"Is this not the image you have of the Messiah, Jesus, the prophet, Jesus? Does this not better suit thy preconceptions? Thy expectations?"

Luca had cried, opening his arms in supplication. Doyle had caught his breath. It was an impressive trick but Luca's sincerity was as about as credible as a TV game show host.

He pulled an extremely small Ciabatta loaf from his robe and a small bottle of wine.

"All shall pass by me and in thy hunger, which has grown as you have sat and watched me toil before my Inquisitors, you shall eat of this, my flesh and drink of this, my blood. And the last amongst you to pass, shall eat and drink as bountifully as the first."

Monsignor Doyle had twisted his mouth in distaste.

Were the hordes of clergymen who had watched and listened to Luca's performance going to fall for such cheap trickery?

As the line of senior Cardinals, Archbishops and Bishops filed past the supposed "Son of God," Doyle noticed the almost rapturous gleam in their eyes as they accepted Luca's bounty.

How could they all be so naïve?

Because of his position as an aide to the Holy Father and covertly, the head of the "Sacred Order of Saint Gregory," Monsignor Doyle was about fortieth in line to receive what he regarded as a black, tainted communion.

He slowly edged closer to Luca Vitalia, just behind a pompous English Bishop who he had heard declaring that there had never been any doubt in his mind about Luca's divinity.

Finally, Declan Doyle was stood next in line to a Cardinal who munched hungrily on Luca's proffered bread and took several gulps of wine from the small bottle.

Monsignor Doyle felt the detonator button in his pocket. His heart was beating like a drum, he could hardly breathe. Then it was his turn and a sort of calm serenity descended over the Irish Priest. He averted his eyes from Luca's, just in case Luca would see his intent from the open windows to his soul.

"Forgive me father, for I do know what I do." Monsignor Declan Doyle whispered as he reached for Luca's bread with his right hand while pressing the detonator button with his left.

Sixty-Three

Walter Wickert's head was in his hands:

"I mean you really have got to be kidding me." He whispered menacingly.

Special Agent Henry T. Burgermeister hopped from one foot to another as his local station chief tried manfully to explain exactly what had happened at the hospital.

"One minute he was there, in a coma, you know. The next he had gone, so had his sister.

The Mom had gone off to the bathroom."

Wickert took a deep breath.

"So, you guys are telling me, that a middle aged woman, smuggled her comatose brother out of the hospital, right under your noses and you schmucks didn't notice a goddam single thing? I mean did she secrete him in her purse for Christ's sake?"

The station chief looked pleadingly at Henry T. Burgermeister who just shrugged:

"I'm sorry, Sir." The FBI Special Agent whispered through gritted teeth.

"This whole thing has been a continuous and consistent catalogue of errors since we first sent you to watch Higginbotham's arrival in the country, Burgermeister." Wickert hissed.

"You lost your man at his mother's house. You allow him to walk right past you to get to a Presidential candidate and nearly damn well kill him and now you allow his body to be snatched by his sister?"

Burgermeister sucked on his teeth and glanced at his station chief who was equally as lost for words.

Walter Wickert heaved a sigh and closed the file.

"I don't suppose any of it matters now, of course. I guess Higginbotham can't damage Luca when some goddam terrorist has already done the job, even if he does ever come out of that coma, which I doubt because Luca fixed him good. Burgermeister take a couple of weeks off, Larsson consider yourself suspended for a month. Now get out, both of you."

The two chastened agents left Wickert's temporary office just as his phone rang. Wickert let it ring a couple of times as he unclipped his "Brigade of Light" pin badge and tossed it into his wastebasket. As the phone rang again, the young FBI officer picked it up:

"Mr Williams, Sir. Yes, I know. Awful news, Sir. Yes, Sir. Washington DC, Sir? Right away, Sir."

Walter Wickert slammed the phone down into its receiver. He had been quite enjoying the L.A. sunshine, but he knew his recall to the East Coast was inevitable given the civil unrest that had broken out in the hours following the assassination of Luca Vitalia in Italy.

Mobs had poured onto the streets of several major cities in both North and South America, fighting looting and burning.

The picture had been reflected all over the Western World, dependent on time zone. Had the assassination taken place earlier then Europe would also have suffered the same sort of breakdown of law and order. The main perpetrators seemed to be the most militant members of the "Brigade of Light" who were disobeying the call of Luca's new official spokespeople, his legal chief, Jonathan T. Sherman and his press officer Carol Anne Riley, to remain calm.

The mob had been robbed of their promised judgment day and the envisaged halcyon thousand-year reign of Christ and they were not happy.

TVs all over the world flickered with the widely varying images of weeping individuals in various states of distress and undress, depending on their penchant for garment rending. Some groups of people sat in circles chanting, holding hands, or candles, while others sang hymns.

The more usual picture, however, was of burning cars and buildings and lines of riot police charging baying, rock-hurling mobs.

Walter Wickert felt his gut churning as he glanced at the screen in the corner of his office. He had been a firm believer in Luca Vitalia. He could feel his bottom lip trembling as the grainy footage of the body of Luca being carried out of Saint Peter's Basilica on a stretcher was played over and over again. Interspersed with President Elmer Ford's succinct and heart-felt eulogy, praising a true American hero:

"This outrageous act of terrorism demonstrates how the axis of evil is not just a political phenomenon, nor is it one of the great faiths and religions in opposition. It demonstrates that men's evil exists in all faiths and it is man's extremism that is the true enemy. Where an Islamic militant failed to assassinate Luca Vitalia, earlier in the day, a Catholic fundamentalist succeeded late into the night. If Luca Vitalia truly was the Son of God then may God have mercy on all our souls."

As he watched his President turn from the lectern in the White House Press briefing room, Walter Wickert shook his head.

Luca Vitalia had been the archetypal American hero, even if it was true that he had been born in Rome, Italy. America was a nation of immigrants was it not?

Luca had been a great TV actor. His long running part in "The Amishers" was the stuff of legend. He had been appealing, funny and cute. Every granny, Mom and kid in America, if not the world, had fallen in love with him, with his big innocent eyes, golden curls and his wicked sense of humour. Then there had been his Pop career, which seemed to transcend all national, racial and gender barriers. Just about everybody under 20 had just seemed to love one of his five album releases, no matter what their cultural affiliation. He ha d had number ones in just about every country on each Continent. Finally his square jawed, all American action hero movie roles had delivered him the remaining demographic: older males.

Luca Vitalia had been the ultimate role model: Hard working, drug, alcohol and scandal free, plus he had been unswervingly patriotic and religiously devout.

Walter Wickert slammed his fist onto his desk:

"God dammit, he would have been the best President we've ever had. Goddam pinko terrorists."

Jack Baring was sat in his own office in Washington DC watching similar news reports.

Had he been honest, he felt quite relieved that some religious nutcase had blown up Luca Vitalia. The guy made Baring want to throw up, although that was a feeling that he kept very much to himself. Luca Vitalia had just been too goody-goody to be true. Something in Jack Baring's long experience in the military and then in Homeland Security told him that Luca Vitalia had not been everything he'd been cracked up to be.

Jack poured himself a generous glass of a nice single malt Scotch he'd been saving.

He held the glass up and toasted the TV screen, where Luca's unfeasibly handsome features were pictured once again.

It was going to be a Happy Holiday season after all.

Sixty-Four

Once the Italian Medical team had confirmed that Luca Vitalia was definitely dead, Aurelio had insisted that any autopsy should take place in the United States.

"I just wanna get my boy home. My beautiful boy!" He had screamed at the Doctors and Carabinieri Officers.

"I don't want him being cut open here, like meat on a butcher's slab. He deserves better.

Where was the security in here? How could some fanatic get to my boy with explosives?"

The thing that had amazed all the paramedics, doctors and police on the scene was how tranquil and unblemished Luca looked. All of his clothes had been blown off in the explosion, but unlike the seven or eight others who had perished, in Monsignor Declan Doyle's suicide attack, Luca was still in one piece and appeared miraculously unscathed.

"It must have been a heart attack." One of the medics had opined upon first examining the pathetic naked figure splayed out on the stone cathedral floor amongst the blood, gore and limbs of the other victims.

"There are no puncture marks on his body, no entry or exit wounds, no burns. Didn't the bomb go off right in front of him?" The medic queried incredulously.

Aurelio nodded his head.

"The schmuck who murdered him, just blew himself up even while he was taking the bread from Luca's hand. I mean why weren't his security men allowed to be with him? Huh? Goddam foreigners!"

The explosion had been reasonably localised. The interior fabric of St. Peter's had suffered very little damage, but Monsignor Declan Doyle had been blown to smithereens, as had those standing in line next to him. The amount of semtex that Doyle had used had been carefully calculated to minimise innocent casualties.

The explosion had traumatised the Pope. He had witnessed the whole thing from a distance of no more than fifty yards. After commiserating with Aurelio Vitalia, he had been shipped off to hospital for checks. The thing that had really shocked him had been the fact that it had been Declan Doyle who had assassinated Luca Vitalia.

Pope Gregory XVII had known the Irish priest for nearly thirty years, ever since Abraham Reichmann had brought him over from Ireland to work as his assistant. He just could not understand why

Doyle had taken such extreme action. The Pope himself had overcome his scepticism and had become convinced that Luca was the Son of God, having met him and now, not only was he upset about Doyle, he was also terrified for the future of humanity.

Father Abraham Reichmann had been so very wrong about young Luca, when he had described his eyes as being evil. Luca's eyes were the eyes of God.

The flashes of cameras and the drone of generators permeated the cold pre dawn air, as the body of Luca Vitalia was stretchered out of St. Peter's Basilica and placed in an ambulance.

Senator Aurelio Vitalia had exerted every ounce of his political weight and influence on the Vatican and Italian authorities and on the American Diplomatic Service to ensure that Luca was to be taken directly to the Aviano Air force base in Northern Italy. A military transport plane was already flying in from Turkey to ship Luca's body home to Washington. He had been in Rome for less than twenty-four hours.

The ambulance arrived at Aviano just before lunchtime, closely followed by a car bearing Aurelio Vitalia, Jonathan T. Sherman and Carol Anne Riley. After a series of tests at the base hospital, Luca Vitalia's coffin was given military honours. The coffin was borne by six Marines and was draped in the Stars and Stripes as it was placed in the C-17 transport plane. The base commander and a guard of honour saluted the body of the Presidential candidate as it passed.

The aircraft took off in the evening just as the sun was setting over the Alps to the west.

Aurelio Vitalia was inconsolable.

The contrast between the Vitalia flight out to Italy, in the opulent luxury of the private jet, could not have been more marked. The cavernous interior of the C17 was designed to carry military hardware, not passengers and the seating was designed to be as pragmatic as possible in its ease of assembly and removal. It was therefore extremely austere.

"I'm ashamed to be Italian." Aurelio wailed from one of the few seats.

Jonathan T. Sherman tried to help Aurelio's mood by pointing out that the assassin had been Irish. Aurelio had just cast the Legal representative a contemptuous, dismissive glance.

"The I-talians let him get to Luca, didn't they? They're as crazy as that Priest. I mean they wait two thousand goddam years for their Messiah and then blow him up."

Aurelio dabbed his eyes with the handkerchief that he usually used to mop his forehead and bemoaned his ill fortune. Not only had his adopted son been the ultimate male pin up and superstar, he had been the perfect politician and consummate religious leader. Aurelio knew that he had been the Son of God. So how was it possible that he had been killed?

Carol Anne Riley had maintained a professional sanguine front in the immediate aftermath of Luca's assassination, but as soon as she had boarded the transport, she had dissolved into floods of tears.

"But I loved him." She sobbed:

"He was the light of the world and now it's been snuffed out, just like that." She clicked her fingers.

"Life's just not worth living anymore."

She began to wail uncontrollably.

Jonathan T. Sherman wiped away a tear as he put his arm around Carol Anne's shoulder.

"We all loved him Carol-Anne." He coughed. "In a brotherly, best friend, sort of religious leader, come guru sort of none gay way."

Carol Anne pushed Jonathan away.

"Oh shut up, you freak." She cried.

"This isn't funny!"

Jonathan looked hurt:

'I wasn't being funny."

Carol Anne wiped her nose:

"You know, I really don't know what I saw in you."

Jonathan T. Sherman suddenly burst into tears:

"Jonju, Jem, Lucy." He blubbed.

What have I done?"

The lumbering military transport flew over France and then across the sea to Ireland as it made its way back to the United States. A lachrymose Carol Anne, a sombre Jonathan Sherman and a seething Aurelio Vitalia eventually fell asleep, as did the Security detail. Some of the Marines on board played cards until they too were eventually overcome by the tedious length of the flight and the lack of entertainment.

Behind the temporary passenger seats, in the vacuous hold of the plane, Luca Vitalia's flag draped coffin was strapped down to the webbing to prevent it sliding around.

The sound was indiscernible from the drone of the aircraft's engines and the clatter of the Spartan interior at first, then it got louder. Banging, hammering, a repetitive knock, knock, knock.

It was a marine who first heard the sound coming from the rear of the plane. He woke a colleague. The knocking got louder, Aurelio Vitalia snapped awake to see one of the Marines walking back down the body of the plane.

"What's that noise?" Jonathan T. Sherman enquired in a sleepy drawl.

"How the hell do I know?" Aurelio yelled:

"One of the soldier boys has gone to check."

It was just getting dark when the mighty C-17 touched down at Edwards Air Force base near Washington DC. A Guard of Honour had been assembled and hundreds of Press photographers and TV crews had jostled for position to get the best and most moving pictures of the Nation's favourite son coming home for the last time.

The President himself, Elmer Ford had made the short journey to Edwards by helicopter to greet the body of the man who had been destined to succeed him and pay due homage. He could hardly stop smiling. Elmer Ford had always been sceptical about the authenticity of Luca Vitalia anyway and he had detested the way he had rendered him a lame duck President with well over a year of his mandate to run.

The C-17 Globemaster slowly rumbled towards its bay, the roar and draught from its engines noisily blowing the chill December rain over the assembled Press and wailing fans. Finally it came to a stop, it's loading bay dramatically pointed towards the crowd.

The engines came to a halt in sequence and in the unfamiliar quiet an order was barked, a bugle was sounded and the bay door of the plane began to lower.

A Marine Guard of Honour slow marched towards the enormous cargo plane. Flashes began to burst and then stopped as a confused silence fell on the airfield as a dark suited Luca Vitalia strolled down the bay door, grinning and waving.

Then there was pandemonium and a thousand flashbulbs exploded at once as a cheer big enough to be heard in New York City erupted.

Sixty-Five

"I just knew you wouldn't be dead!" Natalia Higginbotham gasped when she first heard Wayne's voice on the phone. "That would have meant I'd be rich with all that insurance money." She laughed, and then began to cry at the same time.

"Hey, Nats." Wayne whispered, as Natalia continued:

"The police came in the early hours of this morning and everything. I'm supposed to be flying out to L.A. tonight to collect your body. My Mam's coming all the way down from Newcastle to look after the kids. I did tell them I thought you'd just gone to America for a few days."

"Well done, darling." Wayne muttered, before ruining the moment by adding:

"Does that mean your mam has to stay for Christmas?" He moaned; his voice edged with light-hearted sarcasm.

"Cancel your flight, pet, I'm going to get the first flight home I can, now that Luca Vitalia is dead." Wayne assured his sobbing spouse.

"Fancy that, somebody blew him up in St Peter's, while I was taking a bit of a nap."

Natalia coughed.

"Oh yes, your "bit of a nap," so what exactly was going on with you and Luca Vitalia and what has happened to Dean? And what was all that stuff about lightning bolts that they were going on about on the telly?"

Wayne took a deep breath.

"Look darling, it's a long story. In fact, it's a very long story and I promised you I'd tell you all about it as soon as I get home."

Natalia laughed again, the sheer relief in her voice was a delight to hear:

"Take care of yourself and make sure you're home for Christmas. I've bought the biggest turkey in Buckledon and now that you are going to be coming home not wrapped up in a box, I don't intend to waste it. I'd better go and cancel that flight. I'll get Frankie and Katie so you can have a quick chat to them and reassure them that you haven't gone to join the pet rabbit in the afterlife."

"Phew, poor girl. They'd told her I was dead. They were all devastated." Wayne sighed as he replaced the receiver after speaking to his children.

"Bit premature I think. The rumours of my death have been greatly exaggerated." He laughed. Carrie folded her arms and looked at Wayne, a deep quizzical frown creasing her forehead.

"So come on, are you ever going to tell me how you got out of the hospital, without those FBI men realising you'd gone?"

Wayne looked knowingly at Lucy.

"It was quite easy. I did the same thing I did to get into Mom's old house in Coldwater Canyon Boulevard."

Carrie looked imploringly at Lucy who raised her eyebrows.

"He did his invisible man thing. He just walked straight out past them. Well the one that was sat there anyway. The other must have gone to the bathroom. Terri and I left straight after."

"I wonder if they've noticed yet?" Terri giggled.

Wayne laughed:

"The one outside the door was fast asleep. I don't suppose he expected a man in a deep coma to be slipping out."

He blew out a sigh of relief:

"The best thing that's happened today was finding my car was still just up the Canyon Road. I'd expected it to be towed away. I'd left some very important stuff in it, so that was really lucky."

Wayne wondered how furious Aillen Mac Fionnbharr would be when he found out that his son had lost the most famous of the four treasures of the Tuatha de Danaan, the Sword of Gorias.

"So, Mr clever pants, how exactly is a fugitive going to get out of the country?"

Carrie asked as she sipped a cup of delicious smelling coffee.

Wayne screwed up his mouth.

"Well, I have a plan, but Marco and Marina might not like it."

"What's the plan then?" Terri and Lucy asked in perfect harmony.

Wayne shrugged:

"I'm going to be Marco Vitalia for twelve hours or so, Lucy you could be Marina."

Lucy frowned:

"But I'm not wanted." She stated looking somewhat bemused.

"Oh yeah." Wayne muttered before shouting to Marco who was sat in Carrie's living room watching a DVD movie on the TV with Aoibheall.

"How's that with you, Marco. Can I borrow your passport and pretend to be you?"

"No offence bro, but you look a bit old to pass as me."

"Cheeky bugger." Wayne laughed.

"Leave the details to me."

Wayne was still feeling a bit bruised by Marina's reaction to his return from the dead.

Marina had stormed out of the house as soon as Wayne had arrived:

"I hope you're satisfied now that someone's managed to do what you couldn't." She had spat at her brother.

"I'd hoped that you really were dead!"

Then she had jumped into her car and roared away down Box Canyon.

Wayne had shrugged.

"She'll get over it." He had said.

"So have you and Lucy booked tickets back to England?"

Terri asked, a look of sadness entered her eyes.

"I guess I'm going to have to come over real soon to see all my grandchildren for the first time."

Lucy grabbed her natural mother's hand.

"That would be lovely. I need to find out what's happening with the divorce and what Jonathan is going to let me have, but we do have a nice place in London. Wayne and I are going to book flights back tomorrow, or on Christmas Eve, if we can, of course."

Wayne looked puzzled.

"What do you mean, if we can?"

Lucy shook her head.

"This is a really busy time Wayne, everybody wants to get home for Christmas."

Wayne nodded, suddenly pensive.

"Yeah, I guess so."

"Well I'm gonna cook some meatloaf if anybody's hungry?" Carrie announced.

Outside the sun was slowly sinking off to the west, bathing the distant mountains in strong orange light. Wayne stepped out into the yard to enjoy the spectacle, Lucy joined him, seconds later.

"So, do you think that's it then?" She mused as she watched the shadows change shape in the Valley.

Wayne shrugged.

"Looks like it. Bit of an anti climax really."

Lucy nodded:

"There are riots everywhere. It's a good job the guy who killed him blew himself up, or they'd rip him apart."

Suddenly the near-silence was shattered by the sound of Terri screaming:

"Oh my God, Wayne, Lucy, you've got to come and see this."

The twins rushed into Carrie's living room where a news bulletin had replaced the DVD on the TV screen. Marco and Aoibheall were sat with their mouths open while Carrie had her hand firmly planted over hers. Terri was weeping uncontrollably, her hand over mouth.

On the TV screen a smiling Luca Vitalia was shaking the Presidents hand as the commentary reported the scene at Washington's Edwards Air Force base from a live feed. The ticker along the bottom stated the facts quite simply:

"Luca Vitalia, back from the dead in miraculous resurrection. Can there be any doubt left now?"

Sixty-Six

"I just knew you wouldn't be dead!" Aurelio Vitalia had wept as the ashen looking marines opened the coffin to see a grinning Luca Vitalia staring up at them.

"Heeey!" Luca laughed: " The last time I made 'em sweat for three days, but three days now and they'd forget about you. Entertainment is such a fast moving industry."

He sat up and shook his bleeding fists.

"What does a man have to do to get his coffin opened round here? Is everybody deaf?"

His voice could hardly be heard above the roar of the engines and the rattling and shaking of the contents of the transport plane. Luca's mouth dropped into an ironic lop-sided grin:

"Come on, will somebody help me out of this thing? I could die in here."

One of the marines gave Luca a helping hand to climb out of the coffin while Aurelio, his face as white as a ghost, just kept shaking his head and sobbed uncontrollably.

"They gotta believe it now....." He repeated, mantra like, over and over.

Jonathan T. Sherman and Carol Anne Riley had now made their way to the back of the plane and were standing, open mouthed, staring at their Messiah as he brushed down the designer suit, that Aurelio had given to the funeral directors for the burial.

"So," Luca shouted above the noise of the plane.

"That was most unexpected, but even more convenient."

He grabbed Aurelio around the shoulder and marched towards the austere passenger section of the C-17. His shocked and awed entourage followed. Some were deliriously happy. Carol Anne Riley's eyes shone as she gazed at Luca's pinstriped back, his still curly blonde hair immaculately in place.

"A resurrection? How cool is that?" She whispered to no one in particular, shaking her head in wonder.

Others were more confused:

Jonathan T. Sherman's mouth was hanging open gormlessly. The spell he had been under since he had first encountered Luca Vitalia, had been broken when Luca had been killed and in a moment of harsh realisation, he had understood what he had done and what he had lost.

For several hours Jonathan T. Sherman's degree of self-loathing had only been exceeded by his hatred for Luca Vitalia.

Now he was just confused again. His hatred seemed to have just dissipated. He was suddenly aware that Luca's eyes were on him.

"So Jonathan, my legal eagle good buddy." Luca reached up and clapped his arm around the taller man's shoulder:

"The T. in Jonathan T. Sherman must stand for Thomas, for do I detect a certain amount of doubt in your eyes?"

Jonathan's mouth opened and closed as he mumbled incoherently.

Luca laughed:

"Oh ye of little faith. And after all I've done for you."

He glanced at Carol Anne Riley who provocatively ran her tongue over her scarlet lips.

"I'm sure you two can, patch things up?" Luca suggested tentatively.

"And Jonathan." He looked into the urbane lawyer's eyes.

"I do demand total, one hundred percent dedication in my people."

Luca Vitalia smiled one his best crocodile smiles, his eyes as cold as liquid nitrogen.

The implicit threat chilled Jonathan T. Sherman to the bone.

"You got it, Sir." He mumbled.

Luca smiled pleasantly as he turned back to Carol Anne.

"As for you, young lady. Being dead, albeit briefly, has left me feeling, how can I put it? More alive than ever. I need to speak to you privately for a few minutes."

He turned to one of the stunned looking marines.

"Is there a restroom on this goddam flying crate?"

The marine pointed nervously to the front of the plane.

Luca smiled:

"Good." He grabbed Carol Anne's elbow.

"Come, we need to talk about how we deal with my miraculous resurrection."

Aurelio Vitalia crossed himself as soon as Luca and Carol Anne disappeared.

He turned to Jonathan T. Sherman who had slumped back into his seat, ashen faced.

"This is gonna be so huge. I tell you, after this there won't be any unbelievers left on the face of the earth. Man, that Priest, whoever he was, just did Luca the biggest favour. Word would have crept out about him turning into Jesus, but his dead body was on TV. The whole world saw him, dead."

Jonathan T. Sherman closed his eyes and gulped. His mouth was as dry as desert sand.

"It is truly a miracle." He managed to stammer.

He just couldn't shift the images of Lucy, Jonju and Jemima from his mind.

How had he been so foolish? Carol Anne didn't love him, she probably never had. She was just doing whatever Luca wanted her to do. What really stuck in his throat was the thought that Luca had tried to harm Lucy and he, Lucy's husband, had been complicit in the plot. Jonathan shook his head in an attempt to clarify things.

Luca Vitalia was incredibly powerful, but if he was the Messiah, then his behaviour was not exactly what the Bible had portrayed. Of course, most people hadn't seen the real Luca Vitalia, his media image had been managed to perfection, by people like Dean and Carol Anne. He had been right, there would be no stopping him now.

Jonathan rubbed his forehead. So why, if Luca had so effectively bewitched him before, had he not done so again? Why was Jonathan being allowed to have doubts and concerns about the man he would happily have given his life for, only twenty-four hours earlier.

Jonathan was suddenly aware that Aurelio was talking to him, so he feigned interest and answered a couple of questions that Luca's adopted father put to him, before turning back in his seat and pretending to fall asleep.

The question would not leave his mind. Luca had looked him in the eye, so why was he not being as slavish as before.

The answer came to him in a flash. Luca was weak. The explosion in St. Peter's had been so unexpected and Luca must have used vast amounts of magical energy to maintain the integrity of his physical body. If that energy was limited then he would be weak in other areas. Jonathan opened his eyes to see a rather dishevelled Carol Anne approaching him, while Luca Vitalia straightened his tie.

"Luca says I am so lucky to be with you." Carol Anne simpered as she re took her seat and fastened the seat belt in her lap. She gazed adoringly up at Jonathan who did his best to return her smile as he caught sight of Luca staring at him.

"No, I'm the lucky one." He gushed insincerely.

"Have you planned how to weather the media storm that Luca's resurrection is going to cause?"

Carol Anne cast Luca a furtive glance.

"Oh yeah." She whispered huskily.

"He's going to blow them all away, now."

Sixty-Seven

"He's going to address the nation tomorrow night, Christmas Eve. Yep, he's going to announce that the elections will be held, just to maintain a sense of constitutional legitimacy and the integrity of the system. Yeah Right! Everybody knows the election will be no more than a goddam cosmetic exercise. Yeah, he is going to dedicate his last year in office towards preparing America to be a land fit for the Son of God to inherit." Jack Baring shook his head as he held the phone to his ear:

"Unt zen, ze vorld!" He imitated the sort of fake Germanic accent used in old war movies.

The United States Secretary of Homeland Security laughed.

"Sure, at this rate we're both gonna burn in hell, Marshall. I think maybe our conversions will come way too late. There was a time though when I thought you'd really gone for all this religious hooha, ha! See ya!"

He placed the phone on the receiver and sighed.

What a Christmas this was going to be. The President had invited the World's press to the White House briefing room for six in the evening on Christmas Eve. He intended, there and then, to fully endorse Luca Vitalia as the next President of the United States.

The only other potential rival candidate, the democrat, Janet Regan, had dropped out of the race immediately after the resurrection incident.

The following day, Christmas Day, at two in the afternoon, Rome Time, the Pope was due to announce the World Clergy's decision on Luca's divinity. Monsignor Declan Doyle's suicide attack had rendered that process as inevitable as Luca's Presidential inauguration.

Jack Baring looked at his watch. It was ten in the evening. Just about all his staff had long since left the office. Some would not be back until after the Holidays. What would the world look like after Christmas?

Jack had called off the search for Wayne Higginbotham.

Marshall Williams had just informed Baring that he'd had good news from L.A. The surgeons had assured Walter Wickert that there was no way that Wayne Higginbotham would have recovered from his coma, so his mother and sister must have simply taken the body somewhere else. That certainly wasn't a matter for the FBI or any of the Homeland Security units.

Baring stood and stared out of his window at the City lights glaring garishly in the darkness, enhanced by brightly coloured, twinkling, Christmas decorations.

It all looked so normal. Yet Jack Baring knew that nothing would ever be the same again.

In other parts of the city, rioters had stopped burning cars and buildings to fall to their knees, praising Luca Vitalia. The Brigade of Light was marshalling its forces, ready for the day when their man took over both the spiritual and secular arms of the state.

Jack Baring pulled his heavy winter coat off a coat stand in the corner of his office.

Let 'em believe what they wanted. Jack knew a charlatan when he saw one, no matter how talented he was. He closed his office door and walked out across the floor of his department and out into the freezing cold Washington night.

In Virginia, Director Marshall Williams fiddled with his Brigade of Light pin badge as he sat in his library at home. He had never worn it in front of Jack Baring. Old Jack was a natural born sceptic. There would be no place for such people in Luca's glorious new Kingdom of heaven on earth. Williams smiled. There would be opportunities, especially for those with ambition and who were devoted to the new leader. There would be upcoming vacancies in some of the most senior Government positions and people with recordings of the scurrilous remarks made by the unbelievers, currently occupying those positions would get first pick.

Williams continued to smile as he swirled his Cognac around in the bottom of his glass. He would ring Walter Wickert in the morning and let him know that he would be getting a promotion in the New Year.

Marshall Williams had been thinking about his core team of fellow Vitalia acolytes. They were all good, but Walter was the best even if his dealings with the limey Higginbotham had not been totally satisfactory. How had those women snuck the body out from right under an experienced Special Agent's nose? And why?

Marshall Williams shrugged. It really didn't matter anymore.

Sixty-Eight

Pope Gregory XVII stood at the window by his little balcony overlooking St. Peter's Square:

"We are truly blessed." He said, a beatific smile on his face.

"Blessed to live in an age when Prophecy is fulfilled and the hope and faith of countless generations comes to fruition.

Blessed to live in a world that shall now become the Holy Kingdom.

For today, I announce to all of you gathered here in the Square of Saint Peter and to the billions of you watching on TV, that Our Lord Jesus Christ does indeed walk amongst us once again."

His face saddened and pain creased his wrinkled brow.

"It is, however, sadly one of the ironies of our age, that a man that I authorised and encouraged to discover the veracity of Luca Vitalia's claim to divinity, did so in such an extreme way. It was a most desperate act by Monsignor Declan Doyle and one that I would never have condoned in a million years. I pass my condolences on to the relatives of those that perished in the great Basilica of Saint Peter and I offer my prayers on their behalf.

Yet, is it not a sign that Our Lord moves in mysterious ways?

Monsignor Doyle's inexplicable and inexcusable actions have finally revealed the truth of Luca Vitalia's claim to divinity, albeit at such great cost.

To rise from the dead was Our Lord's greatest miracle and for many, it was the final proof they needed that Jesus Christ was indeed the Son of God.

I believe that Luca Vitalia has just proved the same thing to all of us.

Let us forgive Monsignor Doyle and let us pray for his soul, which must surely be bound for an eternity in hell, given the nature of such a mortal sin.

Let us also pray for those other casualties of Monsignor Doyle's unfortunate actions who have not yet risen in glory with Our Lord, but surely shall be bound to do so.

Now rejoice!

Every man, woman and child on the face of this earth and acclaim Luca Vitalia.

Our Saviour, Our Redeemer, the Light of the World, Lord of Hosts.

In nomine Patris, Filii et Spiritus Sancti, Amen."

The man who had been Piotr Warzowski looked down and checked his notes.

"Mmm" he murmured. "That should do."

His private secretary nodded then bowed and scurried off clutching the dictated notes, which he would make into cue cards for the Pope to memorise.

As the highly decorated door slammed shut behind the secretary, Pope Gregory sighed and slumped into a chair.

Why did he feel so insecure in his decision?

Why did he still not totally trust Luca Vitalia?

From the moment the young man had looked into the Pontiff's eyes, Piotr Warzowski had been almost one hundred percent convinced that the American was the Messiah.

Yet so many things just didn't seem right.

The thing that probably cast most doubt into The Pope's mind was that Father Abraham Reichmann had never been convinced that the "Sacred Order of Saint Gregory" had brought the Son of God into the world. He had described Luca as having "evil eyes" when he had once met him in America.

Abraham Reichmann's right hand man and successor, Monsignor Declan Doyle, was the last man on earth who would have committed the mortal sins of both suicide and murder, had he not deemed his actions to be totally and utterly necessary.

Senator Aurelio Vitalia was, without doubt, a shifty looking gangster. So why would the Messiah have chosen to be raised by such an individual, rather than in the security and safety of the Mother Church?

Would Jesus not have chosen a background of poverty and deprivation, somewhere in the slums of the third world, so that he could be at one with the suffering and the tribulations of his people?

Luca Vitalia's background, once he had left Rome, had been incredibly privileged, with his New England white picket fence and paddock upbringing and his pampered "media star" career.

Luca had excused such an advantaged situation many times, claiming that it was necessary to be well educated and supremely media savvy in the age of global communications, instant media access and the internet.

He claimed that it had been his misfortune to be born in an age where any degree of celebrity was deemed to be so much more important than any breeding, skill, or worthiness.

He claimed that he had deliberately chosen to use his fame to spread his message.

No one could deny that he had not been incredibly effective in getting his message to reach every corner of the world. Luca Vitalia was the biggest brand that had ever existed and he could only get a whole lot bigger.

Piotr Warzowski walked stiffly over to a pad by his desk and knelt down to pray.

He had lived through a great deal of change in his life. He had nearly starved to death in the winter snows of Poland during the latter stages of the war. It had only been by the grace of God and the guiding hand of Father Abraham Reichmann, that he had survived at all. Thanks to that old German soldier he had survived the rigours of communism and the oppressive regime that had crushed the Polish people for over forty years.

It had been through Reichmann's encouragement that he had taken the Priesthood and had eventually become a Bishop.

It had been Reichmann's guiding hand and his sound advice that had seen him rise to the dizzy heights of Cardinal. Once he had reached Rome, he had watched the world change and the certainties of the old order collapse. Yet the stoic old German priest had always been there with his wisdom, his humour and his unquestionable faith.

Good old Abraham! He had been the one constant in Piotr Warzowski's life and his death had upset the Pontiff as much as the deaths of his own parents during the war.

The Pope prayed to the old man for guidance. All he could see in his mind's eye was the white haired old Priest shaking his head, sadly. Piotr Warzowski could not shift the image no matter how much he tried.

Eventually the Pope opened his eyes and climbed to his feet. He walked over to the chair by his desk and slumped into it, his face weary, his forehead creased by a thousand lines.

Everything about Luca Vitalia suggested that he was a Son of God for the digital age, yet as much as the Pope hated to admit it; God had not spoken to Piotr Warzowski at all, let alone to confirm Luca as his son and heir.

God's representative on earth was on his own, despite the fact that all the other denominations; sects and faiths were supposedly involved in determining the truth.

The sad fact was that they had all effectively washed their hands of the matter and were looking to His Holiness for guidance. It would also be convenient for all of them, that should the Pope's choice be proven to be wrong at some future point, then the finger of blame could be pointed at one individual.

The only things Piotr had to go on, were what he had seen, heard and had rationalised following his meeting with Luca Vitalia, balanced against his gut feeling, his own belief in what the Jesus would have done had he returned and that image of the disapproving face of Father Reichmann.

Abraham Reichmann and Declan Doyle had both been convinced that Luca was a demon, maybe even the devil himself and the Pontiff's own cynicism had only evaporated when he had looked into Luca's eyes. Doyle had warned him that Luca would probably mesmerise them all.

The Pontiff had other considerations to take into account above and beyond the ultimate credibility of Luca Vitalia's claim to divinity.

Luca Vitalia's death had seen riots in just about every city in the world, but the news of his resurrection had brought about unprecedented scenes of celebration and rejoicing.

The main thoroughfares of many cities had resembled the scenes seen on VE and VJ days at the end of the war, this time on an almost global scale. The Brigade of Light could now be numbered in billions.

Could one man pour rain on such a parade?

Simply by stating that Luca Vitalia was not the Son of God, a little Polish boy could consign the entire Roman Catholic Church to the history books.

The gathered assembly of Cardinals and the leading figures of the other Great Faiths that he was due to address at the Ecumenical Council on Christmas Day would, without doubt accept his advice, even if it was negative, but even they would then risk being swept away in the tsunami of popular adulation that Luca Vitalia had garnered.

His Holiness Pope Gregory XVII had prepared his speech accepting Luca Vitalia as the New Messiah. He could not see any other way of maintaining peace, stability, the rule of law and the position of the Roman Catholic Church.

In any case, surely he was just being like Saint Thomas. He was just a doubting old man filled with undue cynicism. He had seen Luca Vitalia's dead body and he had seen him waving from the cargo door of the military plane on TV.

How could he say that Luca was not the Messiah, just because he had led a life of opulence and luxury and had used his fame and fortune to spread his message of peace and hope?

How could he disavow Luca, just because he didn't fit Piotr Warzowski's childhood image of what Jesus would be like?

No, His Holiness Pope Gregory XVII would deliver his prepared speech before the assembled senior world clergy and then subsequently, at 2pm on Christmas Day, to the masses in the Square, the Press and to every single form of media that would carry his words.

And as the grim looking face of Father Abraham Reichmann crossed his mind, Piotr Warzowski couldn't help whispering: "And may God have mercy on my soul."

Sixty-Nine

Wayne Higginbotham sat on the enormous rock and looked out over the lights of the San Fernando Valley. He had failed to destroy Luca Vitalia. The Islamic terrorist had failed. The Irish Priest had failed.

Luca Vitalia was literally bomb proof and his resurrection had proved to the world that he really was the Messiah. Wayne's inaction two decades earlier had doomed the world to enslavement and eventual destruction.

It really was the end of days, the end of all things.

It wasn't even as if he'd come close to beating the demon that he knew Luca to be.

Luca had absolutely mullered him, as Frankie would say when his school rugby team had hammered some other poor set of boys.

He had lost the Sword of Gorias, and the Spear of Finias looked like nothing more than a child's plastic toy. Vitalia would die laughing if Wayne tried to use that against him. Wayne put his head in his hands.

So what was he going to do now? Slope off home to his wife and family with his tail between his legs and pretend that nothing untoward had happened, while Luca destroyed the world?

Some hero he was.

Aillen had been soooo right. His entire race had perished for nothing. Mankind would perish for nothing, long before they'd managed to globally warm themselves out of existence.

Oh well, maybe he should just go home, kiss Natalia and the kids, open a nice bottle of wine and forget all about it. It wasn't fair that everything should rest on his shoulders anyway. Why should he have all that responsibility?

Wayne jumped down from the rock, picked up a stone and hurled it with all his might into the darkness.

Going home wasn't an option, was it?

Wayne knew wouldn't be able to live with himself if he forsook his magic again, just to crawl off and find somewhere to die quietly along with his wife, his children, his Mom, his siblings and all the rest of mankind.

Wayne twisted his face, until he was almost snarling.

Wayne Higginbotham had to have one more go at eliminating Luca Vitalia.

The old gunslinger wasn't dead yet, thanks to Lucy. He was going to come back, just like Mohammed Ali in the "Thriller in Manila," or "Rumble in the Jungle" or whatever it had been.

Hadn't Ali lost one of those?

Anway, if he was going to do an Ali and fight Luca again, how was he going to avoid falling into the trap that he had last time of floating like a butterfly and stinging like one too?

How had the Tuatha got it all so wrong?

Why was he not super powerful?

Why was he not like the guy in Father Reichmann's prophecy?

Wayne laughed as he recited the poem that the German preist had written out for him. He could still remember it perfectly:

> *"A child no mortal man shall sire*
> *By mother's blood Royal line acquire,*
> *Shall suckle he no milk white breast,*
> *Shall rise in exile, unwelcome guest,*
> *Shall learn to change his form at will*
> *His shape, his face, his ways to kill*
> *Unseen, unheard, his telling blow,*
> *His doom to lay The Messiah low,*

After all, he was the last person on earth who would ever be born of an immortal father.

His mother was a direct descendent of Brian Boru, the last High king of Ireland.

He had been bottle fed as a child by a couple, who had taken him as a poor second choice compared to their beloved Trevor.

He was a shape shifter and the whole point of his life had been the assassination of Luca Vitalia.

He was God's assassin, for goodness sake.

He was the one!

A shiver ran over his entire body as a sudden realisation hit him like a cold bucket of water in the face.

He wasn't the one.

Michael Sean O'Brien had not been born alone.

He was one of two.

The bloody know it all who had written the prophecy all those centuries earlier, hadn't expected Wayne to be born as one of a pair of twins.

How could he have known?

The genetic information dictating the birth of twins had entered Terri's bloodline from one of her none O'Brien forebears.

A feeling of exhilaration flooded through his body.

His meeting with Lucy had been timed to perfection. Somebody up there really was trying to give them a chance to defeat Luca and he had been dumb enough to nearly go and blow it.

Lucy was every bit as much the subject of the prophecy as he was.

"Wayne, Wayne." He heard Lucy's excited voice as she scrambled towards him through the darkness of Box Canyon.

"I've got it." She exclaimed giddily.

"I can do all the same sort of magic stuff that you do. I was just doing some shape shifting in the bathroom mirror and I realised that we should be working as a team.

Maybe it was never meant to be just you on your own. Maybe the fact that we were born as twins meant that the powers of the Slanathey Moor, or whatever you said you were supposed to be, were split when we were conceived."

Wayne's grin was as wide as the Canyon.

"Funny you should say that!" He laughed.

"You'll never guess what I just realised."

He grabbed his sister and hugged her tightly.

Then he pushed her back and held her by the shoulders.

He stared into her eyes which reflected the twinkling lights of the valley below:

"Look, are you sure you're up for this? We could be wrong and Luca will blast us both into the eternal abyss this time and nobody will be able to drag us out. It's not great in there you know."

Lucy nodded.

"I owe Luca Vitalia. I owe him a nice big serving of cold revenge. We're not wrong. Call it a woman's intuition, call it what you want, but we're going to blow the Vitalia myth so far out of the water that he'll take a hundred years to come down."

Wayne grinned, his teeth shining through the darkness:

"Come on then Slanathey. According to the man on the telly, Luca Vitalia is going to be introduced to the World's press as President Ford's nominated successor tomorrow, in the White House. We have a little stop off to make before we go home to dear old blighty and our traditional Turkey dinners and Christmas Pud. The terrible twins are going to be paying a quick visit to Washington DC."

Seventy

The White House press briefing room had been fully prepared for the arrival of Luca Vitalia. The President had not been this nervous since his own first step onto a stage to announce his own candidature, years earlier. As he sat in the dressing room with powder being slapped on to his cheeks, Elmer Ford couldn't help but feel a huge surge of disappointment. He had been swept to power just three years earlier on a wave of enthusiasm and optimism. The economy was in great shape, the United States had regained a degree of respect abroad and he had been riding high in the opinion polls until Luca Vitalia had come along. Now, to all intents and purposes, he was about to get kicked out of office before his first term had been completed.

As a practising Christian, Elmer Ford was more than delighted by Luca's arrival on the scene, as a practising politician, he was totally dismayed. Had he been honest with himself, Elmer Ford had been quietly delighted when Monsignor Declan Doyle had supposedly murdered Vitalia in St Peter's.

Now he was just going to have to learn to live with his disappointment.

Camera's snapped and a million flashbulbs seemed to flash in unison as Elmer Ford and Luca Vitalia wandered casually out towards the twin lecterns as soon as the President's press secretary had made the announcement:

"Ladies and Gentlemen, the President of the United States of America."

Chairs scraped noisily backward as the collected press representatives stood and clapped.

President Ford smiled and ushered everyone to retake their seats.

After shaking the President's hand in a staged demonstration of bonhomie, Luca Vitalia took his place by his lectern and grinned at the audience.

President Ford's Secretary of State, Candice Cornish, and his Vice-President, Omar Lewis sat nervously in the front row, wondering what was about to transpire.

The President coughed, looked at his notes, then looked back at the audience and the TV cameras behind them:

"My fellow Americans, I am sure you will agree with me, when I say that the events we have all witnessed, over the last few days, are totally without precedent in modern times. Even the world-weariest

341

sceptic must now admit that my good friend, Lucien Vitalia, here, is a very special individual indeed."

The audience broke into spontaneous applause as Luca held up his hand in gratitude, then shook his head and mouthed "no" several times.

The President continued as soon as the noise had died down.

"It is not for me, a simple, humble, politician, from Mobile, Alabama, to say whether Lucien is the Son of God, or not. His Holiness, Pope Gregory XVII is to issue a Papal Communique tomorrow, Christmas Day, in conjunction with the heads of every other major Christian denomination and in consultation with the leaders of the other great World faiths, to say whether they acknowledge Luca to be the Second Coming, or not.

I think it's pretty safe to say we all know what His Holiness is going to say."

President Ford laughed as he glanced over at Luca, whose grin had not even slightly faded. Luca gave a slight dismissive shrug, but his facial expression did not alter at all, as the President turned back to the audience and cameras:

"All I can say is that I know a gen-u-ine miracle when I see one. Some people have asked me, in the past, how I can believe in a God that does not make his presence felt in a tangible way. I always told them it was because I had faith. Well now they have the tangible evidence they were always hankering after, in the shape of Luca here."

There was another huge burst of applause.

The President waited for quiet then began again:

"Now, some folk have said to me, Mr President, what are you going to do now? Surely you might just as well turn the seal of Office over to Mr Vitalia and let's have the Kingdom of Heaven, here on earth, right now. What I say to them and my friend here agrees, is that the United States of America has a democratic tradition, won for us by the blood of our forefathers and by the hand of God, that tradition deserves to be upheld. So we will be holding elections next year as planned. That's the American way."

The crowd applauded again, more politely and with slightly more reservation this time.

"What I will say, my fellow Americans, is that I am hereby inviting Lucien Vitalia to work with me, right here in the White House, to set forward the policies that will expedite the delivery of Luca's intentions in the run up to his gaining the full mandate of the people of this great Country."

Another burst of applause.

"Finally, I have to say this. As a Christian, I am so thrilled to be living at a time when Our Lord returns to the bosom of his people. One thing I can assure you, Mister Vitalia.

This time we will look after you. The only crucifixes in these here United States of America are those worn by the folks who love you. God bless America."

The President raised his hand, then held it out in the direction of Luca Vitalia.

"Ladies and Gentlemen, I give you Lucien "Luca" Vitalia, the next President of the United States of America and Our Holy Saviour."

Luca Vitalia's grin grew even wider as he spoke, his eyes flicking from one person in the audience to the next, then to the bank of cameras at the back of the room:

"Thank you, Mister President. Ladies and gentlemen of the press, people of the United States of America, people of the World. Firstly I would like to thank everyone who has believed in me and has stood by me all the way through my campaign. I would particularly like to thank my father, Senator Aurelio Vitalia, without whose guidance, I would not be the man I am today."

Luca looked over to where a beaming and perspiring Aurelio Vitalia was sitting, wiping his brow. The rotund Senator waved and whispered something to Jonathan T. Sherman who was sat next him.

Luca looked directly towards the cameras:

"I know there have been many sceptics out there who have regarded me as little more than a cheap conjuror, performing children's party tricks and using the machination of special effects to mesmerise an all too gullible audience. I can understand that.

I can understand those of you who have criticised my manipulation of my fame as an actor and singer to serve as a springboard to my political career.

I can also understand those of you who find my promises to alleviate world hunger and poverty and to resolve all conflict, vacuous.

They are big promises.

They have been made before.

I can understand that there are those who still do not believe that I am who I claim to be.

It is a natural reaction to be sceptical of grandiose claims.

It is sensible to test a product before you buy.

Let me tell y'all. Let me reassure you.

You ain't seen nothing but the truth, the whole truth.

Sometimes, all of us get frightened by the truth.

Sometimes, it is more comfortable to hide from it.

Well, let me assure you once and for all, right here, right now.

I am no salesman.

I am no conjuror.

I am no mere celebrity.

I am no purveyor of empty promises.

People of America, people of the World, it is time to BELIEVE!"

Luca punched the air as he shouted the last word at the top of his voice.

The Press audience stood and applauded, but the whoops and cheers caught in the people's throats as Luca Vitalia slowly grew until he stood at least ten feet tall then he morphed into the Christ-like image he had used in Saint Peter's Basilica.

Luca Vitalia held out his hands in a gesture of supplication.

He raised his head and lifted his eyes heavenwards.

"FATHER." He shouted.

"GIVE ME THE STRENGTH TO FIX THIS BROKEN WORLD.

GIVE ME THE POWER TO MEND THE BROKEN HEART,

TO FILL THE EMPTY STOMACH,

TO CURE THE SICK AND THE ILL,

TO COMFORT THOSE WHO HAVE LOST,

GIVE ME THE MEANS TO BRING PEACE AND HARMONY AND HOPE.

GIVE ME ENOUGH LOVE TO SHARE AMONGST ALL THE PEOPLE.

GIVE ME THE KEY THAT SHALL SET ALL MANKIND FREE.

AMEN!"

The gasps of awe and admiration turned into a tumult of adoration.

The President of the United States of America fell to his knees before the huge Christ-like image, his hands held out, clasped in prayer.

All around the World, where people could see a television set or hear radio commentary, people fell to their knees.

The two beautiful angels that suddenly materialised behind Luca and the President, on the small briefing stage, seemed to cement the vision of the Holy scene. Both of the angels fulfilled the classical image of the ethereal, white robed, blonde, curly-haired, androgynous figure. One bore a spear, its white wings were spread out behind it. The other, its wings folded, held aloft a ball that glowed like a lamp.

No one noticed that neither of the angels had a halo hovering above their heads.

Luca Vitalia was so busy mopping up the adulation that he hadn't noticed them at all.

A secret service agent, on his knees, like just about everyone else in the room, barked some questions into his microphone and was asked why he hadn't expected Jesus to be accompanied by a brace of angels?

The President of the United States, the most powerful man on the planet prostrated himself before Luca, who bent down to encourage him to stand up. Then, as the Elmer Ford began to climb to his feet, Luca turned back to face the audience and the cameras, reverting back to his normal size and shape.

That was when all hell broke loose.

Seventy-One

Getting flights to Washington and then subsequent later flights to London at such sort notice, on Christmas Eve, had proved extremely difficult. Eventually Wayne had managed to get two flights that arrived in the American capital somewhat later than he had hoped for and which had cost an awful lot more than he had expected.

The twins had just a four-hour window to get to the White House and defeat Luca Vitalia, before getting back to the airport in time for their subsequent flights to the UK.

The fortunate thing was that the White House presentation of Luca Vitalia was due to happen smack in the middle of that window. If everything worked to plan, then they would get home on Christmas Day, if not, well, quite simply, they would not be going home, ever.

Wayne and Lucy had spent the whole night planning the operation and by the time Terri and Carrie stirred on the morning of Christmas Eve. The plan was fully formed.

A quick call was made to Marco and Aoibheall, who rushed back to Carrie's house in Box Canyon just as the sun was rising over the San Fernando Valley.

There was an awful lot of hugging and kissing as goodbyes were said just outside the house. Terri, in particular, was overwhelmed with emotion as she bade the twins that she had only just seen reunited, goodbye. She regretted the fact that they had not had much time together, but promised that she would see them both soon, along with all four of her posh, private school educated English grandchildren.

"Just make sure you don't go ending up in a coma, this time." She sobbed as she kissed Wayne's forehead.

"Don't let him do anything stupid!" She whispered as she hugged Lucy.

"And don't you do anything stupid either."

She turned and fled into the house.

Carrie hugged and kissed Wayne and Lucy.

"Go get him." She urged them, her fists clenched and her eyes displaying a ferocity and determination that Wayne had never seen before.

"Go get him, both of you." She turned to Wayne:

"Take him down, Wayne. Take him down good. Do it for James. He'll be watching you, you know. His spirit is with you, it has been since the day he died."

She too started to weep.

Wayne took her hand.

"Don't worry, we will succeed and trust me, James Malone will be avenged."

He hugged his late best friend's widow again, then as her eyes brimmed over and tears rolled down her cheeks, she too turned and walked back to the house where James Malone had been murdered by Vitalia henchmen, all those years earlier.

Marco Vitalia blew out a heavy sigh and shook Wayne's hand.

"Good luck, bro." He murmured: "Just make sure you are right about this whole thing. I'd hate to go down in history as the kid brother of the man…" He stopped and grinned at Lucy: "And the woman who, like, well, you know, went and killed the Son of God. I mean look what happened to the Jews after they killed Jesus."

Wayne laughed and hugged the little brother who was so much younger than him and had been raised so far away. He slapped Marco's back fraternally. The fact that they hardly knew one another, in reality, was irrelevant. They were brothers and that was all that mattered.

Wayne grimaced as he pulled back from Marco:

"Tell Marina, you know, if we do defeat Luca and you know, prove he isn't what he claims to be, then tell her I love her. Same thing if he blasts us to smithereens. If, on the other hand, he does turn out to be Jesus and I've been wrong all this time. Well, I guess I owe her an apology. Tell her I'm sorry her brother turned out to be such a dork!"

Marco nodded and bit his lip as the twins said their goodbyes to Aoibheall and then jumped into their rental cars and sped off up the winding canyon road.

By the time the sun was beginning to climb above a bank of ominous looking clouds that were hanging over the San Gabriel Mountains, Marco and Aoibheall Vitalia were taking their First Class seats on the flight from Los Angeles to Washington D.C.

Or at least two people who looked very like Marco and Aoibheall Vitalia were taking their seats.

Lucy struggled to hold her shape as Aoibheall and had to visit the planes restroom several times during the flight to spend a little time as herself and ensure that she looked exactly like her little brothers wife when she emerged. She was still a novice when it came to performing such strong magic.

The time difference of three hours between L.A. and Washington meant that it was already late in the afternoon and getting dark by the time Wayne and Lucy, in the guise of Marco and Aoibheall, arrived in Washington.

The Presidential briefing was due to begin at six. The media had promoted the televising of the event as the biggest TV sensation since a wee Scotsman called John Logie Baird had first decided that pictures could be transmitted through thin air and the human race could finally enjoy the fruits of four thousand years of civilisation: reality TV, game shows and soap operas.

Everyone knew that President Elmer Ford was going to anoint Luca Vitalia as his successor and was going to effectively cede huge amounts of authority to him.

What Wayne didn't understand about that was the Pope hadn't even given his verdict, although the miracle of Luca's resurrection seemed to have rendered the Pope's opinion almost irrelevant. The gossip from Rome was that Pope Gregory XVII had been impressed enough by Luca anyway, even before the assassination and subsequent resurrection.

Wayne checked his watch as he pulled his bag from the overhead locker; it was quarter to five already. For the first time in many years he felt extremely nervous. He and Lucy hadn't talked much on the plane. Their plans had been fully formed the previous night and both had been consumed by their own private thoughts and meditations, before potentially facing an appointment with eternity.

Fortunately, neither Wayne nor Lucy had hold baggage to wait for. They had agreed that there just wasn't enough time to bother with anything that might delay them.

The pair hurtled through the terminal as quickly as their legs could carry them.

They jumped into a taxi at the rank outside the domestic terminal, after enduring an almost intolerable wait of fifteen minutes in line. Wayne told the driver to get to the White House as quickly as possible.

The twenty-six miles between the airport and the White House seemed more like two hundred, as the heavy holiday traffic and the inevitable hordes of sensation seekers caused the cab to crawl along at little more than snails pace at points.

Eventually, however, the yellow cab pulled up at a security checkpoint a couple of blocks away from the White House.

"Can't take you no further, sir." The cabbie informed Wayne in a thick Eastern European accent.

"This thing with the Jesus guy and the President. The whole town has gone mad!"

Wayne checked his watch again; it was ten minutes to six.

He thrust three twenty dollar bills into the drivers hand as he and Lucy clambered out of the car and ran towards a small line of trees.

"Strange people, Americans huh?" The driver shrugged as he folded the bills into his pocketbook.

"This'll do fine!" Wayne cried as he reached the trees and morphed into his own familiar form. Lucy, fighting for breath, retook her own shape and nodded:

"Let's do it!" She gasped.

Wayne opened his cabin bag, behind a huge ancient American oak tree. He pulled out the head of the Spear of Finias and tucked it in his belt. Then he picked up the glowing, reformed, Stone of Falias and smiled encouragingly at his sister. He nodded and winked at her, then held out the stone towards her like an offering, his hands holding it firmly from underneath. She took a deep breath, smiled back nervously and reached out, placing both her hands carefully on top of the stone.

"Here goes nothing!" She called.

A strange green light exploded around Theresa Thornton's twins, the son and the daughter she had loved and lost almost half a century earlier, as their touch energised the fabled Stone of Falias, the greatest of the treasures of the Tuatha de Danaan. Then, they promptly disappeared into the cold thin air.

An old vagrant, who had been trudging towards a bench on the opposite side of the tree, hoping to find somewhere comfortable to spend his Christmas night, rubbed his eyes uncomprehendingly. He glanced at the bottle of hooch in his hand, shook his head and tossed it into a trash bin on the path.

A policeman standing near the visitors' entrance to the White House watched the crowd gathered outside carefully. His colleagues had formed a human chain and were managing to hold the wailing mob back as they called out for Luca and salvation.

No one noticed the two invisible wraiths as they pushed through the crowd and then squeezed through the police line.

No one noticed the sweeping broom that had been carelessly left by the door, snap, as though stamped on by an invisible foot.

No one noticed the broom handle disappear into thin air.

No one noticed Wayne Higginbotham and Lucy Hetherington as they inched past the numerous security guards, marines and special agents that thronged the White House corridors.

Seventy-Two

Luca Vitalia grinned at the cameras like the proverbial Cheshire cat:

"Mr President, people of America, people of the world. I thank you all for your love and support and I swear, I will do my best to make this world, a much more pleasant place to live."

The powerful voice seemed to come out of nowhere:

"For who, Luca?"

The smile was wiped off Luca's face in less than a nanosecond.

"How many will survive to enjoy your brave new world?"

Luca spun on the spot and turned to face one of the angels, who was pointing a large barbaric looking spear at him:

About twenty guns were pulled out in the pressroom as agents and presidential minders took aim at the angel. The President was bundled quickly and unceremoniously off the small stage.

Reporters in the briefing room audience stood, blocking the TV images that were being beamed around the world.

"Have you told them who you really are, Luca Vitalia?" The angel's voice continued, seemingly oblivious to the guns.

"Put down the weapon!" Someone shouted threateningly and the cry was repeated several times.

"Put down the weapon!"

Luca laughed nervously and held up his hand.

"Wait. Do not shoot."

He shouted at the bodyguards and agents. Aurelio, Jonathan Sherman and Carol Anne stood amongst the reporters, open-mouthed.

"Who are you? What are you?" Luca shouted.

The angel smiled:

"The question is: Who are you? What are you, Lucien Vitalia? For you are not who you claim to be and if you were you would most certainly know us."

Confused agents, bodyguards and police glanced at each other not daring to shoot, just in case they hit the supposed Messiah. TV cameramen pushed forward to try and film through the melee.

Luca held out his arms and turned back to his audience.

"The people know who I am." He almost whispered into the microphone, a benign and confident smile crossed his face.

The "angel" with the spear laughed.

"No, Lucifer, they do not!" It shouted.

"Show the world now thy true form Lucifer, once Archangel of light, yet cast down in his impudence and arrogance, now a denizen of the darkness of the eternal void. Get thee back to the bottomless abyss where thou belongs."

The Spear of Finias slammed into Luca's back as people screamed, several shots were fired, but none seemed to hit the "angel".

Luca's face twisted in pain. He snarled and turned to face his assailant.

"How dare you use my name in vain!" He roared, as he seemed to rapidly grow in size and stature again. He pointed his fingers at the figure before him and lightning like energy blasted out from his finger-tips.

The "Angel" staggered back as the energy engulfed it and held out its hand. The other "angel" clasped the proffered hand, holding a glowing ball of stone aloft like the torch of the statue of liberty. Even as Luca grew, a hail of bullets hurtling towards the "angels" tumbled and clattered harmlessly to the ground, as the stone's green light grew in strength and brightness.

The first "Angel" raised its right hand and pointed towards the growing figure of Luca and a laser beam like ray of green light shot straight into the heart of the would be Messiah.

"That's better! Show them your true nature, Lucifer!" The Angel bellowed as Luca Vitalia's enraged face began to turn red and blisters and boils began to appear.

"Insignificant worms, I will crush you."

Luca screamed as he intensified the energy he was blasting.

The stone grew brighter.

People in the front row began to shade their eyes and slowly the crowd began to back away from the briefing room stage.

Even the security men, the agents and police began to back away as they realised their guns were useless against whatever titanic, supernatural contest was taking place before them.

The "Angels" held their ground, unflinching as Luca's blast grew in power.

The green laser light continued to sear into Luca's chest.

Eventually, he staggered back, seemingly exhausted, and stepped off the stage. His lightning blast stopped.

"I will not be denied!" He roared.

"I have waited too long. This world shall be mine and all shall bow down and worship me. They shall crawl on their bellies like worms, just like their President did. They shall be my slaves and you shall not deny me!"

Luca's eyes went red and he pointed his fingers at the "angels" again.

Whatever energy he was firing at the "angels" now was invisible, the dark energy that had defeated Wayne in L.A.

The first angel closed its eyes and gritted its teeth painfully:

"Now!" It gasped.

The second "angel" brought the stone down to waist height and both placed their hands on it. The stone was now glowing like a miniature star. A beam of green light shot out of it, striking Luca in the middle of the forehead. Luca Vitalia screamed in pain and frustration, then he staggered back, falling over some of the press pack in the process.

Then the Messiah changed and the real screaming started.

Seventy-Three

"Jesus H Christ!" Marco Vitalia exclaimed as he watched the scene unfolding on the TV.

"This is like all in wrestling, with laser beams. I mean this is just so totally awesome! That dude is like the Emperor in Star Wars: "And now Luke Skywalker, you will die.""

Aoibheall, her hand over her mouth and her eyes wide and panicked, shushed him.

"This is serious, what are they? Are they really angels?"

Luca Vitalia and the "angels" were engaged in battle in the White House briefing room and it looked like the angels were getting the upper hand. Not only did Luca have a large spear sticking out of his back, but he had also now fallen off the small stage and over some of the reporters.

Carrie Vasquez clenched her fist:

"Come on Wayne, Lucy, finish him." She whispered.

Terri, sat on the sofa next to her friend, shook her head.

"Do you think the "angels" could be Wayne and Lucy?"

Carrie nodded:

"Sure, James always said Wayne could turn into whatever he wanted. Lucy must have all the same magical powers. It's just all so awesome. Come on, finish the sucker!"

She shouted, jumping off the sofa and delivering an imaginary right hook to Luca's head.

"Mom!" Aoibheall squealed in astonishment.

On the TV screen, a jerky camera was trying to peer above the panicking crowd of reporters.

Luca had climbed to his feet, but it was no longer the handsome, blond hunk, who faced the "angels." Luca Vitalia was beginning to lose his human form. Blisters and boils were welling up on his skin, which had now turned a bright red; his eyes were now no more than black pools of liquefied malice.

"I AM LUCIFER!" He raged. "I AM LUCIFER WHO WAS ONCE THE LIGHT OF HEAVEN AND WHO IS NOW THE LORD OF ALL DARKNESS!"

His voice was now a furious low rumble. Everything in the room shook as though an earthquake was striking the area.

The first "angel" stepped forward and pointed at the demon, standing before it:

353

"That speech is getting boring, Lucie, baby. I've heard it all before. So let me repeat my own little announcement: I am Micheal Mac Aillen, Mac Fionnbharr and I am the last of the mighty Tuatha De Danaan, Lords of Fine Finias, Glorious Gorias, Fair Falias and the Magnificent Murias and this is my sister, Lucy Mac Fionnbharr. Together, we are the Slanatheoir Mor. WE are God's Assassin. The weapon he wields to save the world from scum. Scum like you!"

The demon's mouth dropped open:

"There are two of you? A male and a female? How is that possible? The prophecy did not say there would be two."

The first angel laughed:

"The prophecy was almost right, it's just that nature mixed things up a little."

Each "angel" raised one hand towards Luca, palms outward, while maintaining their grip on the Stone with the other. Two balls of pure energy hit Luca in the middle of his chest. He grimaced, closed his eyes and rocked for a second before he pointed his long nailed, red, index fingers in the direction of the "angels."

"Yes, I know you. I know you both. This time you will not return, whelp, at least you will have the company of your sister, once I have finished with her, properly this time!"

An enormous blast of energy threw the "angels" back, slamming them into the wall.

Lucifer, his scarlet face a mask of fury stepped forward, put one foot on to the stage and fired his energy blasts again with all his might.

For a few moments the brilliant light of the stone, which the "angels" had held on to, faded to little more than a faint glow.

Both of the "angels" were breathing heavily and sweat rolled off their brows, but apart from that they both appeared unharmed.

Then the "angels" looked at each other and before the eyes of the world morphed into a very normal looking middle-aged man and woman. The stone began to gleam again and then shine almost as brightly as before.

"You OK?" The world heard the man ask, sounding concerned. The woman smiled weakly and nodded.

"I'm fine."

On TV screens around the world the brilliance of the stone's glow quickly obscured the features of the couple who had been "angels" but in a house in Upper Buckledon, England, a woman, standing sadly before a Christmas Tree, where she had just placed a pile of presents, recognised her husband.

In Box Canyon, California, a woman recognised her son and daughter, a young man, his older brother and sister.

Wayne Higginbotham and Lucy Hetherington pulled themselves away from the wall and still panting heavily, raised their palms again.

The blasts hit Lucifer right in the middle of his chest.

Lucifer fell to one knee, his face twisted, his head had now grown horns and a long tail had emerged through the rags of his expensive designer suit.

The beast that had once been a cute, curly blond TV star and a pop idol, roared its defiance and fired its beams of dark energy again.

Natalia Higginbotham caught her breath and dropped the last present she had been holding, her husband's.

Carrie Malone squealed and covered her eyes.

Terri, praying quietly under her breath, closed her eyes.

Marco, his fists clenched, uttered an elongated:
    "Whooooooaaahhh"

Aoibheall's mouth fell open and her breath caught in her throat:
    "OH MY GOD!" She screamed.

Marina Vitalia, alone at Terri's house in the Valley, put her hand over her mouth:
    "Oh my God, Wayne, I was so wrong about you, I was so wrong about everything. Dad lied to me all those years. I am sooooo sorry." She cried as the screen disappeared through the blur of her tears.

Margaret Houghton-Hughes, in the Yorkshire market town of Shepton, rubbed her eyes in disbelief. She was now in her eighties and didn't usually stay up until the early hours of the morning. She had made an exception in this case, however. She had always been quite fond of that little American boy, Luke Lively, although he had "gone off" a bit when he became one of those silly pop singers. As for him being the Son of God, well that did seem a bit too daft. Margaret was firmly of the opinion that fame was far more damaging than any drug addiction and many of those who had achieved the highest levels of celebrity had gone totally nuts. Look at that nice little black boy who had become a strange long-haired white man and lived in a theme park, pretending to be Peter Pan.

Margaret put it down to too much sun in that California place.

She had been watching the live coverage of the President's announcement and Luke's speech (now why had he gone and changed his name?) carefully and had been as shocked as anyone by what she had seen.

The momentary sighting of her nephew Wayne Higginbotham, fighting the demon in the White House, had left her open mouthed in shock.

"Eeeeh, well I never! What would our Doris have said?" The old lady gasped in amazement.

On the Channel Island of Jersey, Rupert Hetherington watched the events unfolding before him with a huge scowl on his face:

"Typical bloody Americans." He moaned.

"The Pope hasn't even said he's Jesus yet and they're jumping the gun and announcing he's going to be the leader of the Free World."

As the ordered civility of the presentation, turned into a battle of supernatural forces, Rupert snorted:

"Do they really think we're being fooled by this? It's all done in Hollywood, special effects, you know."

He turned to his wife Melinda:

"The Yanks did this with the moon landings in '69. Never happened. All done in a film studio in California."

He grumbled, stabbing the arm of his leather chair with an outstretched finger.

Melinda was sat opened mouthed:

"Darling." She whispered.

"One of those angels is our Lucy."

Marshall Williams sat in his office, with Mac Brown at his side, and watched the TV with a rising level of incredulity.

"What the hell?" He had gasped when the angels had appeared. Then his mouth had fallen more and more open with every single development.

"They've let goddam terrorists get into the White House. Where the hell is Jack Baring? Why don't they shoot them? What the hell is going on?"

When Luca had climbed up from the melee on the floor in his changed shape, Mac Brown had uttered:

"Eugh, that's not right!"

Marshall Williams, tears rolling down his face, listened to Luca's declaration that he was in fact, Lucifer, in mounting dismay and disbelief.

"Holy cow. That sucker's not Jesus." He gasped, plucking his brigade pin from his lapel and tossing it into a trashcan, again.

"That sucker's not normal!" Mac Brown agreed with a look of disgust on his face.

Walter Wickert, watching in his hotel room, shook his head and sobbed like a baby.

"Why?" He repeated over and over again, before taking his gun and placing the barrel in his mouth.

Henry T. Burgermeister at his home in Thousand Oaks, punched the air triumphantly:

"That's how that sucker got past me so many times. He ain't a guy, he's an Goddam angel for Chrissakes. I knew something was up with him."

Jack Baring and President Elmer Ford watched the proceedings from the safety of the Oval Office, where the security staff had bundled the President as soon as things had started to go wrong:

Jack had a cell phone pressed against his ear.

"None of them gets out of there alive. Do you hear me? We will not have angels and demons running around the White House."

He barked, while a very pale looking President of the United States of America stood trembling pathetically next to him.

Pope Gregory XVII, having completed his Midnight Mass duties, stood horrified in his private apartment, as he watched what was happening on the TV screen before him.

His speech, eulogising Luca Vitalia would be consigned to the waste-basket, even if he did defeat the "angels."

So Lucien "Luca" Vitalia wasn't Jesus after all, but Lucifer, the fallen angel and Cardinal D'Abruzzo had failed to recognise him, even his name had been a giveaway.

The original "Sacred Order" had played mid-wife to the archenemy of God.

Piotr Warzowski had seen armies of darkness before. He had seen evil and had survived. If evil was triumphant on this occasion, then he would lead the resistance.

He would lead the fight in the name of Father Abraham Reichmann who had been right in his evaluation of Luca Vitalia all along and in the name of Monsignor Declan Doyle, who had bravely sacrificed his life in a valiant, but futile attempt to correct the massive mistake made by the original "Sacred Order of St. Gregory."

Jonathan T. Sherman, standing next to Carol Anne Riley, stood stupefied in the middle of the now silent press pack.

"Lucy?" he whispered feebly as he recognised his estranged wife in the moment before the glare of the stone obscured his vision. He started to walk forward but was knocked aside by Aurelio Vitalia who was charging towards Luca like an enraged bull:

"Luca." Aurelio screamed:

"My son. Let me help you." He reached out to pull the Spear of Finias from Luca's back, but Luca turned and swung his right arm round, catching the rotund senator with a massive blow to the head and blasting several reporters into the walls, as his energy blast was misdirected.

Wayne and Lucy both fired their own energy at the demon, which screamed and fell to its knees:

"I will not go back to the abyss!"

It wailed as it tried to summon up one last consummate burst of energy. Even after using enormous energy reserves to hold his body together in the aftermath of the explosion in St. Peter's and then to resurrect himself, Lucifer was still incredibly powerful.

The Spear Of Finias was also draining his reserves, but he was still certain he could destroy the last survivors of that race of weaklings and cowards. He had destroyed their entire civilisation for goodness sake, what could two do against him?

He poured all his venom, malice and hatred into one last mighty blast, which hit the Stone of Falias, and carried it straight out of Wayne and Lucy's grip and shattered it against the back wall of the briefing room.

The demon roared in triumph.

"Now you shall both suffer a fate worse than any death."

The twins turned and looked at each other. Lucy smiled sadly and grabbed Wayne's hand.

"We tried." She whispered.

Wayne grinned.

"Who says we've finished." He cried as he pointed his right hand's index finger at Lucifer. A thin beam of white light shot out and hit the demon's left eye.

The demon screamed as the inside of its head seemed to explode:

"Noooooooo"

Wayne laughed.

"You beat me last time with dark energy, I've been learning how to use light energy, good isn't it?"

And at that precise moment, a pampered, mild mannered, American Lawyer drew the spear protruding from the demon's back and rammed it right through it's black heart.

"That's for making a total dork out of me and for what you did to my wife and to my family. You, you, asshole!"

Jonathan T. Sherman snarled and twisted the spear.

Lucifer screamed:

"I curse you!" he cried, pointing at Wayne and Lucy.

"I curse you with the curse of your ancestors. I curse you with the immortality you thought you'd escaped from. Watch everyone you love and will ever love, die around you, mourn and weep for the rest of eternity. None shall know of thy victory here. Thou shalt have no profit from my doom. Live forever in regret. This shall be my revenge."

There was a blinding flash of light and another blood-curdling wail as Lucifer, Lucien "Luca" Vitalia, disappeared in a cloud of sulphurous smoke.

Seventy-Four

Billions of people around the world wept as they watched the demon disappear.

Many wept as a feeling of utter desolation and disappointment overtook them. They had invested so much faith in the ability of Luca Vitalia to fix all the world's problems. Now that he had been proven to be a monster in disguise, their hopes and dreams had been shattered. The world would go on as it always had, scarred by conflict, terrorism, violence, poverty, hunger and disease, all the issues that Luca had promised to fix, with a wave of his divine hand.

Many wept with relief when they realised how close they had come to allowing a creature of unimaginable evil to seize all religious and secular authority on earth. In the pantheon of megalomaniac, unscrupulous, murderous dictators and autocrats who bestrode the pages of the world's history books, Luca Vitalia would have made the rest look like petty, infant miscreants.

Some wept because they now had to believe in such things as angels and demons and their atheistic, scientific beliefs had proved to be incapable of explaining what they had just witnessed and that begged so many other questions, of course.

Then there were those who wept simply because good had triumphed over evil and that definitely and definitively proved that there was a God, an Allah, a Buddah, or a Krishna.

Dazed and confused press photographers and cameramen captured Luca Vitalia's spectacular demise for posterity and while all attention was on the demon, the couple who had appeared as angels, simply disappeared into thin air.

"I thought we couldn't do magic without the stone?" Lucy gasped as the invisible couple sneaked through White House corridors, desperately trying to avoid physical contact with the masses of people who were running around like headless chickens, shouting into microphones, cell phones and headsets. Eventually they reached the exit and ran, hand in hand, out of the doors of the White House through the crowds of policemen, FBI agents, and paramedics rushing in and the press desperately trying to get out.

"Mind you don't trip over the cables."

Wayne whispered to Lucy as quietly as he could.

"The Stone amplified our powers, we can't do as much without it, but it was shattered thousands of years ago and the Tuatha de Danaan still managed to do loads of magic. The magic is in us, not the stone."

He laughed

"And I picked up a few big pieces, as we were leaving. We still have some shards of the Stone Of 'Falias', Lucy."

The couple eventually emerged as surreptitiously as possible, behind the same oak tree that Marco and Aoibheall Vitalia had disappeared behind.

A drunk vagrant shifted and snored in his sleep on a nearby park bench, oblivious to what had just happened in the White House and to the fact that it was Christmas Eve.

"I don't think I'll be able to maintain Aoibheall's shape all the way to London."

The exhausted Lucy gasped.

"Did you see Sherman, by the way, he was magnificent."

Wayne looked confused.

"Who?"

Lucy coughed:

"Oh, of course, you haven't met my husband. He was the one who pushed the spear right into Luca's heart."

"Oh, yes."

Wayne replied hesitantly, his brow creasing into a frown:

"I thought he was your ex husband?"

Lucy shrugged:

"Maybe he just redeemed himself. I think he saved both our butts. I do hope he's OK. I didn't see him in all the confusion."

Wayne laughed.

"Yeah, he wasn't bad was he, then again, you did pretty damn well too. I think he'll be fine."

He glanced at his watch.

"Come on, we'll chat later. We'll be lucky if we get to the airport in time. Let's concentrate on getting a taxi before doing anything else. We've got a plane to catch and I've got an appointment with a family I love, a turkey and a very large glass, or two of a particularly nice Chateauneuf de Pape."

Lucy grinned:

"Me too."

Lucy Hetherington slept for most of the flight to London, a blanket over her head so that her slip in shape from her Aoibheall disguise was not noticed. By the time Wayne and Lucy had rushed on to the 747 every

361

other passenger was sat, belted up, waiting impatiently for take off. The final boarding call had echoed through the terminal building just as the twins were passing through security. They had run to the gate as though Lucifer himself was on their tails. The glares that greeted the couple as they entered the wide cabin were almost as hostile as those that Luca had cast them. Fortunately their expensive seats were right at the front, so they were not forced to take the walk of shame down the aisle to the rear of the plane with hundreds of their fellow travellers glowering angrily at them.

"Not much Christmas spirit here, then." Wayne had whispered to Lucy who had just slumped into her seat. Her only response was to sigh contentedly.

Lucy was exhausted almost to the point of collapse. She still wasn't used to wielding magic and it had taken up almost every single ounce of her energy. The rush to the plane had been the final straw. Her relief at being able to finally relax was probably the best feeling she'd ever experienced.

Wayne couldn't sleep.

His mind raced as he reviewed what had happened. Had it not been for Jonathan T. Sherman, Lucy and he would probably have been blasted into oblivion. It was funny how normal mortals had always seemed to help him out:

Frank Higginbotham's incredible vault over the wall and his terrific haymaker of a punch that sorted out Francisco Pizarro.

James Malone crashing through a window, to save him from the burning cellar in Shepton.

Bishop Donleavy handing him the brandy, which he had managed to use to immolate De Feren in Dublin. ·

Jonathan T. Sherman standing tall and proud, ramming the Spear Of Finias straight through Lucifer's heart.

When he thought about it, Wayne realised that Luca must have been wearing some sort of body armour, so the spear had not penetrated his body deeply enough to do him any real damage, hence why he had fought on so hard and so well.

When it came down to it. Wayne's final victories had always come down to raw human courage, sheer guts and unselfish acts of outstanding valour, rather than magic.

Wayne stifled a tear as he remembered his adoptive father, Frank and his mate, James Malone. He wondered what had happened to the brother in law he had never met. Had Jonathan survived?

Lucifer's disappearance had seemed to involve a fair amount of pyrotechnic effects. Wayne sighed and closed his eyes, remembering just in time to throw his blanket over his head.

Seventy-Five

Katie and Frankie Higginbotham and Jonju and Jemima Sherman were hanging on the barrier at Heathrow Terminal Five, as Wayne Higginbotham emerged into the arrivals hall from customs, a small rucksack slung over one shoulder.

Katie had vaguely recognised the two third form kids from Pangfield College, where they were known as the Yankster twins. She had approached them tentatively and asked if they were Lucy Sherman's son and daughter and that if they were, then she was their cousin and so was the annoying younger boy climbing on the railings.

Lucy Hetherington emerged just behind her twin brother and screamed with delight as she saw the children. She rushed towards them and scooped them up in her arms, swinging them round and round despite them being teenagers.

"Merry Christmas." She cried over and over again, her smile a beacon of delight.

Melinda Hetherington stood by the terminal coffee shop and smiled happily, a smile that turned into a grin and then sobs as she was approached by and hugged by her dear adopted daughter.

"Ho Ho Ho Happy Christmas." Wayne shouted as he stooped to hug his children tightly. Natalia stepped forward, tears streaming down her face:

"You have some explaining to do!" She sobbed as she hugged him and kissed him as though he had come back from the dead, which, as far as she was concerned, he had.

"I promised I'd tell you everything, didn't I?" Wayne grinned.

"But, I still bet you won't believe me."

Natalia shook her head:

"I saw what happened in the White House." She whispered into Wayne's ear,

"and the whole world saw what happened in Dean's yard when Luca put you in a coma. I think after what I've seen and heard over the past few days, I am ready to believe anything."

Wayne kissed her lips tenderly and smiled:

"Well that's going to make things a bit easier then."

Lucy, once Melinda had released her, was introduced to Natalia, Katie and Frankie, while Wayne and his family were introduced to Melinda and her grandchildren.

Melinda put her hand over her mouth and she wept uncontrollably as she appraised her daughter's long lost twin:

"We always wondered what happened to you, dear." She sobbed as she looked at the man she had last seen as a baby, with unfeasibly large pointed ears, in a convent's unmarried mother's home cot, well over four decades earlier.

Wayne smiled and hugged the old lady.

It wasn't the right time for questions about the past.

It had all worked out well in any case.

Wayne wouldn't have changed a thing.

Well, maybe a couple of things………

But now it was a time for celebration, a time to enjoy a late Christmas lunch and some rubbish on the TV.

Promises were made about get-togethers and family bonding sessions as soon as possible.

Wayne and Lucy hugged each other as they said their goodbyes and exchanged all their phone numbers.

Lucy looked deep into his eyes:

"We may be parting, Wayne Higginbotham, but you do realise we're together forever now. They'll never split us up again."

Wayne smiled as he gazed back at her.

"I hope by together forever, you're not referring to the demon's curse. It won't happen, you know. He once cursed my magic, saying it would only do harm and that turned out to be wrong didn't it?"

Lucy nodded:

"No, I'd forgotten all about Luca bloody Vitalia and I don't want to hear his name again."

She gently touched Wayne's lips and as her eyes filled with tears she pecked him on the cheek and then dashed after her mother and her children as they walked towards the terminal transport bus, to take them to their Jersey flight.

"She's not quite what I expected." Natalia whispered, with one raised eyebrow as she linked arms with her husband as they walked towards the short-term car park.

Wayne raised his eyebrow in turn:

"And what did you expect?" He responded sardonically.

Natalia pursed her lips:

"She looks young for her age, much younger than you."

"Thanks!" Wayne sighed:

"Probably Botox."

Natalia playfully pulled his arm in admonishment:

"And her ears are nowhere near as big and pointed as yours."

Wayne shrugged dismissively.

"Daddy paid to have them done when she was at Roedean. Anyway, tell me about what you've been up to while I've been away."

Natalia snorted derisively:

"I think you're the one with the story to tell. Come on, you promised. Surprise me!"

"Dad, Mom says you were on the telly last night." Frankie cried gleefully.

Wayne shrugged.

"Nah, must have been someone that looks like me. What on earth would I be doing on the telly?"

He winked at Natalia, who raised a sceptical eyebrow again:

"Like I said, you're the one with one hell of a story to tell."

Seventy-Six

Pope Gregory XVII lit a candle, then bowed to the statue of Christ and turned to walk away down the aisle of St Peter's Basilica. Construction workers, repairing the damage caused by Monsignor Doyle's suicide bomb, bowed their heads in reverence as he passed.

Tourists had not been allowed inside the Basilica since the bombing and His Holiness enjoyed the splendour of the unusual peace and quiet inside the most important church in Christendom.

His Christmas Day declaration that Luca Vitalia had been Lucifer himself and that God had saved the World in the nick of time by sending two angels and by empowering one man to perform a superhuman task, had been greeted by a massive resurgence in Church attendance and conversions to Christianity all around the world.

The Brigade of Light had dissolved as quickly as it had formed and believers, of whom there were now many more, returned, chastened, to their old denominations.

Piotr Warzowski had decided soon after witnessing the events in the White House on the television, that he would be campaigning for the immediate canonisation of Father Abraham Reichmann and Monsignor Declan Doyle. He knew that Monsignor Doyle would be a harder case to present, considering that what he had done had been described as an act of terrorism, but he had tried to save mankind in the only way he knew.

Even the Pope himself, God's representative on earth, had succumbed to the bewitching influence of the fallen Archangel and any attempt Declan might have made to persuade him that anointing Luca would have been the ultimate act of folly, would have been pointedly ignored. Monsignor Declan Doyle had been forced to take extreme action and brave action at that.

In his hastily revised Christmas Day message, The Pontiff had admitted to the World that he had been on the verge of making the greatest mistake in history. The Pope had admitted how easily the demon, in the guise of the clean-cut young Presidential candidate had deceived him, despite the fact that he had been a sceptic until their meeting.

He had then delivered a sermon on how evil often lurked behind beauty and that what had happened proved how insidious celebrity culture had become.

Pope Gregory XVII had one secret about the Vitalia saga that he still wished to keep, however, a secret that he would never divulge to the world. The part played by the "Sacred Order of St Gregory" in allowing Lucifer his foothold on earth. They had made it possible for him to be born by spending hundreds of years eliminating his potential enemies and they had almost ensured that his plan had succeeded.

Indeed, it had been the new "Order's" last act that had generated the most hysteria about Luca Vitalia. His death and subsequent resurrection had obviously not been planned and poor old Declan had played right into his hands by carrying out that noble, selfless act.

Pope Gregory took a crumpled piece of paper out of a pocket in his robe:

> *"A child no mortal man shall sire*
> *By mother's blood Royal line acquire,*
> *Shall suckle he no milk white breast,*
> *Shall rise in exile, unwelcome guest,*
> *Shall learn to change his form at will*
> *His shape, his face, his ways to kill*
> *Unseen, unheard, his telling blow,*
> *His doom to lay The Messiah low."*

He wondered if any of the prophecy referred in any way to Jonathan T. Sherman, the preppy, bespectacled, American lawyer who had delivered the telling blow to Lucifer.

Pope Gregory screwed up his wrinkled face as he contemplated the possibilities. Maybe one of the "angels" was "God's assassin?"

The Pope shook his head, screwed up the piece of paper and cast it into a bin.

"Have more faith, Piotr." He chastised himself. It had obviously been God that had sent the angels. Jonathan T. Sherman had just happened to be in the right place at the right time and the prophecy had been just plain wrong.

Pope Gregory XVII shook his head as he wondered how many had suffered and died over the years, just because of a few lines of a worthless little poem.

How could people believe in such nonsense?

The Pope scratched his head and wandered off to his private chambers.

The Epilogue

Wayne carefully replaced the final rock on the cairn and then wiped his hands on his jeans. Aillen Mac Fionbharr was still busily engaged in introducing Lucy to her endless line of immortal ancestors, as the mystical green mist swirled around the mountaintop.

It was the second time in a couple of days that she had endured a huge family reunion. Yesterday, she had met some of Terri's brothers and sisters, her Aunts and Uncles and some of her cousins. Katie had been there with her husband Dermot and daughter, Fiona. They lived at the old cottage, which had been Daideo's, which was where the reunion had taken place. John and Molly O'Malley had come up from Oughterard with Patsy and his wife and children.

Colm had flown over from New York to check on the poor woman who had entered his bar in the week before Christmas, like a little lost waif in the snow and Terri had flown in from L.A. with Marco, Aoibeheall and a very contrite Marina.

It had been Jonathan T. Sherman that had appeared to be the main attraction, however.

Lucy had forgiven her husband his infidelity with Carol Anne Riley as soon as she had realised it had been engineered by Luca Vitalia. She had also forgiven him for falling under Luca's spell. He was only a mere mortal after all, even if he was probably the most famous man in the world now, since the American media decided to play up his role in the final destruction of the demon Lucifer.

Wayne had also forgiven Jonathan his betrayal of his sister, especially when Jonathan had presented him with the Sword of Gorias, which he had been looking after for Luca.

The Sword he would return the Getty museum, the Spear he had just buried in the cairn.

Wayne smirked as he watched Lucy's face as she was presented to a series of ancient warriors that looked as though they'd just stepped off a "sword and sandals" film set. After what had seemed like an age, Lucy came to the end of the line and was given a long hug by Queen Oonagh, the consort of mighty Fionnbharr. When she stepped back out of the mist into the thin January sunlight, her expression was wistful and distracted.

"Wayne, I just need a minute, you know, some time to take all that in." She gulped tearfully, as she wiped her eyes, turned and wandered to an outcrop, overlooking Daideo's cottage in the valley far below.

Wayne nodded and waited for his father Aillen who was drifting through the mist towards him, a huge grin splitting his elven features:

"The Council of the Wise have granted you a new title my son:" Aillen boomed, gleefully:

"You are now Prince Arthur, Slanaitheoir Mor."

Wayne looked bemused:

"What?" he asked, incredulously.

Aillen repeated the name and then explained that the name "Arthur" had been given to him, because he was only half of the great Saviour of the prophecy of the Tuatha de Dannan.

Aillen roared with laughter until the tears rolled down his face.

Wayne raised an eyebrow:

"I think you need some new jokes in Tir Na Nog, father!" He said with more than a hint of disdain.

Aillen slowly stopped laughing and put his hands on his hips, his face took on a serious look:

"I am very proud of you my son. You have completed the third and by far the most demanding of your tasks and have thereby fulfilled the witch's prophecy. You have saved mankind. For very many years, I did not think you would ever do it and then I will confess, I did not believe you could do it."

Wayne gave a short wry snort:

"For a many years, neither did I. In fact for a few hours I was convinced I'd failed, but I guess that was the advantage of my destiny being split into two equal parts."

Aillen MacFionnbharr nodded:

"No one had forseen such a thing, not even the witch Fenalla of Gorias had seen that one coming. Your sister is a fine woman. I can see much of Theresa in her."

Wayne laughed.

"Yep, she's a fine woman ok. She's now famous all over the world as the wife of the most celebrated hero in American history: Mrs Jonathan T. Sherman. She's the spouse of the demon slayer and the mother of his children. Ironic isn't it?"

Aillen nodded thoughtfully.

"Look after her, your sister has a lot on her mind."

Lucy was walking slowly back across the boggy mountain-top towards the cairn where her supernatural father and her brother were stood, her face solemn, her eyes tearful.

She disappeared momentarily, as natural mist swirled across the peak obscuring just about everything.

Wayne had saved the question he wanted to ask his father most until the end.

"Father," he began, rather timorously: "Luca cursed Lucy and I with immortality. It's not true, is it?"

Aillen smiled sadly: "Only time will tell my son. Only time will tell."

The last true Prince of The Tuatha de Danaan then bade his children farewell and told them that if they ever needed him to return to the cairn standing so high above Lough Mask. He would be there.

Then he disappeared in a swirl of green mist.

Somewhere singing could be heard, an ethereal sound of such beauty that both Wayne and Lucy started to cry.

Once they had recovered themselves and the song had faded, Wayne Higginbotham and Lucy Sherman carefully clambered down the steep, slippery, grassy slope of Buckaun to the shelter of Daideo's cottage. Everyone else had gone off to Maire Duke's pub for lunch.

Wayne and Lucy had promised to join them after their sojourn up the mountain.

A picture of Tom Mick a John O'Brien sporting his best, checked flat cap, dominated the kitchen of the cosy little bungalow.

"What was he like?" Lucy asked.

Wayne smiled as he gazed fondly at the picture.

"Don't forget, he was getting old when I first knew him, but he seemed like a nice old fella."

"Are things Ok now, you know, with you and Jonathan?"

Lucy took a long sip from her own mug and then gazed out of the window.

"I guess they will be, one day, when all the fuss dies down. Right now I have to make an appointment to see him, somewhere in between all the TV chat show and magazine interviews. Can you believe they are even talking about movie rights now?

"Jonathan the Demon Slayer."

Wayne spat his tea back into his mug as the twins both burst out laughing.

"Buffy the Vampire Slayer" definitely had a better ring." Wayne opined through his laughter.

"Oh well, who needs fame and fortune. I think we've both done pretty well. Two funny little babies with big ears, yelling their lungs out in a convent nursery, totally unaware that the roller coaster of life was going to take them off on two very different rides, but that we would share a common destiny. Would we change anything?"

Lucy snorted and shook her head.

"Come on, let's join "Jonathan the Demon Slayer" and his fan club over a pint of cold Guinness." Wayne suggested as he placed a drained mug of tea on the draining board.

"Why not?" She chirped cheerfully.

The twins jumped in Wayne's new Range Rover, which he'd driven over from England in and sped off down the lane and on to the Lough Road to Maire Dukes.

As he was driving, Wayne turned and looked at his twin sister's face. He had not had time to really study the finer points of her features before. It was amazing just how strangely familiar she seemed to him, even though they had been separated for well over forty years.

Yet Wayne had to admit that she looked a million times better than he did. She turned, embarrassed, conscious of his stare.

"Are you using magic? You know, to tighten things up a bit?" He asked cheekily.

"How dare you?" Lucy responded indignantly, before breaking into a grin and adding:

"Of course I bloody am. What's the use of being able to do magic if you never use it? Being able to shape shift is every woman's dream. It's so much cheaper than surgery and so much more flexible than botox. I can take twenty years off, every morning!"

The gleam of a brake light from a car in front caught in her eyes and they glinted wickedly red.

"You know, we are Gods. We could rule the world, if we really wanted to." She whispered mischievously. Her scarlet lips began to curl in a devilish smile.

Wayne shrugged and turned back to look at the road ahead, he slowly nodded and began to smile too.

"We couldn't do much worse than the bozos currently in charge, could we?" He said as he raised one sharply pointed eyebrow.

Lucy pressed one of the SUVs radio butttons. The voice of Queen's Freddie Mercury poured out of the multiple speakers:

"Who wants to live forever, who wants to live forever...."

Wayne Higginbottom and Lucy Hetherington glanced at one another and then burst out laughing and they laughed and laughed and laughed.